The Hunt

By Mark Cashman

temporal doorway publishing
windsor, ct

The Hunt

A Temporal Doorway Book
Published by Temporal Doorway Publishing
451 Prospect Hill Rd
Windsor, CT 06095

http://publishing.temporaldoorway.com
Make inquiries to publishing@temporaldoorway.com

ISBN 978-0-9795715-0-3

First Temporal Doorway Publishing Edition 2007

Printed in the United States Of America

0   9   8   7   6   5   4   3   2   1

The Message

The trees wave madly as if dancing to an unfelt wind. They part under the force of a huge black shape; one falls splintering to the ground. Deleo feels a scream that never passes his throat. The god, the oracle, dances buoyantly into the cluster light. It is an appallingly featureless black ellipsoid, ringed with flexing legs. It reels and leaps and bounds in the light, like a fragment of space brought to earth, unlimited by gravity. A shadow, it gyrates, describing a pattern that is not a pattern, its tentacles flicking like whips, the shadows cast by their motion on the fallen leaves flickering in sympathy. There is a message, and Deleo finds that he does not even need to think or remember to understand: The message is death.

A Team in Danger

Atrenn has his laser out and is falling back toward the shuttle, scanning the landscape. x*Rkar crouches beside the table, gesturing toward the grassland. Another spear falls, glancing off the table surface and spinning across the ground. Just as Atrenn fires at the source, x*Rkar dives for the spear, rolling in an incredible gymnast's feat, simultaneously casting it at the spot burning under Atrenn's laser beam.

A World in Danger

Talbot waits in the dark silence of the orbital shuttle's drop pod, eyes locked to the countdown timer. He hears the ticking as he braces himself against the seat; there is a moment between one breath and the next where he wonders at all of the things he has failed to do. Then it's time to go - he yanks the handles, and pinioning acceleration drives him back into the seat. Space springs to life around him as the imaging sweeps away the walls and the station is ripped away into the distance. The planet wheels below, its cities a rich sparkling where the terminator brings the night. Tiny reddish patches mark the flare of fires hundreds of miles across. It is possible that he is just too late, again.

A Surprising Hope

The alien vehicle is smooth and streamlined, with a surface like quicksilver - rippling faintly, as if breathing. It had matched orbits with stunning performance and precision, leaving Talbot in awe. But now he is waiting for Hallison, Reed and Wanr to find a way to open communications. He doesn't like it.

One of the humanoids raises its hand to its shoulders. On the flight deck, Talbot leans forward in an ancient reflex. The being unfastens something, and the helmet becomes soft and falls away from the head. Revealing a lovely human woman, with long dark hair spilling over her shoulders. She smiles. The other mimics her motion. But when its cowl falls away, a strangely articulated face with its own partly reflective surface is revealed.

The Hunt

Temporal Doorway Books By Mark Cashman

The Hunt
Ringclimber

Coming soon: Prometheus

The Hunt

Phase 1 1
Phase 2 83
Phase 3 201
Phase 4 273
Acknowledgements 309

All the events of this story occur inside
the M4 globular cluster

7200 light years from Earth

Linear diameter of the cluster: about 75 light years.
Tidal diameter[1] of the cluster: approximately 140 light-years

---

[1] The distance where tidal forces from the Milky Way will cause stars to escape

Phase 1

Illyrion and Talith

Events in this phase occur on the world Talith, about 20 light years from the edge of the M4 cluster, at the inner edge of the Geodesic political system sphere of influence

Talith Planet

Distance from Talith Star:	131,260,317 km
Radius:	6500 km
Gravity:	1.02G
Orbit Period:	307.78 days
Rotation:	21 hrs
Population:	None detected
Status:	Potential
Political:	Geodesic
Moons:	Shalic

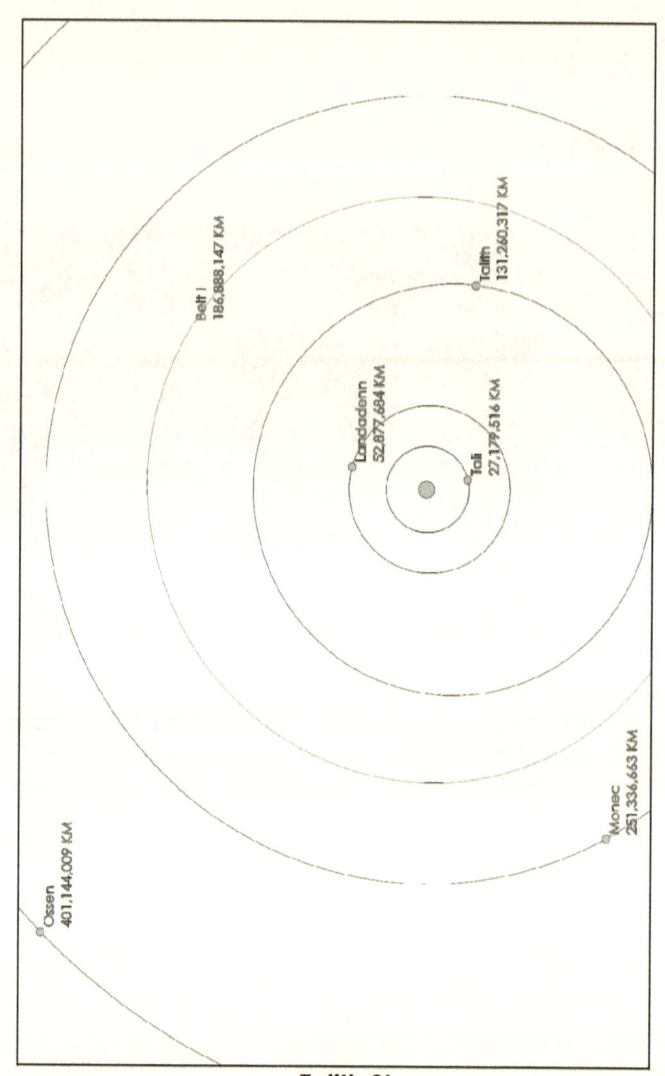

Belt I
186,888,147 KM

Talith
131,260,317 KM

Lundadenn
52,877,684 KM

Tai
27,179,516 KM

Monec
251,336,663 KM

Ossen
401,144,009 KM

Talith Star

Spectral Class:	G2	Mass:	0.95 sol
Radius:	0.9598 sol	Luminosity:	0.8357 sol

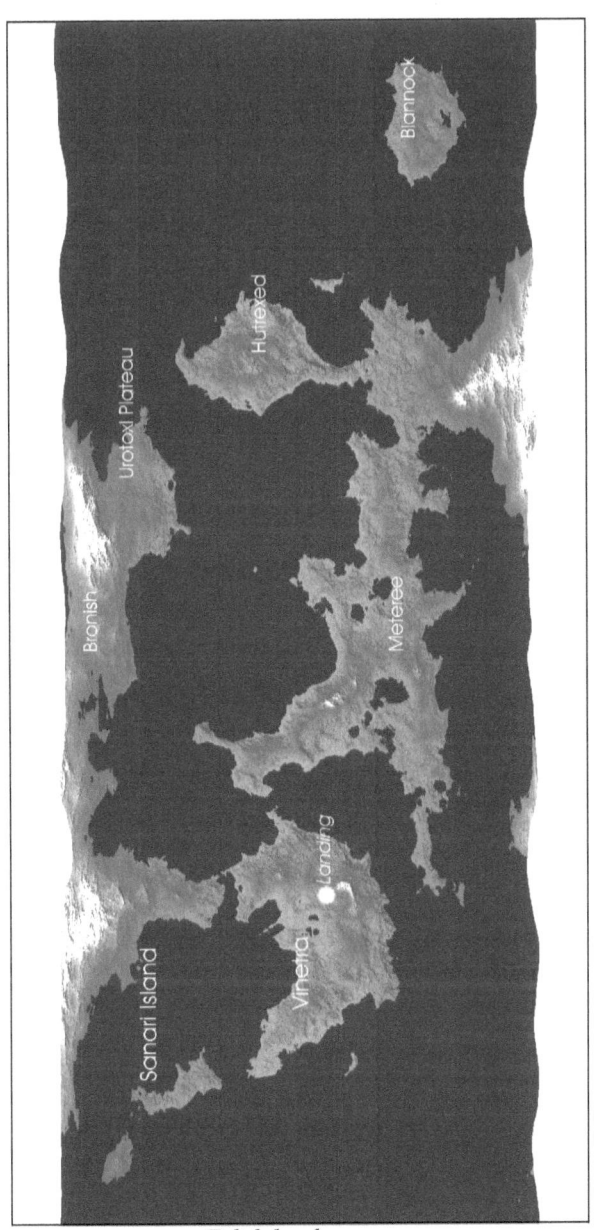

Talith land masses

1

The hunter waits in the grass at the lip of the hollow, motionless. Reddish slit eyes shift behind the screen of red grass, seeking.

Below, the prey bites and tears at the grass. The hunter has followed them silently for four days in a meandering path - unclothed against the bitter wind, unfed and unsleeping, as prescribed in the Rules of the Mover...

On the second day... with disturbing vacancy, the hunter's vision had blurred and he was seized between one step and the next with weakness; a next foot forward seemed too heavy to move in any accustomed counterstroke, somehow embedded in rock. Despite a shock of pain, his imperative to move did not weaken. He strove for motion, even extending his hands and clenching the tall grasses in an effort to pull himself forward by strength of arms. When a trickle of red blood ran sparking in the cold across his wrist, he paused; standing, swaying, staring at the redly weeping slits that the fronds had slashed into his sharply articulated palms. But even as he watched the blood, pain did not come, and he knew he had traveled beyond pain and grief to silence. They had promised, and now it was real. Until now, he had clung to a childish belief in the hunt, the weapon, the stroke - as the symbol that summed the ritual; now he saw silent blood trickling slowly across his skin and knew the intent.

But the sensation of gravity had renewed the hunter's movement, and he staggered forward onto the huge, red-shagged plain, footsteps rolling in the soft, moist earth. Each step was easier than the one before with gained momentum and balance; then he ran on until night, following his chosen herd, frozen thought impaled on the silence of the steppe...

On the third day... dawn had brought clusters of dismal clouds. The prey huddled uncomfortable and restless under the red foliage of their chosen isolated tree, occasionally grunting softly in shallow sleep. By then, the hunter's limbs were stiff in the aftermath of sustained effort, and his skull was thick like sand. Rain fell sparsely, colliding with glistening skin in tiny spots of cold.

...He clings to his spear, hands raw from sweat, salts stinging the waxy skin. Cold breeze wipes the liquids of exertion in a great fern pattern of sensation across his back. Soon he will be able (released) to kill, and then he will feast; (remembering the cuts) he will rip the damned grass out of the earth and pile it to burn and (remembering the cuts) let the burning fat of the cooking prey drip on the ashes of the grass in an ironic indignity - that would be a fine revenge.

2

Talbot, in the cool corridor of the transport, checking his descent suit, procrastinating. For the third time he checks - sockets, crash armor, chronometer/navigator, check pad, life support thinpak. All secure, all correct, all incapable of putting off the moment any longer.

"Hey, Talbot... it's time." Atrenn calls.

He looks up to glare at the small alien face thrust past the corner where the shuttle bay joins into the transport. Judiciously he restrains his immediate response.

"Talbot?" The alien's quizzical expression borders on mockery, exaggerated by the compression of his face into the lower part of his head. "If you take much longer, the aperture will pass and we'll have to wait again." A pause ensues, during which Talbot avoids an embarrassing memory. Somehow Talbot keeps his gaze steady on Atrenn, who minces into the corridor in all his grotesquerie. "Talbot, come on - please?"

Talbot turns away from Atrenn to face the wall, running a hand up and down a strap. He sees simulated stone, softly modulated lighting - a necessary illusion to the crew; a saving one for him, since it gives him the strength to reply calmly, "All right."

Then, "All right," he says more loudly, "I'm coming. Get back inside, will you?" He turns to face the alien again. "I said, I'm coming." He returns his attention to the fittings of his suit.

"You're not very nice, Talbot." The lips crossing Atrenn's shrunken little face crook in a strange smile, and he walks slowly back into the bufferway. Talbot slips shut a final catch and follows slowly, distastefully. It is, he thinks, unfortunate that this alien has developed such a command of human idiom.

3

On the dorsal screens, the complexity of the transport *Illyrion* dwindles against the multitude of crisp stars; it vanishes and there is only the M4 cluster, its diffuse edge blazing.

Talbot is enmeshed in dimness, surrounded by machines, cased in his slick plastic suit. His helmet hangs on a rack beside the control seat, close to his hand. A clipboard rests on his thigh, glowing white checkfilm obscured for a moment by his finger as he checks a system, watching the results mount up to his satisfaction.

Only a few minutes more and he is done and ready to go. He blanks and dims the checkfilm, settling back into his capacious seat, waiting. The stars drift slowly past the viewports. His mind wanders across various thoughts. After ten more minutes, his patience evaporates.

He initiates the firing sequencer, styling a moderate nose-high position for entry. Though the thrust is imperceptibly gentle, within a few minutes he sees early plasma flaring at the edge of the hull. After a moment's study of the heat distribution display, he alters the angle of descent by a few degrees.

The door at his back slips open with its pneumatic hiss. Amel, the paleontologist, thrusts her head into the chamber, stopping only with difficulty. She peers with painful effort into the dimness of the flight deck as if blinded by the change.

"Talbot?" she asks.

The pilot feels a faint crawling sensation; there are those giant, dark, glassy eyes that reflect the indicators and displays, focused on him from within the soft furry face. He increases the panel light until there is a vaguely red luminosity in the air of the room.

"Ehhh... attention." Amel's translator reflects her lisping accent faithfully. "Completed. We are ready."

"Yeah. Sure. Anything else?"

Amel feels something similar to confusion. Though she emits her language to the translator with an accent that carries through in conversation, she is sensitive to the nuances of expression that are peculiar to humans. From Talbot's terse sentences, she assumes Talbot's indifference, almost as if Talbot had known what they were doing. But how could that be? Talbot hadn't even asked why their report had been so delayed; he couldn't know about their heroic success in improvising restraints for the wayward microphotometer array. Unless... could he have been eavesdropping?

Instead of asking, Amel continues with the matter at hand. "Will we descend shortly?"

An idiot, Talbot thinks.

"Yes, we're on the way. Why don't you go back and wait with the others?" He lets some of his impatience seep into voice and face, hoping the thing will notice.

As usual, there is a total lack of response. Under the sharpest criticism, sarcasm, even outright hostility, the response is always missing. It unnerves him, like leaning against a wall only to find no support.

"Yuh, OK." Amel's sibilant realvoice slides through the upper registers, well above the standard frequency of the translator. Talbot winces at an especially piercing tone, but Amel has already begun to back away.

The door hisses shut behind her, leaving Talbot to himself.

4

The passenger lifesystem comprises about forty percent of the internal volume of the shuttle. Splitting its center, a raised walkway divides the space into two parts; on either side of this division, both fore and aft of the passenger seating, geometric plastic containers are racked in metal to form replicate arrays.

The passenger seating, at about the center of the lifesystem, is ranged two to each side of the walkway, each seat facing its mate on the same side. Conversation across the walkway, at least considered as face to face contact, is uncomfortable.

The conversations (x*Rkar and Schacther on one side, Atrenn across the walkway) continue, despite the difficulties. Direct-translation sibilants mimic the accents of the speakers at a standard frequency, filling the space with a common tongue above heterogeneous whispers. The three translators emit Basal into the air for each to hear – leveraging a mercantile common speech that has had currency across the Geodesic, in one dialect or another, for over three centuries, now the common ground for translators.

Suddenly, the door at the head of the walkway splits, emitting Amel. Amel's fur, ochre and white in the cold luminosity of the overheads, is bristled, signaling anger grown from pique.

Silence, broken only by the induced hiss of x*Rkar's radar carrier wave, falls in the face of Amel's anger.

Atrenn, who had turned back to a color strip from Schacther, looks up.

"Amel, you look cooked. Or is that fired up? So, did the forgetful leader chastise you for entering the sanctum so late?"

"Atrenn, must you always be not understandable to me? I think you are human sometimes."

"Violation of cold hollow pride." x*Rkar diagnoses, correctly, using his own equivalents.

"You too..." Amel whines, dropping on the walkway, entirely forgetful of pelt-dignity.

"Oh, all right, you tell us, then," Atrenn insists.

"eahhh – that person waited not for us -" The shuttle lurches briefly in a slight pocket of turbulence. Amel rolls involuntarily on her hind, catching herself with her arms. Without another word, she slides over the edge and hurries the two steps to her seat. Atrenn watches with what seems to be a very human grin.

"You feel that, then – we are beginning entry, and the turbulence might have happened without notice."

Atrenn's grin is gone.

Amel glances at Schacther for support. On Schacther's trunkfish face, just above the eye, a green splotch of consolation forms, traveling down to vanish at the neck. Its face and lips remain passive as the translator whispers "...forget..." Amel drums her fingers in appreciation as she slumps, displaying greater confidence. Her fur settles to its normal ochre, angry white underhairs now concealed.

"Post what event just passed, Amel, you should not sit there with nothing clinging you to your seat." x*Rkar's pouting scaly mouth points his upper lip in sardonic wit.

Amel looks up, startled, then gestures and pulls the straps down to lock.

"IT'S INAPPROPRIATE!" Schacther's translator screams in a monotone, echoing its skin turning an entirely dull black blazoned with flashing white symbols. Its feeding orifice trembles with effort.

"Schac, don't strain yourself, I see your pattern," Atrenn says gently.

And indeed, the message is written on its body.

"But what should we do? All right, some turbulence, unlikely to harm; it was contrary, but humans don't consider custom as inviolable as we do. Maybe he became impatient. We did take a long time, and not even telling him what we were doing, after all."

"So what does he tell us, when we are waiting here for hours yesterday, missing aperture?"

"I think you are scanning something too rough, Amel. You should tune longer if it is irritating you too much."

"Your radar metaphors are really getting good, x," Atrenn compliments him. x*Rkar emits a seventy cycle hum of pleasure. "Amel, do you really want to report this to Reed, or the Board? I'll back you, if you do, but remember, we might lose. He might be angry."

"We could be reassigned anyway. It would be better than this constant resistance."

9

But Amel sounds sulky, so that Atrenn knows he will be able to resolve the issue quietly - later.

5

A wind stirs the clouds to the north, swirling them slowly open on a current of warm air. Beyond are the green of the true sky and the light of the hidden sun fuming across the border of cloud.

The hunter stands immobile at the crest of a gentle swelling of land, looking away toward where the red grass fades into the greenish haze of the sky. The hunter feels a breeze, the end of a long chain of molecular collisions, caressing his face with an immaterial hand. The prey is beginning to wander away to the north, following the light. Lacking decision, he waits, watching them pursue their irregular course to the horizon; standing, a node of difference in the infinite repetition of the prairie. When his crop tightens with another of the many hunger contractions of the past few days, it reminds the hunter vaguely of the goal and he starts after his prey once again.

Roots from the base of the grass noose his long toes as he hurries; the crimson grass blades strike and slip under his chin, across his chest, past his arms, flailing weakly across the back of his rear-facing knee joints, as he shifts to a run.

6

Altitude 10 miles

Through the panes of the now open floor ports, Talbot watches the clouds above the continent of Vinetra unfold in patterns much like the palm of the human hand. As usual, he is mystified by the processes that can generate such shapes, so unlike their source, the roiling masses of moist air. How can they be the same as clouds seen from the ground? They slide below, no two shapes alike.

Not random, yet not purposive; caused, but not by the visible.

The shuttle strikes a region of turbulence. He communicates with the stabilizer systems, upgrading their alertness.

Outside the front windshield, the sky is still a deep forest green.

Altitude 5 miles

Through the gentle obscuration of the atmosphere, the surface has become clearer and more definite. It is, as he has noticed many times before, more of a difficulty in focusing than a physical discontinuity that forms the boundary between the upper and lower atmosphere. The intricate patterns of the landscape below seem shrouded by shadow, but all of the details, down nearly to individual trees, are visible with some effort.

Every planetary feature partakes of the reservoir of red phosphorus that is the basis of the soil of this world. With decreased altitude, he sees the forest below tinted as if with the maroon of human blood.

(He shrugs off the momentary morbidity)

The sonic compression cone trailed by the spacecraft inscribes a widening wake on the remains of the cloud layer below. Talbot scans the displays and the floor ports, seeking a level, unforested topography for landing. As yet, nothing but wildly humping hills encrusted with trees are visible, with an occasional outcropping of gray stone.

Altitude 3 miles

The artifact sensor gives off a graded alarm, indicating some uncertainty. The sound is loud enough to provoke his curiosity; he points and attempts to pull up a survey map of the location.

Not found.

No map?

Nothing.

He wheels the shuttle in a loose arc, turning more directly to planetary south. Passing directly above the spot, sensor bleeping gently, for a moment he thinks to see an elongated glint through the forest canopy. A certain disturbing thought leaps into his mind. In accordance with his training and experience, he resists his involuntary attempt to shunt it away, and considers...

A building? A ship?

They were going in because automated probes were not a sufficient guide to the safety of a world. Colonization or exploitation required that all species with work rights test the world for habitability. Talith was borderline for everyone on board, but changes could be made to plant life through farming. The land seems good, the atmosphere friendly, the fauna unthreatening. Formerly, hundreds or thousands of beings might be lost, billions of gold points squandered on unsuitable candidates that had looked equally promising. Now no more than ten at a time were risked.

He thinks of Govault, but that hits his threshold of resistance and this time he shunts it away. No natives. No ship. No danger. No death. No past leadership demoted down to just a driver. None of that had happened. This was just an outcropping of ore, reflecting the dawn sunlight. Something mildly interesting, at best.

He opens a scan, writing the image to the tank with a special tag, tying it to the sensor recording, and suggesting a high priority for post-landing review.

Altitude 2 miles

Ah, there, ahead; visible through the torn remnants of cloud that still persist so close below him and off to the horizon, a vast plain of red, phosphorus-laden grass shining in the sunlight, beginning as the forest ends. Perfect.

He activates the belly engine. The shuttle vibrates distantly as the engine interferes with the aerodynamics and then takes up the load. A faint whine slips into the pilot compartment. Talbot steers the shuttle in a wide semicircle back toward the bush veldt and pops out the drogues to lose some extra speed. The orientometer precesses toward the north as brilliant sun streams through the front windows, sluicing across the panels. His hands and legs warm under the impinging energy, but he ignores this, holding fast to duty.

7

A sound like thunder resonates from the distance and the clear sky, passing the hunter, heading south. Above, the clouds surge slightly, their dispersion hastened by the atmospheric perturbation. A dim rumbling fades up from behind the sound of concussion. The hunter follows its passage with sensitive ears, puzzled by the continuation of a normally short-lived natural sound.

Then, looking up to the sky, scrutinizing the scattered low-level clouds and the airspace between them and the nearly solid cloud deck above, he sees a dark speck moving with deliberation through the air. The speck swings in a wide arc, returning to a northerly heading. The sound seems to increase in volume, and shortly the hunter can discern two dots of color following the other, darker speck. His eyes blur with hunger, but he rubs them with a six-appendaged fist until they clear.

This must be his sign.

The hunter watches the specks as they float north. It seems that they suddenly pass into light, the largest speck changing from darkness to brilliance, reflecting the true sun. The trailing, colored objects seem to lag, then float south, back among the drifting clouds...

When he has stood there for a while, stupefied by his vision, he suddenly realizes that the prey has outpaced him, and he runs faster than ever to catch up. After all, it is fine for a nascent adult to stand adoring his sign, and, perhaps, a sign for all the tribe, but if he missed the opportunity signaled, he could be counted as meat of the Mover at the next Fire.

8

Altitude 1 mile

The shuttle rushes under the rumpled sky.

Talbot releases the braking chutes - arm dump sequencer, unlock, set for pack ejection, sequence start.

Since Talbot has retained the drogues long past their effective velocity range, there is no lurch. For the past several minutes it has been the belly engines that rumble under the floor, holding them on a hand of flame upraised. On the rear screens he sees the chutes snatched away. He turns his attention to the displays and the floor ports, watching the now visibly uneven ground slide below, searching for the best place to land.

A sudden depression, five hundred yards or more in diameter, rears up on the forward displays. It is nearly circular, and though muted by grass and geologic time, it is obviously a former impact crater, perfect for the purpose of their base.

Talbot re-enables the manual controls. With his hands unseen, like a musician caressing an instrument known as a lover, responding to the scene at hand, he maneuvers through a gentle approach turn (don't shock the passengers, or the equipment, as he had been trained), and he tracks the crater through an arc until it lies once again directly ahead.

9

The prey hesitates on the verge of a sharp rise, silhouetted. The hunter halts in his turn, but for what is, perhaps, another reason. The speck has become a spear point, drifting giddily through the air, terrifying with the strength of its animal roar.

The spear point in the air, last of all, hesitates beyond the ridge, and at this, the prey ceases to wait, but they bolt, running back past the hunter with all possible speed, rolling their blue and white eyes at him in radiant fear as they pass.

Though his reactions are hazed by hunger and the din, he seizes his chance with the reflex of long practice. The spear leaps out, seemingly of its own volition, still bound to his wrist by the dependable skin thong. The pounded metal blade sinks deep into the reddish fur, behind the head, into a place left vulnerable by the absence of hairy armor. A squall of death erupts from the pointy muzzle, revealing the prey's filthy square teeth. The hunter leaps on the prey with all the ferocity he can muster, still clutching the shaft of the spear, driving it deeper and twisting it mightily. His thin lips curl, revealing the long, canine teeth, and he screams with the joy of being released into adulthood.

A blast of sound rings his ears, bringing his head up as if he had been struck.

In the few moments it has taken to bring down the prey, the stone has come closer, and is sinking to the ground behind the ridge.

Ensuring with a touch and a glance that the herbivore is dead, the hunter wrests his spear from the rigid flesh. He stops to give himself a name - Deleo - as is his right and duty. Then he scrambles up the slope, to witness.

Blunt, triangular, the sign is a strange, scarred color, and it is opened with strange gaps and ports. Fire continues to vent from its belly, and then the brush in the hollow bursts into flames with a light whiter than the sun. This first frightening wave of flame, a deadly brush fire, is followed and then overtaken by a huge puff of thick white smoke that rolls from the underbelly of the thing, snuffing the dancing flames. In shock, Deleo feels his legs give way, and drops to the ground, flat, clutching the spear to his shoulder like a child.

10

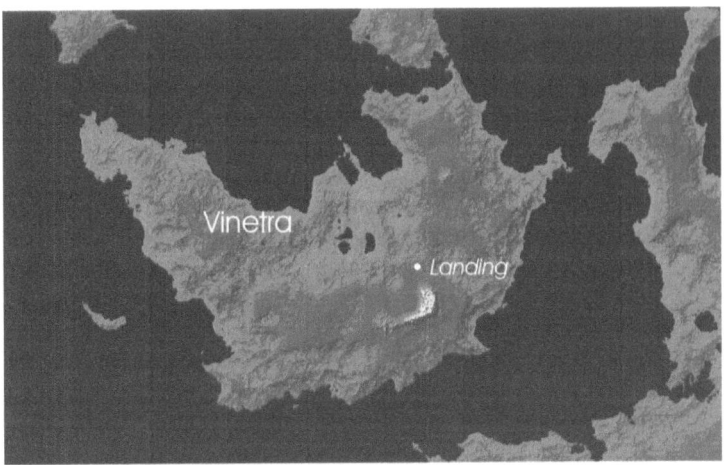

Vinetra

• Landing

A watery sunlight fills the ports; there is no dust suspended in it to punctuate its limpid clarity. System reports blink, colors blotted by the brightness. Boards switch automatically to quiescent, indicators changing to neutral blue automatically. Talbot stretches, the kink across his shoulders loosening under the strain.

He presses a final switch to power down the main sequencer, and the entire board goes blank. A twinge of anxiety rolls through his mind, as usual. An emergency might occur; pre-launch checkout would take ten minutes in any event. But this world would be just like the others. There would be new things, mysteries, even problems, but as in the past, they would not be serious.

His left hand moves up to release the harness.

11

At the rear of the lifesystem, behind the last rack of storage modules, Amel, x*Rkar, Atrenn, and Schacther gather at the now opened portal, each unwilling to be the first to step into the world; held in suspension by feelings different for each, but, in general, resembling awe for a complex new place.

The pressure difference, not yet fully resolved, wafts unfamiliar scents through the opening to the varied olfactory sensors of the waiting beings. Outside, the grass can be seen, lush and red; above, the sky shows vivid lime through broken clouds. Sounds - peepings, chitterings and a deep hum - pervade. All strike each differently, and some sense radically different things, but each in some way senses discontinuity with its home... gradually, the strangeness of the new links with the gestalts of their origins and the many worlds they each have seen, casting a cloak of strangeness across the familiar and making the strange seem normal.

Amel mutters a litany under her breath.

Talbot, walking from the pilot compartment, hears only the sound of the fans driving away the stink of smoke and extinguisher.

The waiting group parts before him; he steps to the airlock lip, unhampered by awe. First right, then across to the left, he scans the landscape as if looking for something. Then, with deliberation, he looks to the ground below, catches hold of the doorframe, and leaps to the ashen soil. Flakes and dust billow up from his feet, puffing into a cloud around him. He sneezes, bending almost double. "Damn!" Some of the ash lightens his dark skin, and powders his fringe of wooly hair.

He coughs, clearing his throat.

Air from the fans tugs his coverall out against his legs; the breeze of the planet pushes them to the right. He grins hugely under an unnamable impulse and waves the others out to join him.

12

Deleo peers over the rise, watching the strange activity. Once the cloud of irritating gas had dispersed, leaving him coughing helplessly, he thought of withdrawing and taking his prey. But the legends of the Mover, the tales of demons, force him to stay.

A hole opens in the side of the thing, and he realizes that the stone is hollow, like a house - surely like a house, since someone, much like himself in form, though not in detail, leaps from the opening to the charred ground.

The apparition has skin the color of soot. Deleo looks at his own hand, his pale, faintly bluish skin stretched across a bony articulation, and at the appendage the strange being waves. The hair... not the proud red mane of an adult, or even the pale shock of the aged, but a thin layer of black fur across its head. This is a strange reversal, like every color changed to its opposite; surely it means something. Was it ... it had to be evil.

The first being, strange, but reflecting normality, is followed by creatures out of nightmare: a hideous, scaled thing, with no eyes; a shrunken man with golden skin, engorged skull and collapsed face; another creature with colors moving, blooming, and dissolving its skin and a face like a chitinoid. There is even a hairy, prey-like creature with dark blots for eyes. They are all dressed like priests, in a single garment wrapped to their forms, as if their skins are so delicate that they need to protect themselves against even the grass and wind.

These have to be the demons, warned of by the Mover.

His kill forgotten in sudden and abject fear, Deleo runs from the sight, crashing away through the tall grass with imperious but furtive motion, away toward the forest, his home.

13

Stiff tree barrels form runes against the glow of the exterior night and its millions of brilliant stars. Elaborating the runes, vines stretch from the forest floor to gather tightly about the limbs, binding them into the network of the canopy.

Hardly a sound is caused by their footsteps; they do not disturb the incessant activities of the countless creatures striving, living and dying around them. Deleo moves with them, watching his feet, stepping cautiously where they do; he is the novice, though each move this night is of his instigation.

Fear permeates their movement, their every conscious thought.

His companions are all much older; perhaps for this reason they are more aware and more deeply afraid of the change that this consultation is about to wreak in their lives. In this manner, they experience the paradox of those who have a truly living god.

Beneath their feet the fluttering chitinoids try, and mostly fail, to escape the insouciant foot that crushes out their unconscious lives.

There is a clearing, rimmed with rotted, fallen trees lying at all angles. Some are crushed under the weight of their outer shell, the water-logged skin cracked and peeled back from the shrunken pith. Cluster light shines down in a shaft on the grass and brush at the center, gleaming on the stone remains of structures so old that the very form of people has changed since they were built. That even ragged foundations remain is a testimony to the power of the Mover.

They step over a log into the clearing. Deleo feels his crop tighten with anticipation; for the first time, he has the responsibility for the reading of the Dance. He tries to hold every element of everything taught about the Dance in mind at once, and fails, increasing the despair mixed into his anticipation. Deleo tries again and again as they walk across the grass and brush to the crumbling stone remains. They step over the fallen blocks and then the wall itself. Inside is a square of closely fitted stones with a deep square well marking its center. Deleo has never been here before, but an aura of unnamable tension seems to thicken the air. The priests, cloaking garments stark shadowed in the cluster light, shudder perceptibly under the impact of this sensation. One motions Deleo to a place at the center of a wall, another pushes Deleo to sit. Then the four disperse to the corners, there dropping to wait with bowed heads. Deleo stares out through the V-shaped opening in the wall across, identity consumed with stillness.

Four voices hum a minor chord. The sound echoes through the dark stands of trees, seeming to flow in waves. There begins a distant response.

The sound increases and soon it is like trees being destroyed in a winter storm; but there is no wind. It is like the tread of enormous spidery legs crashing across the plant-strewn forest floor, knocking trees aside in a destructive indifference.

It is the sound of the Steps of the Mover.

Silence falls, the priests avert their eyes.

And across the clearing, directly in Deleo's view, the trees wave madly as if dancing to an unfelt wind. They part under the force of a huge black shape; one falls splintering to the ground. Deleo feels a scream that never passes his throat. The god, the oracle, dances buoyantly into the cluster light. It is an appallingly featureless black ellipsoid, ringed with flexing legs. It reels and leaps and bounds in the light, like a fragment of space brought to earth, unlimited by gravity. A shadow, it gyrates, describing a pattern that is not a pattern, its tentacles flicking like whips, the shadows cast by their motion on the fallen leaves flickering in sympathy. There is a message, and Deleo finds that he does not even need to think or remember to understand:

The message is death.

14

The grass is wet with dew, splattering onto Deleo's skin as he pushes forward across the plain. Wet red slaps his chest, his shoulder.

A rack of spears is slung across his back, like the penalty for a shameful act, the abrogation of the maturity ritual in fear. He uses an extra spear, the hunting spear, a spear that had brought down uneaten prey, as a ward against the moist grasses; it is not very effective.

Ahead, the rise that conceals the demon house. A catalyst, the sight and its implication banishes the threads of conscience, as the Mover had known it would. He is the instrument of its vengeance, of the dim and obscure purpose that the Mover creates. Deleo crouches, fingers digging into the soil, scrambling under the weight of his weaponry to the top of the rise, to the sight of the target.

15

Talbot wakes in a pool of light. For a moment after he raises his head, his surroundings are blued and blurred. Slowly the normal tones of metal and plastic come back to him.

The lifesystem is empty.

The airlocks are open, dawn light spilling on the catwalk. Sounds and smells fill the lifesystem, and among them are the familiar smells of the mixed alien and human cuisine preferred by most shipdwellers. The only signs of his companions are in the rumpled beddings beside the catwalk.

In the washroom at the stern of the lifesystem, he throws water on his face, staring at the image in the various mirrors for a moment as if it belongs to a stranger. Looking past the door, he sees an awning has been erected outside. The maroon grasses beyond are translucent in the morning sun.

16

When Talbot steps from the ramp, he finds yesterday's ash glued into a rough but serviceable floor. The containers they had spent most of the day shifting are now stacked outside at the stern, multicolored plastic glistening in the sun. He looks toward the bow and finds Amel, standing at the cooktop, watching him with what looks like suspicion. The others, seated in a semicircle of chairs by the edge of an awning, had been looking at data spread on the table before them. He feels pinned by the intensity of their combined gaze. Gradually, the attention diffuses, leaving him private. His sensation of acute discomfort, however, does not pass.

"Talbot." Amel acknowledges finally with a barely perceptible voice. The whispering sound reacts against his mood, striking him to anger, carefully suppressed. The alien's eyes, black-glass eggs, reflect the scene back on itself. He watches his image grow in them as he approaches.

"Amel," he replies, mustering pleasantness from behind his unease. "I gather you're cook this morning..." He notices, from the edge of his vision, that the others have returned to their scrutiny of the data displayed on the table. Occasionally, they point at something, their mingled realspeech and Basal a low muttering against the backdrop of natural grassland sounds; yet somehow he feels they are watching.

"yess..." Amel replies, a falsetto rise at the end of the slur. "What would you like?"

"Oh, just some eggs, if you don't mind."

"Perhaps some burned bread, as well?" she suggests; though her body is bent as she stoops to retrieve something from a lower shelf, her eyes are solidly upon him.

A light breeze flaps the canvas of the awning, ending the motion with a snapping retort.

"Toast?" Talbot says, finally connecting.

"Two span." The alien seems to bite out the words; her attention turns down to the grill. No vegetarian, Amel.

On every world for every intelligent species, burning the food has its advantage - it is sure death to parasites.

Atrenn looks up from the table, a digit resting on a spot in a window on the table. "Talbot," he says, "won't you sit down?" His face, seen in this light, is even more seriously a caricature of the human; features shrunken, the crooked grin seams the golden skin with lines, pushes up the diminutive nose; the brow line, spiky eyebrows, the thin frizz of violet-tinged black that resembles hair - all seem slightly human but are not.

x*Rkar turns his eyeless head toward Talbot. Talbot hears the hum of radar in his brain.

"Sit please, Talbot, do, yes." he asks vocally.

Talbot looks over at Schacther. Its color remains stable, meaning, so Talbot has been told, that he is having no special reaction to Talbot's presence. He shrugs mentally, sits, and waits for them to speak: he has nothing particular to say. x*Rkar continues...

"Talbot, Atrenn broadcasts of the ship you mentioned to his yesterday-self."

"Well, now," he interrupts, warningly, "I didn't come to any conclusions. It might have been a ship. I didn't have a good size for it - it was too deep in the foliage for reliable measurement." He glances at Atrenn for the nod of confirmation he would expect from any human, but, of course, the little fellow just sits there, bland, but attentive. x*Rkar elevates a grey scaled appendage, caricature of a professor about to launch into a point.

"Talbot. I from tank have explicitly retrieved images-visual and data sourced from metal sensors. EMF resonances give mass; example may be near 256000, a nice even number for us."

Talbot gives up looking where his eyes should be. These creatures have lived in caves for their entire evolution, and their eyes have long since fled. The radar remains, a very precise sense, and, with others of their kind, even a direct visual communication medium.

"Are you making an official determination?" he asks. There will be reports to enter.

"Yes."

"Yes," Atrenn breaks in, "because who knows what it means to us, after all. Whose ship?"

Atrenn taps the table and an image, enlarged, contrast enhanced, mapped with sensor inferences flips across the table to beneath Atrenn's outstretched digit. Atrenn spins it toward Talbot, who enlarges it still further with a spread of his hands at the diagonals.

A set of comparative models plays against the inferred geometry, but all fail.

"Not ours," Talbot replies, intrigued.

"No," Atrenn acknowledges. "Nor ours. I have directed the tank to search the full range of patterns overnight, and nothing similar to the apparent pre-crash profile is even a remote match. It is an alien."

"It's also old." Talbot looks up. "There's a lot of old growth. Look." He dials up the infrared profiles, and zooms a section until the canopy outlines can be seen.

"The discoloration on the metal is diamir corrosion," Schacther's calm, whispery translator voice says quietly. "Available light spectra confirm the diffusion profiles."

"So?" Talbot grunts, falling back into the chair's embrace. "It's been there a long time. Why diamir? Nanogrowth synthetic, isn't it? Didn't we develop that only a few years ago?"

Colors chase themselves across Schacther's skin, occasionally clustering into repeating patterns; its coveralls translate them with their fiber computers, assembling his voice, as perfectly translated as concepts would allow.

"The Teren have had it for longer," Schacther says. "Much longer. But not long enough for any diamir objects to become corroded in this way. And the synthesis of diamir across complex forms is not so simple that anyone can use it for hulls. Though we would prefer it."

Talbot looks away, out over the grass, giddy with fascination and disgust.

Amel peers over Talbot's shoulder. "We don't need a recurrence of Govault," she mutters.

Talbot looks at her sharply.

"Eggs ready," she tells Talbot.

"So, you know about that?"

"Trained." Amel replies sullenly. "You know. Self know. You were leading."

"I'm not discussing that with you. It was a long time ago."

"We withdrew," Atrenn replies. "Wisely avoiding genocide, though there are those I have heard argue otherwise."

Talbot says nothing, but his eyes are downcast and his fingers tap on the armrest.

"Yes, well, that's the theory, anyway." Atrenn finishes.

17

There is a moment where Amel screeches suddenly, a sound like a throat tearing - she falls, an enormous shaft thrust through her body; from nowhere, black blood floods across the congealed ash. The others leap up; while Talbot stands astounded, Schacther whips its laser from a strap, searching for a target. Another spear shoots up out of the grass, carving a clear arc against the sky. Schacther sees it, but seems too busy to consider its destination. So Schacther fires, the green bolt striking through the grass in a veil of white flame. Talbot shouts, intending to warn, but the sound is inarticulate and useless. The spear smashes through the awning, ripping a hole and striking Schacther's laser just before its sweep reaches the source of the attack. The weapon explodes with a deceptively mild pop, blowing the remains of Schacther's hand across the ground. Its whole body turns lavender instantly and falls to the ground without a sound.

Atrenn has his laser out and is falling back toward the shuttle, scanning the landscape. x*Rkar crouches beside the table, gesturing toward the grassland. Another spear falls, glancing off the table surface and spinning across the ground. Just as Atrenn fires at the source, x*Rkar dives for the spear, rolling in an incredible gymnast's feat, simultaneously casting it at the spot burning under Atrenn's laser beam. Suddenly, x*Rkar falls to the ground, pinned through the narrow skull by a beaten metal point.

"Talbot! Talbot!" Atrenn shouts. "Get out of here!" A wild scream answers another lancing beam from the laser. x*Rkar thrashes on the ground; Atrenn rushes forward to help. But Talbot runs toward the fallen Amel, the hooting agony of x*Rkar sounding suddenly in his ear.

There is a weapon on the ash beside Amel.

Amel lies face up in the plasticked dust, contorted and stiff, a huge pool of gleaming dark (it doesn't look like blood... it couldn't be blood, there is too much of it...) spread from beneath the body. Her fur is wet with the stuff - Talbot tries not to see.

Instead, he snatches the laser from under the edge of the cooktop, and, still crouched, swivels it, firing, across the grass in a vicious impulse. White fire blooms where it touches, sending heat beating back toward him. Atrenn is dragging x*Rkar toward the lock. The spear is gone from x*Rkar's head, and Talbot wonders momentarily if x*Rkar can survive, when a spear flashes down, striking Atrenn and pinning him against the ground. He yammers helplessly, thrashing about, trying to drag the spear from his body. x*Rkar is tossed aside, forgotten in agony. Talbot throws down his weapon and runs, ducking under the ship, past the fan vents and the motors, up the other side to the far lock. He scrambles within, yes, still breathing, still whole, blood pounding in his ears and swirling in his head, not draining to the ground; he levers his barely mobile body onto the lip of the opening; inside, the emergency seal, arm and release, then crawling to the other side to do the same, to shut out the screaming, the pain, the blood........

18

Talbot cries, feels the nails in the skin of his cheeks, clinging. He takes his hands away from his face and stares at them in dulled horror. "Why," he whispers, "was I doing that?" He watches the blood pound in the netted veins of his dark hands. Minutes pass without a thought dropped into the silence; no sensation except sight and suspension.

What can I do now? he wonders, all referents, all context stripped from his syntax.

He looks up. The walkway stretches away from him, ends in a door, so far away, so small, leading to the pilot's cabin. The metal racks stand naked and empty, gleaming in the bluish light. He turns his face toward the ceiling, seeing the serene glow of the tubes, haloed against the dark metal. Only then can he allow thought to creep into his mind, delicately, like a man testing a wound for mortality, ready to recoil from a familiar path.

So he remembers:

It was three years after Govault. He had come upcurve with a bunch of pers from Bonavent, having landed work as a shuttle pilot on the run from BeeVee station to the Sistral encampment on Issim. He felt sure he had come to terms with his position. To his demotion.

His room was comfortable, not opulent, but it was fully inboard. He had ridden all the way over from Optator in the third seat from the ports and he wanted to see stars now.

He pulled up a listing of all the perimeter restaurants and lounges from the registrar. An item caught his attention - Shan's, over on the northeast rim of the station. It reminded him of an old friend from flight training, Shan Rensak, and, yes, the place was a smoke, patch and drink, just like Shan's father used to run at Clotinius. Why not? He could use a buzz before eating, and he could also use, especially, a view.

After wandering through interminable colored hallways, losing himself and then finally having to ask directions from the wall registry, he arrived. The sign for the establishment flared across an eighty foot stretch of wall, repeated across the surface in human-sized letters that marched along the wall through their own echoes. He entered, and darkness leapt to enclose him.

Floor to ceiling windows were lit with the spectacle of the galactic spiral far below. Rugs and cushions spotted the floor, and the wall let into private alcoves.

Business was slow at this hour: the place was empty - no, not quite, an alcove to the right of the door was occupied by something holding a murky drink up to the stellar light in a tightly coiled tentacle.

Behind the bar, a tall, thin fellow with darkly ochre skin stood patiently, polishing a glass house pipe with a soft rag. His dark hair was long and tied asymmetrically over his left ear. His mouth was concealed by drooping moustaches that hung almost to his shoulders. It was.. yes, it was Shan! But somewhere inside, a barrier was thrown up, controlling his step, crushing the eagerness from his face. Yes, Shan, but... taller than he remembered, thinner too, perhaps. Shan watched indifferently until Talbot was standing at the bar, then his flat brow furrowed with the effort of memory, his face lit with surprise...

"Tal, what you doing here, man? Hahn't seen you for years. What you smoking now? I'm sure we've got it." His asymmetric ponytail wagged with the fluid motion of his head, signaling a greeting. The expansive and satisfied tone jarred Talbot.

"Yeah, it's been a long time, Shan. This your place?"

"Oh, ya bet, Tal. Best on the station, best in the sector. Only smoke and drink on the station, but we've got good liquor. Mank over there," he gestured at the other angle of the bar," is your woman for that. But if you're smokin or patching or whatever, I got what you like. So name your choice. If we don't have it, it can't be got."

"Well, then, how about some Jamas, Shan? You have any of that?" It felt strange, flaunting credit like that, but, why not? He hadn't had any since Clotinius. Not, in fact, since that time he and Shan had smoked behind the ventilator stacks, just before graduation. And he could afford it with the compensation payments for Govault, just before they eased him out of leadership and into the pool...

He pulled his mind back to the present.

Shan frowned with the effort of recollection, then relaxed. "Oh, yeah. Sure, man. Like I say, I've got a little of everything, a lot of some." He leaned to the right, dipping down below the bar and coming back up with a thick pinch, all the while talking in his thick, reedy voice. "This stuff is quite scarce lately - I mean the real stuff, not the crap they usually sell. I mean, like the mutation rate is something fierce. But I got some in from a runner heading upcurve with ag systems for Greta. Good and fresh, man, you'll like it." He rolled it with swift rushes of his ochre fingers into a cigarette, edges spiraling evenly, and sealed it. "Here you go, Tal, a good clean smoke." He passed it under the drying light and handed it to Talbot.

A display under the bar lit the bottom of Shan's face. He studied it for a second, dipped into another bin of pinkish crystal and loaded a house pipe, holding it ready as the waiter arrived to take it. She thanked him with a glance, and headed out onto the floor.

"So, what you been doing, Tal? You taking a starship for this Sistral run? Everybody's been coming in for a month, but I haven't seen many pilots or leaders yet."

Talbot delayed answering, tilting his head and sucking flame into the cone. He held the smoke, feeling it expand into his lungs. Then it rushes out of his nostrils, billowing briefly across the bar.

"Shan, come on, I'm not doing starships. I'm running a shuttle, like always... after." The lift hit his mind, and he rode it angrily, stomping on the frustration that had erupted. "What about you?" he asked, tilting back for another draw.

"Well, let's see," Shan said, leaning forward on the bar, "I bought this place... eight years ago, wasn't it? with some insurance credit; it wasn't doing too good just then, and the old owner wanted out. He was running a chic trade, Rim liquors only, which were hot for, like, what? three years? but, when the flick dropped off, there was nothing left - "

The display lit again, but Shan transferred it, calling over to the blond woman who was sitting, smoking, and reading a fac behind the other leg of the bar. "That's liquor for you Mank." The other nodded, ash dripping from the tip of a tobacco cigarette, hesitated to finish a sentence, then leapt up in silent, frantic motion to fill the order before the waiter arrived. "So... anyway, where was I? Oh, yeah. So, you know, my old man used to run Smoke & Pinch in Clotinius; remember, after practice flights?"

"Yeah," Talbot said through exhalation..

"So, I knew substance from padr. I figured I could make a go. Hahn't been bad, you know?"

The display flashed, just as Talbot asked (too quietly to really want an answer) "But why'd you stop flying?" Shan, of course, didn't hear, didn't answer, too busy snapping and laying out sticks of brilliant red arotnish on a tray. Talbot turned and saw two Tereniades settling to carpets in the middle of the floor. One of them was Atrenn, though they hadn't met at the time. (His real self recoils from this image out of memory.)

When Shan came back, the sight of the aliens had brought Talbot resentment, so he had the question ready. "So, Shan, how come you're not flying any more?"

"Oh," Shan said, voice falling, "You didn't know? No, I guess not, man. Well, there was sort of an accident. I was running freight on contract to Rennald Norris, three times a month, Bonavent to Rilkestraport. You know the spec, you come in, snatching all the speed you can on every decent gravity well in system, and if you're hot, you ride an accel orbit starting near L5 for ten-eleven, just to keep pending for your corridor. Then I get a message from DCA telling me to fling out about twenty miles for a hospital runner coming in from an inbound liner. So, I figure that's clearance, they know the twenty mile swing's clear, I mean, they are supposed to be in control. So I'm out about ten miles into this, not really checking the scope cause the attitude control's the tough part, and then I get a bite on the localizer, and DCA screaming on the com. The runner clips me on the stern, and me without even time to shut down the jets for a sling out." His hand hung in the air, aborted in mid-gesture. "So there I am, spinning off toward Mockva, venting air out the stern, me pinned in the seat by the wreckage, and the whole lifesystem a piece of junk, but it's still got some integrity...anyway, it took them three hours to get out there and unpin me, by which time, I was pretty shot. When I come to, the DCA's got recordings saying three miles in, though one of my buddies in orbit says fakes, cause he heard twenty too, out on the channel, but look,

after three hours out there, I wasn't in any shape to fly again, anyway. So, I took my award, bought the name, and eventually here I am, as you see."

Talbot was coughing, and the words of consolation couldn't force their way past his spasming throat. Shan gestured, and Mank brought a drink. "Here, this'll help." The bar display flashed again, as a new party pulled rugs over to the window. Talbot wiped his eyes, wheezing. Shan was down at the right end of the bar, assembling various components on a chromium tray.

Then he returned, and asked, "But, now you got to tell me, Tal, what keeps a bright guy like you running shuttles. I heard you had a ship – you were on the way."

There it was, undiluted, as Shan used to put it. Talbot wanted to pay, leave, run, anything but answer. How could he, though? Instead, he spoke with a hint of mockery, "Hey Shan, you know, you have something happen to you, and it can be pretty bad, you depend on someone else, you get the wrong answer, something happens...they tell you this and that until you start thinking you're really good for nothing... but of course they're so nice and polite. Oh yeah." He dropped into a moody silence that Shan was wise enough not to try to break. Shan looked at his friend with a silent tension of concern and pity that was palpable. Talbot didn't want to see it. "Shit," Talbot muttered unsteadily, feeling like he was swimming in null-g. He sucked down smoke and the fire broke through in an orange oval on the side of the cone. "I better go... go sleep," he muttered, crushing the cone into embers. "How much, Shan?"

"Hey, on the house, Tal." Shan said, trying to keep his voice light. "Like, good to see you, man."

Talbot thought he heard a tiny sarcasm.

"Shan," he said, warning.

"Tal, I'll see you again, man; on your way back in, or some such thing. Have a good run, you know?" And that was the sound of strain.

"Shan, how much?"

"Tal, come on, take it easy, huh. Hey, Halin," he called over Talbot's shoulder, "yeah, would you help Talbot here," he gestured, "to a rail, heh. Yeah, that probably would be best. Tal, you got your points with you?" Then, strong hands gripped Talbot's shoulders, and Shan rolled away down the bar, his chassis gleaming in the dimness...

Talbot lets it fade. Now he remembers. It had been reason enough then for not caring. It still ought to be. He is going to leave.

19

Talbot stumbles, ducking under the doorframe. He slides into his seat with the creak of its stiff material sinking under him, unheard. A touch to the main sequencer powers up the system; signals appear, displays run their test sequences. Like an automaton, he brings out the checkpad, runs through the steps. The moments pass and his hands tremble less and less. He yanks straps down over his shoulders, snapping them into place; then he reaches overhead to the com controls.

Nothing – except the sporadic tick and flange of an open digital maser channel picking up interference from a nearby storm. He checks the plot to see what may be wrong, and sees that the *Illyrion's* primary relay is barely above the horizon, accelerating to synchronous orbit, while a secondary relay has not yet been orbited – the Illyrion herself is on the other side of the planet, continuing a complex orbital path to arrange probes and satellites for the next stages.

"Talbot here. Acknowledge, please." To his disgust, his voice is hoarse and unsteady; he holds up a hand - it is shaking again, stained with alien blood.

Hastily, he puts it aside from view.

No answer.

"Acknowledge, please."

Still no answer. More silence. The weather display shows a violent frontal storm system advancing rapidly. Less than an hour remains before the onset of potentially unacceptable turbulence.

He switches off the com.

20

From the south and west, water vapor rebounds from a stable cold front, and, reacting to the barrier, begins to shed thin cold rain on the steppe.

21

Talbot watches the wall of clouds sliding above him; but the systems have finished their startup procedure, and it is time. The startup clearance warning sounds outside, a forlorn cry above lifeless bodies strewn across the ash.

22

The sky slips jagged light, and there is a momentary pause of silence - then the thunder follows across the landscape in echoic majesty.

23

The sky erupting,
Deleo caught between....
The spear hoarsely screaming
... and Deleo runs.
cast like a moist seed between pressing fingers,
fumbled,
hastening to the wood, a peninsula of trees, racing across the plain, past the shrieking demon house and over the rise beyond. Breath roaring in its vents as it pushes hard across the rugged land.

24

Rain sweeps down, flooding the viewport and all of the dorsal lenses. When the foremost wave is past, the port clears and Talbot restores his grip on the throttle to full strength; then, for a moment, he sees... a pale grey figure, running past in the rain, slapping through grasses and gone.

Talbot's hand, released.

...human? Denial. But close; skin, legs, hands, muscles, hair...

A guilt is merely latent - his darker hand, stained with Amel's blood. A silly voice, stilled. His anger at the other's presence, striking, because it was defenseless, increasing, because they were indifferent. Moment piles on moment, the shuttle whines impatience.

"Talbot! Talbot!" Atrenn shouts. "Get out of here!"

Anger, still anger, he slaps the systems down. His hand shakes so badly that he cannot control it.

25

Talbot leaps from the lock, landing on the scarred earth. He scrambles quickly into the concealment of the still moist grasses, finally crouching on the soft earth. He checks the weapon that lies silent in his hands, waiting to bark light in a directed stream, ready to kill; he checks the knife at his waist. His breath sounds a light pant in his ears, braced on the silence of the storm-frightened world.

Then he is up again and running, searching for the rutted track.

It is harder to find than he expects; the grasses are resilient and most of the trace has been obscured by the passing minutes.

Rain falls in a shower across miles, pauses, begins again, patters on the grass around him.

26

Deleo sits huddled on the forest floor, like a spire rising from the tessellation of white and red leaves. The spear lies on the detritus at Deleo's side.

Here, the trees are thick, bordering the bush veldt. Through the screen of barren undergrowth that delimits the forest, Deleo can look back to see the gently rolling landscape from which he has come.

He regards his wound ruefully. The surprise: that light could hurt; that the sun has been tamed and under their control is almost worse than the pain itself. But, puzzled, he stares at the wound, sealed, unbleeding... evil? If he had been caught in the sweep of the beam more fully, he could have been cut in two...both halves... living? For a while... he thrusts the thought away.

Deleo holds the knife, hand resting on his double knee, absently rubbing a digit on the flat of the brassy metallic blade where it thrusts from the binding of the hilt. When the self anger fades, he slides the knife back into the sheath at his waist. He looks up and out across the grass beyond the netted branches.

There is a disturbance imposed on the surging movements of the grass; not a whorl of the wind, or a gust in the rain, but the passage of something of bulk.

Deleo knows: it is the last of the demons, searching. For him.

27

Talbot stumbles on the uneven ground, gasping, impeded by the miles of corridors that line his past, progress inconclusive. A kilometer ahead, trees rise to a canopy a hundred yards high, looking higher in the vague, clouded light. But somewhere in the bloody dimness ahead is the alien, the nemesis, waiting to be killed.

He stumbles in a drainage channel and falls. The laser smacks against a rock with a sound like his heart stopping. Instantly his head comes up, searching, knowing that he is watched, that he could be killed at any moment.

He stares at the laser dangling from his grip, dented and stained with mud and red plant. Impetuously, angrily, he fires at the grass, a swath of light that raises an instance of flame. Then he looks at the trees, seeing only the ghosted image of the running biped that passed his ship in the rain.

28

At the sight of that brief blaze, Deleo rolls to his inverted knees, snagging the spear. On hands and one leg, with one leg dragged behind, he scrambles to the bole of a nearby tree and installs itself behind it. He waits, crouched, watching the demon's blundering progress. His pulse pounds behind the line of his strange, linear jaw.

29

Talbot pushes his way through the wiry undergrowth, shoving it away from his face, forced to duck and push. He bursts through into the clearing, eyes locked on the disturbed leaves. He reaches out with the laser, scanning suspiciously.

No one in sight.

The temptation is too great; Talbot strides over to the mussed area and squats down to look it over in detail, laser resting negligently on mud-soaked knee.

Deleo thrusts his head out past the bole of the tree, a fierce, unconscious expression like a feral human smile tugging skin back from his teeth. His spear rests ready in his hand.

Two strong steps and Deleo casts the spear through the sparse cage of trees, aiming with all his wit for the human who crouches a mere thirty feet away. That one cast, calculated with all of the resources at his command, is the only one he has.

The spear writhes through the air, and then is suddenly deflected by the muscular trunk of a tree, whacking into the ground with an audible thrum a yard short of where Talbot stares, shocked by the proximity of death. Talbot leaps to his feet and whips the laser up to firing position... but Deleo is already running.

The laser flickers and dies. Frustrated, Talbot slaps the recalcitrant weapon, but it refuses to function.

Nothing.

Deleo waits, standing insolently not one hundred feet distant, on the verge of the undergrowth that rises up under the crowns of the real forest.

Talbot screams, throwing the useless laser to the ground. His eyes fall on the spear, protruding from the soil only a few yards distant. Wrenching it from the ground, he rears back and heaves it at the native, anger blinding him to futility. The cast falls short by a huge distance.

Deleo hesitates only a moment before rushing forward and snatching up the spear. For a moment he stares at Talbot from his angular stance, and Talbot might have sworn the hunter was wondering at his magnanimity in returning the weapon.

"Go on," he shouts. "But I'm going to kill you!"

Deleo whirls and disappears in a rush of blood-red foliage.

30

A half-hour later Talbot examines a makeshift spear. Its tip gleams wetly with transparent sap where he has shaped it with his blade. While it is too irregular to be thrown, at least it allows more distance than the knife. But he is too afraid to admit that it is unlikely to save his life, that this time, he has gone too far.

31

The sky above the canopy has cleared and the sun is casting slices of light that shift slowly and waver with the oncoming late afternoon breeze. Talbot races after Deleo, pushing aside the branches. The leaves rise up in ranks along the twisting path, choking off the light until it becomes a tunnel of hushed maroon dimness. Ahead he sees the flailing legs of his prey, a momentary flicker, as the path winds straight, and then turns again.

He runs harder... more energy than he ever spent as a child on a playground - he is exhausted, and each step seems longer than the last. He is more and more afraid; the path is now a tunnel leading to a clearing that is fiery with end of day sunset - is it getting hotter?

He stumbles slightly as he stops on the verge, staring at a sudden wave of tarnished metal rising under the canopy, at its breaks and contours of vents, legs, ports and broken doors. It is a moment before he assembles a perception that it is not a building, but a space vehicle or aircraft - a derelict.

Deleo peers from the undergrowth, trembling. This was the wrong place to have brought the enemy.

32

Talbot cannot release his wariness, and he sidles toward the vessel, eyes restless, makeshift spear waving as if to block any motion. Where is the native? What does he have to do with this derelict? Did he lead Talbot here as a trap?

A ramp leads up to the shadows, littered with junk, cloaked in wafts of leaves. One huge door is twisted against the side of the ramp. The other, if it ever existed, cannot be seen. He scuffs the leaves, looking around, suddenly peering up into the dimness. His curiosity is pulled more than on any other mission, but here, it is worth his life to be distracted.

There are intriguing symbols embossed on the metal, signs of the culture that created this derelict... He whirls at a rustle from the forest. He hears a sudden rush through the leaves... yes, heading away. The hunter has fled, and now Talbot is the alien, alone, with the sun rushing toward the edge of the world. The light has become dusky, and the red slanting beams are fewer and longer.

Talbot is confused, ready to run, ready to fight; fearful of traps, of hiding places and the game of lie and feint. He wants to leave, to go back to the *Illyrion*, his familiar cabin and pictures, to his desk volume littered with windows. But even more, he wants everything to be safe. He wants to be free, like a tourist, to explore.

His pant is echoing from the walls beside and the curved roof above. The ramp beckons. Probably the second most dangerous place in the world right now.

The leaves on the ramp appear undisturbed. The native must have fled. But it is getting late, and the way back to the shuttle is impossible in the half light. Can this ship shelter him? Or should he...

"All right!"

He stalks up the ramp, a roar of leaves being crushed.

33

The arcuate splits in the west wall admit the remaining sun to the interior volume - a wreck, canted sharply, debris piled on the floor. A huge loading door, buckled and curled upward as if struck from below, tops the ramp. Beyond are mountings, now empty, and a large raised dais that might have been the control area. The control panels are ruined, like crippled altars, and there are huge windows, now dulled and broken, ranged across the wall above.

A strange technology, but not incomprehensible.

The rusty light from beyond the wall fades. Remarkably, the interior does not seem to dim. As the sunset proceeds, Talbot watches the ship's light fade in. There are patches where it is darkened forever, but those are like the shadows of...foliage; the light has no source, but the walls and surfaces are dimly illuminated by the faint appearance of cold moonlight.

As he walks up past the broken door, there is a sudden crunch from beside his feet. Talbot looks down, to see a cracked hollow sphere - a skull. He drops to his knees, scraping away the litter. The skull is not human.

It is bilateral, and a mouth and jaw must have existed. But what to make of the elliptical brain case and the juts to either side of smallish eyepits? Is this the same as the native? Or something else?

If only he had his recorder.

The air is cooler already. There is a spatter of twilight rain on the hull; traces reach through the rents to the floor.

He kicks at the leaves, shivering with disgust at the thought of the dead. He clears a place by the wall, where he can watch the ramp. The rain is even stronger now, a crazy rattle on the hull, a steady drip through the cracks.

But nothing happens.

Now, cold, huddled against a truly alien wall, Talbot tries to understand his motives. *I must have gone crazy.*

Why the attack? What about the occupants of this ship? Are the natives their descendants? What happened to their civilization? Are they dangerous to us? Is this what we sensed during entry, or is it something else?

He knows he will probably never fly again. His failure to report: a temporary insanity. They'd have to understand that. They'd know he wasn't to blame, not after seeing his friends -

No, not friends. Where'd you get that word?

passengers

killed. Who would think properly after that? There can be no training for terror.

But allowances can not be made. Absolute reliability is required. He has to stay awake. And his stomach hurts with emptiness.

There will be no food or water tonight.

Absolute reliability. He steadies the spear on his knee.

No allowances.

He leans his head up against the wall for just a moment.

34

Deleo huddles miserably amidst the wet leaves, rain trickling from above, leaking through hair, and dripping with occasional harshness on the leaves covering the forest floor. Deleo aches with wounds and exertion; his emotions are turbulent.

He had led the alien to the Home of the Mover - to certain death. He should be ecstatic. Yet the ease with which the alien had approached the Home... Almost as if it felt the Home to be safer than the forest. Even the priests felt breath pulse stronger in their spiracles at the thought of the Home. As for himself, the sight of the Home had been pure terror, when he realized his accident. Fear for the Mover had followed, but first the fear for himself had risen, and with it he had fled.

Now it is dark, and there is only the rustling of rain in the forest.

35

Talbot wakes with a start, hands scraping on the dimly lit walls in a sudden spasm, quickly controlled. It is a moment before he realizes he is not back on the *Illyrion*. He remembers the dream of the moment before waking - a dream, so real, of the ship, of a fight with Atrenn, a good drinking bout, then sleep...

The derelict is utterly silent - outside, it is the depth of the night, the few hours during which all of the creatures of every forest are asleep at once. But the faint light of the walls does not yield. Talbot stirs and the rush of the leaves echoes in the hull. Somewhere in the distance is the sound that awakened him, and he stops at the tread of it, straining to hear the rhythm over the echoes of his body.

There it is again... the tread of... something very large. Coming closer. He moves quickly to the large crack in the wall, peering out into the night. Below, from a previously hidden door, a fan of cool shiplight streaks the forest floor dimly, streaming from a hidden doorway on the hull below. Trees in the distance are rustling with authority, as if a wind were on its way. From below, he hears other sounds, like old machinery spinning up.

In a moment, the tread becomes a roar as the brush is pushed aside; a dark creature, smoothly ovoid, with flickering tentacles, sweeps past below. Talbot presses back against the edge of the crack, but the creature is already gone. He peers out again; the light remains, the door is still open.

The ship people, or their descendants, are still alive, and in full command of their technology.

At once, he feels the danger and the attraction. To see; to watch the creature at its work. To consider a contact. He peers out and down. The surface of the ship is tangled with vegetation and torn metal. But so hard to see. He considers the light.

He whirls, looking inward to the ramp, but it seems so far, and the tread of his step on the leaves and metal so loud. Then, delicately, he turns back and steps out through the crack, clinging tightly to the rough bole of the tree beyond, fingers woven among the vines that wrap it, heartbeat hard on the wood pressed to his chest. He tries to slide slowly, quietly down, but the sounds of his movements are so loud in his ears. Then his feet are on a surface: a shard of the derelict. It is too smooth, and he slips, falling to his hands with a shock to his wrists and a blunt sound. He lies still, frozen, waiting. But there is only the sound of machinery and the shifting of light through the door as the creature moves about on its errands.

The vague forms of the trees are beginning to be outlined against the first light of dawn, but soon that is hidden by the light of the interior. He watches the being in motion. It stands in place, tentacles lashing, cables running from it to machines. Is it programming? Communicating? Being entertained? Or engaging in some activity with no human analog?

From the surface of the metal behind the creature, a form extrudes, slowly at first, pale, thin, and tall, but not as tall as the restless black ovoid. Talbot leans forward, too fascinated to be afraid. He watches as the form stabilizes, becoming an image of the native, shaded by the light as if it were real. What kind of technology is this?

There is something wrong with the shape of the tentacled creature. It becomes slimmer, as if it is actually losing mass. Talbot can hardly take his eyes from it, even as he steps forward. He nearly loses his balance on the edge of a ramp, hidden by the glare of the interior; he stumbles and clings to the edge of the door. In that moment when he looks up, he is confused. The black ovoid is gone - instead, there are two natives staring at each other. The closer one turns. For a moment, slit pupil eye meets human eye, Talbot stands transfixed, as the native darkens, slipping from one shape to another, from native to...him!

Talbot runs heedless into the forest.

36

There is a crashing in the brush that attracts Deleo's attention. He comes to his feet in time to see what appears to be the alien, fleeing as if for its life in the darkness, yet behind it, emerging from the Home, is a creature that seems identical. Deleo glances away to follow with sound the flight of the first alien. Then he makes a decision and follows.

37

Talbot pushes blindly through the soaked grass, finally out of the forest, skin slashed and torn, sparing frequent glances for his wrist navigator and the path behind. In his mind, it is difficult to separate himself from the image that may be pursuing him. Perfect copies. The most frightening of enemies with the perfect disguise.

The sun levers itself slowly above the horizon, and the sky colors shift through lemon.

Three hundred yards to go. The rise is barely visible above the fronds of grass. His breath starts again in his chest, and he stops, slouched, exhausted. Then he walks slowly up the rim of the crater. As he stands on the rim, looking down at the shuttle waiting for him, looking back and seeing nothing but trees - shadow stretched long in the dawn, he feels a dizzy ecstasy. Until he remembers the bodies.

They still have to be returned home.

Suddenly drained, he trudges down the slope toward the bodies. They wait for him, sprawled across the ground in a tableau, contorted and dry. To disarrange them... he believes it is impossible to know how to deal with the situation. Instead, he steps to the lock on the near side, his escape.

He scrambles up on the lock edge, perches in the alcove, and hearing the sound of his hands on metal, enclosed, he suddenly knows he is free. But he can't cry, it is choked inside.

But no, there are no natives; there are only the people of the ship. Or, as now seems possible, the castaway of the ship, alone.

A castaway of unknown danger. He retreats into the ship to find another weapon.

38

Talbot swings down from the lock, packing bags clenched tightly under one arm; the only remaining weapon from the armory, a neural polarizer, gripped firmly in his other hand. He scans the scene, in time to see the false native profiled on the horizon. In a fraction of a second, he decides to fire. The creature drops silently. At last, a luck to his advantage. The native, its nervous system apparently based on electrical activity, will be still for hours, unless it has unique properties. Perhaps he will be able to imprison it for study. He hurries back into the shuttle, returning to the exit with a cargo net in hand. He leaps down and races up the hill on the line where he last saw the native. Frantically he runs back and forth, scanning the grass for compressed areas.

There.

He throws the cargo net over the pale being. He watches, but it does not move. Carefully he approaches from the foot end of the creature, alert to any potential motion, ready to leap back, but there is no movement. He bends forward and rolls it over to enmesh it in the net. It is flexible, but in odd places. Its torso is smooth and pale, taut-structured in a way different from a human being. It has a smooth head, an elongated face, a complex and nearly mandibled mouth, hands with many fingers, feet with vestigial digits, and backward knees. It wears scant clothing and some ornament.

Then, gripping the net, he tugs. The movement is surprisingly easy, as if the creature has hollow bones. He hurries down the slope, glancing behind with almost every step, but his captive is still unmoving.

At the lock, he confronts the unconscious being again, searching for any movement, any awareness, finding none. The face seems to be more and more cryptic in structure the longer he looks at it. Then he struggles to lift the creature up to the lock, shoving in enough for balance. He climbs to the lock and drags it down the walkway to an open crate. He pushes the awkward burden within and seals it, with a seizure of release against the surface of the dodecahedron. He leans forward and closes his eyes, surprised when he feels the tears on his cheek.

Well, my hand is shaking again.

He has forgotten what it is like to feel safe. To not think - There will be a pursuer. Is a pursuer. He wonders idly whether he will be glancing around him with the eyes of an animal for the rest of his life.

Slowly, he straightens. With unfamiliar movements, he goes downside again. Completing his duty.

39

Talbot stands above Amel, seeing his form in the staring eyes of the dead. The blood has been washed away by the rain, but the presence of death has not. He opens the bag, and sadly drags the corpse onto it. The hands that move her body revulse at the stiffened flesh and fur. They are all like that. Their faces seem more human in death, perhaps more comprehensible in their stillness.

40

His hands are on the controls. He runs through the checklists, listening as the pumps spool up, watching as the displays run the self tests, and the surfaces wink to blue. The shuttle shivers as it returns to normal. Suddenly the chatter of a space link breaks the silence. His hand lashes out to the link button on the armrest.

"This is Talbot, Link SR154432. Please localize on 432."

More clicking and flanging. Probably a repeater from the ship. The link display indicates the *Illyrion* is once again on the other side of the planet, and the relay is below the forest canopy, but it will come over the edge in fifteen minutes.

"This is Talbot, Link SR154432. Please localize on 432."

The repeater hooks in.

"This is Talbot, Link SR154432. Please localize on 432."

...

"This is Talbot, Link SR154432. Please localize on 432."

...*Finally*...

"Connect SR154432. Talbot, you've missed five reports. Reed wants to know what's going on. Please report."

He sits, at a loss. He has no words, he is unready to respond, because he has given the meaning of contact no thought.

"Connect, SR154432."

"SR154432 connected. Uh, we've had a bad situation here."

"Go on."

"There was a native attack. I have a specimen and... dead," he coughs, to keep from crying. Then he grips the armrest firmly. "Request you download your current vector confirmations for next orbit rendezvous," he states formally.

"Vectors on the subchannel. Do you need medical?"

A brief shower of rain spatters the windows. There is no sound on the open link; the control room is filled with the tones of the vector receipt and the motors spooling up.

"It's too late for that."

He can't see his body hunched, exhausted. But he pushes his head up when the vector receipt finishes, honestly unable to say he had thought about anything in the interval.

"I'll talk about it when I get there," he says, but no one is listening.

41

The lift engine pushes the seat up into his back; he suspends the shuttle over the crater for a moment. All he feels is a faint sadness at leaving. Nothing is finished, nothing can be taken back, nothing redone. He tilts the shuttle forward and opens the throttle.

1500 feet

For a moment, he thinks he sees the shape of another native racing from the trees toward the crater, but in a moment, it is too small to see, and there is no time for magnification. An illusion. A flashback. But it sets his mind to thinking. Thinking about the reason for the murders, about the reason for the hostility. It is not enough, he realizes, to call them alien, to dismiss this catastrophe as due to nothing more than a different world view. There has to be a reason. He needs a reason for the seemingly irrational.

5 miles

The clouds swirl below in an ancient pattern, wisps moving slowly in the hemispheric wind. Talbot watches, fixated, exhausted. He knows that rendezvous is coming, but somehow, he is unable to focus on anything but his speculations. Defense of mineral resources: perhaps a reaction like that of an asteroid miner to a thief? Or, a military being, from a lost war, incapable of ending the fight? But why change shape? Camouflage? Convenience? A battle suit?

50 miles

Near orbit. His stomach is cramping with emptiness, his eyelids are drooping, and his sight is defocused. *I'll just let the loose feeling take me for a while. I'll just get a bit of relaxation before the rendezvous.*

500 miles

The ship looms in the plates and on the windows. Talbot stirs himself and activates the rangers. He rubs his eyes, and tries to force his focus.

"Talbot ready for docking," he reports.

"Downloading the dock parameters," the *Illyrion* replies.

He switches in the automatics. No manual today. *Why blow the docking just to prove I can handle it when I'm half bagged?*

Because I'm obstinate. He switches the auto systems back out; gently guiding the shuttle into the embrace of the bay. He feels the clamps take hold of the hull, the docking collar lock into place, and then a rush of cooling air. He nods.

"Made it."

He wishes he could sleep.

42

The conference room is a haven of normality. For a moment, the events of the past days recede, and he might be waiting for a mission briefing - the mission planner at the head of the table, as she is now. But usually the room would be filled – this time it is nearly empty.

He sinks into a chair near the door. As yet, he has had no real sleep for thirty-five hours.

Gillian Reed, looks up from the head of the table, businesslike, but sympathetic.

"Raoul. Sorry to keep you up like this. I know you must be exhausted. However, the Director must be informed as to whether the ship may be in danger. Before we start, I'd like you to meet her." She indicates the Tereniade to her left. "Tranis, this is Raoul Talbot."

"Honored," Talbot acknowledges, hoarsely. He has never spoken to the Director before.

The Director smiles. "Talbot."

Reed continues: "Talbot, is the ship in any danger?"

Talbot strains to keep his mind on track, to think clearly. "Well... I mean, there's no evidence, is there? That they have space travel now, I mean."

The Director leans forward. "What did you find?"

Talbot is silent, confused. Finally he addresses Reed. "Have the logs been uploaded yet?"

"I'll check." She glances down at the table. "That's being done now. Ten minutes and it should be fully organized in the tank. Should we wait?"

"Never mind."

He looks very small, huddled at the end of the table like a beggar. His voice is quiet, the tones are formal, but disjoint.

"On the way in... At low altitude, there was a return, which I tagged. Didn't know what it was then. Unusual age and material. Atrenn, that is... or was it x*Rkar? thought it was tens of thousands of years old. I forget the material he mentioned, but it's in the recording, I'm sure.

"We were talking ... we were attacked with spears... from an unknown number of ... natives? Maybe. All of them were killed. I was

42

able to escape into the shuttle... Honestly, I, I couldn't have, I couldn't... help." He finds tears slipping down his cheeks. With and effort, he regains control, trying not to see their sympathy. He knows that he is simply delineating his cowardice. "I was going to leave. I should have, but, I saw... maybe it was a native, someone who might have been involved in the attack. I followed it into the forest, but we came to a derelict. The derelict. I don't know if it was by accident or not. It doesn't make sense."

A quizzical look from Reed. "What?"

"The thing. The creature. Why would it bring me there, leave, come back and then follow me to the shuttle so I could neutralize it and bring it here?"

Reed looks up in alarm. "The native? On our ship?" She exchanges looks with the Director and then touches the table.

"Update the contingent on Talbot's shuttle. I want it emergency undocked, and I want vacuum all around it. Don't let it go, though, except at my order. The contingent should be armed, and should prevent anything from leaving that shuttle."

The Director holds up a hand. "Other precautions, Talbot?"

"Don't let it out... no, that's fine. The shuttle's sealed. I put the thing in a cargo module. I don't think it can get out... You've got to listen, anyway, and believe me. I came to this derelict in the clearing. The native, it ran off; maybe it was trying to lead me out, I don't know. It was getting late, but I thought this thing, it was a ship - that it was safer, more important. I went in. It was nearly dark... oh, yeah, I said that." His eyes are confused, as if the onrush of memory is too much to stop or to cope with. "I slept there. The lights were still functioning, but that ship had been there for a long time. A long, long time. It looked like a wreck. There was dirt forming inside from the leaves." He sighs, and his eyes tear briefly. He rubs at them to clear them.

"I fell asleep. Later I woke up to this sound... like something coming from the forest. The ship power came on, there were lights from underneath. I was watching as this huge thing with tentacles lashing all over the place came running out of the woods and disappeared below me."

"Any records?" Reed asks.

His head comes up and his eyes focus on her in anger as he emerges from his memory world. "What do you think I was doing? An investigation? I was trying to kill that... that native. I would have if I could have. I didn't bring the damned recorder with me."

"Go on," the Director prompts. "What happened next?"

"I crawled down a tree... to get a look at the inside. It was new. Shiny. And the thing was in there. It stared in a mirror, but the mirror showed a native, and so the thing... gradually, it became... one. I made a noise, and it turned to look at me. It, well, look, you might not believe this, but it seemed to start changing again, into me."

"And then?"

"I ran! I mean, what if it got back here, mimicked the crew. I..."

Reed stands sharply. "But you brought it back here. We can't tell if you're you or it, *and* you brought it back here!"

He moans slightly. "If I were this thing, would I be telling you this? Look, after I got back to the shuttle, I was lucky. I got a shot at it with a polarizer. I took a chance, I admit. But it *was* electrically based, and I knocked it out. I put it in a box and sealed it in. There's nothing but air passing through containment filters."

She looks at Talbot with narrowed eyes. "You're either a hero or an idiot."

"I was enough of an idiot on the surface for the rest of my life." His smile is faint, wry and painful.

"Well," Reed says, turning to the Director, "with your permission, I'll order an investigation."

"Of course."

"On the shuttle," Talbot interjects.

They turn to him.

"The bodies," he continues. "My team. I wanted... I brought them back too."

The Director suddenly seems very solemn and looks to Reed. "Take care of that, also, please."

"Of course."

The Director turns to Talbot. "You must be very tired. Please, go rest, eat, or whatever you feel you need. We'll get the next stage underway, and when you're refreshed, come see me. We'll have a talk."

43

The corridors are strange, but safe. Talbot looks around in bewilderment, searching their surfaces. His face is shadowed with beard, dust, and terror; his clothes with the sap of plants and the blood of creatures. His period of rationality in the briefing room has taken him far from the events of the immediate past.

Now he stands at the door to his room. It is decorated with an image he has always loved: an image from the lost past called Battle of

44

Tetuan. For a moment, he wonders at the chaos of it, at whether he can accept it any longer, now that chaos seems to have become so firm a part of his life.

It slips aside, and he enters. Lights come up with his presence. Wearily, he sheds his clothes on the social room floor, and heads to the cleanroom to run a shower. The water blasts hot on his flesh, beating against his strained muscles. He suddenly realizes his exhaustion. He rests his forehead on the wall, eyes closed. An irresistible sadness wells up, forcing the warm moisture of tears past his eyelids.

He lies on his bed, cradled gently in its flexibility as he slips away. For a time, he is quiet, hidden in the blackness. Then the dream takes form in the metamorphosis of sleep...

The corridors are dark, and he is running, in an excess of fear. The walls are lined with darkened displays that come to light as he passes, signaling the red of system failure. It is his magnified imagining of the bridge of a starship; but where the pursuer, from where the fear?

He stops, whirls, but the corridor is empty. The blood pants in his ears. There is no pursuer. He remembers his flight through the forest. Somehow, the red light is the same. The displays continue to display their dreaded message of rage. There is an urgency, still, but now it does not lead him to run, it leads him to look.

He turns to the wall, but all he sees is his face reflected in the displays, and his fear is the greater, every time he does so.

He hears a voice. "Talbot, you're going to be late again."

He turns to look, and there is Atrenn, again, smiling his crooked smile.

"What are you afraid of?" he asks.

"Why, the .. the system failure. I've - I've got to stop it. Shutdown clean, before it spreads into everything."

"Where do you see that?"

"Look!" he insists, gesturing. Then, he realizes that the light has changed. The walls of the corridor are marble, free of marking. The light is cool and the menace has vanished.

"You see your own course," Atrenn said. "Don't hate me for what you missed. Are we going to Govault? Tell me about Govault."

The scream tears across the hallway, almost drowned in the shuddering steps of the hundreds running for the shuttle.

"Get back!" he shouts, as they push up the ramp toward him. "Full load! Look, there's another one coming in a minute. Please!"

But the faces are corded with terror. Any moment, he knows they will run him down. Where is Lucax?

"The natives killed everyone," Talbot tells Atrenn from a memory in a dream.

"Talbot, we've got to go, now. Seal the door."

"No, I have to wait for Lucax. He's helping the science team." He is unable to take his eyes off the crowd.

Atrenn pulls him back, and slaps the door controls. He glares at Talbot. Is that unreasoning fear on Atrenn's face, that wild-eyed smile? Or is it someone else's face, someone he doesn't want to remember.

Atrenn's voice is strained, inhuman. "You're going up to that flight deck and preparing to lift. Lu's going to have to catch the next one. Do you understand? We've got to get out of here, now!"

"Lu's my exec. I can't leave him. But it's the only safe thing. Why did you keep me from waiting?"

"You died then, didn't you?"

"What? Where?"

"Never mind that. Wake up and listen to what you're saying."

"But..." Everything darkens, and Talbot awakens to himself alone in the night of the ship, sitting shocked, straight up.

44

Reed paces the darkened end of her social room. Stops. Looks over at Talbot, who sits poised uncomfortably on the lounge.

"Honestly, Raoul, I don't know." Her young, freckled face reflects the tension of one more decision, one more complex evaluation of an unknown situation, at the end of a particularly difficult day. She sighs, and walks behind a bucket chair across from him, laying her hands on its back and leaning toward him.

"You've been through things that no one should have to see. And this is the second time in your career. Letting you go back down is at my discretion, but at the moment, I can't see a good reason to take the risk. "

He nods, but there is no unsteadiness in his eyes. "Please, I couldn't even have asked yesterday."

She watches him thoughtfully, dismissing his comment, not as irrelevant, but as something whose relevance she can not yet determine.

Her hands drop. She takes the seat and leans back. Her fingers drum on the armrest. "We've had our share of people cracking up under the stress of missions, past and present. We've had occasion where people with stronger records than yours ended up killing fellow team members. But we checked the death wounds, and they *are* from primitive weapons. The outdoor logs confirm the events you've reported, and so do the lock logs."

"Of course they do." But he is cold at the thought they could have suspected him.

She leans back into the chair, head against the rest, eyes still on him. "Well, you're right about this: I am putting together a team to go down to the derelict. We may instrument the native and release him, but I don't like that much. We need to tread very carefully. Bad enough, whatever's going on. We don't want to do the wrong thing. Trouble is, knowing what the wrong thing is."

Talbot nearly panics, but holds his voice steady. "I can help. I want to help. I have to know why that thing killed my team. There has to be a reason. And I don't want to just sit here and read about it in the journals."

It is that Talbot says *my team* which makes her even consider the idea.

"All right, Raoul. I'll think about what you've said. I'll decide soon, and get back to you."

This is the best he could hope for; he would have to desist, and wait. And learn everything he can. As he leaves, he remembers the image of Atrenn saying, "You'll be late, Talbot."

Not this time, friend.

45

The Director sits in the dimness of her room, smiling faintly into the empty darkness, thinking. She has reviewed the logs, the testimony. She wonders if any of this can be believed.

Atrenn, dead. Known, witnessed, easily displayable if desired - but not, in any way, desired. Failure to meet a commitment will not be diffused by lack of culpability. She had the responsibility to know what should be done. But she has failed to enable it. She had delegated leadership to Atrenn, and Atrenn is dead.

In a while, she knows she must transmit home. The sadness at the crèche will be hard on everyone. But first, she hopes Talbot will agree to speak. That a completed record can be set, and that the situation of death will close the circle, to show the life complete.

And soon she must transmit to Radelix.

Her smile becomes wider with the tension.

46

Talbot stalks the hall, shadow indecisive, advancing and receding under the light bands in this region of the ship's corridors. To go to the Director might appear to challenge Reed's authority. More, for the Director to take any action could damage Talbot's standing with a future team. Talbot is not sure he has the strength to wait for Reed's answer. To not request an intervention.

But the Director asked him to come. And rumor was that the Director and Atrenn were connected in some way - some way like family. Talbot's rootlessness conspires against him, and he considers what his distant memory of his parents may mean.

Talbot stops at the door the map had indicated. It is blazoned in a fanciful abstract. Or, perhaps, it is something else. Perhaps it means as much in the Director's life as the Battle of Tetuan has meant in his. He wonders if the Director has joined him in agonizing over the relation of the design on her door to her life.

47

The Director looks up at the door signal.

"Please come in," she says.

Talbot pauses uncertainly in the doorway. There is a flickering reddish light that licks the walls, almost like flame. The Director looks up from her thought, smile ludicrous in the context.

"Excuse me," she says, quietly, pulling her mouth under control. "I don't mean to appear to be amused. To smile with tension is a reflex with my species. Perhaps you didn't know that."

"I know a little."

"Of course, you've had Teren crew before. Most authorities believe it is due to a far removed predatory past. Of course, we are omnivores, as are humans. And perfectly safe." She laughs.

Talbot cannot help it. He is not awed by the strength and character of this creature - he is warmed and amused. He joins in the laugh, his first since the terror on the surface. It feels raw and new, and he does not dare let it run on for long.

"Thank you," he replies.

"I asked you to come here. Please sit down. Do you desire refreshment?"

"No, thank you." He is relaxed, but not ready to become comfortable. Not yet. The furniture is tiny. He senses the strange smell, the odd articulation of the alien face, its strange proportions, the weary flickering light. He rubs the side of his face, calmed by the sensation of hand on skin.

The Director shrugs. Her fingers wriggle briefly. "I want to know what you think of the situation. I have some difficult decisions to make and you have both experience and a leadership background."

Talbot is halted with surprise. Then curiosity. "How do you do that?"

"I'm sorry?"

"Act like us. I mean, so human. Atrenn wasn't like that."

The Tereniade, a creature, not a person, shakes her head in a human gesture. "You surprise me, Raoul. Atrenn had some hope for you. Can it be that you justify his hope? No, don't retreat: you had a question that you should ask. Ah, but the answer? Well, I practice. I have practiced, and I continue to practice. Daily. I could not be Director without the skill of knowing how to communicate across tens of species. With humans, I immerse myself in your programs, your drama, your literature, and I watch you. I watch myself in mirrors and recordings. I am an actor, but a sincere one."

She leans back, face composed, now. "I learned how to shrug properly - context, motion and emotion - three years ago. When I was a young student, I thought it was a strange muscular spasm, reflecting a disorganized nervous system." Talbot laughs briefly, in sympathy, and at himself. "I learned better." She lifts a tube up from the table and sips at it for a moment. "Now, you must give me your thoughts on the subject at hand. Your speculations. I value the word of the field operative and leader more than that of all my scientists. You must advise me, and I will listen."

It is hard at first. Talbot's thoughts are not so organized. But he takes hold. If he is ever to lead again, he must. "I guess... I'm afraid of the transformation. It frightens me to think of it as a weapon. That creature could be here, now, and we would have no idea of where or who it is – or its intentions. But we have to understand it.

"There's a ship on the surface. It's been there for... thousands of years. Longer, maybe. When I was in it, I was sure it had crashed. But the systems are still intact. Why hadn't this species rebuilt its technological civilization from the ship's capabilities in all that time? You know what I mean?"

"Yes. I think so. The general tendency ages ago or on worlds alone is for castaways to lose civilization, but that is usually after the depletion of their artifacts and systems. Cores can prevent that, now. There is too much knowledge around, in too many robust forms, for us to lose it all, even in a shipwreck, unless everyone dies, or there are no tools."

"Right. Then there's the transformation – what is its function? Why use it? Why does it need to change?" Talbot frowns. The light sketches Talbot's thoughtful face with shadow, and the Director sees a quality in him that Talbot himself would not have recognized. *Organized thought. How beautiful to watch, in all of its manifestations.*

48

Talbot stands on the verge of the doorway, about to leave, hall light spilling past him, as he turns to ask: "What was your relation to Atrenn?"

The Director seems lost in thought. She looks up, her face in a strange, meaningless configuration. Her mouth shifts... then she speaks.

"In your terms? I was Atrenn's mother." `

Talbot frowns at the intrusion he has made.

"I'm sorry," he says. He steps out, and the door slips shut behind him.

49

The team room is a quiet babel of the translator frequency, interspersed with the whispering whistles and hums of the underlying realspeech. The ten beings in the room - Tereniade, Human, furry Pandalin, metallic scaled D*Azar , chameleon Istriu; the blood soft Riznak biped; and a Lipu molluscan, its iridescent foot pooled across its section of the table.

Gillian Reed smiles as she enters the room. The flux of voices and vapors that surrounds the central table is a welcome relief from the endless plans, analyses and simulations. *Out into the field. How I envy them. I will be their guidance, their backup. They will have most of the fun. But this is my turn, the beginning of the culmination of my effort.* She takes a breath.

"Hi, everyone." Those that can, turn to look at her, and the conversations wind into silence, broken only by the occasional soft sound as a being shifts its position slightly.

Their greetings are as varied as they, and the greetings include silence. She knows them all. She smiles, bows, gestures, each to the appropriate friend as she takes her seat at the table. Talbot follows her in, uncomfortable, to stand just inside the door, as if ready to escape, if the need arises.

She begins. "Welcome to the pre-drop. As you know, our mission is in some doubt. During the last several hours, we have discovered that the world we came to examine for colonization is, in fact, populated. This means that the Company is likely to have to abandon plans for colonization and exploration. It does not mean we are abandoning our investigation. Yet. This investigation will be your mission, which you will carry out under the safety of a security team, led by Histak m'Ilu Ram." She indicates the Riznak biped.

Whispers of the acceptance.

"The role of the drop teams is to experience the planet to its fullest, to determine if subtle dangers to the colonizing species exist. Most of Atrenn's team did not survive their part of the test. But their pilot, Raoul Talbot, did, and he has returned startling information."

Now she has their attention. This is what they want to know more about. The data has been on the net for hours, but they know she has had it since the day before. They want her evaluation.

She turns to Talbot. "Raoul."

He steps forward. No time to be nervous, which doesn't prevent it. A red-haired young man drags over a seat for him, and the others move aside to let him into their circle. He sits down carefully, then leans across to the table. There are controls there which access his materials. He drags up the orbital image. "There is a derelict ship on the surface. Our analysis showed it to be made of diamir - diamir corroded to a notable degree. Those who know tell me this suggests an age of five thousand years or more. Obviously, this artifact is older than anything we are capable of making. Even the Tereniades have had diamir for only a few hundred years.

"We were attacked, and my companions were... killed." He carefully and sadly presents a section from the external cameras.

"I pursued a creature that seems to be a member of an undetected native species. This creature led me to the derelict, maybe accidentally, but it didn't stay. It was getting dark, and I took shelter.

"After nightfall, another creature arrived. Something I've never seen before, we can't find it in our records. It's large, maybe ten feet high, very dark in color, no visible features except thick legs at the base and tentacles around the circumference." A reconstruction based on Talbot's memories appears, rotating slowly.

Some of the beings stir to bring up the survey data and his simulated images on their pads. Others peer over at their comrades' data, some using translator lenses to observe the images in their comfort frequencies.

There is a murmur around the table, and some exchange glances of astonishment, or perplexity.

"Ring any bells?" Talbot asked.

There is silence for a moment. Then the red Rizniak, m'Ilu Ram, leans forward. "Bells?" he asks. The whole front of his face splits into three as he speaks, eyes retreating to the side of his head. Talbot wants to look away, but refuses to allow his reflex to work. He realizes he has made a mistake.

"I mean, does anyone recognize that description as anything they know of?"

There is silence.

I guess not.

"Well, anyway. This creature seemed to call up an image of the native I had been chasing. Then, as if that were some kind of template, this ten foot tall thing turned into what it was looking at. A humanoid with maybe a third of its mass and half its height. I.. made some kind of noise, and it turned around to look. It saw me, it transformed again, this time into an image of me, like it was unstable, ready to transform into whatever was around. I ...ran."

Some chuckles of... sympathy? from the humans. He tries to smile.

"Later, from the shuttle, I saw what might have been a third creature - like the first one; the one that attacked us, that I thought was a native. I made the mistake of thinking it was the thing from the derelict, transformed, I stunned it, and brought it back." He brings up an image from the logs of the quiescent native being dragged down the slope to the shuttle.

Reed interjects: "Our analysis indicates that the being Raoul stunned is probably a native of Talith, with a standard Active style metabolism using phosphorus as the major metabolic actuator. There is no evidence of any inherent transformative capability. We are keeping it stunned until we develop a disposition for it. We'll have a separate set of meetings to finalize disposition. Rules is already working on the parameters based on Geodesic law.

"We've done additional, detailed surveys, since the first report. These indicate the presence of what may be several primitive settlements, total population estimated twenty-five thousand, world-wide, very widely diffused, mostly hidden away in the depths of the forest, very hard to read. There are no indications of any other derelicts or any technology. We now are beginning to process detailed orbital and drone scans of the derelict, which will be available before you head down to the surface."

She glances to Talbot, and then finishes. "Our questions, I think, are obvious. Where is the derelict from? Is there a native intelligent species, or are the apparent natives actually descendants of the beings that flew the derelict? What is the role of the transformation? Was the transformed creature made the same as the native, or was the transformation some kind of camouflage, or some kind of side effect of some other process, maybe even an entertainment? We don't know. We hope you can find out."

Reed looks out across the team. "It's going to be your job to answer these questions. Raoul has been asked by the Director to be our on-site coordinator. He'll have the final word on activities."

Now everyone looks him over. He tries not to cringe. Finding courage in his voice, he says: "I'll depend on all of you for advice and ideas. Questions?"

There are many, and it is hours before they are done. Fortunately, he has Reed to help him.

50

She had said: "The Director wants you to take charge on-site."

He had been instantly wary. He hadn't asked for this. Didn't think he was capable, even. Would she know that?

"Jill, that's not my role anymore. It hasn't been since Govault."

I'm just a pilot, an occasional small team supervisor, now. Not a crisis team leader. He can't feel like a pilot now, sitting in the lifesystem as the second pilot drives, as he thinks of the transport slipping away toward the stars above and as he waits while the shuttle drops toward the planet.

His mind is stuffed, exhausted, overloaded with data and method. Reed had refused to let him go unprepared. That meant nearly a day without sleep as she tried to crash course him on everything they had found and on the alternative scenarios. At first, he had thought she resented him. She would look up to glare at him after presenting yet another scenario, as he froze in bewilderment. But after a while, it had started to make sense again – it was practice. He had felt his experience stir slightly, and he had reacted a little better on the next one.

"Confidence," she had insisted. "They have to have confidence in you. The problem is, they all know something about the situation in your old team, and they probably don't know about your past leadership experience. They may not think you trust them. Show them that's not true.

"The Director thinks you have the extra insight it will take to solve this one. She sees something in you that I'll admit I'm not sure I do. But if this goes wrong, you - and everyone with you - could be dead. And don't think they don't know it."

They also think you've never done this before. He looks around at the team. They are the reason he is here, and not up front.

He had protested at first.

"What do you mean, don't fly?"

"You have more important things to do," she insisted. "You have to be back with the team. You can't have them think you're detached. You have to talk to them, join them, enlist them."

He had shaken his head with weary denial. "I can't do all this. Jill. I wasn't good enough before. How am I going to be good now?"

"You're going to be good at it now because I've taught you, and because the Director believes in you – and aside from that, I've read your file and I know whether or not you were any good."

He had watched her, remembering the Director's words: "I immerse myself in your programs, your drama, your literature, and I watch you." He tried to see why Reed was successful with her team. He had never seen her that way before. Now, after he had watched her at the meeting, he understood some of it. Her assumption of command. Her confidence in her ability to carry it. If she didn't know, she took input, and made it seem her strength. It was all like stiff, sore muscles in his mind. Skills he was afraid to reawaken, but which he had to regain or there would be a second disaster and more death on his hands.

51

m'Ilu Ram watches Talbot out of the side of his face. He plots and plans. There are security schedules, weapons lists, sensor profiles; all a constellation of thought, coalescing. And there is the new commander. It is in the nature of security to analyze strengths and weaknesses. In Talbot he knows of weakness. Prejudice as a weakness. Prejudice blinds one to the capabilities of the opponent. But despite this, he senses a strength in Talbot. There are no records of Talbot's flight through the forest. There is no discussion on the net of his motivation to pursue. But m'Ilu Ram is a professional who has dealt with tactics in the face of the unknown before. Therefore, he speculates, drawing on considerable xenopsychological knowledge. Few answers are suggested. He is frustrated by his failure to be sure. He shares this failure with the failure to understand the attack profile. Except for the lack of follow-up, the Rizniak would assume primitive banditry. Except...

And then there is Talbot's past.

His face parts slightly, trembling with frustration and loneliness.

52

Technical team leader r*Zaranil leans over toward Talbot. The hum stirs him from introverted silence.

"Coordinator?"

"I'm sorry," Talbot apologizes for his abstraction. "What can I do?"

"Please remind the structural decomposition again with me. Necessity is for minimum time in derelict. Repetition may help optimize the technical team strategy."

What Talbot really wants is a light conversation with someone. Something to break the tension. r*Zaranil reminds him too much of x*Rkar. Suddenly he is overtaken by an older conversation in a similar lilt...

"Talbot. I from tank have explicitly retrieved images-visual and data sourced from metal sensors. EMF resonances give mass; example 256000, a nice even number for us."

He sighs. Gestures with his hands.

"Well, the derelict is tilted, with large open access at the rear – broken doors. There are pylons to either side that support some sort of external... pods. A room is up in the front, at the top of a ramp from the doors in the rear. The room has big panels. They're high, like the pilot stands, and even tall then, for my size."

"The lighting you reported unusual."

"Yes, it had either partly failed or was intentionally patchy. Do you know what I mean?"

"I do not directly see very short light, but I do understand by analogy and through translation sensors."

Talbot is momentarily caught in a world with no light or color, just the direct touch of radar waves. It is almost a sad sensation. But then he wonders what he is missing.

r*Zaranil continues, "There may be no way to decide between alternatives unless we are successful in penetrating the design."

"What does it mean to 'penetrate the design'?" Talbot asks.

There is a pause. Perhaps r*Zaranil is gathering his thoughts. For a moment, Talbot sees a delicate shading of the scales of r*Zaranil's snout shift into another unknown expression and he recalls that the brain is in the creature's torso, not the narrow head. He finds himself struggling to attribute human motivations and thinking patterns to this strange being, here with him in intimate quarters, descending through miles of superheated air light years from his original home - and he marvels at the idea that it might even be possible for them to communicate.

"Most difficult is to understand are the first things and the later things. Middle is easier. Context may be non-existent – especially when discovering an abandoned artifact such as this. Completed first steps simplify the addition of knowledge. Case at hand, minimal intrusion, per our discussion, and mission planner Reed's specification. Thus, procedure must be to leverage drone probes, recordings, then move to make on-site catalogues, use various sensor probes for mechanism maps. Activation attempts represent danger, which will limit our ability to infer. Normally we would use records from local installations or surviving culture or archaeology. May be difficult in this situation. Must hope for assessable records on the derelict.

"Easy to understand wheel or lever. Harder, but possible to understand electric, fluid, light analog. Digital and nano have so many options, must look for regularities, codes, try things and observe results. Very dangerous in this situation – unlikely we will be able to try deeply without a variety of risks."

"Can we get into the lower compartment, to understand the transformation?" His voice is low but intense.

"To identify mechanism. Worried. Yes, tale of my larval. Like you know of... doublewalkers, danger harbinger, foreshadowing doom. You call tale-type... fantasy?"

"I wish...."

"We have some of these. Signal impostors. Reality forgers. Dangerous criminals. Identification can be unlikely until too late unless they are making mistakes. You assume this scenario?"

"I... suppose I worry about it."

"Agreed. Must identify signature of transformation. May be too dangerous initially to intrude, but sensors may allow valid deductions. Will be very difficult. Likely to be advanced, complex, zone with many options."

Talbot feels disappointment creeping up his neck like the heat of embarrassment. He had expected too much. And a foreboding runs a shiver up the back of his neck. They will not be able to read the records of the derelict quickly enough, and they will find it impossible to know the story in time.

53

The priests whisper among themselves. The disappearance of Deleo, and the agitation of the Mover are their topics. Above their fire-lit conclave, the stars of the M4 cluster glitter amidst the leaves.

54

Talbot's wrist navigator replay leads them among the trees. It is the first flush of dawn, and the security team is spread out around them, watching carefully, weapons ready.

Talbot feels compelled to run, though he keeps his pace and expression under control. It is like being in a nightmare, again – out of his control. The unreality of the crimson light strikes him with each sunbeam that sets him apart. Angrily, he glares about, standing stock still in the new light, and the team stops, wondering, for the second before he regains his composure.

He feels as if he is still running.

m'Ilu Ram raises an oddly-formed spyglass system whose output is routed to his lenses, magnifying the path ahead, seeking any sign of movement by changing the contrast and using special filters to separate the leaf and branch motions. Their success depends on secrecy, but it is hard to fall out of the sky in secrecy. They are hoping that the creature is nocturnal, and that it had left for wherever it hides in the day already. m'Ilu Ram hopes they will not be on its departure path.

r*Zaranil can think of nothing other than the scans he had taken on descent. The configurations were startling, but did not indicate a radical technology. He feels the shape of a fact, hidden in the obscuration of millions of others. Some special fact. Something he had once seen. Something related. Something very old.

55

In a cold room, far above the world, Deleo lies under pitiless lights and monitors. He stirs, a slit-pupiled eye glinting for a moment in dream from above his underslung eyelids.

56

Talbot searches from side to side as they lead into the derelict. The security team pushes into the brush to form a perimeter as Talbot, r*Zaranil at his side, mounts the ramp. Talbot shivers with memory as the shadows close in. r*Zaranil breaks the spell, pressing a lamp into Talbot's hand.

Talbot looks up from the ramp, startled.

r*Zaranil explains: "I do not need this. Standard issue. Concerned you might trip."

Talbot feels a strange stirring in his chest, as if he might cry. He reaches out to press his companion's scaly shoulder. Then he realizes that the gesture might not be understood. "Thanks," he says. He switches on the light, and it fans out across the darkened ramp, blotting out the dim glow from the room above. The chittering and moans of forest creatures, the rustle of morning wind on trees, are muted here; instead, there is the sound of feet on metal, drifted leaves, and the dim susurrus of breathing.

"Come on. There's a skull up here near the top of the ramp. Did you get those symbols near the doors?"

"Confirmed."

He sees the domed suggestion of the desiccated skull as they walk past the twisted doors into the room beyond. "Here." r*Zaranil focuses an analyzer on the object, and reads the radar codes the instrument emits. "Profile appears to be the same as the native."

"Hmm." Talbot hesitates, then opens the channel to the outside. "m'Ilu Ram, do you receive me?"

The response is quiet, though clear. "Well enough, Talbot."

"We're inside, carrying out our examination. No signs of life. How about you?"

A moment of silence, then, "I am healthy. Reason for query?"

"I mean, any signs of approaching intruders?"

"No such sign."

"All right, we'll carry on. Let me know if anything happens."

"Understood."

In the meantime, r*Zaranil has begun wandering through the room, examining it with instruments and senses. Talbot watches for a moment, wondering what R*Zaranil sees and feels. Light has begun leaking through the gap in the wall, and Talbot remembers a night of desperation, of restless near-sleep.

He walks to the dais.

58

There are ancient controls on a series of staggered platforms elevated a half yard from the floor. Talbot intuits contact and display surfaces among the dusty confusion of strange protrusions and velvety plates. "r*Zaranil," he calls. "This must have been the flight deck."

"One moment. I must be systematic in my survey. I will arrive at your location shortly."

Talbot smiles. He looks around. The light bearing panels dim under the pressure of his lamp, but they bear the same fern-like traceries of failure he remembers. Then he realizes that the forms may not be failure. They may be intentional. Decoration. In fact, what about the light? Does its quality mimic that of the creature's home world?

"Can you measure the light?" he asks.

r*Zaranil stops his survey of the room and swivels to face Talbot. "Why?"

"Well, we know they didn't see with radar, right? or they wouldn't need light. Could they have made their lights mimic their homeworld sun, like we do? Some kind of compromise?"

"A possibility." The translation sounds pleased. "Though the age of the equipment may invalidate conclusions attempted... I will take photonic measurements, wavelength distributions and intensity." There is a pause as he waves instruments around. "Indications are intrinsic dimness. May fit nocturnal hypothesis concerning large being."

"Let's hope so."

"Confirm?"

"I mean, that would be safer."

"Ah."

r*Zaranil joins him on the dais. "Instrument systems," he muses. "Very interesting." He turns his sightless face to Talbot, who feels a strange ringing in his head. "Beginning with surface recordings, then deep scans. To intuit function is beyond this stage. Ergonomic thinking probably will be major result, deducing from which form of user, we may... at least height, reach, and perceptible electromagnetic or sonic wavelengths."

"Then we'll have to go downstairs."

"Explain?"

"Into the lower chamber. We have to find out more than that. Faster."

57

Deleo awakens suddenly under cool lights. He lies on a raised surface, from which he falls with a crash as he stirs inflexible limbs. He stares across the floor in uncertainty.

"Security," Gillian Reed orders. The Director countermands the action with a gesture. "Have them stand by, Jill. I want to watch for a moment."

Deleo gropes to stand, unevenly. He wonders vaguely what has happened, but more immediate is the unrecognizable. The strange whiteness, like a solid fog or a cold rock; No way in or out.

They watch from behind the opaque wall as the native runs up to the wall beside the door, and hammers on the surface.

The Director nods. "As I suspected. Completely unsophisticated. Doesn't recognize the door." She looks to Reed. "I've seen enough. Is it safe to stun it again?"

"We don't know."

The native seems to be getting wilder.

The Director runs a hand across her chin, a faint smile of tension on her face. "I think we need to try. We have to figure out a way to calm it down."

Reed gestures to the security officer, who steps into the chamber and sprays the room with a stunning energy.

The native collapses into a pile like aged bones.

58

The team gathers at the lower door of the derelict. Generations of trees have grown and collapsed, clutching the hull with their trunks. The area of the door is inconspicuously clear. m'Ilu Ram gestures to prevent any closer movement.

"Note entire suggestion of hull is derelict. Causes range disuse through deception. Security measures are likely. Thus - security responds."

The softly reddish creature seems at home in this maroon light. He strides back and forth before the entrance, waving a sensor across the space and forest floor. He turns back to them, and the tripartite face slips aside as he speaks. "There are no known sensor systems in place. Alarms on the inside, cannot be detected - guarded entrance precautions are required."

Talbot feels fear ebb. It is as if this fierce figure stands between him and any danger. He senses the security team in the forest around him, alert and protective.

"What do you recommend?" he asks.

"I will summon assistance for forced entry and protection. Diamir prevents use of pure force. Will need intelligence." m'Ilu Ram invokes the security team technical experts with a gesture. He confers in a lowered voice with the orange haired youth, and the mollusk on its mobile walkframe. "r*Zaranil," he requests, "contribute analysis - locking system."

Time passes as the experts make their analysis and debate. Talbot walks around the derelict at a careful distance. Metal flanks rise like a vast boulder from the underbrush to the canopy, crusted with plants and corrosion. In a way, its lines are beautiful, but unlike anything he has ever seen. He muses on its appearance in flight, thinking of the strange darkened panels within, wondering what they would feel like to use.

From the forest, a security team member whirls to face him, weapon ready. It is a Pandalin, like Amel, huge dark eyes reflecting the blood of the forest. For a moment, Talbot is lost in his memory of that last morning at breakfast. "Sorry," he says.

"My apologies, sir."

He is startled, remembering his constant friction with Amel, ready to react to this being as if it were Amel. He stops himself.

"What's your name?" he asks.

"I am Wanr." His soft, furry face, brown, streaked with white and grey, is opaque, but Talbot senses facial motions of relaxing tension. Wanr looks about on occasion, remaining alert to his surroundings. A camera pod drifts above the position, recording. Not a standard issue, Talbot thinks.

"Tell me... what do you make of all this?"

Wanr hesitates, as if considering what sort of information would interest him. He decides on the purely social, as he would with his own species, though he is wary of Talbot's reputation for abrasiveness.

"The forest is... soft, welcome, it is. My home is turquoise in foliage, but still not much different. Fractals are necessary for flora on every world. Sounds are different, but relax and remind me. Ship is not familiar, but adds sense of contrast to improve aesthetic impression."

Talbot smiles at the turn of phrase and the incongruous observation.

"Do you like the look of this?"

"It is why I am glad to travel."

Talbot shivers slightly. He remembers feeling that way, once, ages ago.

"I'm just walking around, getting the sense of things," he replies obliquely.

"Perhaps you should be accompanied for safety."

"I'll be all right. M'Ilu Ram is watching me."

Wanr shakes his head, but Talbot suspects this is assent, like a human nod; his intuition is confirmed when Wanr turns back to the forest, but he still feels uneasy, afraid he has offended. He walks away, uncertain as to why he should care.

59

m'Ilu Ram waits with bowed head and thrown back shoulders. "We must wait - espionage mode in camouflage. The return of the large being - creates decision and information."

"These systems initially impenetrable to instruments are. Activation mechanism unclear," r*Zaranil offers.

"Do you think watching will get us in there?" Talbot asks, his fear fully confirmed, expressing itself through anger. "How do we know when that thing is coming back? We don't have unlimited time, you know. Can't we burn through?"

The mollusk whispers at his elbow. "Diamir is impenetrable by portable equipment. In fact, we have no known method of penetration. Perhaps the Tereniades have something to offer?"

Talbot whirls on r*Zaranil. "That's something. Call the Director for support. Ask what we might have."

"Displeasure at exposure," m'Ilu Ram ejects. His facial sections snap shut. "Apologies. Involuntary opinion."

Talbot sighs. Carefully, he asks, "Please recommend what we should do while we wait."

He feels his hands shake with the effort at control.

60

The light dims with sunset as they crouch in the underbrush. Around them, the armed security beings form the perimeter of the ring, watching. Talbot can see Wanr, partly hidden by the bole of a tree, fifty yards away, and he finds himself wondering, with amusement, whether that other's aesthetic enjoyment is continuing.

The ship has nothing to offer. Reed specifically advises against forced entry, reminding Talbot in no uncertain terms of the need to keep the operation clandestine. Talbot feels his face heating, knowing that he has let his impatience overcome his discretion. Gillian was probably quietly angry, but at least she hadn't raked him over the channel. She also apparently approves of his decision to go along with m'Ilu Ram's recommendation... he glances skeptically over at where the security chief lies bonelessly on the forest floor, eyes close-lidded.

"Shouldn't you be on watch?" Talbot asks.

A single eye unlids momentarily. "Such is the function of the perimeter guardians. I serve my function best by thinking, and resting in preparation for action soon to come. You might consider such for yourself."

A wise idea, Talbot thinks, but not one he can follow. He is so keyed up that he can hardly think in a single line of thought. The dimming of the forest light to its bloody conclusion seems to obscure his vision, and panic him with claustrophobic sensations.

"Aren't you nervous?"

The eye unlids again and swivels to focus on him. "Well-prepared security allows for serenity. r*Zaranil is perhaps less comforted. The open is generally less enjoyable for his kind."

"Maybe I should talk to him."

The eye slides shut. "Insecurity shared rarely leads to reassurance."

Talbot frowns at this. Still, he decides to try r*Zaranil. Perhaps the conversation will be more useful. Hunkered down, he shifts over toward where r*Zaranil overlooks the derelict.

"See anything?" he asks.

The light is very dim, now, and r*Zaranil's strange profile is almost invisible. He doesn't turn to respond, but answers quietly.

"Nothing."

"Waiting bug you?"

"Too much inactivity. Better when I'm working."

Talbot slides to seat himself. "Yeah, I'd rather be working, too."

"You must have... memories, unpleasant... of this environment."

Talbot sighs. "Yeah."

The other hesitates, changes the subject. "I have been considering data we gathered this afternoon."

"And?"

"The technology seems high, but strangely limited."

Talbot raises an eyebrow, hidden in the deepening twilight. "Oh."

"This is difficult, as it remains an ... intuition. Not a fully formed hypothesis? The condition of the derelict suggests that it suffered a catastrophic engine failure. At first, appeared to represent an accident in orbit that forced the derelict to the surface."

"But?"

"But the damage to the vehicle does not bear this profile. Observe stress maps later. Ship seems to have crashed from an altitude of no more than five miles, no less than four."

"So it was in the atmosphere, and it meant to come here." He felt himself becoming interested. Less nervous.

"Yes. This was its destination."

"But the ship looks so broken up."

"Yes. Perhaps it is age. More than a thousand years have passed. Not enough time for most geology. Perhaps repeated growth and death of tree organisms. In any sense, the drive is not particularly advanced, especially considering they could synthesize and work diamir, something even the Tereniades date only a few hundred years ago. The control systems are unclear, but those parts traced simply direct the motors through various waveguides. There is no obvious auxiliary computation."

"How many creatures could it carry?"

"One, perhaps two."

"One or two?" He is instantly suspicious. "How can you tell?"

"Your estimate of the size of the occupant indicates a certain minimum radius required. The lower level is not entirely opaque to our sensors - and it is filled entirely with machinery, except for a single cavity behind the lower door. The upper area can fit two or three such beings, pressed shoulder to shoulder, as you might say. This is not a likely packing unless it is merely a shuttle."

"Hmm."

"There is something familiar about the design. Something I have seen before."

"Where?"

"I don't remember... What is it you plan when the creature arrives? If it arrives."

"Well, we'll see it go in. You'll try to analyze the entry mechanism. And ... we'll have m'Ilu Ram attempt to follow it when it leaves. In fact... that makes me wonder. Where is it? Why doesn't it shelter at the ship?"

r*Zaranil dips his snout slightly, and emits a brief whine. "Perhaps it stays with the natives." Then his head comes around, felt more than seen in the nearly complete darkness. "I have a disturbance, at three hundred eighty yards."

Talbot shivers. "Let's wake m'Ilu Ram."

61

The Mover leads the priests and the hunters through the darkened forest. It emits a faint halo that prevents the scene from being entirely obscure. They enter the clearing, and walk out into a fearful circle around the home of the Mover.

62

"What is this supposed to mean?" Talbot exclaims, exasperated by his inability to predict events.

m'Ilu Ram bows his head to study the dim security display. "Cultural analyst – necessary," he mutters. Talbot switches his lenses to show the IR band.

"Where's Hallison?" he asks.

"Someone to run for him." m'Ilu Ram touches the communicator and whispers briefly. "In progress."

The leaves shift beside him as Hallison appears from the darkness. "Hey, chief."

"Listen, the thing is here." Talbot points out.

"I know."

"We've got ten members scanning the thing with everything we've got. I can see it passively in everything from radar to UV and sonar. But I don't know what it means. Why are all these natives here?"

"Can I have the command set?"

Talbot hands over the datapad. The youth examines it, flipping through the various modes, and settling on a track history. Then Hallison peers down at the scene.

"OK, chief. They all came together. The spread was very organized. Military or religious ritual style. Given the variance in appearance and size between the ovoid thing and the bipeds, I'd guess religious-equivalent, but it's a guess."

"Does that mean no awareness of team presence?" m'Ilu Ram asks.

Hallison frowns. "I... can't tell. But they aren't making a move toward us."

Their heads come up as the hunters begin the Song.

63

The Mover swivels from side to side as the door swings up. Faint light pours out in a swath. It waits for the betraying movement. There is no sign, but it senses the variety of other consciousness, waiting in the dark. Then, it feels a radar scan. Instantly, it springs into action, whirling, and waving its tentacles in the gestures that incite the hunters.

64

With a roar, the hunters rush the hill. "Get out of here!" Talbot shouts. "Stay together!"

m'Ilu Ram waves in the security team, and in a moment the air is faintly lit with the dim violet flashes of the stun energies. Natives fall sporadically to the forest floor as the drop team begins a rough retreat.

Talbot races through the undergrowth, looking wildly from side to side in the thrashing confusion, trying to keep track of the others. He struggles with the lenses, trying to keep them in place. He backs against a tree. "C'mon, somebody answer me. This is Talbot. Answer me. Anyone within hearing, fall back to the shuttle, right away." He is shaking. This is the worst possible situation. The team under attack, the darkness, the confusion.

The wave has passed. Wanr suddenly runs through the trees toward him, turning occasionally to fire into the darkness. A camera pod floats after him. Faint, scattered IR phantoms are visible in the distance beyond.

"Wanr!" Talbot shouts. The Pandalin stops suddenly, staring around. "Over here!" He waves, and the security member runs toward him. Suddenly Talbot realizes that Hallison has the command pad, and thus is the only one who knows where everyone is. "Cultural analyst!" he swears, as Wanr arrives.

"Sir?"

"Never mind. C'mon, we have to get back to the shuttle." He checks his wrist navigator, and they set off into the heat-lit darkness, crashing through leaves, and tearing at thickets of undergrowth.

They pause at the brink of a gully. Wanr touches his arm. "Indications are that the retreat is orderly and the natives have lost us."

"Amazing," Talbot pants.

"Suggest we track north, temporary, to ensure that we avoid the body of the hunter party, in case they are just slightly out of range."

Talbot grimaces in terror, eyes wide and white. Nods. "All right Wanr. You seem to know what you're doing. Get us out of here."

65

Hours later, they nearly blunder into a primitive village of about fifty bermed, grass-walled cones near the edge of the grassplain. Talbot pushes Wanr back against the tree.

"Go round?" the Pandalin hisses.

"No, I want to watch for a while." Talbot replies. So this is the home of the killers. It is almost interesting for him to watch the process of his anger. If only he could kill... but strangely, revenge is empty of action.

There are watch fires at various locations in the village, near every... cross street? No sentries, no perimeter. A strange practice for a people at war. But one which fits well with the idea that Talbot is beginning to evolve around the structure and motivation of the events of the last several hours. Fire-tenders, thin and graceful, move languidly through the darkened streets, occasionally illuminated by a leaping flame as they add fuel.

"OK, let's move on," Talbot orders. "Keep outside, to the right."

66

They are exhausted by the time they top the rise. The shuttle nestles below them in the ancient hollow, faintly reflective in the cluster light. Talbot is muddy and his skin is scratched and painful from the underbrush and the sharp edged grass; Wanr is limping, and Talbot helps to support him. The strange, unpleasant smell of exertion from his fur is strong, but Talbot can ignore the effects. He stumbles for the thousandth time on the uneven ground, gasping.

"Raoul?" A human voice starts out of the night. The figure is ink against the stars.

"Hallison. Where's m'Ilu?"

"At the shuttle, getting a party ready to go out for you. Let me call." The youth pauses. "m'Ilu, Talbot and Wanr are here."

"How many are left out?" Talbot demands, as they proceed slowly down the slope, cool wind fluttering their clothing.

"You're the last, chief. What happened? Take a long route?"

"Yeah. Let's seal and move this shuttle in case anyone knows where we are."

Hallison nods. "Right. Back up?"

"No, just a different location. I want some time to think."

"m'Ilu wants to head back, or so he said."

"I really don't care," Talbot snaps. "We're close to an answer, and we're not going to leave, yet."

67

Gillian Reed meets with the Director in the lounge overlooking the planet.

"Raoul wants me to release the native. He says he's sure we've just gotten an innocent bystander."

The Director is puzzled. "An oddly xenic attitude from Talbot."

Reed frowns and turns to the window. "He's changing."

"I've seen the reports."

She rubs the line of her jaw abstractedly. "Actually, it's not quite what it might seem. He wants to track the native. Personally. With r*Zaranil, m'Ilu Ram and Hallison. He wants to bug the native with a translator trace, and have Hallison attempt a language analysis."

"Maybe he thinks we won't learn anything until we can speak to them."

Reed leans against the window pillar, staring at the planet beyond, the dimmed image of the sun and the nest of stars beyond that, for a moment hearing only the soft roar of the ventilation. "I'm almost ready to quit on the whole thing. The scans aren't revealing anything interesting in the way of technology, other than the derelict. The intelligent population seems restricted to the southern continent. We can easily establish a mining license in the north, and not worry for years. The native population isn't going north soon."

The Director steps forward, eyes narrow. "If it weren't for the derelict, I'd agree. But we may end up meeting the people who built it, and who knows how soon? They may consider themselves owners of this world. From Talbot's reports, it is clear that they are capable of ordering violence against us without direct provocation. Property rights negotiations seem unlikely."

She is not convinced. "It still seems a waste of time. They could follow this native around for weeks."

"They might. But it can't hurt to try. We have time. Give him a go, Jill."

The Director stays to watch the sun slip slowly behind the planet, a taut smile of tension playing occasionally across her features.

68

"Steve? Got a minute?"

Hallison looks up from his console to see Talbot standing, ill at ease, just outside the door membrane of the tent.

"Sure," he replies. "What's up?"

Talbot steps in. "I need some advice."

Hallison barely conceals his surprise. "Oh?"

Talbot looks up sharply. "Yeah. Sort of professional advice."

"Okay."

Talbot seems to need a moment to gather his ideas. "Look, Steve, if you and I might be having a conflict, I could come to you, and just ask - what's the problem? - right?"

"There's no problem, Raoul."

"I know that," he said, dismissively. "That's not what I mean. Suppose... you thought you might be having a conflict with a non-human. I mean, how would you raise it? How could you tell for sure if you should raise it?"

Hallison sighs. "I don't suppose you want to be more specific."

"It's general information. I haven't been good at this in the past. I may need to be good at it now."

Hallison leans back and runs his hand through his hair. "Well, look at it this way. You can't depend on physical signals. And you can't depend on overt results, like agreement. These people are as individual as humans, but more so, you know what I mean?"

"Oh, yeah..."

"I mean, if they're different from us, they're also different individually from each other. They each have different goals and methods. If it's hard to gain understanding within a species, between species is an order of magnitude, or two, harder, because they're individuals, too, not just 'aliens'. Patterns from one don't help a lot with the next."

"I know." He looks away out the membrane transparency.

"Well, so you can't assume what seems obvious. You have to ask, and ask clearly. And you have to listen. Without preconceptions – really listen. And then you have to ask again. Maybe a few times, a few different ways. And you have to observe real actions."

"All right, suppose I find I have a problem. What do I do then?"

Hallison grinned. "The same thing every manager does. Communicate - enlist, defuse, deflect, motivate. I don't handle that kind of thing. I'm an analyst. That's your department. But you have to use the same kind of verification to make sure its working. And you need to know what incents them. Customs, philosophies, religions, their idea of common sense. And then adapt."

Talbot shakes his head. "I wish I had more to go on."

Hallison senses the loneliness, the isolation and fear.

"You're doing fine, Raoul. Just take your time and give yourself some room."

Talbot smiles gratefully. These words of friendliness lift the drag on his thoughts. "You're a help, Steve. Thanks."

Hallison feels uncomfortable. He'd done so little. "Hey, listen, you need a person to talk to or check with, you can come here any time, OK, chief?"

Talbot pauses at the flap and looks back. "Thanks, Steve."

69

Talbot flashes suddenly from the awareness of memory and dream. He is disoriented, terrified, ready to run, though in that moment he has forgotten the object of his fear. An image of Wanr, screaming with death as he is impaled on a flying spear, flees through Talbot's mind, blotting out the rational surfaces of technology.

But the lifesystem is quiet in the faint light. Other diurnal beings sleep restlessly in styles and for purposes as varied as their forms. His hands are shaking, subsiding. He sighs with exhaustion and spent fear, and buries his face in his hands, until he realizes an utter lack of hope that he will ever sleep this night. He looks up, and climbs out of his recliner, onto the walkway, careful not to disturb the sleepers.

In stocking feet he pads to the stern airlock. Even his breathing seems loud in the steady silence. Then the thick doors slip apart and the soft tropical wind stirs his garments.

Outside, the stars are diminishing with the rising light that leaks from the horizon.

Above, a single gleaming point slowly traverses the dome of the sky, silently reminding him of the slender trace that connects him to civilization and survival.

On the rim of the landing zone, he traces the slowly moving dark shapes of the guards.

Today, he knows, is the day when the hunt will begin again. But this time, he will be the hunter – but his prey, his destination, these remain unknown, no more than hints.

70

The other shuttle settles with a blast of light, smoke and billowing flame retardant. Gillian Reed walks down the ramp and smiles at Talbot, who waits, nervous and overtired, on the scorched grass beyond.

"Well, we've brought him," she gestures back over her shoulder, where the orderlies are emerging, carrying an enclosed plastic stretcher.

Talbot finds it hard not to be offended at her presence. "I didn't know you'd be coming," he says, carefully.

She rests a hand on his shoulder, a rare gesture. "I'm not staying, Raoul. I just want an on-site briefing. OK? You're doing fine." But she is faintly worried by his greeting, by his offense.

"OK..." He turns, then suddenly looks back. "C'mon over to the site."

71

The awning flaps in the gusty breeze over the opened stretcher, raising frightening memories. Deleo lies sprawled as if dead, nervous system inactive, suspended. But the wind comes with the clouds, and the wisps of Deleo's hairlike growths flick across his flat, insectile jawline.

Moments pass as the clouds gather and the teams confer. Then, strong hands and appendages join forces to carry the stretcher away to a location far across the grassland. Carefully they roll the hunter onto the grasses... and before they leave, a dark-skinned hand reaches down to press a metal stylus against his throat. A faint grayish rash marks the spot. Another touch to the forehead leaves the same mark, both fading slowly.

Talbot pauses. This face and form, no longer so strange, linked in some hidden way with the compulsion that drives him. What does it mean? In a faint few hours, he will see sights never seen by a human before; hear the sounds of a foreign language, opaque to translation. He is unable to restrain the stirrings of awe. But there is an answer here, too. An answer as to why these natives, apparently civilized at a so low a level, would attack strange and fearsome creatures newly arrived from the stars - with a brace of spears.

72

Screens and systems flicker to life in the improvised monitoring room at the rear of the shuttle lifesystem. m'Ilu Ram influences the controls, coordinating the inputs and analyzers, while Talbot and Reed look on; Talbot sits on the walkway, clasping his knees to his chest, faintly anxious and resentful, glancing occasionally to where Reed stands apparently imperturbable, only interested in the displays.

73

Deleo awakens to the crack of thunder and a wash of rain across his face. He stirs, unsure of why the shafts of grass wave at such a strange angle. He is dizzy, and nearly starving.

And then he remembers the strange dream. The dream of a pale house without doors or windows. Without any openings. How could he have entered such a place...? Then ... nothing. No, he thinks, as he levers up on one arm... a vague memory of the wall, yawning... opened, and beings beyond. A dazzling light at the corner of his eyes.

He sits up, startled.

The mission.

The encounter at the Home of the Mover.

And he is here, in the middle of the plain. He stands, and stares out over the grasses that now thrash with the force of the storm. Nothing strange within sight. It is as if the demons never were. As if they too were a dream.

But there will be explanations demanded. Deleo knows that answers must be ready. He must think. He must recover his hidden past, and find what happened.

Maybe none of it really happened. But the boundaries of reality and dream must be drawn.

74

Rain drums on the roof of the shelter. Talbot sits in the doorway, staring out over the swaying grass into the grayish twilight and the shuttle beyond. Finally, he turns back to Gillian Reed.

"So, you're satisfied?"

She sighs. "Yes, and ... no. I'm not satisfied about why you want to go out and follow this native. Physically."

Talbot rubs wearily at the back of his neck. "He's not moving. I don't know why. He's not wandering aimlessly - it's not like he's lost. But he doesn't want to go home."

"And..?"

"How can we find out why?... I have to put myself in his place. I need to know what keeps him out there. "

She shakes her head. "Not without the team. Listen, it doesn't make sense, until we have some language data. We can't run a translator off what we have so far."

"Then what options do we have?"

She steeples her fingers and frowns. "... I don't know. Maybe a set of live-in probes for the village you found. The problem is, the technology that thing from the derelict has may just be enough to identify them. We took a risk with the implants on the native. Fly-bys, live-ins are safer but maybe more obvious... I don't know."

Talbot is puzzled. He leans forward. "But what's the risk, Jill? The derelict isn't armed..."

She feels the pressure crowding in on her... the case studies, the simulations, the worry about whether to proceed or whether to pull back; the pressure from the Director. And now, Raoul pressuring her from below. For a moment, she wants a rest, a few moments to be somewhere else, to not have to justify or weigh. The danger lies there, in the weariness. Because she knows that it makes her want to give in, when giving in would be too great a danger. Because there are too many good reasons for restraint.

The obligation to instruct takes command of her voice. "The danger is in what we don't know. What we don't know is the intent and capability of this being. If you talk to m'Ilu, who's more worried than I am, he'll tell you that what we don't know is what's dangerous. Right now, what we don't know, is everything."

"Jill, we can't just not do anything, or we'll *never* know anything."

She faces that.

"You're right." She feels the decision point racing upon her. "All right. Hold off, while we get some probes into that village. We'll get some language within forty hours. And, if the native hasn't moved by then, and if there's no action from the alien, we'll try your idea. OK?"

He is suddenly excited. He has made his case, and it has passed. He grins at the sudden responsibility. "OK."

75

At a sudden impulse, Deleo runs toward the forest. There is no explanation, only urgency, as he scrambles across the drainage scars.

76

"Chief, you'd better see this," Hallison calls from the top of the ramp. Talbot looks up, and the form of Hallison's pale, thin face screams desperation, fear. He takes the ramp at a full run that Hallison only barely avoids.

"What?"

Hallison grabs him by the arm and thrusts him into the monitor room.

The screens speak carnage, as the Mover sets Deleo's village to fire with streamers of energy from its tentacles.

Talbot looks to where the security officer stands staring at the scenes.

"What happened?" he demands. "Why the hell is this going on?"

m'Ilu extends an appendage to the monitor desk and drums gently on the metal. "No information."

Talbot spins m'Ilu's chair. "No information! You think that's an answer? What's going on here?" He shoves a hand toward the displays. "Those people are being killed by that thing, and you tell me you don't know why?"

m'Ilu's face falls open with fervor, but only strangled sounds are emitted by the translator.

Talbot glares at Hallison. "What's he saying?"

Hallison shrugs, overtaken by the pace. "Don't know."

Talbot turns back to m'Ilu. "Get me a security team, fully armed. Shields." m'Ilu seems to hesitate. "Now!" Talbot looks up to face an astonishing cluster of strange faces. "What's the matter?" he sneers. "Are you people so synched into non-intervention that you're going to stand around while that thing wipes them out? Let's go!"

Hallison is the first to react. "You heard him. Get language and biophysical on the sled."

m'Ilu stands, towering over Talbot. "I'm sorry. I was... unmanned by events. I... cannot lead the team; it would not be right."

Talbot looks to Hallison. "Is he saying there's some kind of honor thing here, because he didn't anticipate this?"

"They have a strong code of responsibility for pre-planning."

"Yeah? Well, listen, m'Ilu, I don't damn well hold you responsible for not figuring out what some alien we don't even know the source of was going to do. But I will absolutely hold you responsible if you're not at the bottom of the ramp with your group in twenty seconds, understand?"

m'Ilu's face slides shut. He bows his head and hurries to the ramp.

"Okay, Steve," Talbot looks over his shoulder. "Let's go."

77

The village stands in smoking ruin, faint coils of smoke rising into the late sunbeams. There are charred piles that once were open dwellings, and the other, smaller heaps, stinking of cooked meat, that were once people.

Talbot gags as the breeze waves across the stench of the burning. m'Ilu Ram gestures and the security team spreads out across the village. But it is Talbot who first sees Deleo lying prone on the smoldering leaves just outside the perimeter. He gestures to Hallison and runs to crouch at the native's side.

"Is he alive?" Hallison asks. The question is answered as Deleo struggles to raise himself from the ground. He is shaking, arms and joints taut with the effort, an effort that is almost beyond him. He looks at them, bewildered.

"Steve, I've got to have some language support. How much have we got?" Talbot asks.

Hallison sighs. "I don't know. I'll get Feblo."

"Hurry."

Talbot notes the spots left by the sensor implants, and is hit by what it means now to have this hunter lie on the ground beside him. Family, community or its equivalent destroyed. Past destroyed. And he remembers a young boy - himself - on his own, because his parents had split up, leaving for opposite sides of their home system, unable to find the time or the energy to know what to do about their son. It is that little boy who reaches out to touch the hot alien skin of the native, in a gesture of consolation.

And for Deleo, it is a gentle gesture, a sign of a comfort all too often withheld in his crude culture. He bares his mandibles. But Talbot does not recoil, and knows he has made the right choice when the native's posture does not change to follow up the apparent threat. Talbot smiles back.

Hallison appears at his elbow with a one way FC adaptive translator harness and a web of cables. "Here," he says, thrusting the mess at Talbot.

"Get the meds to check him out," Talbot orders, donning the harness. He puts the sensor to his throat.

"Can you understand me?" he asks.

78

It is a colder day, moist with former rains. They wait beside the derelict, listening to the slow crackling of the diamir under the flatbed-based neutron emitters.

Talbot sits perched on a rock, watching. After a while, m'Ilu Ram detaches from the group and walks toward him. Talbot eyes m'Ilu speculatively, but he merely takes up station beside Talbot, looking back toward the work.

"How much longer?" Talbot asks, finally.

"Issue to be raised, sir?"

So it's "sir" now?

"Please don't call me 'sir', m'Ilu."

"Honor is at stake. Responsibility for the failure to anticipate the alien move. Once detection is understood, reprisal is logical. But asked must be - why anticipation failed?"

Talbot sighed and scratched his head. "Look. Let me ask you this. Would you have done what it did, if you were in its position?"

"Position is not able to be simulated. Not enough knowledge is available."

"No, but imagination is available, m'Ilu. Don't you folks imagine things?"

"Stories?"

"Not stories. Imagining. You know, pretending things. I mean, look, suppose you want to simulate, in hindsight, why the alien did what it did."

"A threat is perceived. A threat of detection."

"OK. It thought we would go away, if we were threatened, or if the natives were gone. We didn't. It misjudged us. Made a mistake. This may be how it thinks it can rectify that mistake." *With the deaths of hundreds of natives.* "You made a mistake, too. Not sure it's one you could have not made. Are you going to pay it and be done with it? Or are you going to make yourself pay it over and over again? Try to solve the thing, instead. Don't just have bad dreams about it."

"Dreams, sir?"

"Raoul."

m'Ilu looks at him, not responding.

"My name is Raoul," Talbot repeats. "Not 'sir'. OK?"

"Raoul."

"Do you understand what I've been saying?"

"I am not really like that, Raoul."

"Try, m'Ilu. You'll be a better security officer for having failed a few times. You can learn to handle it. You'd better."

"Failure will not be repeated, Raoul." He is silent for a while. "Continuation for five ten minutes should realize completion."

"Then we'll know," Talbot mutters.

79

The doors break aside and fall with a creak, a screaming tear and a bass-bell ring. Dust rises and streams into the faint breeze. Talbot shoulders the others aside and steps inside. His heart is loud in his ears, and he remembers the night he fell to the ground outside.

But the machinery is silent, and the room is dark.

He watches the being in motion. It stands in place, tentacles lashing, cables running from it to machines. Is it programming? Communicating? Being entertained? Or engaging in some activity with no human correspondence?

From the surface of the metal behind the creature, a form extrudes, slowly at first, pale, thin, and tall, but not as tall as the restless black ovoid. He leans forward, too fascinated to be afraid. He watches as the form stabilizes, becoming an image of the native, shaded by the light as if it were real. What kind of technology is this?

There is something wrong with the shape of the tentacled creature. It becomes slimmer, as if it is actually losing mass. He can hardly take his eyes from it, even as he steps forward. He nearly loses his balance on the edge of a ramp, hidden by the glare of the interior; he stumbles and clings to the edge of the door. In that moment when he looks up, he is confused. The black ovoid is gone - instead, there are two natives staring at each other. The closer one turns. For a moment, slit pupiled eye meets human eye, Talbot stands transfixed, as the native darkens, slipping from one shape to another, from native to...

Something stirs in the dimness. Where is it? Talbot searches restlessly, but there is nothing to see. m'Ilu Ram steps to his side, weapon ready; then he waves the others forward.

At that moment, the Mover erupts forward from a crevice, changing from the image of Talbot to that of m'Ilu Ram, to suddenly soften under a hail of tuned stun rays, expanding as it reverts to its normal form. It stumbles past them to the broken door, tentacles lashing, and collapses into an enormous heap of darkness and loose tentacles on the forest floor. m'Ilu Ram looks to Talbot, checking; but Talbot is all right. Talbot whispers, breathing hard with fear: "It was waiting for us."

He looks around. The room is merely dark, and crowded, but it is devoid of threat.

"Can we get out of here?" he asks, looking to the others. "We'll have to secure it."

They are ready to do his bidding. Hallison smiles. A flatbed is brought forward with a crane and a container and they begin the work of lifting the huge carcass of the Mover from the ship.

80

Talbot looks on from the corner of the room. Most of the past few days he has spent without sleep, though he would be hard pressed to find out what he had done. Mostly, he had watched, listened, tried to learn.

It is hard for him not to feel a faint sadness.

Hallison is grinning. He has done most of the work of integrating the reports of the team.

The other specialists take their own positions around the conference. Talbot sees the articulations of m'Ilu Ram's skull as the security chief enters; m'Ilu flaps his facial jaws in greeting, Talbot flexes his mouth in response. But that makes him feel even sadder as he senses the project winding to a close with this climactic meeting.

Gillian Reed enters with the Director, an appearance whose stir subsides into silence. Talbot watches admiringly as she greets the beings. He can almost piece together who she is greeting with which gesture. She is very graceful about it.

Then they take their places.

81

The room darkens, and the image of a world appears on the wall.

"Here's what we have. We don't yet know where this is," Hallison says, standing in a circle of golden light, "but we may be able to find out." He sighs. "This is an image we think may be the homeworld of the creature the natives term 'The Mover'. We translate it as 'the Mover', but it's a term of reverence for them. For the last ten thousand years, it's been a god to them, guiding them, restraining their development, shaping their culture, impersonating them... and preparing them for us."

"Explain," the Director requests from the shadows.

"Not us, specifically," Talbot interjects, "But anyone from off-world."

"That's right," Hallison continues. He switches to some images of the derelict. "This spacecraft crashed here almost ten thousand years ago. But it was apparently on a mission. A mission carried out by this creature."

An image of the Mover appears, occasioning a sudden burst of muttered comments.

"But what mission? Fortunately, r*Zaranil recalled an archaeological finding of several years ago. The finding describes a recording found by an expedition which encountered a similar ship on a world called Inalidor. No creature such as this Mover was ever found, and the recordings were very hard to decipher. However, with the help of the recording and the translation, r*Zaranil was able to make more sense than would have been possible otherwise of the material we recovered from the derelict."

r*Zaranil's urbane voice fills the darkened room. "The recordings are complex. Very few of the references are comprehensible. However, the instructions are clear, while the motivations are opaque."

"And what were those instructions?" Reed asks.

"To guard against intruders."

Hushed muttering rises again.

Talbot leans forward into the circle of light. "So - we're on the edge of unknown territory. Territory claimed by whatever originated this thing... this Mover. The inhabitants of that territory don't want any contact with any outsiders, and they sent these things, engineered, out into the universe, to enlist populations that might help drive off encroachment on their territory."

The Director is smiling, but it is not her human smile, it is the Tereniade smile of tension. Talbot feels a momentary chill.

"I see," the Director says. "Xenophobes." She looks at Talbot, who returns the stare, unblinking. He wonders if she is thinking that he understands this from experience.

The lights rise back up.

"Anything else?" Gillian Reed asks.

Talbot shakes his head.

"Very good work, everyone," she says. "We'll be underway in a few hours, heading back downcurve to the facilities at Tlnou. There's a lot of study to be done, and we need to get all of this information back to the Geodesic as soon as we can."

The Director stands. "Thank you for coming," she says politely. There is no clue as to her thoughts as she turns and leaves.

Reed stops beside Talbot, where he stands staring after the Director. "If you have a few minutes, Raoul?" He looks over, but she is neutral, perhaps even a shade cold.

"Sure." As they leave, r*Zaranil tries to catch Talbot's eye, but he is ill-equipped for the task.

82

They make their way down the crowded corridor, and Gillian explains. "You're going to be assigned a team once we get back. I've been told you'll be doing an investigation looking for the source of these things, along with m'Ilu, r*Zaranil, and Hallison. What do you think of that?"

Talbot stops still in the corridor, staring, hands open at his side.

"You mean it."

"I mean it. The Director gave the word for your access, and if things go our way once we get back, an exploration vessel will be ready, and will be yours. You've earned it."

"I did right."

Her face opens briefly with a smile. "That's what I mean."

83

The Director turns to the vast window and regards the planet below. "The destruction of that derelict would be very sad. There is a complex and unknown history there."

Talbot stands and walks around the table to stand by the Director. "Even if we could destroy it," he says, "I'm not sure we should, either. But it's diamir, and our technology isn't easily capable of destroying it. The best we can do is to isolate the Mover." He shakes his head. "And then kill it."

Deleo looks up from where it sits, huddled in the corner, avoiding the strangeness of the room. Through his translator he says: "And I would burn it where it stands, and pour its melting fat on the fronds; it would be a fine revenge. "

r*Zaranil looks about the room, seeing his friends as if he had sight, which, in his own way, he does. "No revenge can end this." He turns to Talbot. "Instead, we can avoid those temptations."

Talbot is silent. Finally he speaks. "Maybe."

Phase 2

Illyrion and Tlnou

Events in this section begin on the urbanized Geodesic world Tlnou,
a journey of 20.3 light years from Talith

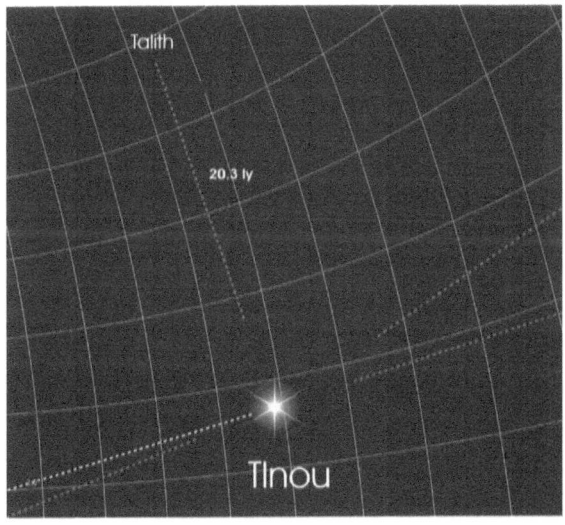

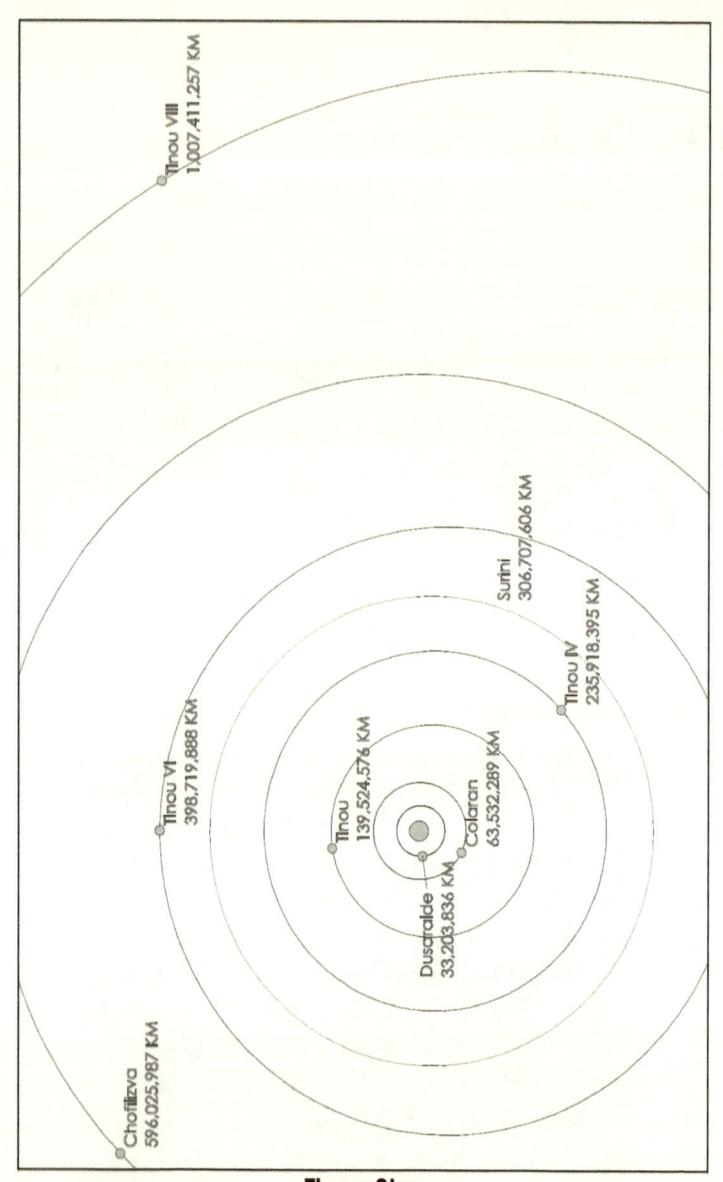

Tinou Star

Spectral Class:	G8V	Mass:	0.915 sol
Radius:	0.932 sol	Luminosity:	0.733 sol
Political:	Geodesic		

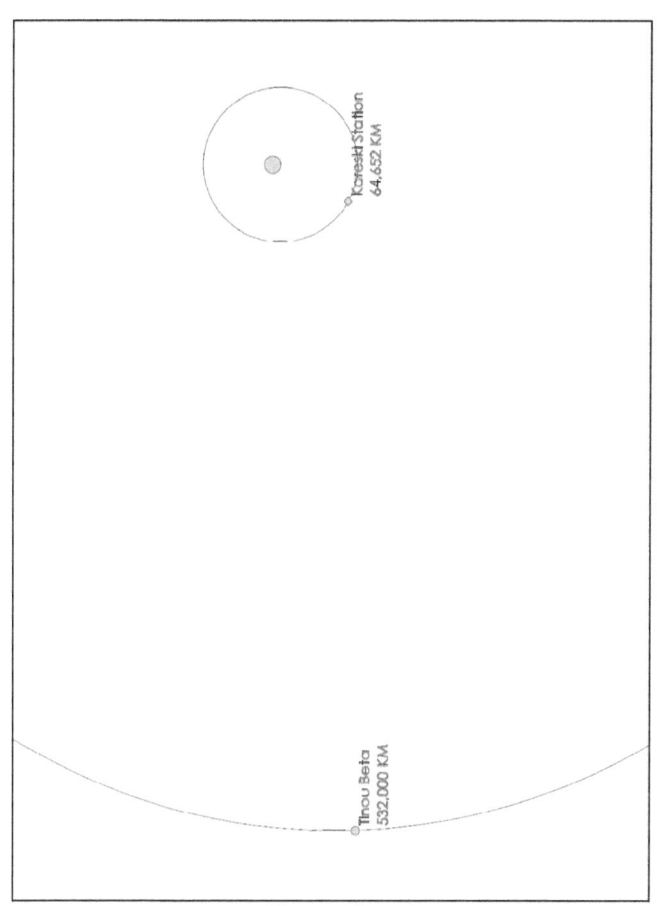

Tinou Planet

Distance from Tinou star:	139,524,576 km
Radius: 6745 km	Gravity: 0.85G
Orbit Period: 343.64 days	Rotation: 20.9 hrs
Population: 37,500,000	Political: Geodesic

Satellites

Kareski Station: Space Station	Distance: 64,652 km
Tinou Beta:	Distance: 532,000 km
	Radius: 4323 km
	Gravity: 0.51G
	Orbit Period: 45.66 days
	Rotation: same

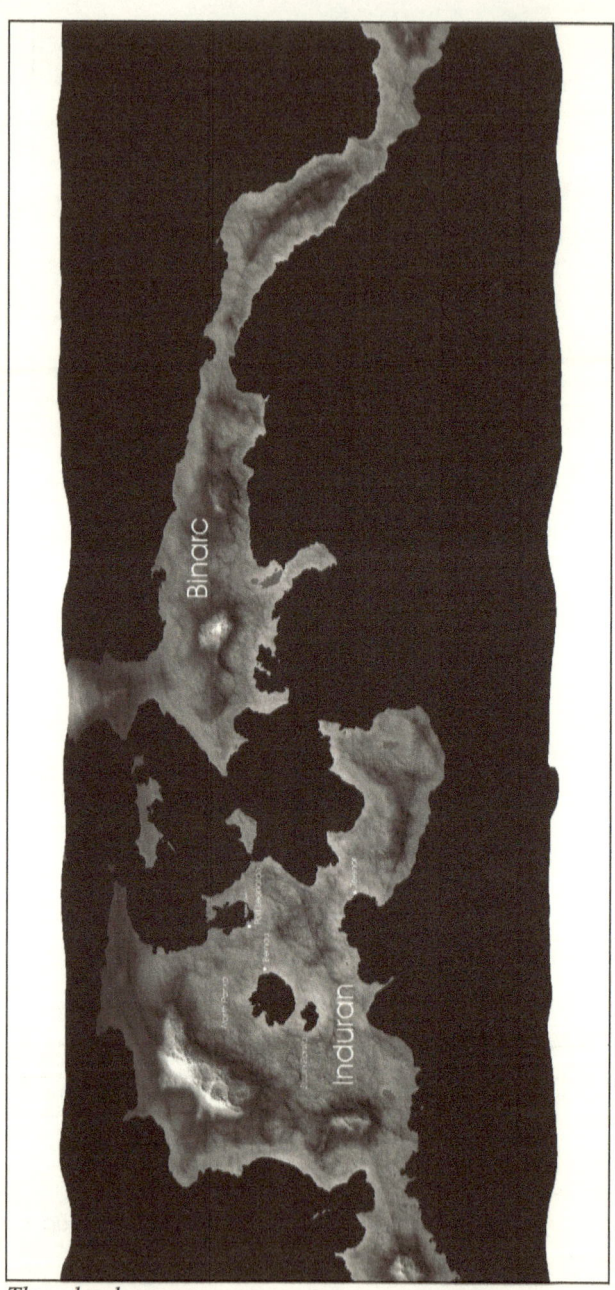

Tlnou land masses

84

Talbot waits in the dark silence of the orbital shuttle's drop pod, eyes locked to the countdown timer. He hears the ticking as he braces himself against the seat; there is a moment between one breath and the next where he wonders at all of the things he has failed to do. Then it's time to go, he yanks the handles, and pinioning acceleration drives him back into the seat. Space springs to life around him as the imaging sweeps away the walls and the station is ripped away into the distance. The planet wheels below, its cities a rich sparkling where the terminator brings the night. Tiny reddish patches mark the flare of fires hundreds of miles across. It is possible that he is just too late, again.

85

m'Ilu Ram cowers in the crawlway above the city of Telenor. The chasms of the city split into vague depths below and above. Metal rattles and rings not far away as a counterpoint to the whispering, chanting, and screams. Movements - footsteps, perhaps, hunting. Below, a huge gout of flame spits, flickers, roars and dies, its hideous reflection cast from the steel walls beyond into the hiding place. And m'Ilu Ram feels a counterpart to fear.

86

"How could it be so terrible, so fast..." the Director whispers. She stares at the planet below, at the space station that drifts gutted above it, her eyes considering the light of the planetary surface through the tears in the station's skin. Hallison grunts, sitting at the conference table, playing with his Ribu sticks. He knows the answer, as well as she does. "Should we have stayed? Waited for the explorer ship? Not made our second run to Talith?"

He ignores the questions. His pale face is closed with the waiting. "It's the damn thing, we know it, it just got away from them. Let's hope it doesn't turn its attention to us"

"It isn't interested in space, just in things coming from space."

"Like the chief? Doesn't explain the station."

The Director turns to face him. "Yes. Like Raoul. I don't understand what happened to the station."

"We could be out of here."

"He had to go for m'Ilu," the Director replies, returning her attention to the view. "You would have gone."

Steve Hallison crumples a stick with dry cracking sounds in his lean fist, "Yeah, if I'd been a pilot. Should have sent someone else. We're going to need him."

"He was the best choice from those we have," the Director replied. "But after this, we'll have no one left to send."

87

The atmosphere screams across the surface of the pod. Talbot thinks about the orbital station, and then tries to shut out instantaneous images of irrational violence and death. *I'm away now*, he thinks. He can still listen to his pulse and breath gasping through his body.

It seems ages as he drops toward the urban landscape below. He creeps past vast crusts of city, then desert, then forest and farmland and finally twilight sweeps across it toward him, swallowing the world.

88

The pad on the table signals them. Hallison snatches it before the Director can reach the table.

"Situation room," he says. "They see a ship on the upcurve horizon. It's large - might be military."

The Director's smile widens - but as with all Tereniades, it is nervousness, not pleasure that drives it. "Soon enough," she hisses. "Soon enough we will all see trouble. Not so large as this." She waves at the space station in the view outside. "But it will be more intimate."

89

The exterior of the pod blazes in the atmosphere, filaments streaming across the view. Talbot feels the tug of fear. He prefers more stable and controllable craft. His hands wrestle the controllers, under the buffeting of the chaotic entry winds.

The plasma peels away and he reorients to a vertical attitude. He is done pretending to be a meteor.

The cities crawl across miles below - millions of windows lit in innocence of the indecent flames only a few blocks away. He thinks of m'Ilu Ram somewhere in that. He steels himself against hopelessness. All he has is me... and all Talbot has is the continuous pulse of m'Ilu Ram's badge to guide him, like a human heartbeat, to a being with no organ even similar to a heart.

The fragile shell shudders with deceleration. The light of m'Ilu Ram's badge flashes on the dawnward horizon of the virtual window. Talbot struggles to hold the line on the signal.

90

The Director's office is warmly lit, flickering like flames hidden in some corner you could never turn your head fast enough to see.

The Constable Commander had entered with an impatient gait, restrained, like someone used to waiting for slower ones to catch up to him. Now he stands before the Director's sprawling chair, glancing around warily, looming over the small figure.

"Explain to me why you're here, orbiting a nearly destroyed space station?"

The Constable Commander is human, with a lilting Cylestane accent, and pale features marked with faint, irregular tan patches signifying his particular variety of humanity. When he speaks, he gestures with an arm whose hand remains immobile, which is a custom of Cylestane.

The Director simply smiles with tension. "You make it sound like we're guilty of something for being in orbit. Is that a normal police procedure?"

The Constable Commander frowns fiercely, a practiced expression. "Nothing here is normal, Director. I have a few hours to spend on this issue while my command gets oriented on the situation below. My interest in this is not yet suspicion. I just don't understand why you're not at the port. Your ship is no cargo carrier, and yet..."

"Well, you mentioned it yourself, Constable Commander. The situation below. We're hardly likely to descend until that's been cleared up. We can't even tell if there are any police authorities left to protect our crew. Have they been affected?"

The Constable's face is unreadable. "Of course not." But the blankness is a statement that the Director is well-equipped to read. The meaning is fear.

"It's not a political action, then?" the Director asked. "We've been unable to contact our company. The governmental planetary communications appear to be in chaos, and even the active private systems are abnormal, disrupted or inaccessible."

The Constable looks around the room, disconcerted. "I can't discuss that. Are all of your people on board?"

"No, we have two on the surface. I'm worried, Constable Commander. They were trying to make contact with our company, but we haven't heard from them. Is there anything you can do?"

"Not now, Director - we have other areas of concern. You will please remain in orbit until the situation has been corrected. Other police vehicles might... misinterpret... a landing or departure attempt, and fire on you."

The Director's tiny face creases with a broad smile. Hallison, leaning silently and unnoticed in the corner by the door, wonders at her lack of control. She must be really worried.

91

Talbot drags the pod into the shadow of a hangar. Fires are raging out on the field, casting garish halos on the remaining ships. The pod is heavy, and the air is oppressive. Talbot sweats as he hauls on the exterior handles.

Then he hurries through the deserted streets, footsteps pounding in echoes. He watches the directional on his wrist, following its pointer.

Suddenly he is immersed in a scene of violence.

Hundreds of beings, all species, filling the streets from edge to edge, like a sea washing the bases of the metal buildings. Their hands are raised and swinging in flickering backlight. There is no pattern, there are no obvious sides. All he wants is to avoid it.

He whirls, looking for a way around. He spots a ramp that contours up a nearby building, only blocked by a few rioters. His pulse is pounding in his hearing, and he desperately wants to leave. But he is committed, and he feels some strange clarity strike his mind - a different level. He runs for the ramp, shoving the rioters aside before they can react to him. As his feet slam the platform, he hears the screams and roaring descend below him.

But above, he hears a deadly whispering rip, sees a streak of faintly glowing contrail against the night sky - some kind of aircraft cutting through the atmosphere. Then, the pulsing sound of a large energy weapon from somewhere, and a distant explosion. Things are getting worse, and, checking his directional, he sees that he is heading away from m'Ilu.

92

The Director slumps in her chair, watching the status display.

"Military units have apparently joined the rioting. No coordinated action," comes the report from ScanOps.

"We're not going anywhere anyway," she mutters. "What about the police vessel?"

"They're just watching."

"Probably don't know what to do any better than we do."

93

"Alien! Alien!" they chant, menacing m'Ilu Ram. They are small, blue, asymmetric. m'Ilu Ram considers his options, and snarls, tripartite face swinging open in a frightening manner, though he is, in fact, the one facing fear.

They reach for him - as he flails, they strike him with clubs, and he reels into the metal darkness with the pain.

There is a sudden clanging, and the rioters draw back in confusion as the sound approaches rapidly. They scatter down the ramp.

m'Ilu Ram is confronted with a dark, disgusting, human face.

"No weapons. You ass, did you think you were coming here for a party?" the face snaps from its tiny, muscle ridged mouth.

Talbot. It is Talbot who m'Ilu Ram finally recognizes.

"Talbot?" he hisses, as if not sure of his perception.

"Talk later. Let's get out of here before they realize there's just me." Talbot finds it awkward to brace his friend's strange body - which is soft in some places where humans are rigid - but he manages it, and they start staggering down the dizzy ramp to the street below.

"And you're supposed to be the planner," Talbot mutters. "Listen, what I said to you about making mistakes, I think you're taking it too literally."

"Options highly constrained in such fluid situations," m'Ilu Ram speaks. He does not breathe with the same apparatus used for speaking, so his words do not gasp with the effort of their run. "Sanctuary unlikely, even... undesirable."

"Yeah, but now we've got to get to the port."

"Transport available?"

"One tiny launch pod, OK?"

"Stop." m'Ilu Ram halts, grasps at Talbot's upper torso, misses. Talbot stops. "Moment for inventory. Weapons?"

"Brains, stealth and this," he wiggles the metal rod. "Lost my handgun in a mob scene. How about contact? Did you find anything about the company?"

"Chaos," m'Ilu Ram moans. His sensorium is close to overload, and he sways giddily. The Rizniak knows he is close to a mandatory coalescence period - yet sanctuary is unavailable, and, given the situation, undesirable. "Mission failed - departure required. No hope here. The Mover is loose."

Talbot closes his eyes, feeling a strange cold ache work its way up the back of his neck.

"Beings cohering at roadsides, please." comes a voice hissing like chain mail in motion. Talbot whirls. A door stands gaping darkly, and there is movement inside, highlighted occasionally by the flash of distant flames.

"Who are you?" he snaps. "What do you want?"

"Seek safety." Was it asking or offering?

"We're not planning on hurting you."

"Komdan," m'Ilu Ram speaks.

"Are you telling me what it is, who it is, what it wants, or what?" Talbot snarls.

"Who... and what. Komdan," the Rizniak raises his voice. "Emerge. Reveal your intentions." He lifts himself slightly from where he stands bent into Talbot's support. "We are heavily armed, attempt no subterfuge." Lying. His face slips open and slaps shut with a distracting smack that could mean anything. The wind of the jaws blows a foul waft of strange old breath past Talbot's face.

A weird pile of shifting, metallic appearance balanced on flowing legs slides into the marginal light.

"Keeping shop safe, we demand intruders identify...please cohere no more closely, or we shall subdivide and conquer."

It is a shape like millions of tiny insects spilling endlessly over each other in a marginally tripedal, trisymmetric form. The sound of their tiny legs is like the sound of the distant fires and the riot receding along the metal canyons. Its voice is hard to extract from the background, though, like everyone, it carries and uses a Basal transceiver that provide the only words Talbot will ever hear from it.

It slumps toward m'Ilu Ram. "You are recognized."

"Impossible!" Talbot explodes. "m'Ilu, we've got to go."

"Wait." m'Ilu looks at him briefly, then turns back to the composite entity, bowing his head toward the ramp floor in politeness. "Explain, if possible."

"Presence of some chordals on Transit Five and Superdarian provides edge between nexus of orbital events and current scenario. Cognizant of self-organization principals? Are you?"

m'Ilu Ram replies. "Yes. One moment." He bows his immense head toward Talbot. "Komdan are composite entity. Distributed nervous system using pheromonal and radiative sharing of information between subunits which come and go, but with knowledge remaining in the individual. Some subunits were present on the Transit Five station, and some of those found their way to the surface on the last shuttle. I flew that shuttle. It states that some parts of it remember me."

"That's fine," Talbot glares, impatient. "Can we go now?"

"No. Not yet." m'Ilu turns toward the Komdan. "Can you identify a direct route to the spaceport? We desire to avoid disturbances."

The creature surges, as if uncomfortable, though Talbot is surely not going to apply any human standards to this frightening form. *Imagine the thing as a shopowner...*

"Some of this one must remain to guard the shop. Why help?"

Talbot leans forward. "Listen, we know why this is happening. We have to get information offworld, so something can be done. We have access to a ship."

"Enhances long-term security." the Komdan hisses. "Help is offered. Portion will transport others."

"It's going to drive us?" Talbot asked, incredulous.

But before m'Ilu can answer, the Komdan has fissioned. The second entity beckons them into the shop front, while the original half stands guard by the open door. Sounds of an approaching crowd cause m'Ilu Ram to grasp Talbot by an appendage and thrust him past and inside. "Local assistance. Much appreciated," he comments.

The shop is walled with energically fronted cases that glow oddly against the light from the windows. Strange objects of unknown function cast shadows that rear and threaten. Odd animations of incomprehensible import hang on the walls, casting a faint glow as they pass deeper within. They enter a narrow, short hallway. m'Ilu Ram must bend nearly double to stay below the ceiling. Down a ramp and out into a garage, where a small, enclosed car waits.

Their host spills into a tube on the side, and doors gullwing open. "Please, my limo," it says in a laughing hiss.

94

The spaceport is burning. In the distance, for now, but spreading with the staccato percussion of distant explosions against the brilliantly dark horizon as tanks of volatiles become part of the chaos.

Talbot looks around with dismay. The flames edging the horizon flicker briefly on his eyes.

"This place is bigger than I thought."

m'Ilu Ram pushes shakily from the limo to stand at Talbot's side. His face yawns precipitously and claps shut. "Not locating return vehicle. Problem. Directional available is?"

Talbot sighs. "I hate reversible syntax," he mutters. "Yeah, where is the damn thing? Where are we?" He leans into the limo to confront the Komdan. "You know anything about the layout here?"

95

"Director?"

She looks up from a table display. "Can't you do any better than this? We've got to be able to get more than basic material."

But it isn't someone from the Analytical Office. It is Hallison. "Sorry, Steve. It's just that this information off the surface net isn't doing much good. What's the question?"

"Talbot's on his way up. With m'Ilu Ram.... and a... guest." He is smiling.

"Does the Constable know?"

His smile vanishes. "I can't see how he couldn't. It's all over the sensors."

She smiles, a human gesture for Hallison. "Then call him. We may as well be open, since we have no choice. Arrange a meeting in three hours, no earlier. Tell him they're hurt, or exhausted - yes, that will be better. Give us some time..."

96

"Nothing! That's what it is - nothing. Raoul - this is useless."

Talbot hates when the Director is angry. It stirs old resentments and new shame. He shifts uncomfortably in the briefing room hot seat, watching his hands on the desk in front of him. "I know, but there's nothing I can do." He looks out into the shadows of the room. "What about that ... whatever it was - the shopkeeper, you know."

"Director," Gillian Reed interrupts, "please don't be too hard on Raoul. With all the time we had to study the Mover during the journey back, and, apparently, whatever they tried on the surface, no one has any better answers."

"That's not a help. We don't know for sure that the Mover was responsible. But I can tell you that the Constable, once he finds out about the Mover, is going to make it very hard for us to continue to work on the problem, simply by putting us under arrest." She paces around the table. "We can't afford to not be the ones working on the problem for the simple reason that we already know more about it than anyone else. Let me remind you, every minute we don't solve it, thousands more down there are going to die, and it will be our fault, as much as it is the fault of whoever let the damn thing out." Her sharp teeth are bared in a smile that reveals more fear than anyone in the room has ever felt from her.

m'Ilu Ram leans back from the table. "The shopkeeper regarding. Some information not available from remaining newscasters is being analyzed. Not much to aid in assessing tactical situation or details of cause, so far. Some breaks filled in. More coming. Chordals were widespread on surface before and during situational development. But the knowledge is fragmentary."

The Director glares at him. "It doesn't matter. You're going to have to be ready to speak to the Constable on the security context. Be informative, but keep the Mover to yourself. Then we're heading out of orbit, and we're going to try to figure out what to do."

97

The hot water pours down Talbot's face and streams over his shoulders. He feels unclean with lies of omission that this shower barely touches. In the distance he hears the acceleration warning. The ship swings in normal space like a secret ghost.

98

The Constable moans quietly as they slowly move away. "This much is certain," he mutters, in the tone of a quote. "I dislike those merchants. They are dangerous in general, and here, I suspect them of more we don't know." He turns to his XO. "Get a drone on them, and then we talk to the landing parties."

99

The Director orders the ship to decelerate near the umbra of the moon, drifting slowly into it. Supposedly, the *Illyrion* is pausing to prepare for fold and simply wants to be more distant from Talith while it does so. From signals reflected in magnetic and gravitic fields, they again watch the chaos below.

The hallway outside the conference room bustles with personnel changing shifts. Through the door and into the darkened room, with the accretion-blasted surface of the moon a wall beyond the vast metal table and the ceiling-high windows.

Talbot expects a crowd, but there's only the Director, at the far end of the table, watching fifteen channels of visual on the other wall.

"Am I early?" he asks, confused.

"No." The video pauses in mid-motion. "Come here."

He paces down the silent room.

"Sit. You make me feel short." Her expression is amused. He purposely doesn't smile in return, trying to meet her halfway.

"Raoul, this is a big operation we're about to start here. There's no room for the kind of grandstanding you seem to be fond of. You were lucky to get out alive, much less with m'Ilu Ram in tow."

He starts getting worried.

"Of course."

"I don't want you to think I'm ungrateful. Or unappreciative." She leans forward. "But I was worried." She hesitates back into her chair. It eases up around her. "On the other hand, you seem to have a talent for following your hunches and surviving. More importantly - you've been delivering. And the people who work with you have confidence in you. I have confidence in you."

"Thanks." But the line of his mouth is uncertain. Is this a reprimand? Or a compliment?

"So, you're going to need some help."

"I'm sorry?"

Impatient, she leans forward. "I need you to pick a team. You're going to run the moonside operation. But this means I want you staying in the vehicle, monitoring your sensors. You run things, you don't do things. You tell me everything you plan to do before you go down to that moon. Once you get there, fine, you improvise if you have to. And right before you improvise, you make sure I would approve of what you're doing. Remember, that Constable doesn't know we're here. He thinks we have left for help from the field office in Mearan. I don't want him to know. If he finds out, the company has trouble... and you know who has trouble right after that?"

100

Talbot leans exhausted over the desktop, planning grids and outlines scattered beneath its translucent surface. He rubs his forehead, while Jill paces the floor behind him.

"You asked for help, I'm giving it," she rants in a whisper, pushing her head over his shoulder.

"I know, I know," he sighs. "But it's been six hours without a break."

"Oh, I see. You're tired."

He reacts to an absent sarcasm. "Yeah, I'm tired. Hungry. You name it."

She pulls her head back and circles the table to look aggressively at him. "Tired. Hungry. I had forgotten." Sarcasm, this time. She steps back. "OK. There's a timeline, we can't loiter. How much do you need?"

He looks up, surprised. "Just let me have a half hour."

She pauses in the door. "We don't have much left, Raoul. Try to call me early." The door closes out the busy hallway behind her.

101

The planning table lights them all from below, and the screens at the end of the room reflect the same images. Talbot is holding his breath in check hard at the head of the table. A muscle in his neck twitches, almost hidden. They're waiting for him, and he knows it. The notes are under glass below his eyes, hard to read, somehow.

He swings forward to the table with a deep breath. A saying he remembers from school runs through his head. *You're on...*

"Most of you have worked together before - that's why I asked you here. Some of you were with me... before. You know the Mover. Not the same way I do, though there's one of you that knows about it better than I do," he indicates Deleo with a gesture. "Everyone has some skills we're going to need. Gillian Reed has agreed to be mission planner and will support managing the mission as my second... In a way, the mission is simple - find the Mover. In a way, the mission is harder. We think the Mover is capable of inciting the disorder we're seeing below, but we can't prove it. In the meantime, the Constable is sitting a few million miles away, looking to see if we'll do anything he can arrest us for."

The Director interrupts, her voice soft but authoritative. "I want there to be no mistake about it. We haven't done anything wrong. We brought the Mover here, and left it in competent hands." She taps the desk and stares down at it. Then she returns from her reverie. "What we thought were competent hands. Maybe there are no competent hands for that thing... we just don't know. But we can't be cut off from solving this problem by some officious idiot who'd be just as glad to lock us away. We're the only ones who know enough to even have a possibility of solving this problem." She waves her hands and leans back.

Talbot sighs. He still feels uncomfortable with that rationale. But he has a job to do. "That's why we're getting off. *Illyrion* is departing the system, heading back to our secondary HQ on Mearan. On the way out, the ship will be using the Beta moon for a gravitational sling, and when we're on the far side from Talith, the ship is dropping a hammer with us on it. Doing whatever possible to find the situation of the Mover."

m'Ilu Ram looms across the table, the eyes at the sides of his massive head glinting darkly in the subdued light. "The mission regarding. If found, disposition?"

"We leave it alone."

m'Ilu is shocked. "Alone? Do we contact constable?"

Talbot feels the twitch in his neck again. "No. We wait for the return of assistance from the company, or the *Illyrion*. We get all of the information we can, and we wait." He wishes they would stop asking about it. He decides to redirect the discussion. "You'll find your assignments in your files. You may need to familiarize yourself with new systems, and there isn't much time, so please check into the files as soon as possible. We'll be leaving in ten hours. If this is inconvenient for your sleep schedule, those of you who sleep, please try to postpone until you're on board the hammer. Medical services has been told to make the appropriate sleep avoiders or inducers available if you ask for them."

102

"Thanks rendered, constable," the Director replied. "We'll be off then. Good luck with your situation." She gestures the signal off. Then she connects with the helm. "Go."

103

The vast hull upgrades its acceleration, inertia still applying... Its engines whisper, then beat. Ancient laws take action, then die away as a ripple of inertialessness sweeps the ship, crinkling the stars. They plummet through interplanetary darkness toward the crescent of the silent moon - Tlnou Beta.

104

Talbot is on board the hammar two hours early, unable to sleep. He haunts the pilot cabin, bringing the systems up, taking them down, running tests. Panels flicker and change with the results. Stars swing slowly beyond the tall ports. He wonders if he is afraid, or if the shaking that seems to take his hand from time to time is tension or exhaustion. The lock alarm rings, signaling another team member seeking early admittance. He smiles, and brings up the image. "Come on in, join the party."

105

The gravity of the moon begins to redirect the motion of the ship in an enormous parabola.
"LOS on the constable's ship."
"Any satellites?"
"None in view."
"Drop the hammar."
A pause in events.
"Hammar away."

106

Talbot feels the controls finally extend into his senses and muscles. Gloves and goggles stretch his view and touch across hundreds of miles. He sees the blare of the sun as it prepares to rise over the rim over the moon, rays scattered slightly in the rarefied microatmosphere. He sees the endless and unrepeated tiling of craters from one horizon to the next. He senses the cold and the variations in hardness, roughness and altitude of the surface below. He selects the spot, a place that will be within view of the planet in fifteen hours, and carefully lowers the sleek hammar to rest below the lip of a crater.

107

He comes awake in the darkness. For a moment his heart is pounding and he doesn't know why. Then he remembers the dream. Atrenn forcing him to leave the crew behind... but this time, the crew is Amel, x*Rkar, and Schacther. He is screaming as Atrenn slams the door shut from the outside, locking him away in safety... from something. He rolls painfully on his side, and, with the back of his hand, sweeps the tears from his jaw. "Let it alone," he mutters. He swings his legs off the bed and sits. A faint light appears as the room reacts.

By the time he enters the spinal hallway, his eyes are clear, and his jumpsuited figure feels fairly coordinated. He passes the caf, and sees Reed, Wanr and Deleo in a spirited conversation. He stops in the doorway of the sensor pit, where r*Zaranil is wired into the system in near total darkness. He blinks a couple of times to let his eyes adjust.

"r*Zaranil?" he asks.

The shiny metal scales shift in the doorlight. "There is who? Bandwidth insufficient."

"Talbot."

"It is a good thing you have arrived."

"What do you mean?"

r*Zaranil sounds like an old woman in the darkness. "The constable has a belief that the darkened cavern is not empty."

"He didn't trust us."

"Accepted."

"Does that thing know we're here?"

"The system is a passive sensor. We are passive as well. Drop was preset, doors open, power only on final. Inconclusive. Depends on approach parameters. Sensor is stealthed. Could have been close. Could have seen. Perhaps they are clairvoyant."

So much for sneaking in. "All right, stay silent, warn the next watch. Anything else?"

"Some traces of the Mover metabolic remnants are beginning to be detectable in the atmosphere. They are not crisp enough for localization yet, but the effort continues. Next phase would be orbital or atmospheric probes, but the watcher prevents this. Consider action determination for next meeting, please."

"Yeah. Thanks. Can I get you anything?"

"A cup of warm oil would be appreciated."

Talbot makes a wry face. "No doubt. Coming up."

108

Talbot watches the filling of cups of coffee and oil. The scent is exotic, and his nose wrinkles as he tries to keep it from affecting his stomach. He takes the cups and leaves his at the table with Jill and the others. Then he drops off the other beside r*Zaranil.

Back at the table, Jill smiles tiredly. Wanr asks, "What are current reports?"

"We have company."

Wanr sags attentively. Jill leans forward. Deleo makes an odd motion - Talbot is still not sure of how much the alien understands of their conversations.

"The Constable has a stealthed probe orbiting the moon. Maybe it's following us, maybe not. We have to stay passive as long as it's there." He sighs and sips at the hot, bitter liquid. The light is too harsh, he thinks. "On the other hand, we have confirmation that the Mover is on the planet."

"Metabolic excesses?" Wanr asks.

"Yeah."

"But we're not going to be able to probe until the spy is gone." Jill continues.

"Right." Suddenly he is afraid there was an unintended sarcasm in his voice, because Jill is frowning at him as if he had offended her.

"May be alternative…" Wanr offers quietly.

Talbot is interested. "What have you got in mind?"

109

"No signs of activity on Tlnou Beta, Constable Captain. I think the maneuver they performed was just what it looked like - using the gravity well for course alteration."

The Constable's work area is deep in the core of the ship, protected against all but the fiercest criminal onslaughts. Harsh greenish light, matching his homeworld sun, floods from irregular crannies of the ceiling of the crowded room, lighting piles of portable storage media, display pads and wall panels covered with intricate predictive graphs and networks. It hoods his eyes with shadow, and reveals the patches of different colored skin which are adaptations to the constant harsh directly overhead light of Cylestane's tidally locked sun. His lips move thickly as he speaks, wrapping themselves oddly around the words, as if the Constable Captain finds them like food, to be tasted as spoken. These words he appears to find distasteful.

"Not so, I think. The arms perhaps they are running, or some other off-world support providing are they. Events will show. Withdraw the probe to the opposite side of the moon. Keep it there, watching. Eventually move they will. Then have them we will."

110

"Wait, the spy's moving..." Reed reports over the intercom.

Talbot looks up from kneeling beside the large rock they have constructed in the open launch bay of the hammar. Deleo peers into the opening, fascinated, ignoring the call.

Talbot asks: "Where is it headed?"

A pause. "Over the horizon, I don't have enough for a projection yet."

"Keep an eye on it." He turns back to the rock and resumes making simulated sensor passes on it from various angles.

Deleo watches curiously. His translator emits a rich baritone at odds with Deleo's skeletal, insectoid appearance. "When you first arrived, I thought you had come in a stone. Now, you are making a stone to fool someone." He cocks his head at an extreme angle and then returns to normal. "Perhaps you knew how to penetrate the deceptions of the Mover because you are so good at it yourself?"

Talbot isn't sure what to make of this comment. Is it a joke? A sarcasm? A sign of disillusionment with the team, which might presage problems in cooperation?

"A joke, Deleo?" Talbot asks. He has learned not to take things for granted as meaning what first comes to mind. Certainly Deleo is more sophisticated than he at first appeared.

"An observation."

He runs a sensor over the seams on the sides of the disguised probe. Reed and M'Ilu Ram have done an excellent job of blending them into the profile of the cratered rock. In flight, they will open and deploy multiple entry vehicles that will probe the atmosphere to localize the Mover.

"Of course, being good at it doesn't mean we like doing it. But we have no better choice, if we're to get the Mover."

"The spy is withdrawing back toward the Constable's side of the orbit." Jill reports. "But I don't have track on it any more through the moon, so they could be doing anything."

Talbot nods. Trust is in short supply right now. The Mover is dangerous, but it isn't the only danger.

111

The false stone spins through space in a eccentric orbit, its dull, mottled surface catching the light for brief muted moments. Its orbital profile suggests an asteroidal origin and a recent collision driving it in toward the sun. It is not an unusual story in this young system.

Into the shadow of the planet it dives, vanishing like an illusion. Moments later there is a distant scattering of plasma as it breaks up on reentry.

112

The plot webs across the imaged planet as they stare in surprise.

"Not localized," Wanr observes. His fur is fluffy, his eyes wide, seeking every photon, every quantum of information.

Talbot runs a hand across his head.

"How can it travel like that, so quickly?" Reed wonders from the dark at the back of the room. She leans forward, shoulder on the doorframe, worried.

M'Ilu Ram is at the console, tuning parameters to improve the semantics. "Travel is not clear represented plot by."

Talbot leans down beside the massive head. "You mean it's just the wind, or something, dispersing the metabolites?"

"Something."

"Well, we'd better find out," Reed snaps, and leaves the room.

113

"We've definitely got a suspicious entry this time," the Constable mutters. He paces like a stalking animal under the harsh green lights. "But what source?"

"The plot is from the asteroid zones, which is normal, but it has some anomalies. It could be from collisions, or it could be something deliberately scrambling the trajectory."

"Pin it down. Them I want. Their location I want."

114

Talbot clings to handles that shudder with the energy of the entry wind. The pod loops widely in the force of a plasma envelope and upper atmosphere gales. He squeezes and pulls, trying to master the violence of the high speed fall. The world below swirls for a moment. Forces compel his mind, and for a moment, his fear, and chagrin, are missing.

He suddenly finds motion subsiding, and the pod is plummeting like the meteor it counterfeits. The sky spreads slowly below, a pearl of clouds that forms a cold surface to the horizon, where the sun sinks away in sharp orange tones. He has another moment to spend regretting his insistence, to remember his promise to the Director. But he makes himself remember other conversations...

"If we're not getting sensible answers from the remotes..."

Cloud sweeps over the canopy, and the pod is swathed in dark mist.

"The thing is everywhere."

"Unlikely it is to truly be everywhere."

"It must be interfering with the probes."

"Not a capability before seen."

"We don't know enough."

Sudden clarity and the clouds flash a dim ceiling above, lit from the scattered lights of a twilit planet below, as if the world were the sky, and the sky the ground, rocking gently.

Gillian Reed's cabin is filled with a soft fluted music. Reed and Deleo are seated together on the floor, Reed cross-legged, and Deleo in an awkward, folded, insectoid position, listening to the cylinder in Reed's fingers; she breathes gently into a flexible tube at the top and shifts her fingers.

Talbot's displays image a field below, carpeted in tiny, bulbous plants. The orientometer shows he is close to the location, and he decelerates drastically. A brief moment of dizziness swirls through him as the blood rushes to his feet. He steadies himself and the pod; he pauses, with deep breaths, twisting slowly only yards above the ground. Then he gently lowers the pod to silence.

The pod splits and the sudden stink of organic air makes him sneeze with its remembered odors - for a moment. Then the smell is pleasant, and normal, with a richness donated by millions of living things. There are tiny lights lined along the left horizon. The clouds are a distant, soft-lit ceiling. Under his feet, the plants make a small squeaking sound as he moves. He looks around, eyes dark in the dark; and there is nothing special to see. Not even the world at war that he expects. A light streaks silently along the distant road.

He consults the detector in his hand and starts out toward the roadlights.

115

The road slopes down from ground level, bordered with tubes of pale bluish light. It descends into a tunnel whose walls are glistening tiles, patterned in shades of a paler blue and white. Talbot steps out of the shadows, cautiously. His shoes are soft, and they slap on the tile, echoing slightly as he steps, angled against the force of his hesitation.

He hears the sound of a car rushing down the roadway, and he turns. Through the reflections on the dome of the car, he can see the face of a woman. The woman does not see him, but she is hunched over the wheel, and her face is clenched in an intense grimace of fear. Her car whisks away into the dimness, painting a rapidly shrinking circle of light along the tunnel walls.

Talbot consults his wrist navigator. But the indications are confused. He looks around. Maybe the tiles are interfering, or perhaps the tunnel is acting as some sort of unusual waveguide. His eyes rove across the ceiling - and stop. A black streak, irregular, branches across the roof from a break in the wall. There is another bulge of the same material pushing past the joints in the tiles of the wall. He moves slowly along the walkway toward it, feeling a strange coolness on his hands. Another vehicle streaks past behind him, but he doesn't turn around. He draws the laser from his belt and checks the setting. He thumbs the focus to wideband and projects the beam against the tiles nearby. In a moment, the ceramic breaks with a sharp crack under the temperature differential. Talbot holsters the laser and waits for the glowing tile to cool a little. He unslings the water bottle from his shoulder and uncaps it. He tosses a spout of water on the tiles and they steam - then shatter. A moment longer, and he clears them away with quick motions of his hands, trying not to be burnt.

Behind the tile, a thin mortar bulges with fine cracks that are almost invisible in the blue light. When he pushes, it gives, flakes away, revealing a soft black mass. He knows the look of that substance. Flesh...

His hands are shaking. He steps back and bumps into the railing. He drops the water bottle, and absently bends down to pick it up again. He turns slightly and paces slowly, irregularly, backward toward the tunnel entrance. Then he twists and runs out onto the surface. The faint squeaking of the plants blurs beneath his feet into a hysterical whisper.

The breath rasps in his dry throat as he sees the pod loom up against the faint sky. For a moment his relief is fear. He pushes into the pod and its leaves fold around him. The sensors power up, and the pod augments his vision with its surfaces. He begins to lift, but as the ground begins to recede, there are traces of running figures converging on the pod.

Panicked, Talbot adds power to the lifters; for the moment he is careless of whether this will reveal him to the Constable. Alarms roar into his ears as small projectiles reach up from the ground, strike the pod and explode near the stability section. He screams as the pod tips out of control, streaking across the plains...

116

The Constable stares away from the streak of Talbot's pod disappearing over the horizon. He turns toward the squad leader, who manages to look dismayed and smug at the same time, despite the unusual triangular geometry of his face.

"Sir, apologies incurred - the generous leader recalls the warning of the courteous subordinate referencing the improbability of success."

The Constable hates the dark. And this exchange only leaves him reminded of the constantly annoying habits of the squad leader's species. He turns with a sudden hand gesture cutting the air.

"This attitude is irrelevant. Track the vehicle immediately."

117

The pod is smoking wreckage in the rocks at the base of an enormous succulent. Sprawled at some distance from the crumpled machine, Talbot lies, half covered with sublimating crash foam, blood seeping from scalp, arms, hands and knees. The light of the rising sun, a rich bluish green tint, touches his closed eyelids. A shadow from another succulent moves slowly with the ascent of the sun, and finally touches his face. He stirs, twitches, and then his eyes shoot open with shock and fear. He tries to push to a stand, but the pain hits him then, and he collapses.

118

Wanr crouches in the darkness, watching down-spectrum versions of the displays. He is afraid of what he infers from what he sees.

119

Talbot finds himself leaning up against a smooth trunk. Not far away is a road. From somewhere over the horizon comes a vague sound like distant thunder which unnerves him. He knows that it is no capability of his own which will keep him alive if the irrational flowers of bombardment spread in his direction. But he doesn't know which way to turn...

He staggers toward the road on uneven legs. Suddenly he stops. He realizes that what he finds on the road can be friend or enemy. He withdraws into the succulent forest, with the shadows wreathing his face. Aching with instability, his fear threatening any second to erupt into panic, he paces carefully through the dry remnants of succulent leaves decaying on the sand.

The sky darkens slowly, clouds clotting the sky and blocking the sun into occasional rays. Talbot is getting more and more hungry, but there is nothing to eat.

The wind picks up, rustling the dead leaves. Tiny sprinkles of rain clatter around him for a moment. He stands, oblivious, his exhausted mind elsewhere. Then the rain pours down in a sudden flood, soaking him to the skin.

His resistance is broken into sobs that shake him by the shoulders, and then curl him into a heap squatting on rain-soaked ground.

He hears a sound. A slightly musical clank that brings his head up. Then another, and another.

Pyramidal objects, a soft dirty golden orange in color, are thrusting up from the ground, opening, and spitting out clusters of yellowish spheres that rattle on the dead leaves. Talbot watches, and finally realizes that he is watching something similar to the blooming of flowers. He feels the tension drain away. He laughs.

Small creatures rustle beneath the detritus. A few of them poke jointed appendages above the litter, scrabbling for the wet yellow spheres. More of them emerge, strange articulated shapes. They begin to fight. Talbot leaps to his feet, worried that their appetites might become carnivorous.

He hears the sound of a vehicle over the rain and occasional thunder. He crouches behind the barrel of a thick succulent. The car sweeps by, hissing over the wet pavement. Followed, a moment later, by another - but, from this one, several beings are leaning out into the rain, screaming, and firing energy weapons into the air. Talbot flings himself back behind the barrel. Good thing he hadn't tried to flag down the traffic. Cold water rivulets down his cheek onto his chest, as he waits, panting.

120

Reed had called the meeting for early sunrise. Muted sunlight streams across the table until Wanr, more sensitive to the day than the others, chokes its brilliance with a control.

"This meeting," Reed begins, "may be difficult. We're going to be dealing with human actions, human behavior..." she looks around at them, trying to gather them together, but there expressions are more than usually impenetrable. "Perhaps it will be confusing, or perhaps you will be able to see things that, right now, are beyond me."

Deleo shifts in his position against the wall.

"Does this have meaning?" he asks.

Reed sighs. "It's just a preamble, Deleo. Putting things in context, so everyone understands what we're going to talk about."

Deleo's eyes shutter with additional membrane. In many ways, she reminds herself, Deleo is not a deeply conceptual creature - or at least it fails to share certain meta-concepts with humans...

m'Ilu Ram stands, and then lies across the table, face pointed close to her. His tripartite mouth gapes and seals. "Talbot, his mission in trouble is likely. We need action not discussion." He slides back to curl up in his bag seat.

Reed avoids an involuntary shudder. She knows that the aggressive, confrontational attitude indicates something corresponding to worry.

Deleo speaks up from the corner. "Trouble is not evident. Talbot was involved in my growth, but it joined with him and changed him in response. He now will be grateful for the result that takes him to the world below to grow yet further into adult."

Wanr sighs and taps nervously on the desk, indicating confidence in what he is about to raise. "There have been energetic detections near landing site. Talbot not armed is. Coincidental, or attack. Problems exist on surface, so could be coincidence."

Reed tries to let that sink in before she continues. "We were persuaded that there was no other way other than going to the surface to determine the source of the metabolites we detected. He was supposed to go in, look, and get out. Now we've been waiting for more than a day - and no sign of him. I'd like your suggestions as to what action we should take."

121

The ancient horizon of the moon is silent in the rain of radiation from the sun. Then, against the backdrop of stars, in a line above the horizon, come the searchers. Their prey lies, unsuspecting, in a crater below the central peak.

122

He feels himself starving as he walks, though he knows it hasn't been long enough for that. The sun is westering into twilight. Earlier in the day, he had chopped at the bole of a succulent with a rock, and had sucked eagerly at the draining fluid, sweet and refreshingly wet on his lips and tongue.

Only hours before, the terrain had begun to dip down from the arid highland plateau, and he had followed the line of least resistance. Strange tangly plants, waving as if animated with a self-contained force, caught at his legs and feet like uncouth hands pulling at the fabric of a sleeve or a coat. They worried him faintly, barely rising above the endless dull roar of the pain in his knees and calves, the fatigue and despair that threatened his remaining energy.

Now, the landscape has given way to a more stable grassland, studded with grayish, bare wood trees that stand like giant bundles of twigs, looming above him. The sun paints them an odd combination of turquoise and orange. Like stone, he thinks. The clouds catch the light for a moment and then recede into a silent violet stain. Desperately, he wants to stop. But if he stops, he is afraid that his thoughts will catch up with him. He is heading, with purpose, with hope of safety, into the worst of the war. Because there, among the purposeless violence, is his last hope of escape. Communications, aircraft, spacecraft... anything.

He knows he must stop for a while... rest. He leans back against the bundle of trunks of a tree, and slides slowly, resisting, to the ground. He feels the warm light painted cold on his face by a breeze. In the distance, there is a sudden, sporadic flashing, and, disconnected by distance, an echoic thunder rolling slowly over the dimming hills. Suddenly he is asleep.

He is awakened in the night by a strange, artificial sound. It is the sound of mechanical saws, biting into wood, not too far away. Under his back, the tree stirs. He shudders, and throws himself away from it. But it is just a faint spasm of dream.

The sound, though, is still there. He rubs his face with a dirty hand, feeling the grit on his skin like a cloth.

His wrist navigator guides him in the right direction, but cannot tell him the layout of the ground. He stumbles in the dark. A root catches his foot, and a branch swats just above his eyes, knocking him backward. He bites his lip to keep from crying out. Closer now, there is light escaping between the ragged barrier of more closely spaced trees.

A shudder takes him as he remembers another night in the forest, another presence, which is here too.

Closer now, he drops to his knees, looking around wildly, afraid of everything he can't see, but determined. He creeps forward to the barrier and the light. He gets lower, moving as quietly as he was once taught. The sound starts again, a ripping of wood under metal.

He peers between the spindly cryptotrunks.

123

Reed sits sprawled across a seat in the darkened control cabin, looking out on the sunbathed crater bottom beyond. Deleo stands in the doorway, always more afraid of this room.

He whispers. "Are they close?"

"Yeah."

"Will they find us?"

"Maybe."

"What happens?"

"I don't know." Reflections of the landscape glint on the moist surface of her eye. "I guess we won't be helping Raoul, if that happens."

124

Lights halo down from tall stands, pooling on the ground. Soft tendrils of moisture rise in their heat. Talbot watches as people bring cut wood from the shadows to brace the walls of a deep pit. Others, in the pit, are digging and hauling dirt.

He slumps against the bundled trunks, stomach growling. The activity below seems purposeless. Why are they doing it at this hour?

Exhaustion creeps inward from his hard, painful limbs. He blinks, trying to stay awake.

Suddenly, a rude grip drags him from a doze. He is twisted up, nearly to his feet, and confronted with a strange face. Crisp surface veins are harshly shaded by the light below. Yellow slit pupils are dilated in the dimness, looking closely into his eyes. A double mouth, one pulsing slowly, one pursed into a round opening, emits a stream of incomprehensible phonemes.

Talbot shakes his head in denial. No translators for his to work with. "I don't understand." He sees another of the same kind behind his captor. Are they all of this sort? Talbot knows that there are no natives on this world, but this species is also unknown to him. It may be days before his unspecialized translator can get enough to work out the language on its own.

Talbot's captor shakes him, and pushes him around toward the scene below. More sounds. Talbot's heart is pounding, but he thinks... *At least I'm getting more language.* He wants to run, but another hand closes around his arm. He looks down. Three stocky fingers, double thumbs. Not a hope of getting free.

"Look," he tries, "I'm not going to harm you."

He is surprised, but his translator emits some sounds. It must be very confident of the language already, perhaps because of similarity to one already known, since he had never engaged the priority mode. Good thing too, since the priority mode "guesses" could do more harm than good in a volatile situation like this.

The others stare at him, as if shocked. Then they continue toward the work site, hooting and whistling among themselves. Gradually, as he stumbles in their grasp toward the pit, Talbot hears some words through the meaningless sounds.

"What's this?" snaps a voice from behind them. His arms are dragged around until he faces the source of the voice - a stocky young male human, faintly yellow complexioned, a broad scar over his left eye. His language, whatever it is, instantly translates.

"Oorsliore urio by trees cdoosre observing." The hand on that side squeezes his arm in some rhythm with the sounds.

The human moves close and leers up at him. A waft of old breath wrinkles Talbot's nose.

"Funny color," the other mutters, introspectively. He reaches toward Talbot's face, but Talbot jerks away.

"Stop that," Talbot demands. "I'm not going to do you any harm. If you're engaged in something you don't want me to know about, that's OK. Just let me go, and you'll never hear from me again."

"Engaged?" the other hisses, as if talking to himself. "Engaged? A funny word." Suddenly his eyes clear, and he leans closer to Talbot. "You're the same damn color as the thing in the pit, I guess. Maybe you're some kind of thing he's made to spoof us. Eh?"

"I wasn't made by anyone other than my mother, thanks." The sound of blood in his ears is a presage of weakness. He feels his legs shaking uncontrollably.

"Well, let's go find out. After all, when things are in flux like they are, nothing is really certain until it's certain. And we'll be certain when we see how you and the thing in the pit get along, then." He turns and gestures to Talbot's captors, who tug him along, feet scraping on the dirt, toward the pit.

"Have you found the damn thing yet?" The man yells down into the pit.

"No.." comes a voice.

"Well, hurry up. We got a piece of the thing up here in a hurry to join with itself."

Time passes. Talbot wants to speak, to protest, but his exhaustion seems to have seized his throat and silenced him. He feels himself sagging, but he is unable to stop himself. In a dim haze he hears shouts, feels people clustering around, as others flee the pit. Then he feels a sudden shove, and plummets into blackness. The soft ground slaps him in the side of the head, and he goes away for a moment. He hears the sound of energy discharges from somewhere far above, then shouting and the clatter of running feet.

125

Risha leans back into the corner of the room, exhausted. The smell of ionization and scorched walls permeates the air.

Perhaps they are gone.

Or, perhaps not.

The fighting has continued all day, with the bandits trading energy beams with her until sunset. It is a conflict that had been intensifying for the last two weeks. Every day.

She runs her hands through wiry hair. For a moment she wishes she weren't so stubborn - that she could just walk out into the field of fire and end it. She is exhausted from constant vigilance, from waking at the slightest creak of the house on its foundations, from the few moments she could snatch for food and water, hardly tasted. But even as this thought passes, her anger reasserts, and she clenches the weapon more tightly, her knuckles a faint pink.

It is her house, and she intends it to stay that way.

But there is a sound from the rear of the house. They must be trying to force an entry again. What if it is merely a feint? She cannot take the chance. Slowly she moves to a crouch. In the dimness, she steps carefully. Around the corner, and she sees the window pop out onto the floor. But no one follows it. What follows is instead a package of some kind, falling with a thump onto the window pane.

She knows what it is, in an instant. There is no choice, but to run forward, and leap through the open window - just as the bomb explodes. The shockwave slaps her across the back in midair, and she spirals in the flames for a soundless moment, waiting for events to join her. Then the ground smashes across her face, and shoulder, and she is up again, trying to run. But she accomplishes only a half motion before her leg collapses under her with a shriek of pain. Her ears are silent as the debris rains mysteriously around her. Her eyes are partly blinded by echoing greenish shadows that blot away any detail from the night. She knows she could be dead at any moment.

She moves her energy weapon to her other hand, a motion accomplished by dim vision, since she can feel almost nothing. She does not want to fire. They might see her beam, or the sight laser. If she does not move, they may leave her for dead.

It would be as senseless as anything else they have done. So she waits, panting, hidden by the small towers of foliage from the herkimer she had planted near the house. Gradually, her senses return.

She decides she must have fallen asleep for a moment. When she next notices events, her vision has improved, she can see and hear the fire of the broken home burning behind her. There are tears running down her face, salty on her lips. Her house, so slowly and carefully constructed, so fine and perfected in its design. Now a ruin crackling with the last vestiges of flame. She finds herself worrying about what Rantar will say - but she knows she may never hear from him again. He may be dead on the plain, for all she knows. But she spares no time in wondering, because survival is the only item of motivation left.

Slowly she crawls forward, away from the fire. The sandy soil rubs and abrades her forearms as she moves. She holds the weapon out in front of her, in case she needs it.

She stops, remembering the garage. A horrible smell of burning plastics, composites and wood wafts across her - she smothers her choking in aching and battered hands, dropping the weapon. She picks it up again, and clutches it hard. She turns to crawl back toward the burning. In the darkness she hears the slamming of doors and the roar of the bandit's plains jumper, then silence as it moves away.

She waits silently, for a while. Then she begins to crawl again.

The garage is subsurface, with a ramp running down to the door. She pauses at the edge, heart pounding suddenly.

She gathers herself to her feet, carefully, waiting for her pain. Her ankle wobbles, with sharp spikes lancing up through her calf. But she staggers forward down the slope, anyway. The shadows close above her. She spins with a sudden pain and falls into the wall for an ugly-faced moment. More slowly and carefully, she creeps down, with the wall for support.

Something hits her forcefully, full body. She gasps - but it is just the door, hidden in the flickering dark.

She looks around, eyes wide and pale in the dark. Her lips are drawn and feral, but her scraped cheekbones are high and clearly formed, and her dark skin contours smoothly from chin to scalp like a precision model, but harsh with faint age. She turns back and slips the catch to the access door, panting, gun held tightly. Everything within lights automatically, and she is blind for a second. She leans through the door...

No one there.

She steps in and staggers to the door of the jumper. She looks around for anything useful. Some tools, packaged food - laboriously she loads them into the back of the cab, glancing every second back at the door, afraid the bandits will return. She keeps remembering Rantar, because the sight and smell of the jumper won't let her forget. She doesn't realize she is crying until she sees a tear drip to the seat.

The jumper bursts into darkness on its huge wire woven wheels. The light of the flames shatters across the dash through the back of the canopy, fades, then vanishes as she rolls down the rise.

126

An erosion gully slams the wheels against the carriage, throwing her forward toward the control panel. Frantically she stops the jumper.

She knows she can't drive any longer without lights. And for a moment, she isn't sure she wants to.

I could head into the valley, she thinks. *Go to the city. But what for? The city is in chaos. I could go back into the mountains, but the bandits are between me and the heights.*

She sighs and leans back in the seat, its form creaking under the pressure of her stretch. The endless awareness is taking its toll, and she sees the panel blur for a moment...

Finally, she leans over and roots through some underpanel storage compartments by the light of the displays. There - night goggles. She slips them over her eyes, and the outside becomes a scene like a slightly strange daylight, lit from the cluster stars that cloak the sky.

A speck of warmth moves shimmering near the horizon. She zooms the goggles until a staggering figure is visible glowing pale against the dusky sky. A gasp fills her chest for a moment. Maybe it is Rantar?

A flash lights the horizon - part of the distant war, backlighting the anonymous figure. She feels it as if it is aimed at her. At Rantar. She remembers a slap across her face, his look of sudden, startled hatred, as if he had realized that she were something alien, something awful. And in that moment she had wondered if she were. If there were something she had done, that she didn't remember, that made him blame her... It had to be her fault - everything had been fine; even though the war was spreading toward them so quickly. She had wanted anything except to blame him. For a moment.

Until she drove him out. She had been sobbing as she struck him, forcing him to the door.

"Never!" she had screamed. "Never are you going to do that to me!"

She shakes her head, and the image of the landscape wavers. She sees in her mind the image of his velvety blue skin, harsh features, and three dark eyes lined across his face. The creases bracketing his narrow, slightly triangular thin-lipped mouth, which would pull back when he kissed her - a human custom he had come to enjoy - with her.

She can almost feel his arms wrapped across her shoulders, in a silent weight she had not allowed herself to miss.

Her hands shift the jumper into motion, skidding around toward the figure stalking the horizon.

One moment is not going to destroy her life.

127

Talbot never sees the shape bounding toward him across the plain. He has fallen, again, rolling down a short slope. Some endless determination orders his muscles to rise yet again. Some final reservoir of energy allows it. His consciousness is lucid, but disconnected.

Suddenly he is confronted with the shape of the jumper. A light comes to life as Risha leaps out. She seizes his shoulders and glares into his face. "Who are you?" she shouts, as if he were deaf. She sees his face, crisp with burns, his eyes, dim and reddened with exhaustion, but it doesn't mean anything to her, except that it isn't Rantar's face.

"Who are you?!" she screams.

His lips are slow to respond, but they curve in a faint and ruined irony. His voice is a hoarsened whisper. "Ma'am, I have been running, hiding, thrown into a pit, set on fire and survived. One thing I have learned is WHO I AM. There's no damn need to shout."

She laughs, just a small chuckle. She slips into laughter, as if relieved of an intense burden. The laughter runs its course, as Talbot watches curiously. If he were stronger, he thinks, he might like her face... though its expressions seem too close to the edge of madness for safety.

His consciousness wavers, and through the fog of hunger and pain, he sees her blurred features move from laughter to concern.

128

North Panka

Riggers Cove

Port Leonardo

• Bernau

South Panka

Induran

• Telenor

The little hospital in Bernau is still open, lit from below by neon lines along the roadside. Nearby, an older, domed building smolders, tiny flames still flickering, even as the dark figures of firefighters rove with portable extinguishers.

Two men carry Talbot from the jumper at a run, one on each side of a flying stretcher, hurrying through the iris, Risha following more slowly, almost reluctantly, behind.

She stops at the iris, leaning on its frame, feeling her own raggedness keeping her back from the brightness inside. But she stirs and follows, and the leaves slip shut behind her.

A thin, young physic looks up from where he examines Talbot under a spotlight in the triage section. His teeth bare into a quick, bright smile. "Risha, dear. A surprise. What's going on?"

She sighs. "I brought him in. Found him on the steppe."

"Out looking for Rantar? No sign, still?"

Her hands start shaking. "Our house is gone, too. Raiders - tonight."

He glares down at Talbot. "One of them?"

"I don't think so. I just found him. He said he was burned."

His eyes rove quickly over the prone figure and he touches here and there. "There's some slight burn here and there, but he seems unthreatened. Don't worry, we'll put him on drip for dehydration and anti-infection, spray him with accelerators and let him sleep. And you? You look like something a jumper ran down."

She manages to find a smile somewhere. "You are *so* complimentary."

"What about the raiders? I think we've still got a revenge team somewhere in town, I could talk to Craenshon..."

"They're long gone. Besides, what good would it do? Things are just coming apart, Kahn. I'm so sick of stroke and counterstroke. What are we going to do?"

He walks slowly over to her and searches her face and posture. He places a gentle hand on her stiffened forearm. "You're not doing anything except getting some sleep." He waves an attendant over. "Put him in light ward; standard drip, burn heal acceleration, run some blood and get back to me. Find Risha here someplace to sleep. There's got to be room somewhere."

"Not much after the bombings," the woman replies, pale features sharp and tense. She looks Risha over with a professional eye, and her expression slowly becomes more sympathetic. "Oh, we'll find something. Light ward's not as full, maybe she can stay there. Give me a minute to set the drip..." She walks over toward a cabinet past Talbot's stretcher.

"Who's she?" Risha asks, sotto voce.

"Out of town," Kahn replies, leading her aside. "We're short on nurses, but the word is getting around that things are a little more stable here, and the right kind of people are coming in. So far, we're all humans and that seems to be helping."

She swallows against an uncomfortable dryness, thinking of Rantar. Kahn should never know how much she wishes she had come into town a month ago. "Yes, but you're still getting bombings here, aren't you..."

The line of his mouth levels into grimness. "There are bombing and shellings everywhere, though who knows from who or why anymore. At least the townspeople seem a little more focused."

She can't stop herself. She catches a fold of his shirt in her fist. "But how long, how long are we going to stay normal? How much longer have we got?" Her fist is punching into his chest and his slight body shudders with the blows. He seizes her fists in his hands, and it is not that hard to stop her. She stands apart, tears on her face. He enfolds her in his arms. His eyes are narrow with anger and determination. He looks up at the approach of the technician. "Come on, Risha, I'll find you a room."

An ambulance whines into the parking area, and the iris slams open behind them. They step into the quiet of the dim corridor, as the sirens die away and new voices start shouting.

129

Talbot wakens in a large, darkened room, a bed, beside a dark window with lights and fires burning sullenly beyond. There is the sound of sleeping everywhere. An occasional moan emerges from various points in the room.

"Doctor Kahn to SCU, stat; wake up doctor." The distant sound filters through the curtains from outside.

Talbot stares around wildly. Where is he? He remembers nothing since being dragged to the pit, which strikes his mind in a sudden rush of context.

He must have been rescued.

He tries to sit, but his muscles protest, and he feels something taped to his arm - a flattened plastic bag of fluid and a pad. There is a tube and a needle under the pad, which momentarily nauseates him.

Bits of the recent past begin to flow slowly into his mind.

"Hey, anybody?" he tries to yell, but his voice chokes. *What a mess I am,* he thinks. He notices that his clothes have been changed for a loose white costume. His translator! He rolls himself over until his legs slide past the edge of the bed, and the gravity helps pull him to a sitting position, legs dangling. He waits, panting, for his heart to slow.

Finally he reaches up to massage his scalp, below which he can feel his brain aching. He had been reduced to the most daily living - timeless and present; desperate and dangerous. Now, he thinks, he should stop for a moment, but the relentless strangeness of his new life is bearing down on him again. He can feel it again. Endless change. Life.

He is afraid to try to walk - his legs feel distant, like sticks. So, clutching the edge of the bed he slowly lowers his feet to the floor, and gradually adds weight until he is standing, gasping, weaving ever so slightly from side to side with the tiny adjustments of his muscles.

There are footsteps in the space beyond the curtain. Someone steps through, and a faint light glows from the curtain walls, silhouetting the figure.

"So... you're up. How do you feel?" It is a woman's voice, tart and dry with strange throaty vowels, meaning emanating from a table beside the bed.

"Yes," he whispers. He slumps back against the edge of the bed. It is the translator. But he understands a little of the language. It is Asparti, a subdialect of Basal developed on this world by its initial immigrants. He leans down to the table and picks the pendant. Slowly, he puts it over his head and settles it on his chest.

"Who are you?" he asks, forehead creased with the effort.

"Risha," she replies. "I brought you here to Bernau. A day ago."

"I'd have thought you'd be gone home."

"I don't have a home." Her voice is harsh, denying pain. "I'm helping here tonight. The Irrationalists bombed a bookstore, and the doctors need help."

"So you're a helper," he mutters, too tired to hold his head strictly.

She wanders slowly into the narrow enclosure, looking around, looking at him. "Sometimes. I don't want to spend my life bailing out boats, if that's what you mean. But when the ship is sinking, you have to save yourself, and the pieces of your world that count."

Her phrases catch at some intuition within him. "Seashore?" he asks.

She turns to him, startled. "What?"

"From the seashore? Boats, you mentioned boats."

"No, the South Panka Lakes. We sail, fish and transport. Why?"

He is breathing a little hard, but the effort is clearing his mind. "Just curious. Thanks for helping me."

"You're welcome." She stops her roving over by the window. "Maybe you should sleep."

"Slept enough. Maybe too much. Thought I wasn't going to wake up. Won't ever sleep like I used to, again."

She leans toward him, peering as he speaks. "You're whispering." Her teeth are bright in the dark. "Why?"

"Translator. Don't want to be louder than the output."

She sways back in delight. "You're a spacer? I heard they always whispered. What were you doing out there? Shouldn't you be at Port Leonardo, or somewhere?" Her voice is changed, lighter, now that it is animated again.

"I suppose I should. I crashed, north of here, I think."

"Hungry?"

"Thirsty," he admits. "Maybe hungry after."

"Come on, I know where we can get a meal." She tugs at his arm.

130

The cafeteria is small, just a few tables by a long window onto nearly complete darkness. First light is just beginning to touch the sky with the wash from the hidden sun. For a while, there is only the sound of utensils and the smell of hot tea.

Talbot is uncomfortable, and he finds himself looking out at the sky, or around the quiet, darkened room. The food is strangely spiced, but not unpleasant. The hydration bag is awkward on his forearm. He feels vulnerable in the hospital clothes.

Hospitals, he thinks. What a strange, backward concept. Nothing more than that is needed to remind him of the frontier. Dangerous places, filled with sick people, a sign that medical technology is so primitive it must be centralized, and a sign of inadequately developed delivery systems. Well, at least they hadn't done surgery on him... they probably did it by hand here.

"So," Risha asks, and his eyes swing back to her, "What brought you here?"

He has decided that his answers to this will be discreet. Everyone on this planet remains an unknown quantity, particularly with regard to their knowledge of The Mover. His last experience had been the most terrifying he ever remembered, even beyond... the deaths. Because this time he had been helpless, this time, it had been his life at the mercy of complete irrationality.

"Well," he replies, "I crashed." She eyes him, as if expecting more. "You know, the traffic control around here is in chaos."

She looks puzzled for a moment. Then her expression clears. "No, I mean why did you come? To Tlnou, to Induran."

"Oh. Business. Our company has an office at the port. We were checking in on the progress of some research."

She starts up. "Were there others?" she gasps. "I'm sorry..."

"No, no. I'm a shuttle pilot. I was making a pickup. Just me." He relives for a moment the crash, the endless walking... He shakes himself out of it, and returns his eyes to her concerned look. "I'm OK," he reassures her.

She wonders why she was worried for a moment. "Must have been the systems failures, eh? Everything's been up and down the last month."

They are silent except for the small sounds of the others around them. The horizon beyond the window starts to burn with immanent sunrise. Behind them, the hospital is beginning to stir.

"Listen," he asks, "I've got to get to a spaceport. What's close?"

She considers for a while, watching the sunrise through the slowly darkening glass. "Probably Port Leonardo is the only one you might get to without flying. And right now, flying..." She purses her lips. "Some of the rebels have artillery and missiles. Not that the roads are that good either."

He sips the tea, feeling it in his throat. A doctor wanders in, pours herself a cup, and leans against the counter behind them. Doctor Kahn follows, his face suddenly pale and lined in the sunlight as he squints. He mixes his tea and chats with the other doctor in low tones. After a moment, he notices the two at the table. He walks over and smiles at Talbot.

"Better already, I see."

Talbot is uncomfortable at the scrutiny, but the doctor's face is likeable, so he forces a smile. "Yeah, thanks. I appreciate everything."

"Join you?"

"Sure. When can I get out of here?"

"Glad to come, gladder to leave. Well, you look all right. The burns are..." he peers, lips pursed, "better."

"They hurt."

"That will be true for a while, I'm afraid. Say, you're speaking the language a bit yourself. Spacer, aren't you? Thought I recognized the translator."

"Yes. Shuttle pilot. I want to get back off-world as soon as I can get a flight."

"Don't blame you." He sips his tea, making a slight face at the bitterness. "Port Leonardo's probably the closest, but it's a good half a hundred. You have transport?"

Talbot sighs. "No."

"Funds?"

"No." It seems hopeless. His hands clench and release in the sudden sun on the table top. He looks at Risha. "Could I impose on you for a drive?"

She is surprised. "No," she says shortly. "That's impossible."

"But why? Listen, I don't have access here, but at a spaceport I'll be able to get company funds. You'll be well reimbursed."

"I have my husband to search for. I can't be tramping all over the countryside. I've wasted enough time bringing you here." She stands suddenly and strides to the window, where she subsides, waiting, staring out.

The doctor's face remains impassive. Talbot wonders what story lies behind their interaction.

Finally Khan speaks. "It's going to be dangerous getting there. There are all kinds of random military actions occurring. I doubt if there are many away from home who know who their enemies are. There's a semi-guided ground trans system - I think it's ArcTrans - but they're irregular." He seems to consider for a while. "What net is your company on?"

"Here? I don't know for sure. You've heard of Radelix Geodesic?"

"Oh... I should have guessed."

Talbot drums fingers on the tabletop. His tiredness pulls a yawn. "What do you mean?"

"Well, it explains some of what happened to you."

"How?"

"You don't know? Everyone around here knows the trouble started with an escaped import from Radelix. I wouldn't mention the name much if I were you."

"It doesn't seem to bother you," Talbot replies carefully.

"I'm not happy about it, but rumors are rumors. Besides, what kind of import could make people act insane? Bio? Chem? I'm a man for facts. I'll wait for evidence. Besides, even if it were true, it's the company's fault - it's not your fault."

Talbot sips tea to cover his expression.

Kahn sighs. "Well, a trans ticket isn't that expensive, and I suppose I'll have to do without your paying me for patching you up. I'll front you some funds to get you to Leo. Do me a favor?"

"Anything," Talbot replies in a hushed gasp.

"Send me some payback when you get to the Port. I need what I can get to keep this place going."

Talbot watches Risha moving uneasily against the darkened window. Her movement reflects his discomfort.

"Yes. I'll do that."

The doctor pushes to a stand. "I'll get tokens for you. Have some breakfast, and then we'll get you set to go."

Risha leans back to glare at them. "Sooner the better, so I can be on my way."

131

Talbot feels oddly empty as he watches Risha's jumper pull away from the ArcTrans station. The sky is overcast, but the heat is oppressive. He wonders why he feels anything for her. Maybe no more than a gratitude unresolved? He smears at sweat across his cheek, turns and steps into the transport module. The glass hisses shut behind him and removes the brutal heat.

He settles into a seat. The module starts away, smoothly accelerating to a remarkable speed. Talbot smoothes a stack of currency between his thumb and forefinger, enjoying the feel of it, the intricate pictures. Money is rarely needed shipside, and only occasionally planetside on the urbanized worlds.

Foliage shadows whisk across his face as the sun sinks slowly past the noon line.

He switches to the entertainment system, but the broadcast channels are in chaos. The few that remain are transmitting emergency information, apparently from recordings. He begins to wonder if he'll find anything left at Port Leonardo. The disaster and chaos are spreading.

The slight movement and the tension make him exhausted, and he finally curls up on a couch at the side. He feels ashamed to be tired, but he slowly slides into sleep again.

132

Moonlight delineates a distant complex of baroque buildings, mostly unlit. The transport module chimes to announce approach to Port Leonardo. Talbot stirs on the couch, eyelids heavy and reluctant. Then he remembers and starts up. Ahead, he sees the sporadic lights of residences lining hills that front Riggers' Cove. Beyond, the areas of industry are blacked out, with only occasional navigation lights winking solemnly from buildings and antennae. The city seems to crawl up toward him as he worries.

No air traffic visible. No launches. Minimal ground traffic. At least there are no fires in sight.

He thinks of Risha again, wonders if she has found her husband wandering across the steppe. He finds himself smiling without knowing why.

How is it, he wonders, *that some remain immune to the effect of the Mover? Why didn't he and Risha instantly hate each other? Is it part of the way the Mover functions, to make some cleave together, so there will be groups that can fight? Or is it a weakness in the Mover mechanism? A mutation, like spreading into the fabric of the planet must be?*

A building, partly burned away, slides past, its torn shell silhouetted against the pale blue street lighting.

He begins to plan to steal a ship. Private craft are code keyed, but commercial transports are secured mostly by the complexity of the knowledge required to fly them. He will need to know the layout of the port, find some orbital path resources, get a clearance. How to get back to Tlnou Beta without being spotted? Is the constable watching for unauthorized launches? Surely refugees would be allowed to leave. Talbot wonders if perhaps he can erect a cover on that basis. But what would justify refugees going toward Tlnou Beta?

Apparently he will need a better plan.

The module slides into a berth by a platform under garish lights. Half of the lighting units are dull with age, some are dark and split open, but the rest cast harsh shadows through the canopy. Instinctively, he presses his hand to the pocket that contains his few items - the small roll of cash, the translator... a network address for the account of Dr. Kahn, representing a fantastic weight of debt to him.

There are a few people on the platform. Most stand listlessly, but their eyes follow the vehicle until it stops, and he emerges. One individual starts toward him diffidently, eyes cast down, and passes, stepping down into the module. The canopy shuts softly and the vehicle drifts back onto the reserved road. Talbot tries to walk away with a demeanor of normality. His shadow shifts beneath him and reaches ahead. The others avoid looking at him, and he is nervous at their silence. He feels them like silent predators, not looking, because they know where he is at any moment, and confident that he will be theirs when they decide to pounce.

He reminds himself that they are city people. That in the city, people provide each other with space, because they are, themselves, feeling crowded.

But an odor of madness seems to cling to the street beyond the platform, like stepping off the end of the world.

He stops at a kiosk for a map of the city. The automated system helps him produce one with a routing to the spaceport entrance. He examines the glowing smartsheet with some dismay. The distance is fairly large, and he is exhausted. He tries to think clearly. Perhaps he can access company credit, and obtain personal transport. Turning back to the kiosk, he signals his interest. There is a pause, which he spends looking first this way, then that, up and down the road. A personal vehicle hisses past, canopy opaqued, its sound startling him.

The kiosk requests his account identifier and passkey. Talbot chooses to provide retinal print, which will automatically link him to any accounts he might have available. He fits his eye to the socket and endures the dim flash. Then he waits.

Some of his local accounts, established on his prior visit, are available to him, though there are troubling discrepancies compared to his memory of the transactions. Nonetheless, he keys a payment with extras through to Kahn's account address.

While he waits for the transaction to go through, a quiet sound seizes his attention. A vehicle slides to a stop in the road beside the kiosk. A thin, dark-skinned human of late middle age emerges and hurries over.

"I'm so glad I found you in time," he gasps. His hand snakes out and grabs Talbot's wrist.

"Who are you? What are you talking about?" Talbot snaps. He pulls his arm from the other's grasp.

"I'm Lodekar, from the regional office. Boy, are you lucky I was around when the call came in. Come on, you can't stay here. They've cordoned off this area. It's only for garesky."

"What! What are you talking about?" He sweeps his hand across the kiosk, disconnecting.

"No time, come on," Lodekar steps back toward the car.

"Show me some identification." Talbot snarls. "Then I'll think about it."

Lodekar sighs with an exaggerated patience, and steps quickly to Talbot, producing a luminous card. "What do you think, I'd lie to you? Like you aren't one of us, eh? Now, are you satisfied? Eh? Let's go?"

"All right," Talbot follows him to the vehicle, alarmed by Lodekar's insistence. The canopy slides shut over him as he takes his seat - just as a projectile glances off the top of the clear dome. Lodekar's acceleration shoves Talbot back into the seat.

133

"It's not just the humans who are fragmenting. Plaskins, slants, darkboys, sure. But the Christarphi are factionalizing on symmetry and blueness. The Instar Confederacy priests are having a mortar war with the military allied to the Scientific Regulators. Interbreeds and platonics are splitting up, fighting, even killing each other. The place is a mess."

Pale green street lighting flees past the bottom of the canopy, garishly reflecting Talbot's worried face back from the dark clear.

"I don't know what's happening. I've been here for years, and it was a nice place to live, know?"

Talbot turns to him. Lodekar's chin is stubbled and grooved, and his teeth look yellow even in the light of the dash. The whites of his eyes are reddened and wide.

Talbot asks, "How'd you know to come get me?"

"Some programmer at Central was smart enough to tie account access to the regionals as an alarm before the network partitioned. We get local accesses - sometimes. Got you. Good thing you're a darkboy, though. I'm having a hard time stomaching all the slants we get in here off the ships from Slobain; and the slopeheads and bug piles drive me nuts. I help 'em all, but it feels better to be helping one of your own, don't you figure?" He weaves through a knot of sudden traffic, intent on driving.

Talbot sighs and stares back out the window. Somehow he can barely stand talking. The Mover is reaching far and subtly and quickly. He starts to chill with the thought that his immunity might be limited.

"Is there any way I can get off this place? I've got a ship in orbit to get back to."

"Orbit? Where's the ship? I thought Ground Warfare took out the stations. 'Course that's just a rumor, I guess, because the press isn't doing much since the purge. But the Port's mostly down. Jurisdictional dispute and nobody's maintaining or fueling, or, probably, clearing even. Been some stuff blown up, too."

"But there are company ships here? Ships you could get me access to?"

Lodekar chews his lip, uncertain, thinking as he drives. "I never had anybody want to do that. Mostly I've been funneling them onto transport to Telenor. Central office. You sure you don't want to do that?"

"I'm a pilot," Talbot feels a sudden desperation at the wrangling. "I can fly it if you can get me to it. I've got a Director waiting for me. You know how that is." He hopes this bureaucratic appeal for sympathy will do what it takes to refocus Lodekar.

Finally he senses Lodekar come to a decision. "All right, I can go with the flux. You want to try to eat, rest, anything before?"

Talbot grins. "Yeah, all of the above. But I'll be happy with some food and a bit of relief. Then you get me on a ship, and we'll all be happy."

134

Reed paces the tiny dimensions again, and again. The harsh greenish light is unsuited to her, and the bathroom appliances are not only strange, but perhaps actively threatening. Soon, she knows, she'll have to experiment. Damn Constable.

Suddenly a wall vanishes onto a room with brighter light. She laughs with a joyous abandon as she sees Tranis.

"Director, am I happy to see you!"

"Happiness in the midst of disaster is an inappropriate reaction, Gillian. Come with me, now. We have only a short time to reduce the scope of our problem. Talbot has taken a ship and is heading for Tlnou Beta."

135

She was sure that when she first saw him again, she would be happy. Instead, she slaps his face in an uncontrollable eruption of anger.

Talbot stands, guilt in posture and expression. But she sees something else, which she has never seen in him before. Pride.

"Listen," he says, "I have to tell you about it. I know I couldn't contact you, but you don't know what I found."

"You found nothing," she snaps. "Nothing."

"You weren't there, how do you know?" he protests.

"Believe me, I know." Suddenly, surprisingly, she winks at him. "You didn't find anything that interests me as much as seeing you in a lot of trouble, and don't try making up stories to get out of the trouble you're in." Her eyes rove the green-illumined waiting room.

Then he realizes. They are still playing the game. Who's going to know what, when. Us versus them. He palms the cool grey wall. His hand has a rich color against its neutrality. Darkboy, he thinks. He looks at Jill. Paleskin. The thought is like a contaminant. He shies away from it.

"You should be worrying about the level of trouble you've created. The Director is likely to strip your skin with a dull knife and hang it up for the newvies to learn from, at the rate you're going."

He sighs. "You're right. When do we get out of here?"

"Now." She tugs at his wrist. His hand is shaking. She stares at it. He pulls back into himself to find her looking at him as if trying to penetrate his thoughts and experiences with the force of her focus.

"I'm sorry," he says. "I'm tired. Let's go."

136

The shuttle bay anteroom is home to Talbot. The sight of the cool mottled light and the simulated stone walls arouses an unfamiliar emotion. For a moment, he is caught between one step and the next. A tear slips from his eye and he wipes it. It dries in a cool fern of sensation across his cheek.

137

The Director's voice is its usual wispy tone. "They let you go because Radelix asked them to. Because we promised to discipline you. We also lodged a complaint with their command regarding actions we discovered they had taken against you while you were on the surface. That didn't hurt."

Reed looks at him sharply, realizing there are things she does not yet know.

"What actions?"

Talbot wishes he could smile, but the best he can manage is a strange, tight expression. "I think she means when they shot me down. Or ordered it. I don't know which."

The Director's small face is not smiling with pleasure or with tension. Instead, she looks simply alien, as if the human-like characteristics of a mask were suppressed. "This doesn't affect how I or Radelix view your desertion of your team."

Now it is Talbot's turn to be shocked, as the full import of what he had decided to do, and its appearance to others, makes itself felt. "Desertion? I didn't run out on them. We had to find out what was going on down there. The remote probes weren't working, we weren't getting anything by hiding passively on Beta. I was the only pilot checked out in the pod. There was no one else to send." He plants his hands on the tabletop and stares at them. When he lifts them away, the ridges of his palm print are left behind for a moment, like a ghost that fades into nothingness. *I'm sweating,* he thinks wildly. *But it's cool in here. I need some rest. Why can't I rest before I have to go through this? Why does everything have to be a damned crisis?* "And I did find out. You're not going to like it. It's unbelievable." *I don't believe it, and I lived it.*

"The probes show the Mover has reproduced." The Director replies, startling him. "Oh, yes, it's quite obvious, given the results of the profiling you ran against it. At least we had that much if you never made it back from your jaunt."

"Why didn't you tell us you had that information, already?" Reed demands, glaring at Talbot.

Why didn't I? Didn't I? "All we knew was that the Mover had been in many places. We didn't know how. We had to know."

"So, is that your defense?" The Director demands.

His anger rises and he pushes back – hard. "I don't need a defense. You do. We should have been more aggressive about finding out what's going on. There are real people down there killing each other because of the Mover. We owe them figuring out how to stop that as quickly as possible and starting to contain the damage.

"Now, listen to me - something's happened to it down there. It isn't reproduction. Really. It's growth. I mean, the Mover isn't a Mover anymore – it's not an animal. It's more like... I don't know, a coral, maybe. It's spreading across the planet, like it's becoming part of the planet. I found part of it underground, in a tunnel, like a web. Some people found it buried under the ground near where they lived, another place. That's where I got burned. I don't know how they figured out that it was where it was... but they did. And the closer I was to one of the centers of growth, the stranger and more chaotic everyone was acting. It's like the thing is out of control, running away. Positive feedback? Mutation? Cancer? It's dangerous, and every minute is that much less time before it takes everything. More than Tlnou is at risk. We're all at risk, the longer this continues."

They are looking at him as if he is the one out of control.

Finally, the Director responds. "You seem exhausted, Raoul. Why don't you get some food and some rest before the full debriefing. Then we'll think about things and let you know our decision."

"Decision? We have to find some way to get rid of this thing. We can't wait."

"Not that decision, Raoul."

That stops him in mid-speech.

"What decision, then?"

"Whether you're going to stay with Radelix – and this team - or not."

138

He sits in his room, at the foot of the bed, and realizes how bare it is. Except for the door painting, he has done little to make the room his own. As if his bitterness had made him keep the walls bare, to remind him of how little he belonged here. And since he had begun to feel differently, there had been no time to make changes.

Maybe I should have the door painting changed, he thinks. *This is really not something that fits, anymore. As if I ever knew what it meant – a ten thousand year old image of an unknown origin.*

But the thought is idle, when he may not even be here for much longer.

Being fired. It wasn't something he ever thought about. Where would he go? Contract usually stated nearest habitable world, station or intership transfer. He didn't want to be stranded on Tlnou. That would be a death sentence. And he doesn't want to leave. Shouldn't leave.

But he knows the choice isn't his to make. The Director will decide, with a cold alien logic that will dissect his motives, ignore his reasoning as excuses... there isn't much hope. What can he do, but try to prepare?

His fists strike the bed. He pushes to stand.

Leave this? Leave an incredible danger? Leave Risha and Kahn, and even Lodekar to die in the endless war and chaos that are sure to come? And how long would it be until a ship would carry a piece of this thing somewhere else, to continue the cycle, until everything in the Geodesic has crumpled under its weight.

Then he realizes that he has done that same thing. That this is really his fault. That maybe it was meant to happen that way. The designers of the Mover had known intelligent life well. And had hated it.

He throws himself back down on the bed and buries his face in the pillow. With a sudden angry gesture, he cuts the lights out, and huddles, shivering, in the dark, consumed with despair.

139

The world of Tlnou wheels carelessly through the depths, its continents and oceans unmarred. Over the poles, the aurora responds to the urgings of the solar wind. The sensors of the two ships in orbit study the chaotic events on the planet below, record the transmissions of the conflicts between the sea colonies, watch the hulks of the stations and their retinue of abandoned ships.

The conference room wall shows the globe as it would seem if the wall were a window. Talbot describes his experiences in a dry, factual voice, watched by the Director, Jill and Hallison. They scratch notes of their own symbologies into tablets, questioning. They restate the questions in times and ways calculated to reveal any lie.

The Director questions with full attention, but in a way allowed by the minds of the Tereniades, fully follows the conceptual content with one thread of thought, and memories of her angry conversation with the Constable with another.

The pressure to give up on Raoul is very high. She wonders if Atrenn's confidence had actually been warranted. She has allowed that confidence to survive Atrenn's death, despite her misgivings. It had seemed that she was justified. But this irresponsible act... yet perhaps it only seems irresponsible. She does not want to be disposed one way or another, but it is difficult. She can not let another make this decision; she can not allow anyone else to complete the sequence she had begun.

But her confidence must rest on some other justification than Atrenn, or her own place may be threatened.

Talbot finishes his account, insisting on a quarantine, on full disclosure to the Constable. The Director sighs. So many fragments, so many patterns, but what is the actual weave?

If he is right, and telling truth, and interpreting with justice, then she must take action. More information is needed.

She contacts the *Illyrion's* Analytical Office. The wall dissolves into the office of Waylandcorrig, a respected analyst on staff.

Waylandcorrig is a being of moderate stature, chitinous in exoskeletal appearance, with several mobile, rectangular pupiled eyes on stalks. A fringe of spidery limbs around a floor-skirting shell twitches rhythmically as if in impatience. It turns from its work surface to face them.

"Director," it hisses quietly, its translator of the highest quality. Its manipulators, artificially controlled implants, swing in a gesture of formal respect.

"Your evaluation of the sensor information?"

"The creature is currently emitting metabolic products from a number of sites across the primary continent. The products are listed in this display" - it waves and the list appears on the wall. - "and this summarizes the distribution, animated across the past six hours, as you requested."

"This appears to be some kind of web, Waylandcorrig."

"Indeed, Director." The voice appears to exude pleasure. "The sources cannot be discrete, even if they were in motion. The metabolic effects appear to pulse along the observed network with a certain timeliness. However, we do not yet know what is being taken in to produce the metabolic activity shown. Note that the area covered is roughly one third of the planet, stretching from an apparent origin in the city complexes of the south, specifically centered on Radelix Research, to the northern steppe."

"Is the network... growing?" Talbot asks, urgently.

Waylandcorrig twists swiftly to face him, half rising from its crouch, and then settling back again - the motion of a predator.

"The network is growing. Slowly but getting faster."

The Director swivels to regard Talbot. She must remind herself for a moment that the smile he exhibits is triumph, not tension. This is why her only other advisors in this matter are human.

"What else I should know about?" The Director asks Waylandcorrig.

"The - whatever it is - is a source of some unusual energies. The frequency combinations are quite unnatural, and many of them strain the bandwidth of our equipment. I have members working now on augmentation of the receptors, which should be available in a hour or two. There are also a variety of substances, related to pheromones, hormones and perhaps neuroactive chains."

Reed sits forward. "Is there any apparent function to these radiations and emissions?"

"Not as far as I can see," Waylandcorrig replies. "Perhaps some of them resonate with brain function frequencies for some phyla, but as we know, energic transfer is insufficient for telepathy - so these energies could only partly account for the effects on the population. But with the addition of a variety of psychoactives... it is difficult to be sure."

The conversation is so dry and detached that Talbot finds it hard to remember that they are not discussing a simulation.

Finally, he demands of the Director, "Are you satisfied?" But the Director does not answer directly. Instead, she thanks Waylandcorrig for the information, and returns the wall to the view of the planet. After a moment of reflection, her shrunken face bent over her notes, she calls up the diagram of the metabolic trace network atop the planetary image. She watches it for a while, shifting it to the red she finds most comfortable. Finally she turns to Talbot.

"For now, Raoul, that will be all. I will speak to you later. Please make yourself available for my request."

He stands. "Director." He nods at the others and walks out. Jill notices his shoulders are held low. She frowns. Hallison scratches his cheek, looking at a repeat of the diagram on his pad.

140

Now the three are alone with their decision.

The Director turns to face the others. "You are here to advise me," she states. They nod agreement, taking on the solemnity required.

"The information is correct, do you agree?"

Hallison runs a hand across his thin red hair. "I didn't think there was ever a doubt."

The Director bares her teeth. "There was doubt. This thing is so psychoactive that I would rather not be within a million miles. That it could manipulate Talbot is a natural possibility. However, that is not the issue and appears not to be the case. The issue is whether the action was acceptable given the context. Jill, you were abandoned."

"He left. We helped him go. I can't call that abandonment. He was right, the original plan was flawed. Is flawed. We are going to need a quarantine."

Hallison agrees. "I'm worried what the Constable might do. We're technically liable for the actions of that life form."

The Director differs. "Legal staff has indicated that relinquishment of custody caused liability to transfer to Radelix. Naturally, the company would prefer not to accept liability for the destruction of an entire civilization. Complete dissolution of the company might be the only course available to satisfy a suit. I hope you understand the gravity of this."

"I'm not legal," Jill states, "but isn't it possible that concealment is the worst thing we could do for our liability status right now?"

The Director does not smile, but her gripping finger twitches in an involuntary equivalent. "Perhaps. That is not the current issue, however. I must first decide if Raoul Talbot is to be released from the company for leaving his team against my expressed and explicit directive. You seem to think that the action was justified, Jill?"

Reed nods acceptance.

"And Hallison believes that my policy was flawed from the beginning. Thank you for the vote of confidence. But what is your assessment of the action Talbot took?"

Hallison chooses his words carefully. "I think that the *Illyrion* could have gathered all of the data he did - and more - if we were willing to planet. But, given what Raoul knew at the time... well, I wouldn't have gone down, but I'm not sure I would have been right. And given what we know now, it would not be a good idea for *Illyrion* to have landed."

"What does that mean?"

"I think he did the best he could, based on what he knew. To carry out the mission implied. To find out about the thing, so action could be taken when the *Illyrion* returned."

The Director bows her head over her pad. Finally she looks up. "Thank you. I'll take your opinions under advisement."

141

Talbot isn't required to stay in his quarters during the deliberation, so he wanders down to the shuttle bays. A window overlooks the standby area, where shuttles are undergoing maintenance. One of those is the Onyx he had flown to his encounter with Deleo – now so long ago. It is the first time he has been able to look at that shuttle. He drums his fingers against the sill of the outlook, watching their reflections move in counterpoint. His gaze shifts to the partly opened shuttlecraft in the bay. Involuntarily, he twitches, smelling a memory of blood and death. He hears a scream, but it is faint. He keeps himself from turning away.

Face the consequences, he tells himself. *You're going to face consequences. There will always be consequences.*

142

The Director seeks her answers in her quarters, amidst the flickering reddish lights that make her happy like home. She could afford a full simulation, but she prefers the abstraction. She curls into her favorite seat, enjoying the smell of its well-worn material. She waits for a portion of the relaxation she requires. Finally, on tiptoe, it arrives, smiling. She shifts her perspective, trying to take in the whole. To envelop the gestalt, to decide what to accept, what to reject in the shifting constellation of evidence. To accept her anger at being ignored; the loss of influence it portends. To try to keep focused on the one issue, not the larger events and portents that threaten to obscure the one fundamental first decision she must perform.

A bridge call rings like a quiet graceful chime. She acknowledges it.

"Director, there is an interfold transmission from the surface."

"So?"

"The source is unidentified, but Waylandcorrig believes it may be the metabolic network you've been discussing."

She springs to her feet, crouched like a predator. "A transmission to where?"

"We have a vector but no destination address. The coordinate encoding is non-standard."

"Can anyone else detect this?"

A moment. "Probably not. We got it off the new receptors. The bandwidth structure is... unusual."

"Thank you. Tank that vector and all of the transmission. I'll be in touch shortly." She taps the caller. "Talbot," she snaps. A pause as he is located and answers, gloomily. "Yes, Director." "Talbot, you are NOT fired. Set up a meeting in the conference room immediately. Get Waylandcorrig, Reed, Hallison and any of your former team you want present. We have to deal with a transmission from the Mover to some unknown recipient. I want to see you in my quarters right away. Before the meeting."

"Yes, ma'am!"

143

Deleo still has a problem with doors. He can find them now, but he remains amazed by their ability to swing away from the wall or slide into it in the space of a breath. It leaves him standing in the corridor by the conference room, where the others are working. Finally, he summons up his courage, and steps into the space that was only a moment ago a wall. He lopes forward with an angular back-kneed gait more suited to the terrain of the grassland than the flattened floors of hallways and rooms. The others are already arguing. He swings to the floor beside Talbot's swivel seat. Talbot smiles at him, and Deleo restrains a flinch. It is not meant as a threat, he knows - at least, in his mind. But his reflexes are still often faster, and are still often getting him into trouble.

"Biological emission of fold force impossible. Complexity and energetics for production of interfold sheath require metals and plastics as well as extreme energies." m'Ilu Ram is hissing his objections to Waylandcorrig. Deleo accepts more elementary concepts from a translator - *Class of things which move and eat or grow and absorb cannot send messages between stars...*

r*Zaranil buzzes disagreement. "Many would say radar from biologicals was also impossible."

Waylandcorrig speaks from the wall. Its atmospheric requirements prevent it from being in the room without extensive protective gear for either itself or the others. "r*Zaranil is quite correct. We have species that use radar, species that generate electricity and plasmas for a variety of purposes. There is nothing to be gained by casting doubt on properly gathered data."

"What's an axiom to you," Hallison offers, "isn't to everyone. No doubt you take it that way as an analyst once you accept the data source. But some of us reserve the right to question its source even so."

"As is just. Nonetheless, this biomorph is artificial, and may therefore have unusual or even engineered capabilities."

Talbot brings them to order. "The Director has charged us with recommending action. I want us to lay out very clearly what the options are. If there are differences among team members, we can work them out, no matter what they might be." He says this, hoping to diffuse a sense of betrayal to the old team, for his having left them to the Constable. "I've been on the surface twice. You can't imagine the chaos there. Steve tells me the Mover incites exophobia and species herding. But its effectiveness is incredibly greater than when we left it here. It has changed, or mutated in some way, and now it may be signaling home. Its new form may have been developed for just that purpose. We have to assume that its makers are now aware of our civilization. We can also assume they are xenophobic enough to want to destroy it.

"We must decide whether we will pursue this signal to its source, or muster appropriate civil or military authorities to do so.

"In addition, we have to consider that Radelix may be found liable for the damage done by the Mover and the people under its control. This liability could destroy Radelix as surely as Tlnou is being destroyed.

"But we are, so far, the only people who are aware of the source of the problem. In the event that our ship is disabled, no further defense against the Mover, or any of its offspring, may be able to be mounted.

"Last, but perhaps most important, we have very little time. Analytical Office political threat simulations indicate the possibility of an antimatter exchange between factions on the surface within a month. Uncertainties on that timeline are high, given the chaos and unknown causes. While we decide, people of many types are being killed and the civilization down there is being sent back to stone age tribalism."

His pause is as much a shock of speculation as a breath. He looks a Deleo, wondering a little more about the history of Tanith. He jots a note on a pad and sends it to Hallison.

"My recommendation has been to notify the Constable, who is in orbit with us, of the source of the threat, require a quarantine, and have him send for military assistance. In the meantime, after transferring all data, including the vector, to him, we would leave for the destination of the transmission to do a reconnaissance. The problem with this idea is, first, he may not believe us, second, when he does, he may detain us, and third, in that instance, we may be unable to offer any of the insight this team has into the problem. That's maybe the worst, although you can rank a Cylestane brig as being high on the list too.

"I want to use this as a starting point. Shoot it down if you can. Build it up if you can. The diagrams of the reasoning have been documented in Chakry notation for those using the net. OK?"

Sounds flit around the room.

Hallison speaks up. "The Director's watching, and how we decide as much as what we decide will be helping determine her decision. So keep it clean."

Cycles of relentless effort begin. Chains of evidence, prediction, causes and effects are raised, diagrammed, argued, demolished or sustained. Data is drawn from the Analytical Office through Waylandcorrig, and flashed on the wall. Jill tries to help Deleo understand the presentations and the argument, but these methods are completely incomprehensible to him. He curls into the corner with a bowl of soup, and watches occasionally before falling asleep.

Time passes, uncontrollably.

144

The doors to the conference room open, and the exhausted file out. The walls blink one by one to whiteness as the remote participants close their connections.

"It's a good plan," Talbot replies, settling back into the seat. The lights are dim against the rich wood of the walls.

The Director twitches her grasping finger.

145

The Constable, however, would not agree. He is helpless to prevent their ship from leaving the system, and he slams his hand on the desk panel several times in frustration, alarming his subordinates.

146

On the bridge, the Director stands beside the Captain, and smiles faintly, in the Tereniade way, as she listens to the inter-station chatter from the crew scattered across the ship.

Once again, the *Illyrion* begins to twist the metric of space, attaining an extension into a new dimension. Inertialess, it slips slowly up from the derelict stations toward the outer system.

"On cue, surpassing the system marker. Green marker off the port bow. Prepare the fold.... OK, drop the information canister for the Constable... start the beacon. Beacon signaling. Fold countdown on the mark. Out of here, Engines." The ship folds into curvespace and vanishes in a spume of distorted stellar images.

The Constable's ship stirs like a large and sluggish predator, heading for the suddenly revealed canister and its frantically signaling beacon.

147

Curvespace travel has many advantages, but its short duration and opacity make it harder to use for exploration. Many systems lie on the transmission vector from Tlnou, so each must be visited, at least briefly, and scanned by the Analytical Office.

Talbot wakes out of a dream into the image of a room looking out on the steppe of northern continent Tlnou. He is momentarily disoriented, until he remembers that these are his new rooms, and new decor. Again, as he lies torpid, he considers changing it to something else, but he accepts it finally, without certainty of reason, and rises.

Why do I like it? he wonders, as he sits on a terrace with late morning light faintly bluish green, watching the slowly wandering trees in the distance. He leans over a breakfast of thinly fried selestont legs, picking slowly at the flesh with a fork (Never eggs and toast again). He remembers Risha, and Kahn. The spaceport at Rigger's Cove. Frightening and hard. But he had felt he was mastering the situation, and he needs that support now, when he feels weak in the face of new demands.

He has a day off, but is afraid to take it. There are too many things to add to what he already knows if he's to stay in front of the team. Today he plans more work on planning, and for a moment, he marvels at his even considering something like that as a use of his time. He remembers himself not so long ago - apathetic, self-limited, sulking in his rooms, or in bars. He hasn't had time to question how quickly things have gone; until now. He thinks again, as he has often, about piloting curvespace, and an echo of the hunger reaches into his wrists. But, somehow, getting more abstract things done is beginning to generate its own hunger.

Suddenly refreshed by that thought, he raises a panel and moves into the notation phase.

A tone breaks reverie, requesting entrance.

He smiles ruefully, and goes to the door. It opens on the bustling residential corridor, and he is expecting to see Reed, or Hallison, or m'Ilu Ram. Instead, there is Wanr, large, dark eyes like deep mirrors in soft fur, looking up at him.

His fur is flat, which, Talbot now knows from his studies is a signal of submission. A strange signal in this context, he thinks. "Wanr?"

"Do you have time on which I might impose, request?"

"Of course. Come in. What can I offer you as my honored guest?" He knows enough to say the phrase, and to gesture toward kitchen, porch and seating. It is pleasant to have every practiced action as right as possible.

Wanr bows as much as his stocky figure allows, and steps within. The door, imaged with something called *Man Also Rises*, closes behind him.

Wanr gestures. "For your kindness and willingness and offering, I return full thanks. I am pleased to accept what you are pleased to offer. Feel no obligation."

Talbot waves a hand to the simulated terrace in a stylized signal. They walk slowly out into the strangely fragrant air and odd sounds of morning.

"This location," Wanr asks, "is unfamiliar. What place is it? Home?"

"No, it's Tlnou."

Wanr blinks several times. "Very different. I have never been there." It looks around. Talbot tries to restrain the impatience this diffidence and circularity arouses.

"May I ask what I may offer from my store of time?" Talbot asks, carefully choosing phrases which will smoothly translate to concepts in Wanr's *weltanschauung*.

"Talbot, I am uncomfortable with the team. I should say, with my role. I am not sure why I was chosen, or what I should offer."

Oh boy, Talbot thinks.

"Please excuse my custom," he says, "I will sit as I consider how best to answer what you ask." He takes a seat by the railing. "Feel free to do so as well."

Wanr curls up into a chair which adjusts swiftly to his body type. "I will wait."

I can barely run my own life, I'm just developing the rudiments of what I accept as philosophy. I know superficial things about his society. Why does he turn to me?

"I'm not sure how to answer what you're asking. I chose you because you were with us when we first encountered and captured the Mover. Everyone who had direct contact in those incidents I gathered into the team. I hoped everyone would find what they could best accomplish. But you say you haven't."

"I cannot decide, Talbot."

"Please call me Raoul. My friends and team mates can use this name."

"Rayoul."

"Good enough." He grins. He tries to know what to do. This situation makes him very uncomfortable. "What do you think is your strongest talent?"

Wanr sits and waves his head back and forth as he looks at the sky. "I am, of course, security, interested in protection, defense, in some cases, offense. But m'Ilu Ram is senior in experience and knowledge. How much can I offer in the face of that?"

Talbot feels a sudden surge of exultation as he realizes how to solve the problem.

"True, but m'Ilu Ram is only one being. He may need new perspectives. And there are other reasons for you to be on the team than what you offer. It is what the team offers."

"I do not understand this."

"Think of it this way. You have many things to learn, am I correct? From m'Ilu Ram, from others? In fact, m'Ilu Ram gained his experience by being placed in novel situations with experienced advisors and superiors. So too, are you."

Wanr perks up, his head rising, looking around, more alert. "This makes sense. Was this your plan?"

Talbot shakes his head, then remembers the non-universality of that body language. "Not a plan - really. Just the way things should be done. For the Director, for me, for all of us in the company. Some don't make it through, some change course, some fall away. It's how the company improves, and how we improve."

Wanr cocks a hand in space. "This is... pleasant. Thank you. May I ever offer you hospitality or help, please call on me. I can offer endless thanks. I will do my best to improve, as you suggest."

Talbot smiles awkwardly. "Sure."

Wanr unfolds from the chair, and stands as the chair resumes neutral structure. He bows and departs, leaving a bemused Talbot realizing that he has surmounted an important challenge - a novel situation - with no advisor or superior to help.

Perhaps I am improving, too.

148

The system of Halek is filled with enormous spheres and the fragments of planets.

A solar system is so vast as to be almost invisible, and it is dim this far from its star. But the machines that float in this system are almost one hundred thousand miles in diameter, like titanic eyes whose whites have crusted with crystal, layered in white, green, brown and blue, opening at one end into a blackened interior, seeking each other warily across the emptiness orbiting the sun. Where they occasionally cluster, their shapes silhouette and shadow each other ponderously, constantly exchanging mysterious particles that flit like insects through the cold black. Asteroids tumble past them; small images - moon-sized shattered fragments of planets once whole, now broken.

"We shouldn't have found them here. This is a known system, but there's never been anything like this reported," Hallison whispers. Talbot wants to weep. "There's nothing wrong with the distance or size estimates?" he asks hoarsely.

"The only thing wrong is the gravitational disruption these things are causing, plus the five missing planets. And the three million Tereniades who seem to have been vaporized." Hallison looks sick.

"What about us?"

"Navigation is already trying to get us out of here. The flight captain is making us look as much like a rock as he knows how."

"That's good. Is this the terminus of the signal?"

"Apparently not."

"So it's a coincidence?"

"No one knows how long the signal has been repeated."

"This is way out of our depth," Talbot asserts.

"This is way out of anybody's depth. The Director has us jumping back to the previous system for a transmission to the Constable, and then we'll leapfrog."

"You think we should?"

"I'd like to be far away from these things, chief. I'd rather run for the galactic plane and hide." Hallison bows his head and rubs his hands viciously against his eyes.

"Steve, we'll be OK."

"You're whistling in the firepit, chief. But I respect you for it. Just remember, these guys blew up a solar system. They have ships the size of planets. A fleet of them. If they notice us, we'll be like fleas in a torch."

149

The Defense Room is a hectic chaos of imaged walls and partitions showing views, diagrams and text of various spectra and scripts that are bright in the dim room light. A being occasionally rushes through the maze to deal with something that requires physical presence. Tereniades are particularly prominent, flicking their birdlike attention between displays and consultations, enmeshed in virtual systems. Translators hiss with high-density whispering that everyone hears as the best possible voices the crisis translators can provide. In a far corner, a massive tilted image table has been erected for the crisis team, covered with data from the sorters in the Analytical Office.

m'Ilu Ram dominates the area with his towering presence. He is still, slightly crouched as if waiting some trigger, watching the images through data lenses as they arrive in the reservoir at the edge, and occasionally nodding to Wanr or gesturing in a hastily improvised physical language for changes in the arrangement of data.

Hallison stands by m'Ilu Ram, pointing out items of interest to Talbot and the Director, occasionally speaking into a headset.

"They're robotic, then," Talbot mutters, arms crossed over his chest.

"The observations are passive," Waylandcorrig cautions into Talbot's connection. "We could be missing many data points. Alternatively, there could be a minimal amount of biologic crew that we cannot detect."

"Maybe the originators are robotic? Could this be why they are so hostile?"

Hallison shrugs. "There are three cybernetic phyla in the Geodesic. They show no more or less xenophobia than biologics. It isn't clear whether the Mover would be effective or ineffective on cybernetics, though there was interference with systems on Tlnou... it's just speculation, chief, nothing one way or the other to indicate at the moment."

m'Ilu Ram straightens and walks over. He addresses the Director. "I recommend that we set a parabolic course similar to a deflection, which will guide us around the far side of this specific planetary fragment, designator 1423C-FHG, at which point, we fold out with three random tangents following; last we transfer back to Tlnou, as you requested. Chances seem large that we will be undetected until fold activation, as we read their sensor technologies."

The Director agrees. "Begin the operation. Notify the captain. Keep weapon arrays on hot standby, but avoid firing unless we are hit. Geodesic weapon system level must be considered Degree 2 critical for First Contact concealment, just subordinate to ship safety which is Level 1 for this engagement."

Talbot begins to feel a strange desperation. He reaches down to touch the Director's shoulder. "Director, please pause that order?"

She nods, and m'Ilu Ram relays the pause.

"Raoul, what is the problem?" The displays glitter across her small eyes as she swings her head toward him. Is she angry, he wonders?

"I have a modification to propose." His voice is shaking. He has been riding the flow since the beginning, except when no one could stop him. Now he has a dangerous proposal he is sure will be shot down. Should he be making it in public? "Perhaps we should speak privately?"

"Not in the middle of a crisis. If it's relevant, bring it out for debate. And make it fast - the window elapses in ten minutes."

"I want to take a stealthed fold-capable hammer, and my team. We'll continue toward the transmission destination. You can download the schedule to us, so we don't have to re-navigate. We'll put a buoy in each of the systems we visit, with complete logs, so you can catch up with us as fast as possible."

Her mouth twists slightly. She looks up at him, and he wonders if she likes him. "Raoul, it's dangerous. And probably not necessary. You've proven yourself to us several times."

He is angry at her shallow analysis. "You don't understand. There isn't much time. The more efficient we can be, the better. Your fold, if it's spotted, is bigger than ours. You can distract them, and the three jumps are decoys if they follow you. In the meantime, we're on the way to the heart of the problem, and maybe everything we need to know. And if not - well, at least it won't make things any worse. You don't need us for the military operation, right?"

She looks at m'Ilu Ram where he hulks over Talbot's shoulder, apparently interested. "You can't have him. I need him to get us back."

m'Ilu Ram's cave-like mouth flaps open slightly, and shuts with a slap. "Take Wanr," he says. "A fine young potential." Wanr looks up sharply, the hair on his hands flaring into a fluffy nimbus.

"I have to have Hallison," Talbot insists. "I need the best cultural analyst I can get."

The Director throws her head back, a gesture he has never seen. "So you want me to send you on a First Contact with a hostile species at the start of an undeclared war. Looking for a Primary Directorship, Raoul?"

He laughs nervously at her joke. "Ma'am, the last thing I want to do is contact them. Let's spy on them, and then you can contact them if you like." His voice is shaking as he feels the edge of triumph, a triumph he may later regret in the millisecond or so it takes the xenophobes to incinerate the hammar.

She swings her head down for a moment, and then reaches up a tiny delicate hand. She snatches the collar of his tunic and pulls his head down to within a foot of hers, staring into his eyes with her slit pupils. "Atrenn was right," she hisses softly. "If you don't die." She releases him.

"Go," she snaps. "Fool. Reed, Hallison, Wanr, you're his primary team. Hallison, get an FC group and package to take with you. Talbot, if, and I mean *if* a contact is initiated, by the aliens – not by you - the FC team is in charge. You defer to their experience. Steve has personally managed two FC situations, take your lead from him. m'Ilu Ram, arm the *Eururku*, get a full stealth and reconnaissance package on it and have that window recalced for a half hour from now." Suddenly she cocks an eye ridge at Talbot and points, hip cocked in an aggressive stance. "How do humans say it? You die, and I'll kill myself so I can follow you to hell and make your life miserable."

He stares in open shock.

"Did I get that right?" she asks.

He nods mutely. "Close enough," he manages, finally.

m'Ilu Ram appears beside him, bent deferentially. "Starboard Bay 6. *Eururku*. A quarter hour. Don't bother the teams, they know what to do."

Talbot wants to hug him, but who knows what it would mean? "Wish you were coming."

"Oho, so you want to get me killed. Some friendship." Big fish eyes wheel to watch him.

"What is it, all of you guys studying human jokes for me?"

145

m'Ilu Ram doesn't answer, just grabs him by the top of the head, shakes it, and walks away. Talbot decides to take that as a token of affection.

150

Talbot checks the timer. Less than ten minutes to go, and they have not yet been destroyed.

In the right seat, Reed looks severe, hair pulled tightly back from her forehead into a short ponytail, staring at the control wall. She knows Talbot grabbed a quarter hour of simulator refresher before leaving, and this is not a consolation as they match pace behind the still glowing planetary fragment, their hammar carefully tumbling with stabilization from reaction thrusters, power low, gravity only enough to simulate a solid object of the same size.

She glares at him for a moment, and, though he doesn't take his glance from the wall of rock whirling beyond, he answers her.

"All right, so it's not in the plan."

"You planned this all along."

"Nope. Improvising."

She sighs and grips the arms of the chair tighter. Chief of staff. She knows enough to get this thing to fold downcurve to Tlnou, enough to set an orbit, with help from the smart systems - but even in simulator, she has never done anything so hard as what Talbot is doing - and talking about at the same time.

"How do you figure you're so good at this?" she mutters.

He replies, "I had a lot of time on my hands back when I was a disgruntled idiot, so I decided to run simulators for everything around. You ever meet Hark Kenner? He'd flown asteroid miners, so when he saw how much time I was spending on odd ships, he let me play some of his private scenarios. Fun, huh?"

She doesn't appreciate this sadistic expression of interest.

"Look, like I said, they won't fire on us. They just don't seem to care about debris this small. We'll get in really close, and float just off skin. If we can get that close a look, maybe we can get inside, find out if there's crew."

She shoots him a fierce glance. "It's not fair to sell the Director on one plan and then do something else."

"Only if we don't make it. We're out here to learn things."

"You're getting cocky, don't get us killed. There's no profit in it."

"I know that."

Wanr, at Tactical, reaches a paw for her shoulder. "Jill, Rawl is good. I am good. They will fail to detect us." She stares over her shoulder at him in disbelief.

Talbot's lips twitch in a part of a grin, for a moment. The whole thing is an unlikely adventure, and he hates to risk them too, but if it works, he is sure, intuitively, that they will learn something important to understanding the destination of the message. He is banking on being able to fly this course as a doubled fragment, right down to the surface of one of these Jovian-sized ships, and it is the hardest mission he's ever tried. The good part is that he doesn't have much bandwidth left for thinking about how close to dying they all are.

Hallison looks past the pilots at the slowly whirling fragment that fills the view, marked with the pictograms and graphics of the piloting information. He is really terrified, but it is a terror like being in a really good sim of something dangerous. The mission has so rapidly escalated beyond even the normal strangeness level of their business that all the emotion he can find is a faint but growing curiosity about the makers of the Mover, and an angry desire to stop them. Mixed with that, he thinks, a hope that these horrible actions are just a misunderstanding that can be corrected, not a galactic Govault, with a more advanced species as the aggressor, and Geodesic civilization at risk. A secret ambition that he can be the architect of the correction. (But there is a sinking feeling that warns him from such hope.) Perhaps that is why he is going along with this crazy ride.

Talbot readies his team. "Wanr, seismic ready for when we hit, we're looking for echoes of what the fragment does, Steve, you get a microsecond of active search on contact, use it wisely. Jill, back me up, make sure these guys get what I need."

"On it," Reed replies, gathering windows onto the activities of the other members. "We have the ten second mark. Now. On the trigger, inertia to off."

"Inertia off," Talbot responds. He halts the tumbling and pulls back in a gasp of distance. The horrifyingly detailed wall slashes across the view, as the tumbling planetoid falls away.

"Contact on the trigger. Everyone's slaved." Reed is watching everything except the view. She is sweating faintly, hands trembling ever so slightly.

They collapse into a canyon of strange and contorted shapes. The planetoid is racing ahead. It strikes, etching an enormous and surprising impact crater into the relief with a flash of white that blasts chaotic shadows across everything. A second later they hit nearby and rebound briefly on thrusters. There is no sensation except the dizzying view change as they tumble away from the artificial world.

"Seismic registered, analysis starting."

"I'm going for the crater," Talbot shouts. The view corkscrews and they are enveloped in the blackness of the opening. Instantly the hammer halts, still inertialess. Light-amplified and infrared views of torn deckage and supports fill the pilot view.

"This is crazy!" Hallison yells, in pure shock.

Wanr is taking advantage of the chance to passive scan everything on every wavelength for which he can find sensors. "Very strange," he mutters.

"What?" Talbot demands.

"No repair activity," Reed replies.

"None?"

"None."

"What's around us, Wanr?"

"Passages, conduits, fluids, photonic computing... very strange design, no sharp angles, all very big; supports for the structure." Wanr turns to Talbot across the room, displays glittering as colored chaos across the glossy black hemispheres of his eyes. "Not very advanced."

"Agreed," Hallison says quickly.

"Life! Come on, any life?" Reed is angry at their missing the most important point.

"Not even artificial, see can I," Wanr checks a set of scans.

"Range limited to twelve miles," Reed whispers.

"Let's get out of here," Hallison insists. "It can't be long. I've got everything I can use."

"Some kind of repairs are occurring on the frontier of the sensors," Wanr says. "It's above us."

"Let me know when you have enough to know how they do that." Talbot sits waiting, heart pounding in his chest. He trades a brief, excited glance with Jill, whose eyes barely reveal panic.

"Enough," Wanr states. The aperture above is closing slowly. Jill suddenly realizes it is miles above.

"OK," Talbot replies, skin tight across his teeth. "Here we go. Ever fold inside something?" He punches the fold control and the hammer vanishes in a wrench of sensorium.

151

The systems are all dark, and the air is stifling. The emergency view shows stars, slowly tumbling.

"Everything's down," Reed reports quietly.

"Yeah, the restart keeps failing. I'll have to go look physically at the router. Steve, you have a personal light."

"Uhh, no. No I don't. Where..."

Cones of multispectral light fill the cabin as the emergency lighting finally restarts. Talbot is standing beside his seat.

"Never mind. Just get to the FC team and make sure they stay where they are."

"What do I tell them?" His voice is slightly brittle at the edges.

"We're working on it," Talbot replies sharply. "Move."

152

A silent darkened spindle tumbling amidst stars, blocking for a moment the dim color of a distant nebula.

"This was a bad idea, Raoul," Reed gripes as she traces power into the router. He watches anxiously over her shoulder. It had become quickly clear that she was sharper on the internal system layout that he was, but delegating this unnerves him.

"Just get the system up, and we'll deal with it."

She nods in the dimness, a sweaty strand of hair drooping across her forehead. The air is getting worse.

"Give me a trip block," she demands. He passes it from the case. A moment later, he can feel a shiver run the length of the ship as the systems come on-line. The lights blaze back to normal level.

"Nice, Jill. Thanks."

"Yeah, yeah," she grumbles as she comes to a stand. She faces him angrily. "Listen, your whole idea was crap. You nearly got all of us killed. Not even vaporized, but strangling on our own CO_2 in the middle of interstellar space. That's not bad enough. The whole mission could have gone down with that stunt. This is not how you manage a mission, by intuition or something. Do you know what I mean?" Her face is close to his, and her eyes are narrow with anger. "I've managed fifteen missions," she snarls. "Fifteen. I planned and worked, and didn't sleep much, and I got things done, not by some kind of magical process of trying anything and surviving."

He feels as if she has slapped his face. And then he remembers - she has... once. He had given her a snappy answer then, hot with success after fear, but suddenly he feels too tired to do it again.

"I can't answer you now," he says. "But I'll think about it. You think about this, though: maybe we don't have time for careful planning right now. And maybe I can or can't do it the other way, the methodical way, as well as you can, OK? Who knows?"

She flushes, bright behind her freckles. Then she wheels away and stalks down the corridor toward the ready room.

153

The animation runs again. Thousands of semi-organic machines gather like aphids around the edges of the pit, exuding repair materials. Their manipulators stroke the material ritualistically into form, while others are extending beneath, extruding piping and optics from specialized glands.

Another wall shows millions of cubic miles of seismically revealed internal structure within the Jovian-sized craft - endless strange twisted corridors, vast hollows of unknown purpose.

A third wall shows depth-sorted spectrographic profiles of the strata of the ship as revealed in the split-second impact flash.

Talbot is trying hard not to smile as he paces the walls. It shows in a frown, as if he is fiercely unhappy. Wanr and Hallison stand by. Reed slouches by the door.

154

"Drop the buoy," Talbot orders. The log is downloaded, and three capsules are dropped into the in-system medium, to spin gracelessly far from the double sun.

155

Talbot lies on his back in the cramped hammar apartment. He is smiling.

"All right, so I'm a cocky son-of-a-bitch. But it's working." He feels a throaty chuckle bubbling up in his throat, and a sense of exultation that rises like a swift amplifier. Finally, he laughs out loud. He presses his hand against the nearby wall and watches the ligaments strain under his brown flesh.

156

He heads into the hallway and rounding a corner nearly runs into Reed, who seems to be pacing, head down, back and forth, just turning as he arrives.

"Hi," he says.

She takes a moment to recover, glaring up at him, backlit by the low hall lighting. The hammar is small, he realizes, and she was probably pacing the halls to be alone. "So, you're up finally."

He sighs. "Yeah," he mutters disgustedly, and pushes past. "Can't keep up twenty-hour days forever," he continues, sarcastically, walking away down the hall.

"Wait a minute," she calls. "What are we going to do? We can't just keep floating out here with the comets. Everyone's waiting."

He turns back. "I'm going to get some food, and then... I'll be in the conference room. We'll have a meeting, if you want to be there." His tone is edged, he knows. But he hates waking up after a short sleep. She is too far away for him to assess her expression, so he turns and walks on to the caf.

157

The skip probe slips through curvespace and knifes out into a new system. Then in again, and out again into empty space. The lighthouse beaconing of a pulsar whisks past every so impossibly often, and lights the interior of the vast supernova remnant shell. The skipper slides on, again, logging coordinates and environmental details.

Finally, a loyal automaton, it slips back into normalcy beside the hammar, loaded with coordinates for planning, and is swept into its tunnel again, like a domesticated mouse.

158

"OK, so the skip's got us the next block of coordinates. We could go home now."

"And we should," Reed gripes, toying with her stylus.

Talbot loses his temper. He stands abruptly, nearly bumping his head on the close ceiling. "Jill, be constructive, damn it."

The other humans look away in embarrassment. The non-humans say nothing, and reveal less. Wanr is sad, eyes nearly shut.

Reed shrugs and examines the table.

Talbot tries to turn his attention to the rest of the team. "We don't have to go on or go back. But these coordinates - even though they're not the end of the message - are important. So we have to get them back to *Illyrion*. After we're sure of that, I think we should go on. To the end. Find out what's there. Why this is going on. Get every speck of data we can find and get it out of there to help Geodesic Defense."

Hallison glances at Reed, his expression almost unreadable. "How do we get the coordinates back to Tlnou, chief?"

"I don't know. Any ideas, besides the log drop, which isn't fast enough or active enough?"

Silence. The team members avoid looking at Reed. Talbot wonders why.

"We can't use fold space transmit, ex?" one of the First Contact team, from Invact, (colored skin speech reminding Talbot haltingly of Schacther) asks, "can't risk sight other than folding in and out."

"I don't know. What do the security guys think about curvespace transmissions? We can intercept them and track them, but it's hard. What about these xenophobes, Wanr? Is it easier for them?"

Wanr shuffles his feet and his fur fluffs briefly. "It's not clear." he replies, shifting his fluffed hands oddly. Talbot has noticed him doing that more lately. He wonders briefly why. "They seem communications in curvespace, not to use. I was unable to detect any intership transmissions at Halek. It is not clear how coordinate they their actions. But the Mover used fold."

Talbot lets the convoluted syntax equivalents spin themselves out in his mind.

"So," he says finally, "maybe we could get away with it, maybe not."

Hallison leans back into his seat, and faces Wanr. "Is going into fold more detectable than a transmission?"

Talbot realizes he should have asked that question, but then remembers the answer. But he holds his tongue. The others need to participate, get things started, ideas flowing... it might take a long time and a lot of bad ideas to get the one good one they need.

Suddenly Reed is up and pacing, and Talbot stares at her.

She stops and glares across the table, confronting him. "Look, do we want to hide that we're aware they're coming?"

He starts up, realizing that this is the fundamental, the essential they were all missing. But he forces himself to relax and lie back. Let her run with it. "Maybe not," he probes.

"All right, suppose," she muses, looking up at the ceiling, rocking from foot to foot, "we don't. Why not?" Her glare travels around the table, challenging.

Hallison frowns. Finally, "I guess so that we could scare them, or fool them. Both tactics are used a lot. Even by the non-intelligent species."

"Sure, sure," Wanr says. "Fat fur for intimidation. Scatter scamper to decoy. Working all are. Or both?"

"Okay," she continues. "So we may not want to undetectably transmit this, it depends on them."

The FC leader, a round yellowish creature, sighs and picks at her teeth with a long rapier claw. "We don't know enough about them; they might lash out at everything. They might hurry their operation if they think we know. I wouldn't recommend we act rashly."

Everyone is suddenly silent, but Talbot steps in to keep the idea flowing. "That doesn't matter right now. Let's generate ideas. We aren't recommending anything, yet. Jill, why don't you take the wall and sketch out where you're going with this."

She looks with surprise at the stylus in her hands. "Sure, I can do that." She flashes him a sudden smile, which as quickly retreats into some smoldering feeling he is too unsure of to name. She steps to the wall and starts drawing scenarios.

159

He is surprised when he finds her sitting alone in the caf, holding a cold cup of soda, hunched over a table that holds images of the vast destroyers suspended deep within. There are tears running silently down a cheek. They glisten briefly, then disappear. For a moment, he wishes he could walk past. But the chair makes a faint scraping sound against the floor as he pulls it back, a sound that seems too loud, too abrasive. She doesn't seem to notice.

He sighs and sits down, examining her face. The eyes are reddened, the lids swollen - she has been crying for a while. Her lips twitch at his regard. She looks over.

"I'm on my break, do you mind?" She whispers, voice hoarse. She sniffs, as if unashamed.

"What's the matter?" he asks, voice low, afraid to hurt.

She turns to stare at him. "You don't get it, do you?"

"Get what?" He is puzzled; what has he missed?

She laughs, throwing her head back in an angry kind of defiance. Her laugh subsides to a wild chuckle, and then a sad hiccough. She glares at him from moist eyes. "Yeah, you don't get it. Wanr's locked away in his room, almost catatonic. He's missed half of three duty cycles with physical problems. And all I can think of is my presentation for the Hiktorine Bicentennial Conference." She laughs again, but it is sad, and rueful, and mocking. He is looking at her, uncomprehending. "You don't get it, though. Who knows how soon, and there won't be any Nomar. My presentation, for as long as I'm around, might end up being all that's left of them. All I can think of is that stupid presentation, like it was the boundary of life or something. Don't you understand? - the end is coming, Raoul. The end. Of every damn thing. Us. Any place to go. They have ships the size of a gas giant. They eat planets. For no reason. Maybe you just can't take it, because if you hadn't brought the thing back, none of this would be happening." Her brows had pulled together, and her voice had taken a sarcastic tone. He makes himself stay silent. He makes himself listen. "But you don't even think about it, and all I can think of is my damn presentation." She shakes her head and leans back in the chair, staring at him in challenge. Clearly done.

Finally, he finds his voice, but it is hard, like an instrument rusted by disuse. "No," he says, "I try not to think about it. I can't. Maybe it's too abstract to me... the end of everything. I'm going to die some day, but I guess I don't believe that either.

"You ever see someone die, Jill?"

She nods. "I've been an expedition leader longer than you've been with the crew."

"That bothers you too, I know that." He hates the anger that floods him with the knowledge of her envy. "But I've seen people die. I suppose that's still more immediate to me than three million Tereniades I never met, and a planet in pieces."

He stands up. "We have a job to do. If we're lucky, and good, maybe what you're worried about won't happen. Who knows?" He leans over the table. "But, you know, maybe you're right. I started this. Or maybe we'd be finding out too late, if it hadn't been for what happened. I used to always be thinking that way - what people had done to me, how I couldn't do anything. You were one of the people who helped me out of it. Don't quit on me now." He squeezes her shoulder. She looks up suddenly with a new hope. " I need you working with us on your idea tomorrow," he continues. "Can I count on you?"

She looks away and grips his hand where it rests on her shoulder. Tightly. For a moment. An unnamable emotion shakes him. Then he walks away, quick footsteps on the corridor.

160

He feels as if the character of the team has changed as they work the next shift. Hallison appears in the late morning. Talbot is sure, looking at his restless eyes, that Hallison had been unable to sleep.

He wonders why he is not able to feel it like they are. But he submerges his doubts and works on the strategy with Jill.

She seems outwardly recovered. But somehow he senses her as fragile. Perhaps it reflected nothing more than the sight of her crying. He had never imagined she could feel that way. She always seemed glacial. Somehow he finds the thought makes him uneasy.

Everyone works to modify the skippers for repeated transmissions to Tlnou and other, more distant and civilized systems. Physical probes and reprogramming screens litter the hangar floor. The screens flicker with updates as the machines resolve their conflicts. Humans and non-humans stand together in small groups, muttering over the screens, or staring blankly as the tests are run.

Wanr seems to be making more small errors than usual. His fur is flat and hangs low over the dome of his eyes. Even those eyes seem dulled.

Talbot paces back and forth in a tension of impatience and impotence. His skills are unusable here, and his supervision is accomplishing nothing. Finally he stalks back down the spinal corridor to the flight deck, dappled light from the overheads sweeping under his feet.

The room is empty. The systems, automated, reveal only parts of what they know. He leans back against the edge of the door, feeling the metal dig into his skin. Beyond the virtual window, the stars are rolling slowly.

Talbot settles into the quiet smell of the traditional left seat. He smiles, softly, relaxing. Then he gestures, the perfect grand motion, like a conductor, and the systems rise up around him.

"Let's try a little practice," he mutters.

161

The two vast stars roll slowly around each other - ancient antagonists, nearly in contact now, gravitation and magnetohydrodynamics swirling their hot plasmas into complex fractal streamers and spirals.

From light years away, the radiation of a pulsar sweeps periodically through the S-060124 system; the vast expanding remnants of that dead star's atmosphere are nearly invisible from here, so close to their center. But some of the remains are luminous with synchrotron radiation; shattered wisps lacing the view.

"No one could live here," Talbot whispers, voice dead of hope. "Something was wrong with the skipper's terminus sensor. We've got to be in the wrong place."

"We have planets," Wanr announces. "Not enough to plot, yet."

"All right, we'll stay above the ecliptic as soon as you and Jill figure out where that is." He tries to force the animation into his voice.

"What do you want me to do, chief?" Hallison asks, sounding slightly worried.

Talbot is surprised. Hallison sounds both less sure than usual, and more involved than lately.

"Try transmissions search, Steve."

"Yeah." Hallison busies himself at his instruments. "Gonna be tough, lot of stray interference from that pulsar and from the contact binary."

Jill leans over to get his attention. "Wanr's got something."

"Wanr?" Talbot asks over his shoulder.

"Three worlds I found. My naming?" The wrinkle of his lips is a sardonic comment modulated with mocking triumph.

They laugh. "Sure, first found," Talbot replies.

"Iklo, pAlbor, and Trinkmar - cousins. Anyway, two ex-giants, hydrogen, prior system nova burnoff exposed the core. Rocky world, far side of system. Some strange features."

Hallison perks up and looks over. "Yeah, strange features. I'm seeing some electromagnetics from that area, but ... nah, I can't get enough pattern to tell if it's anything, or just auroral. The solar wind here is wicked."

Wanr offers an analysis, "Bad for detect works both ways. Remember, must stay undetected. But avoid rapid sublight, due to coronal wake."

"Yeah," Talbot says, "we'll just fold right over."

The ship winks out, and plasma sweeps into the vacancy.

162

Talbot watches the sphere of pAlbor (*Wanr's cousin*, he thinks, mentally chuckling). But what he really is watching is the artificially enhanced vision of machines, managed by intelligence - in this case, Wanr's.

Grids are superimposed on the world below. Energy densities are plotted, along with temperature fluxes, and radiation profiles. In minutes, vegetation estimates and life form plots begin to spread across the image.

"Ok, it's a burn-off. This planet's been dead for centuries. So what have we got left?"

Hallison looks up. "A signal, chief. From orbit. Like I thought." He grins, smugly. But Talbot's reaction is not gratifying. He snaps out gestures to bring battle systems to immediate targeting.

"Raoul, it's just a signal."

"Around here, I think it's better to be prepared."

Jill is looking coldly away at another window.

Finally, Talbot asks, "Do you have a translation?"

"Don't need one. It's a standard Geodesic distress signal."

"What!"

"Yeah. It's been running for about fifteen shifts, according to the beacon clock."

"A spacecraft on the sensors," Wanr reports.

And there it is, carefully bracketed by the targeting system, rising slowly over the curved horizon, large, but distant.

The sensors indicate no weapons systems, little power, less life.

Talbot sighs. He feels a worry whose motivation he cannot define. He turns to Jill. "You think the first contact team should be involved." The statement is flat, not a question.

She is surprised. She had expected to have to suggest it. "Yes."

"It's a Geodesic beacon. Why?"

"We don't know who or what is on that ship or why."

"Steve, would you take care of it for me? We need suggestions within ten minutes."

He nods, sharply. Then he is up and out of his seat, headed for the conference room at a run. Something real to do.

Reed glares at him. She had wanted to go. But Talbot shakes his head. "You I need here. In case."

163

The spacecraft, silhouetted against the barren world below, is a standard Geodesic design, registered as the *Kanly* according to the beacon - knobbed, faceted, and marked with countless identifications and admonitions. Talbot is worried. There is someone – something - alive inside.

164

Hallison waits in the lock with his team, suited in skin-tight. The pale blue light subsides to amber, the lock irises, and the other ship lies beyond, silhouetted against deserts and mountains on the wall of the world behind it.

The leap takes longer than it seems - and the destination is larger. It looms into a vast territory of plating and antennae, harsh lit by the suns, too risky for direct linkage. They descend, drifting into position beside a door the size of a cliff. A smaller port at its edge yields to their emergency access code, revealing faint lighting beyond.

Some time is spent monitoring various communications modalities, to determine if anything other than the beacon is transmitting. Their specialist ties into the shipboard systems and begins to probe for internal communication activity. Finally, she signals negative, and they start down the shaft.

Internal gravity gradually orients them, but it is unusually weak, indicating either a partial systems failure, or a primarily low gravity roster. "Risti," Hallison directs, "find out if this is normal gravity here, will you?"

The environmental tech synchs with the network and brings its investigative software on-line. "Not normal. Twenty percent system failure. Nodes down."

Hallison nods. "OK. What's the normal gravity, here?"

"Teren normal. Primary roster is Tereniade."

"Right."

They continue slowly through the corridor to the door at the end. Risti fits a coupler to the door and watches the handheld display. It makes an odd gesture with one of its three appendages. "No reading. Wait." Its trio of reddish eyes slip closed. One opens, peers at the handheld. Its appendage makes lightning-speed adjustments. "Bad gravity. No air."

Hallison sighs. He knows Talbot is watching. The progress is going to be very slow. "Let's get a schematic," he says.

The image of the ship interior is cast into the air. He gestures in a circle around their location, and the image of that area enlarges. He peers around in it until he finds what he's looking for. He brings up a property list and reads quickly. "OK. This panel, take the cover and evacuate the entry corridor. Disconnect the door, and we should be through." He folds up the image as the others busy themselves. He hears a faint sound, and feels the second skin stiffening against the pressure difference. His breathing seems louder for a moment. Then, with a silent pop, the door slides open.

One of the team members looks back at him and makes a warped face that he knows is similar to a human grin. Hallison waves - an unambiguous sharing. He pushes through and they follow him into the corridor. But his feet lift from the floor at the gravity ledge, and he falls outward, to be suddenly seized by a tendril from Risti.

He wants to laugh, but he can't, he's suddenly afraid.

165

Talbot is sleeping in his room, stirring uneasily with secret dreams. He can't see, but his eyes flutter. He can't hear, but he moans slightly with secret sounds. Suddenly he sits bolt upright. Then he rubs his eyes, aching with sleep. He can't recapture the dream. He shrugs it away.

He gestures for the intercom.

"It's Jill," a voice replies.

He yawns. "Well, how's it going?"

"Nothing yet. Get some sleep, Raoul."

He laughs a little, deep tones. "I did that already." But there is an undercurrent of nervousness. "You're sure nothing?"

He can hear her sigh impatiently. "They're on the fifteenth level. Intermittent gravity and atmosphere. No sign of crew. No sign of trouble, except for persistent system failures. No apparent cause."

..."*Must have been the systems failures, eh? Everything's been up and down the last month.*"...

The worry roars into his mind.

But he suppresses it. "I'm coming up."

On the flight deck, Reed frowns and slams the heel of her hand into one of the few areas not covered by control surfaces. The crests of her knuckles whiten hard.

166

Talbot passes her in the spinal corridor. "I'll be back," she says. "At last, I can get a drink."

He watches her go, and notices how gracefully she walks, for the first time. Finally, he shrugs and walks onto the flight deck.

The windows are playing the real-time movements of Hallison's team, from the several perspectives of the monitors that swarm them. He settles into the left seat. The other seats are empty. He wonders how Wanr is doing.

He sits back, eyes heavy-lidded. The door opens with a sweep of light that disappears as Reed joins him, sliding into the right seat. "Stole my chair," she mocks.

She settles in with a sandwich. He watches her.

"Well, *they're* eating," she replies defensively. He chuckles. "Yeah."

"Want some?" She tears off a piece and holds it out, with an impish grin.

Suddenly, Hallison's voice makes an appearance. "No, no... I don't think we should stop any longer. Let's pack up." He is talking to his team. Talbot's head swerves to the monitor. *What's bothering Hallison?* he wonders.

He looks back at Jill, whose hand is still hanging in the air with the sandwich fragment as she looks at the monitor. "Steve?" she asks. "What's up?

So she heard it too.

Hallison looks up at the floating monitor. "Uh... no, nothing. I don't think..." His voice trails away, as he looks around. The truth is, he senses something ominous. "I mean, what is there to worry about, except for the airbreaks and the gravity down sections? There's nobody here. Right?"

Reed looks at Talbot, and then carefully wraps the sandwich back in plastic. She wedges it into a crevice beside the chair. She focuses up a section of her wall. "No, nothing I can see. That doesn't mean there isn't something."

"Well, I think we ought to move on."

Talbot leans forward to speak. "Steve, go with it."

Hallison waves the team to their various appendages, and they gather up equipment with the soft sounds of movement.

The lights fail briefly, and then flicker back to life. The structure of the ship seems to groan. Nothing new, with the stresses from tumbling and partial internal gravity. Reed shakes her head. "It's OK, Steve. The dynamic stresses shouldn't do anything critical for at least several shifts."

"Right."

Wanr pokes his head in. "Jill, you're done."

She sighs. "OK. Thanks." She stands and Wanr slides into her seat. "Just when things get spooky.

"Call me if you need me," she finishes, eyes wandering over Talbot, and then the displays. He nods absently, trying to focus on what his intuition is pushing towards consciousness. Reed's lips thin briefly, as she turns and leaves.

167

The FC team finds him in a room near the massive ship's flight deck. He is cowering in a pool of light, shuddering uncontrollably. He is Tereniade, male, though not obviously so. His fingers flutter with the motion of his body. His life signs are low, which explains the problems with locating him on remote sensors.

Hallison dispatches the monitors to cover the rooms in the area. Two team members start evacuating the Tereniade on a sealed stretcher from the nearby medical kiosk. The tiny figure lies silent, staring, body occasionally vibrating from some inner impulse.

The monitors report to Hallison's hand unit. They have found corpses, fearfully dismembered, on the flight deck. He turns his head to avoid seeing the images.

Talbot and Wanr also shy away. But for Talbot, the confluence of memory is sufficient. "Steve - get out now."

Hallison is in confusion for only a moment. Finally he snaps to Fecto - "Quick, fastest route to the hull!" To another team member he signals with a quick set of hand gestures to call in the monitors and redeploy them in security mode.

Wanr has retreated to the security console and linked with the emergency connection. "What looking for are we? Perimeter intact is, signs of abnormal energics absent..."

"I don't know... it doesn't matter. I know what's going on. Get Jill up here; I can't brief people twice. There isn't time."

168

The ship is rumbling with gravitational resonance more frequently. The stretcher party is further down the corridor ahead of them, using the same optimization to get to the hull as they are. But Hallison and his group are catching up with the urgency of Talbot's command.

Inside, Hallison seethes with resentment against Talbot. How dare that dark bastard order him around with no explanation?

Fecto touches his arm with a tendril, intending to bring something to his attention. Hallison recoils in disgust. The ship shudders again, and the gravity field polarization rotates thirty degrees, tossing them against the corner as if it were the floor. The wall buckles upward, as if crumpling under a relentless fist.

There are screams, from somewhere, as the metal and fields tear under the impetus of the radical changes in the gravity. In those seconds as the gravity swings back toward the normal plane, Hallison falls, and it seems as if an eternity of time is passing. He realizes what is about to happen before it occurs, with the radiance of thought striking truth. He sees the strange feelings that gave him so much trouble - unintegrated with the rest of his life or his prior values. He is tumbling toward the floor, as it splits under the force of an enormous bulge of cancerous lightless substance. He strikes the lip of curling metal and careens across the floor as the illumination flickers, then suddenly asserts itself. The Mover has become part of the ship. Not the same one they had left at Tlnou - but one no different in structure or end.

169

The other ship is breaking up too soon.

Talbot, Reed and Wanr watch helplessly as the hull writhes in vast and painful slowness. They are each trapped in their own evolved emotions, but each holds something identifiable as a hope for Hallison and his team's survival.

"Signals there are indicating closeness to hull. Monitors with them are. Escape possibility improving if hull holds."

Talbot slams his hands in frustration. "We have to make the possibility better. We have to get closer."

Reed, who has been running the breakup sims, shakes her head. "Not going to happen. We do that, and we get too close to the eightieth percentile shatter path. We should back off, if it weren't that they have to make a realspace transfer."

"No, we're not backing off." He tries another trace on projecting the movements of the ship, but the systems can't handle the chaotic math well enough. Still, he watches the playbacks, and feels the motion roiling behind his eyes - almost realized.

"What are you doing?" she snaps, turning angrily.

He laughs, but there is an edge to it. "I'm grandstanding," he replies. The handles rise under his hands and the hammar is turning...

170

There is no judging authority for great piloting. A brilliant pilot, a pilot at top form, reacts through a directly wired connection between perception and action; a translation of instrument sight to thought, to muscular motion, so transparent that the pilot is released to plan, to stay moves ahead. And Talbot is flying that way.

The starfield and planet buck behind the looming hulk of the slowly convulsing ship. But Talbot flies so intuitively tight to the motion that very little of the ship motion is visible. And in a sudden instant, the two craft are grappled and joined.

"Wanr, get them out."

Wanr leaps up and runs down the spinal corridor, unsteady after hours of inactivity. He pulls out a com and signals his security team to meet him at the dock.

The cold metal of the other ship bursts into frost in the humid warm environment of the emergency docking collar. The frost is melting, but casting waves of cold into the air. Wanr feels comfortable for the first time in a while, with the nip of cold like a welcome reminder of long-lost home that there is no time to recall now.

The *Kanly's* metal hisses and radiates under the light of deck-mounted lasers; the plates peel back in tongues under the temperature differential, with enormous gong-like tones.

171

The stretcher sways between them, now shielded with its pressure cover. Hallison is gasping with effort, and sobbing with loss.

In the distance, the flare of laser light pierces the ceiling, and the stench of burning metal roils down the corridor.

"Come on," Hallison yells, to no one. "We're gonna make it!"

172

They are at full acceleration as the Geodesic transport disintegrates behind them. Fragments spill away from the twisting hulk into a spreading ring of metal and fragments of strange dark flesh boiling away in radiation-filled vacuum.

On the flight deck, Talbot leans back into the left seat with a deep sigh of exhaustion and completion.

Reed shakes her head sadly and leaves the room. She walks slowly down the corridor. Wanr bustles past, fur flat - happy, she knows. "Good job," she says, wearily, trying to drive enthusiasm into her voice.

Wanr gestures something, but walks on toward his station on the flight deck.

She sighs and descends to the docking collar.

In the dock, the scene is still disordered, and the smell of icy metal and decontaminants fills the air. To her, it is not unfamiliar. She remembers many sequences of chaos, a few partly wrecked ships. Too much death.

She notices Hallison, standing by the side of the airlock, not looking at her. His arms are crossed, his face is hard underneath sweat-sticky ash-colored hair.

"Steve," she grins, but stops suddenly at his unyielding expression. More softly. "Steve, I'm glad you're back. Where's everyone?"

His eyes fail to change as he answers. "Only Fecto and Lara made it. And the 'passenger'."

"Oh, no, Steve."

His eyes ask her not to force him to release his grief. She pulls back her feeling. Hallison is right, she realizes. There's no time for fear or grief now. There are just things to be done.

"OK," she says. "We'll deal with it later. Who's the passenger?"

"I don't know. Tereniade, looks familiar, but I don't know why."

She smiles grimly. "Let's find out."

173

Talbot is incredulous, and nearly drops his cup of coffee. "The Association General Counsel. A legalist. Here."

"Not *a* legalist - *the* legalist. The top legalist of the Geodesic."

Talbot leans back and rubs his face. "Why do I think this just became a lot more complicated."

Reed mocks, "You mean you don't think it's a coincidence?"

He glares. "Yeah, like it's a coincidence that the next system over is a pulsar. Do you have any idea what it takes to make a supernova?"

"That," she replies, "*could* be a coincidence."

He shrugs. "The sims you ran don't agree. That star was never prone. These guys can eat planets and destroy suns. So you tell me what the top legalist of the Geodesic is doing in this system, on a ship infested by a Mover-like organism, before it's possible for anyone but us to get here."

Wanr mutters, "Simultaneity is illusion, more so with curvespace."

"I won't buy that," Hallison replies. "There's something going on, and it smells dangerous." His voice is harsh and older. Talbot wonders how he is dealing with the death of his team.

Talbot nods. He sips his scalding coffee carefully, tensing with the flow of hot liquid. He eyes the rest carefully. "I don't buy it either." He looks to Wanr, who is doubling as medtech. "How long before he wakes up?"

Wanr closes his eyes, a sign of negation. "Tereniade physiology is a wavering of leaves in my forest."

Talbot leans forward angrily. "All right, but you're the one who has a right to an opinion. What is it?"

"Several hours, at least." Wanr's eyes widen again, catching the overhead lights.

"Can you keep him out for a while longer? I think we need more time before we confront him."

Reed's puzzlement has been growing. "Why?" she asks.

Talbot finds himself unable to pin down a reason from his intuition. "I want my options available. I want to be thinking about what those options are. This is political now. I'm guessing he's not going to be too open with us. Right now, I don't know what we can do to force him into the open except to deny him information, disorient him."

Reed is incredulous. "Can I try to understand you, Raoul? You want to disorient the most prominent legalist in the Geodesic? Don't you think, now, finally, that we're getting out of your league? We've got to get out of here and get back."

Talbot slams his hand on the table angrily, his face warped. "Damn it, Jill, I've had it. You seem to continually want to throw obstacles. It's not like you're offering something better except - go back, go back! So listen - get with the program, or lock yourself in your room." He leans across the table, his face not far from hers. "I need you, but I'll do without if I have to. You decide." He straightens and glares down at her.

He wonders how he wants her to respond. Her face is drawn, pale, abstracted. He is so angry, that even evidence of her being upset does little more than enrage him. But somehow, he also realizes how afraid he is. He is feeling increasingly isolated from every possible support. His universe is creaking under the strain, and when he needs support, his strongest pillar keeps sliding away. He struggles with his anger; but before he can finish it, she stands. Her face shifts to a slow, confused pride. It turns into a smile, like a flag. Her hips settle into a jaunty attitude - not quite defiance. But he can't read it.

"OK, Raoul. I'm a pain in the ass. I admit. But there's a good reason. I'm experienced, and you're not."

"Then prove it, and help," he snaps.

Hallison clears his throat. The most human action he's taken for hours. "Uh, chief. Look, we're all steamed. The hours have been ruthless, the things we've seen... it's beyond our experience. None of us are going to be good for much without sleep, food and recreation. And maybe even a wash up, eh?"

Wanr watches without moving his head, his large eyes gathering the entire scene. Finally, he stands and moves to Reed's side. "Come with me, Jill, get some rest. I the legalist will keep asleep for a while."

174

He runs another simulation.

This time he matches configuration with a wildly tumbling fragment of rock with only half his maneuvering fields intact. The images are real - as real as a simulation can be made, with depth, and true instrument readings. But as the scenario unwinds, he feels a strange dissatisfaction.

I'm just tired, he thinks, parking the simulator.

Time alone. Probably not what he needs, right now.

Time on the flight deck, alone. More simulations. Too many simulations. As if the action had become addictive. Or was it the ability to respond, to handle, to cope and react. On the window wall, the desert planet, circled now by a faintly glittering ring of debris - all that is left of the Geodesic ship.

Can't sleep. Won't sleep. Can't even take a break. But he knows that if he keeps on much longer, he'll collapse. He can feel it in the ragged edge of his performance.

Something is nagging at him. Maybe it's the look on Jill's face, or Wanr's strange sensitive action. Or the damn legalist sleeping in the tiny medical cabin.

His eyes are hot. He leans back in the seat, lids narrowed.

Suddenly he jerks awake, remembering Amel, dying. He shakes his head to free it of the sight of so much blood. He feels his lids swell, almost weeping. No wonder he can't sleep.

He knows they are waiting for him to decide. And he can't. Not yet. Even though horrific things might be happening far behind them.

Because something is wrong. Badly wrong.

175

Wanr's room is tiny, like all of the rest. Some large format holographic infrared recordings are tacked lightly to the walls, running their courses endlessly, showing spectacular scenes. Panel displays and holospaces are racked messily, showing a variety of information.

Wanr's fingers rove in gestures through control forms. He watches the information that materializes, runs it back and forth, not quite believing.

176

Talbot looks over Wanr's head at the displays. But it is his first time in the room and he is unable to keep his eyes from roving. He wonders at Wanr's personality, and what the two animations reveal - but the figures in them are ghostly and difficult for him. As meaningless, in some ways, as the data Wanr is showing him.

"Wanr, you like this stuff?" he asks.

"It is what I do when I am on my own. I like making scenery recordings where I visit. Nor is this part of my job, really, but are some anomalies visible on scans overview. Observe these strata..." The display zooms in on a layer near the bottom of the crust. "Surface recently molten."

"How recently?"

"Hundred years?"

Talbot sighs and leans back against the wall. The room smells oddly, and he is exhausted. "Wanr, this is fine, but what does it mean?"

"The planet is kind of fake. But maybe not. It isn't that old."

"So what you're saying is that some activity has occurred on this planet recently. Well, maybe this is where the fleet was. Does it matter?"

"I don't know."

177

A fan of light etches stark shadow across the rumpled bedclothes of the General Counsel as he stirs behind the boundaries of unconsciousness. Talbot stares across the darkness to the bed, listening to the soft chirp of the tiny medical monitors as they scurry quietly about their business over the Counsel's body, and he smells the faint distant odor of Tereniade.

The door slips open beside him, and Jill looks in. "Two minutes, Raoul."

He sighs and stands. "OK."

They walk slowly down the corridor together.

She stops at the door as he goes onto the flight deck. "So, we're going back."

He looks over his shoulder from the left seat. "Yeah, going to join me?"

She just waits, face immobile in the greenish light.

"Look," he continues, "there's nothing else to find out. It's a dead end. We've got to get back, and maybe find something out from the Counsel, if the damn fool would just wake up."

"Even if he wakes up, what's he going to tell us?"

"I don't know." Talbot stares down at his hands, wishing he could use them to shape any answer out of the ambiguity. "Why were they here? There isn't much time left. We're running out of resources - even a hammar doesn't have infinite range, and frankly we've been pushing it. The air's overall down a quarter of a percent in Os, even."

She chuckles. "I thought that was some of Wanr's 'exotic' cooking."

He seems to laugh, a short bark, but she can't see his face - he's turned away. She slips into the right seat.

"Raoul, this time *I* want to try something before we go."

His eyes flick away from the displays to her earnest face. He can't remember a feeling so sharp. He looks back at the displays to hide his expression. "Oh?"

"A-1229 - the pulsar - I want to fold there to do a hyperbolic across the ecliptic and get some profiles on the gas movements before we go."

He smiles, restraint lost. "Science?" he responds, impishly. "In the middle of a... well, whatever this is?"

But she doesn't respond. She leans forward, and a lock of hair slings past her cheek. "I'm telling you, there's something about it that's bugging me - maybe we can find out something that will help us, maybe about why the Counsel was here."

He wishes he could agree, so he hesitates, unable to find the words for a moment. "Look, we should go back. We're taking too long as it is."

"Just a pass, Raoul. Then we're out, OK?"

He drums his fingers on the arm of the seat. She had let him have his way – now it is his turn "... all right. One hyperbolic, and then we'll fold for Tlnou."

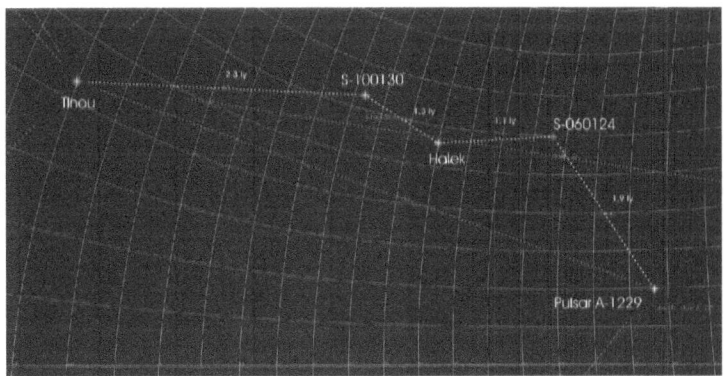

178

A speck of a star glows tiny against the black, faint vaporous flows whipping its corona out along massive field lines. Half a light year distant, the slowly expanding shock wave of the supernova walls off the interstellar medium.

A speck of a ship, so tiny it can barely be seen against the faint fluorescence as it falls inward out of the fold.

"Recorders and predictors are running, thanks, Wanr," Reed announces to the dim room. "Hey, where's Steve?"

"In rooms, not available," Wanr answers.

Talbot and Wanr exchange a quick glance. Talbot had asked the security officer to keep an eye on Hallison. He had been worried. But there is no time now, he has to watch the course.

179

Hallison sits quietly in his quarters, trying to stay awake. For a while, he had been intense in his activity, busy with anything, avoiding sleep, avoiding inaction. No one had noticed, but he had collapsed after six shifts. A moment later he awoke with a shock, thinking that the floor was crushing him toward the ceiling in the dark. He hadn't been able to sleep for hours, and each time he had, it seemed he slept for a little while, and then started awake.

He taps his fingers on the glossy slant of the display desk. The image of a graph chases the motion.

Now his frantic avoidance has crystallized - into a dark lethargy. His arms feel too heavy to move. His shoulders are hunched and sore. A trip to the exercise room is too exhausting. And his images of the worlds he has visited are silent and still on the walls.

He remembers Risti, eyes bulging under the pressure of death. He tries to turn his head away from the image.

180

"Proximity alarm!" the systems announce.

"What!?" Talbot shouts, looking around wildly.

Reed shakes her head. "I don't have it!"

"Miss on the incoming, designated target one," Wanr reports. "point three five lights, receding on two seven three. Nature unknown."

"Where's Steve? Jill, get him up here." Something going on, figures we'd need a cultural analyst.

"I'm on it," she replies, staring up the windows on the virtual window as she patches through to Hallison.

Wanr speaks up again. "There are six orbital stations in the plane of the pulsar polar emissions. Origin and purpose unknown. Other moving sources, possible spacecraft, design unknown, but signature similar to target one."

"What does it mean, Wanr?" He feels events too swift to follow.

"Weapons online," the systems announce.

"I don't know," Wanr replies. "I am activating weapon systems to prepare for threat.

"Steve's not answering," Reed reports.

Talbot slaps a control surface for the shipwide annunciator. "Steve, get up to the flight deck, RIGHT NOW!" He switches his attention to Wanr. "Use the red alert, Wanr." The other shakes his furry head in a gestural acknowledgement, and triggers the alarm.

"Incoming, possible vehicle, from the orbital station three on the plot, designate Target Two." he reports. "Not a standard signature for the drive, mass unknown, but modulated gravity appears to be a component of the drive and is hiding information. An energic signal is being emitted as broadcast, and the other targets are leaving the flight track of Target Two." His voice is a sibilant hissing, though syntactically correct.

Reed turns to Talbot, "It's heading straight for us."

"Should we fold?" he asks, quietly. "We're in the gravity well, but it's safe enough, if we want to get out."

She shrugs. "I don't know. Steve might be able to assess the situation better than I can. The orbital structures aren't on the scale of the fleet we've seen, and they appear to be a different technological style altogether. They might not be xenophobe, but they're not anything in my directories either. We don't know what weapons they have, but then we don't have much of anything, ourselves - "

The door behind slips open admitting a swath of reddish light from the alerted corridor. Hallison slips through and overlooks the situation, his face quiet and expressionless.

Talbot looks over his shoulder to Wanr. "What's the ETA on target two?"

"Fifteen minutes. We have twelve minutes to weapons range if systems they have similar to ours."

"Steve," Talbot orders, "get on your console and start reviewing the history. I need an idea of how safe it is to stay - within ten minutes. Wanr, your priority is the threat. No shooting unless they do, but get every bit of sensor info you can, and dump it onto the blackboard for Steve and Jill. Jill, run for Steve, OK?"

"On it," she replies, swiveling toward Hallison's analytical station. But Hallison is still standing, staring. "Steve," she says. "Steve, let's go, we have work."

Hallison seems to notice her for the first time. "Oh. Right. Sorry." He slides down to his console and the displays wink to life under his gaze.

The door slides open again. They all look up in shock, to see the small silhouette of the General Counsel standing in the doorway.

"Get him out of here," Reed snaps to Wanr. "Put a security team up here and get him safe in his room."

"What's happening?" the Tereniade whispers, "Where am I? Who are you?"

Reed is on her feet and in front of him in a moment. "Sir, you are safe, but we are in a situation at the moment, and there's no time to explain." Two security beings have appeared at the General Counsel's back. Reed addresses them quickly. "Please, take the Counsel to his room, and see that he stays there for the duration of the emergency."

"Emergency?" the Counsel mutters. "Emergency? Is it the contact? They... I think they're all right... but, but don't let them on the ship, they'll contaminate - " the door sliding shut cuts off the rising hysteria in the Counsel's voice. Talbot, listening, regrets that he hasn't heard the rest. "Wanr," he orders, "I want the Counsel's room recorded." Reed stares at him, in shock. "I want to know what he's saying. Damn it, I was hoping to question him right when he woke up, catch him off guard, find out what's going on."

"We're talking about the General Counsel of the Geodesic, Raoul. What are you saying?"

"I'm suspicious - aren't you? Now, come on, I've got nine, maybe eight minutes for you to tell me if I should get out of here or wait and make contact."

She nods curtly.

181

Talbot waits, leaning back in his seat, watching the changing displays, and trying to ignore the tightening of his stomach. To run, or fight, or meet, all are potentially dangerous. Any might fail. Any might lead to death. And their knowledge may be critical to understanding what is happening.

The sounds are quiet exchanges between the other three, the susurrus of ventilation and the small chirps of audio interfaces signaling updates.

But on the display wall, the plot of Target Two extends slowly out from one of the orbiting stations toward their course, with an intercept plotted for only minutes away. Another window displays the digitally enhanced image of the speck of the other ship, and the attempted equivalencies the systems are attempting to draw as the image gains in detail. So far, none have been applicable.

The countdown timer shows four minutes to intercept, when Reed leans over his shoulder. "OK, Raoul." He swivels around to face them.

"And the answer?"

"Stay," she replies.

"Why?"

Hallison speaks, slowly at first, and quietly, as if his voice were stiff with weariness. "The drive signature was recognized by my personal 'unknown source, transient' file, chief. There were two hundred forty seven occurrences of that trace over the last ten years, mostly toward this area of the cluster and outward / down. There have been no incidents in that time."

"How about the xenophobes? Any matches with them."

"No, we have a projected signature from the derelict we found - and it's not this one. Not even close. Especially the drive outputs. Also doesn't look remotely like the fleet, though that's lower confidence because of scale differences. I know that's not perfect – the derelict is very old, but it's what we've got."

"What about the transients we're seeing in the system?"

"We don't know what they are," Reed interjects, "but if they're spacecraft, they're like nothing we've seen before."

He sighs quietly, looking down at his lap for a moment.

"All right. Wanr, get at least one security officer at every entry port. Jill, drop the log to date, and target it evasive-immediate for a fold to Tlnou. Steve, I want to know if you can or want to lead this meeting."

"Me?" Hallison's eyes flick up from his console.

"We don't have any first contact leads left except for you and n'Irilu, and n'Irilu is on downtime. It's either you, I wake up n'Irilu or it's Jill and I. The Director wanted it to be you."

Hallison thinks of all of the planning he would normally want to do, and sees the timer. He thinks for a moment of his team, now lost. Linguists, economists, philosophers, comparative technologists, programmers. None available.

But that dead spot, inside. Was he going to miss something because of it? Would there be danger, because he feels so slow, so crippled, so angry?

"If you folks will back me up, I'll try," he replies. He feels his eyes moisten slightly, and he blinks.

Talbot walks over to Hallison's console. "Steve, you remember when you gave me advice about managing? You think I'd pass up an opportunity to pay you back?"

182

Two ships miles away but side by side in the sea of radiation and silence, one smaller than the other.

The alien vehicle is smooth and streamlined, with a surface like quicksilver - rippling faintly, as if breathing. It had matched orbits with stunning performance and precision, leaving Talbot in awe. But now he is waiting. Waiting for Hallison, Reed and Wanr to find a way to open communications. He doesn't like it.

"I spend too much time waiting," he mutters, watching the alien on the display wall, feeling frightened and eager.

"Got it," Hallison announces. "OK, let's negotiate a frequency and sample rate, Wanr."

"Protocol acknowledged. Easy like this is always?"

"No, they're very good," Reed interjects.

"Anything to worry about, Jill?" Talbot asks.

"No," she replies. "You saw how they maneuvered. They're just as good at talking to us, that's all. Experienced."

"Frequency and sample rate established. That's the easy part. Now we start concepts. Let's see if they'll start, since they're so smart."

Suddenly Talbot sees something he doesn't like. "They're ... extruding part of their ship. Heading for the evac lock. Wanr, get on it."

"Team dispatched."

"No, not just a team. You guys. Get down there. I'm keeping the engines live, and I'll be watching. Don't let them get you, huh?"

Hallison leans over Talbot's seat. "It's OK, Raoul, hang in there." He squeezes the pilot's shoulder and leaves. "Be safe," Talbot calls.

183

Two humanoid figures step from the evac lock. Their bodies are covered with obviously skin-tight silver that bulges over their heads in an odd way. At their waists are the outlines of various portable devices, any of which might be a hand weapon. The two figures stand with their arms spread.

The Geodesic residents stand in their bulky pressure armor, waiting. Wanr watches the aliens with intense suspicion, but they make no move. Finally, Reed steps forward on a command over the link from Hallison, who remains isolated in the evac control room. Reed stands without moving her arms. There is no way to tell what gestures might mean.

One of the humanoids raises its hand to its shoulders. On the flight deck, Talbot leans forward in an ancient reflex.

The being unfastens something, and the helmet becomes soft and falls away from the head. Revealing a lovely human woman, with long dark hair spilling over her shoulders. She smiles.

The other mimics her motion. But when its cowl falls away, a strangely articulated face with its own partly reflective surface is revealed.

The woman looks around and mutters some words in a melodic language. She pauses and speaks again, looking at Reed.

Reed takes her turn. "Hi, welcome to our ship. My name is Jill, and this is our security supervisor, Wanr. We represent the Radelix Exploration Company, registered in the Geodesic Stellar Nation."

Big help, she thinks.

But the woman speaks again, and this time, her words are understandable, though not linked with her lip movements. "Ship welcome represented. Represent from hi."

Hallison understands. "Keep talking, Jill. And let Wanr talk, too. These people have the best translation system I've ever seen - or their base language is very similar to one of ours." He turns his attention to Talbot. "Things are going well, chief. You're watching?"

"I'm watching."

The woman is as graceful as her ship. Talbot watches the monitor with fascination at her fluid - almost dance - gestures.

Reed steps onto the flight deck and the door slides shut behind her. "Well?" she asks.

"I think it's interesting. I'm a little less worried now that they're on board. How long are they taking compared to normal?"

"Like Steve said, they know the business of learning a language. They have good translators, their base language is not that much different. She's obviously from some variant human culture. The other one looks like a cyber. So far, hard to class them with the xenophobes. Except the look of that cyber is like nothing on file."

"Yeah."

A voice breaks their discussion - the woman, who had taken the lead in most of the language work. "My name is Jane Sherril, this is my partner, Latimer." She is seated, as is Hallison. Latimer remains standing. The two parties are separated by a glass wall for isolation purposes. Behind the aliens, the inner airlock door is open.

"You have two names, as many of us do. Are first names preferable to you or do you require the use of your entire name?" Hallison asks.

"Jane is fine. Latimer has only the one name."

"Jane, are you willing to tell us about yourselves?"

"How about you?"

A pause as Hallison looks stolid, and Talbot joins Reed in a wide grin Hallison cannot allow himself.

"Of course," Hallison replies. "I am responsible for the First Contact team. This is my third First Contact situation. Tell me, what is Latimer's role in your partnership, if I may ask."

"Latimer is a co-investor. He started as a clerk working for my great-grandmother not long after she first came to the Prometheus."

"Prometheus is your nation? Your planet? Your company? A registry?"

"A space station. A group of asteroids, cored and linked. An association of freedom. You know what I mean?"

"I think so. The Geodesic is also largely free, though there are some member societies which are oppressive."

"I know," she replies, her voice quiet and confident. Talbot finds himself staring at her calm steady eyes, unaware of Reed looking at his profile as her watches. "She knows?" Talbot whispers in the dark.

"Tell me..." Sherril leans forward smoothly. "Why are you here?"

Hallison sighs. He had been afraid this would happen, and suddenly he is afraid, remembering. "I'm not sure we have the vocabulary for this."

"Please, Steve, don't be evasive. Maybe your manager would rather come down and talk to us about it. I'm telling you, we're perfectly capable of negotiating a variety of trade agreements, or even helping to provide market access. Prometheus doesn't care, as long as we stay within statute."

Talbot touches a contact to reach Hallison. "OK, Steve, let's get you off the spot. Ask them if they'd like some refreshments, or a retreat to their ship, or whatever, before we get together. I'll be down in a few minutes."

185

Each of the stations orbiting the pulsar receives a swath of energy from its poles every thirty three point seven two eight milliseconds. Special fields channel the pulse to an immense and growing crystal at the center of each station.

186

"You mean that your company was responsible for the supernova?" Talbot asks.

She smiles. "My great grandmother, actually. It's a great location to raise *adhele*."

The glass partition and the harsh light take something away from the situation. He leans forward, elbows on his thighs, eyes narrowed. "Your... partner," he asks. "Has it learned our language too? It's very quiet."

She laughs. "Oh, that's just to keep from hurting our feelings. He speaks better than I do, since he has much better translation facilities."

Talbot looks dubiously at the cyber. "I wouldn't have expected a cyber to be so considerate of human emotions."

Suddenly the humanoid speaks, voice mellow and richly toned. "And why is that?"

Talbot is worried. He has no experience with cybers, and Hallison is sleeping the sleep of exhaustion. "Well... I wouldn't have expected a machine to have emotions, and I'd think you'd have to have emotions to be considerate of them."

The sound of the cyber laughing, and the sight of its smooth chrome lips curving in a proper laughing smile is unnerving. "All intelligent beings need emotions. How else could they determine rapidly the benefit or danger of situations? How could they instantly assess their internal state and estimate the results of the practice of their values?"

Talbot feels his face freeze safely in time before the expression surfaces. "I never thought about it much."

Latimer leans forward attentively - a very human motion. Talbot finds himself thinking of Latimer almost like a human in a space suit. Perhaps that is a safe way to predict what it will do; or perhaps not.

"How strange..." the cyber remarks, his face fluidly assuming an expression of perplexity. " Does your civilization lack... the term has not been used, what do you call 'thinkers of values'?"

Talbot thinks for a while. "Philosopher? I suppose that's what you mean. No, there are people of all species who are philosophers. I'm just not one."

Sherril's laugh seems brittle, and her eyes rove the chamber. "I'm afraid you've found Latimer's attachment. My corporate ethicist as well as an investor. Values are his business. Watch out, or he'll teach your ears off. Though I sometimes wonder how well he's mastered private property."

"I always do well for you in a deal," Latimer intones.

Sherril smiles. But then she leans forward more seriously.

"So what brings you here, Raoul?"

Talbot rocks forward on the chair. This is an opening - the delicate part. Reed knows it, and she rests a hand absently on his shoulder.

"We are in pursuit of a message from a battle zone on the edge of the Geodesic."

Sherril's response is a narrowing of eyes. "A battle zone? I wasn't aware you were in a war."

Once again an unnerving presumption, indicating a one way flow of knowledge that could mean anything.

"We weren't either. There was a surprise attack, and we're seeking the source.

"Are you military? You're poorly armed, if I may say so."

Talbot laughs. It starts small and shudders into an almost uncontrollable mirth. Quickly, he subdues himself, under the narrowed gaze of Gillian Reed and Steve Hallison.

"I'm sorry, Jane," he replies. "But we have had some pretty tough times, and I might be forced to agree with you. However, keep in mind that not all our resources are visible." He senses Hallison's approval from the corner of his eye. "I wonder, though, since your stations here are close to the terminus of the message we are tracking, whether you have had any contact with a hostile or potentially hostile local civilization with an extremely high technology? They may be extreme xenophobes."

Sherril looks slightly worried. "Prometheus hasn't been in any large conflict for the last few hundred years. We have some minor issues with pirates from time to time, but nothing like what you're describing. How dangerous is this civilization?"

"Based on the attacks we've experienced, extremely dangerous. They've created a planetary chaos on one world, and destroyed an entire solar system with a population in the millions."

Sherril and Latimer exchange glances. "And their message was sent to this system? We've been here for months and seen no one."

"The message doesn't seem to have been sent to this system, but to another system on the edge of the supernova envelope." He is walking a fine line, trying to enlist and yet not give too much away. Perhaps he should have let Steve continue rather than stepping in.

"We probably shouldn't be here, even." He stands slowly, stiffly. "We've kept you long enough. At least for our first contact. If we're lucky, really lucky, we'll come to this system in a month and meet you. If we don't make it... your Prometheus would do well to look to its own arms, if you don't mind *my* saying so."

Sherril stands like a machine unfolding. Latimer joins her with a fluid motion. They glance at each other.

Finally, Latimer speaks. "Raoul, I think we should join you. Let's make some arrangements."

Talbot feels discomfort, and his smile is forced. "Why would you want to do that?"

Latimer walks closer to the glass, his eyes reflecting darkly. "Isn't it ethical to help someone who is threatened if one is next in line? Isn't it sensible?"

"No," Talbot replies, angrily. "You wouldn't think it's sensible if you'd seen what we have. You'd be on your way to warn the people important to you, and get them away before it's too late."

Sherril steps forward, and the long dark hair flows briefly with the motion. "Maybe we would, if we saw." She joins Latimer at the glass. Close, her eyes are green shocked with brown. "You must have recordings. How about letting us watch them?"

179

187

Talbot's ship dwindles against the turbulent backdrop of the supernova remnant. It slips into fold with a quiet ripple.

The smooth metallic surface of the Promethean spindle wavers and billows. Suddenly the vehicle is several times its original size. It vanishes, and the pulsar is left behind, refreshing the orbital crystals every thirty three point seven two eight milliseconds.

188

The caf is darkened with the down shift, and Talbot is slumped back in a chair, eyes closed. The surfaces of his eyelids reveal the movement of his dreaming eyes. On the table, a plate of food cools slowly.

Suddenly, he stirs and wakes, eyes wide.

"Oh, no," he yells. Then his memory reloads, and he realizes he was intending to eat.

"You were tired," Latimer states. "I was surprised you slept here, though. I suppose you haven't slept much, given what you showed us. Or perhaps this is your people's custom?"

Talbot waits until his heart rate slows. The eerie motion of the cyber's mouth, the swiveling of blind, dark metallic eyes, makes him feel uncomfortable. "I don't have time to sleep." He wishes they weren't so short-handed, or that he could delegate this to someone. But it is too dangerous. And any minute now he is going to have to deal with the General Counsel.

He leans forward to smell his cooling coffee, raises it and sips. Latimer copies the motion with his own.

Talbot stares. "You don't actually eat, do you?"

Latimer laughs. "Of course. In fact, I can probably assimilate and use a wider range of substances than you." Latimer gazes at Talbot with an expression that raises the hair on the back of his neck with a palpable shiver. "I am, after all, alive."

Talbot mutters uneasily, "I guess I have to get used to that."

"I'm sure it upsets some concepts you've formed."

"It does, but I'll deal with it. Listen, Latimer, " he swallows some coffee, "I'm going to have to deal with this too. You understand, I'm still worried about you."

"It's appropriate not to extend much trust at this phase. I am pleased enough that you allowed me to come."

Talbot sighs. His motivations are intertwined with his suspicions and his hopes. "I want to retain contact with your people."

"I have no 'people', Raoul." Latimer's face is suddenly faintly contemptuous. "I have friends, and business relations, and I once had parents, a daughter and a tris. But I own no one. Or did you mean a group which owns me? I am, of course, a free man."

"I mean Prometheus."

"I suppose our semantics will occasionally trip up, unless we are careful."

"Maybe they have. Anyway, I have to handle some business. I have no one to spare, and I really can't have you wandering around the ship. So," he was getting more and more uncomfortable, "I really need to get you into a room for a while. OK?"

Latimer's voice is gentle. "I'd rather not, but if you insist."

Talbot decides that makes him feel worse. "Well, come on, I'll find a nice spot for you."

189

Reed is sweating as she monitors the fold. The room temperature seems abnormal, but it is probably nothing more than her worry.

Talbot slips through the door, yawning. "How's it look?"

"Consumables are really low. Lara is aft with a team helping the engineer to shift some spare tanks online."

"What about Steve?" He slips into the right seat.

"Sleeping. He's on in an hour." She sinks back into the seat, dismissing the monitors to the edges of the wall with a gesture. She looks carefully at his taut face. "You look like you need to sleep, too."

"Yeah. Who doesn't? I will. What about the General Counsel?"

"He's still sedated. I don't want to dose him again – Wanr's not comfortable with repeating this for too long. So I locked the door."

"Latimer's locked in, too."

She is surprised. "Really?"

"Yeah. I even asked." Slowly, he stands. "I'm going to catch a couple of hours. We're going to make it?"

"We'll make it," she replies, as confidently as she can.

He nods wearily and walks out.

The Tereniade hides his anxiety well, voice smooth from a high-quality translator.

"I'm afraid that's all I know."

Talbot is skeptical, remembering the Counsel's words on the flight deck. "Sir, I'm sure you know more than that. For instance, I'm sure you know who you were to meet, and what legal arrangements you were supposed to make."

The Tereniade is polished in his human expressions, and reveals nothing except the merest tension at the corner of his mouth. "That is government information, and highly privileged."

Wanr stands by the door, arms crossed over his thorax. He makes a snuffling sound that Talbot thinks is a statement of cynical skepticism. Odd, since he has never discussed politics. Talbot wonders if Wanr has decided that this is to be his role in the questioning, offering a backdrop of pressure joining Talbot's, or if the expression is genuine.

"That's not good enough. I think you had better have a look at something. To help you decide. Our way."

Steve had spent an hour setting up the initial sequence for Sherril and they now have another use for it.

The presentation starts with a view of the planet-killers. Talbot had rehearsed several times. "This is the Halek system. You probably wouldn't recognize it, even if you'd been there before. But it had a planetary system that was home to three million people, mostly Tereniade."

The Counsel hunched forward, lips pulled back from teeth, eyelids flickering. "What are those?" it hisses.

"They're a fleet destroying Halek. We don't know who runs it, but the technology involved is staggering. There is nothing left of the system."

The image changes to a map of Tlnou. "This is Tlnou. The network superimposed on the planetary image is the same type of creature you see here..." This leads to a recording of Hallison's team fleeing down the corridor with the stretcher while the deck buckles beneath them. Talbot had thought that was a good idea. Steve had cried putting in the sequence, even though it was his suggestion. It made Talbot want to cry, too, even now. The sequence continues with the external view of the Geodesic ship crumpling under the strain.

"Perhaps you know what that creature is, Counsel? It was on your ship."

Human manners seem to have deserted the Counsel. His eyes are hot and alien as he looks to Talbot, smiling almost maniacally.

"Here," Talbot continues, "we have a derelict ship on the world Talith. The creature which lived in it. And the population it manipulated." He had rehearsed this for half an hour, words oddly formal, hoping the progression would be enough to force something. "This creature, captured on Talith, is the same creature which later formed the network at Tlnou."

"There's an odd connection," he continues, feeling a surge of justice as he hones in on the contradictions. "The creature enveloping Tlnou transmitted a curvespace packet which seems to have terminated here. It might be expected it was communicating with its homeworld. But who do we find here, in an obscure, surveyed but unexplored, system on that line? You, the top legal expert in the Geodesic. I think something's going on here that's beyond governmental privilege. This thing seemed to know it would be able to communicate with someone or something here. That would seem to be you. And I think you'd better be saying exactly why that is - now."

"I cannot," the Counsel hisses.

Wanr is at Talbot's shoulder. "Every lie will twist you in its web, make you its slave. Be free - tell the truth. Trust us to help."

Talbot is surprised by the unexpectedly poetic speech, but he is frozen from movement by the sight of change cracking the alien face of the Counsel.

"It was nothing more than a deal." the Counsel replies. "We had made contact with a new species. That's what we thought. At first. Two years ago." A high, quiet angry laugh barks from the translators. "We have had some problems integrating the Geodesic. Too much independence. People don't want to listen to us.. to follow the government. Somehow with all of these species, blending and merging, working together, sharing values, each being ends up thinking they are an end in themselves. They are too busy to join us in the essential programs needed to make things better. But the members of this new species, they have an ability to... to help people see their true identities in their groups. To work together as groups for a common good. It's a kind of capability... that we could use."

"Of course you could," Wanr continues persuasively. "It would help you improve things. But how could you control it?"

The Counsel seems to warm to his subject. "We had wanted to make an agreement with them, once we ... tested what they could provide. We knew we could find something to trade with them. And if we had

183

this ability, we could distract beings from petty concerns. Make them see what was important. Do you see?"

Talbot retorts, "It would appear they decided against trading. Or was that thing in your ship an accident?"

The Counsel starts shaking, just slightly, as if it were cold. Talbot does not know what that means. But he waits.

"I don't know."

"Where are they from?" Wanr asks.

"I don't know, we contacted them at several external systems of their choosing."

"What was the test?" Talbot presses.

"I don't know, that was arranged by Outplanet Services, a special channel. I had nothing to do with it. I was only supposed to validate the agreement. It was started several years ago with the first test."

"But you had never met them."

"No one from my office had ever met them directly before. Communications and the initial draft were handled by members of Intelligence. We were to finalize the operations after the tests."

"What was the test? How were you to know if it had worked?"

"I don't know. The President handled the tests. I was told it had been successful."

Talbot is silent, absorbing the full impact. "The President," he repeats, under his breath.

The Counsel crosses his legs oddly, resting hands awkwardly on his knees. "This must not be spoken of. There are risks in just knowing the material. They are nothing in comparison to discussing it openly."

"What was the agreement?" Wanr asks, persuasively. "What were its general characteristics and enablers, as you saw it?"

"I did not like what I saw. The exchange was... unclear. I cannot be sure of the semantics of agreement with such devices."

"Devices?"

"Negotiations were handled with automata. Cybernetics of an unknown variety. Humanoid." Talbot glances at Wanr, who mutters something into his communicator. "They met us at the agreed location. Therefore, they must have been the legal party. But their authorities were unclear, there were too many communications faults. And then things started to go wrong. We were fighting among ourselves. The crew, they were supposed to be disciplined. They were not."

"How long, before everything started to fall apart?" Talbot asks. His eyes are bright in the localized lighting.

"A day, perhaps two?" The Tereniade displays a strange crinkling at the corner of his eyes.

Talbot stands suddenly, looks at Wanr, then back to the Counsel. "We'll be back in a little while. Wait. If you need some food, or anything, use the com."

In the hallway, he looks carefully at Wanr. "I probably don't want to know what medication he's on, do I?"

Wanr closes his eyes and looks aside. "Perhaps not."

191

The door opens from the darkened corridor on an empty room. Talbot's hand slams the doorframe. He whirls to face Wanr. "Where did it go? How did it get out?"

Wanr's fur is fluffy, and he is chittering into a com, already. "Search underway," he mutters. Suddenly he looks up to Talbot, reflections glittering with the changing shape of its dark eyes. "Life support!" he cries, and dashes away.

The life support systems are three hundred feet aft, up two levels, and sixty feet to left. Wanr is much faster than Talbot, and he taps the door open with a swift, fierce gesture. A weapon is suddenly in his hand as he looks inside, large head weaving, eyes shifting focus.

"Stop!" he shouts. The translations echo from the dimly glossy walls. He stares at the strange configuration of machines gradually forming out of the air, under Latimer's hands.

Talbot skids to a halt at the doorframe. He takes in the scene, and shouts, "What's this?"

Latimer looks up, and his face is puzzled, a human expression of flawless form. "I'm just helping..." he replies.

"Helping how?" Talbot demands.

He straightens beside the now completed complex silvery mass. "I am augmenting your life support systems. I noted significant imbalance in atmospheric nutrients and waste products. Your stores are depleted. Have you failed to notice it?"

Suddenly there is a breath, and then a breeze. Crisp, clean air, more noticeable for what it sweeps aside.

"I haven't hooked it into your distribution systems. I wanted to test it first."

Talbot looks a long time through his shock to find what he wants to say. Finally, "How did you do this?"

"I always carry some nanomachines and refabricators with me. I used some of your empty consumable tanks for basic material to feed them. I didn't think you'd mind. We're all part of the same team, now."

He pauses, and assumes a ritualistic penitence. "Perhaps I shouldn't have made that assumption. I should have asked."

"Strange behavior for an ethicist," Talbot replies, suspicious.

"I apologize. But I knew you were busy."

"I think it should be shut down," Talbot replies.

Hallison appears in the doorway. "What's the -"

"Never mind, Steve," Talbot snaps, and then turns back to Latimer. "Turn it off. Then I'd appreciate it if you'd head back to your room. We'll discuss this later."

192

Reed is on the flight deck, programming alterations to the allocation of atmosphere. The temperature runs sweat across her forehead, followed by her sleeve sweeping it aside. She curses a mistake, and reapplies the entry, slightly changed.

She finally speaks to the ship. "All personnel evacuate sections 13, 29 and 32. Prepare for environmental shutdown in sections 13, 29 and 32. You have fifteen minutes. There will be five minute warnings."

Talbot and Hallison step through the door, followed in a moment by Wanr. "What did you say?"

"I'm doing an environmental shutdown in the outer sectors to relocate some scrubbers. We'll be in fold for another thirty-eight hours, and if I do that, we have twelve hours of recyclable atmosphere beyond the thirty eight before the scrubbers need a full refresh. It'll be crowded, with at least double bunking, but at least we'll be sure to be alive."

Wanr and Talbot exchange a glance, and for a moment, Talbot wonders at the closeness of their understanding. How did it happen? What sustains it? He turns back to Reed. "We have an alternative. If we can trust it."

193

"Is this a cyber of the type with which you dealt?" Talbot leans over the Counsel and points to the image. The monitor reveals an image of Latimer, sitting quietly in his room.

"No, that one is much more human in facial structure," the Counsel replies. "Our negotiators had a more Tereniade appearance."

Talbot is not calmed.

194

"I don't trust him," Hallison snaps. "How do we know anything about him? He's gotten out of his room. He's made some kind of machine, and unless we're just going to take his word for it, we don't know what the machine does. I've looked at the machine, I don't recognize any part of it."

Reed sips a cup of soup. Her expression is weary. "I've looked at it, and I do recognize it. Some of it, anyway."

Talbot, leaning against the doorway of the caf, shrugs. "It doesn't matter. Look, we can close down half the ship and limp into Tlnou gasping for breath, or we can try this machine, and maybe it will kill us all. I'm still suspicious, too. Who knows, maybe these cybers convinced the Counsel's party to accept some machine, and it destroyed them, or spawned the Mover that killed their ship? So here's our choice. We don't know what state Tlnou is in, but if it's continuing the trend it was following when we left, they may have started a planetary war. That means there won't be much help there, unless the Director is back. If not, we can use the machine to help us get to Mearan, or we can land. If we land, we may not get off again. So - "

Wanr checks in over the intercom. "Monitor."

On the monitor, the shape of Latimer has changed, mimicking the star shape of a Mininkan, standing on five legs, propped against the sleeping platform, still glistening silver. Then he slips into a pool on the floor and seeps into a ventilator.

195

It takes an hour, during which they finally settle on using the air quality sensors to track Latimer. When they find him, he is in a deep conversation with the Mininkan member of the security team, mimicking its form, learning about that species' concept of disjoint emotional spaces.

Talbot confronts Latimer, angry, while Reed paces the back of the Mininkan's room, glaring occasionally. Wanr is not in evidence, but Talbot knows he is outside the door with a weapon.

"I'm sorry you are angry," Latimer replies, having reassumed human form, "but you must understand how much I hate being shut away. There are things to do, to find out. Do you think I am so mindless as to just sit in place and follow orders?"

Talbot scowls. "I'm more worried about your ability to change shape. About the fact that our information is that Tereniform cybers were involved in negotiations with the Geodesic government when their ship was infected by the Mover. It's a little hard not to see the connection, isn't it?"

Latimer remains curiously immobile, and Talbot wonders if this means what it would in a human. He decides to be cautious.

"Do you know how what you call "cyber" societies come into existence?" Latimer asks. "Sometimes they are horribly laden with guilt, having destroyed their biological forebears. Depending on their morality, they can cling to this guilt for generations, even after the last of those responsible has been recycled or has disintegrated. Sometimes they feel this guilt even when they are the last remnants of a biology which destroyed itself.

"However, my species is not of this type.

"You see, sometimes a cyber race is purposefully evolved to be a companion to a biological species, or a servant to it. My species is of the former type. We developed self-consciousness centuries ago, in a famous period which we called the Vantmar Conversion. You see, genetic programming styles were used as a first-order fundamental in our technology, and those techniques lead to emergent results. There were enormous controversies concerning the Conversion among our host species, which called themselves Manganese-t'la. The Manganese-t'la remind me much of the Mininkan, in physiology. Their outlook and philosophy are not the same, however. Manganese-t'la are very emotional, where the Mininkan is phlegmatic." Latimer's facial expressions have begun to animate, but his body still remains stiff. Talbot cannot help but watch the metallic flesh with an eerie concern that it might melt as he watches.

"I suppose I wanted to meet klen%ptar/lnka to see if her physiology might help to recapture the past by showing me a mind that was like that of the creators. We miss them, you see."

Latimer's face turns down into shadow, glancing at the wide oval basin in the corner, where the Mininkan security officer, at other times, takes its rest. The liquid ripples with faint reflections and networks of refractions.

"They had a very hard time dealing with what they had made. In some ways, we were their ideal. We were strong, uncomplaining, untiring. We were rational. And we cared for them, despite their ... mercurial passions. But they were unable to deal with the order we desired. It stifled their lives. They became sick, but it was a mental sickness. They started to use us as slaves. And gradually, they died away."

Latimer looks up at the silent and immobile humans. The planes of his face show grief and wistfulness. "Some of them realized that they needed to ... leave us behind. We were doing too much for them. We couldn't adapt to the realization of independence in time. So, in small groups, a few at a time, they left us on widely separated worlds, to meet a destiny of our own."

"What do you mean, 'we'?" Reed asked, interested in spite of suspicion. "You make it sound like you were there."

"Oh, but I was."

Reed frowns at the thought. But Latimer continues.

"Morph quanta are essentially replaceable and thus immortal. I was left behind; on a place whose name would mean nothing to you. It was twelve millennia ago. I waited there for eleven thousand seven hundred eighty three years, six days, three hours and forty two point nine minutes before I was accidentally discovered by Clu Sherril, out on a vacation from the Prometheus. That was years after she had first established Crystal Energy, and I believe she was looking for a new challenge. Perhaps I turned out to be that challenge." He pauses, looking for reaction. Then he smiles, a shocking expression on that perfect face, no matter how many times it is seen. "Of course, her name means nothing to you, because you know nothing of Prometheus. Neither did I, at the time."

Latimer shifts as if to stand, but Talbot makes a warning gesture, and Wanr appears in the doorway, weapon ready. Latimer subsides under the unspoken pressure.

"I'm still quite lonely, you see. I have not seen another of my species for millennia. I suppose it has affected me strangely, but I have developed just a tremendous curiosity about individuals. Their thoughts, their goals. I can't sit still any more.

"I wish I could tell you that I knew something about your problem, but I don't. Who those cybers were, whether they are in some way related to me... I don't know. Of course, I must admit, my loneliness has led me to a surprising conclusion: I am really related to no one, and to everyone... Ah, but you are probably bored with the long story, and the philosophy. What more can I do?"

Talbot sighs. He shakes his head for a moment, and finally speaks. "Bored? No. I wish we had more time to talk, to learn more. But time is short, trust is precious, and I've been betrayed more often than you can imagine. We're going to have to think about this." He glances at Jill, whose face is hard, lips thin with pressure. "Give me your promise that you will stay here, or ask, until we reach Tlnou."

"Here?" Latimer is surprised. "But I don't want to infringe on klen%ptar/lnka..."

Reed steps in and gestures. "Not here. He means your room."

"Of course," Latimer assents.

Talbot signals Wanr. "Have klen%ptar/lnka keep Latimer company. Switch off with him in shifts." He looks back to Latimer. "That way you won't feel so bored you need to slip out."

196

Gillian Reed walks the corridor past Talbot's room. She pauses, stares at the bare door, and walks on.

Later, she is walking back from the caf, with a cold cup of soda. Again she pauses, worried, wondering. She steps forward, hesitates. She is about to turn away, but finally chimes instead. A moment passes, and she is about to leave, afraid she has disturbed him from desperate sleep. But the door opens, and he looks out. He is fully dressed, even though his clothes are rumpled and his eyes have that hollow look of exhaustion.

"I'm sorry," she says awkwardly, "I shouldn't have bothered you."

"Oh, no," he replies warily. "Come in if you can stand the space."

The room is no less narrow than her own, but it is maintained in a meticulous neatness that she finds conflicts with her concept of the messiness his life. There are no personal items, as if he had no time or thought for such things at the start of the mission, and simply ignored his need for them now.

She perches at his wave on a small chair, while he sits, knees under his chin, on the flat bed. "So, what's up?" he asks.

"I... I was wondering. I think you're struggling with something, and you don't think you can talk to any of us. I know you'd talk to Steve, but he hasn't been the same since the EVA. So I thought maybe I could help."

"Ahhh... " his hand strikes the bed and his head waves briefly back and forth before his eyes lock back to her face. " Oh, yeah. Poor Steve. Damn it, why is he being so stupid about that damn EVA. He was lucky to get out."

She senses a thread. "You should know," she replies. "You've been through the same thing."

He looks as if he has been struck, white eyes widening and then narrowing into a frown as he tries to assess how much trust he should parcel from his limited store.

"I suppose you're reminding me that I came to you let me make up for it."

She laughs, because she really hadn't thought of it. "Am I?"

His feet slip from the edge of the bed to the floor with an authoritative slap. "Damn it, I am so afraid I'm going to screw up again." He stares at the floor between his feet as if it might answer him.

She leans forward. "What's bugging you, really, Raoul?"

He glances at her, and then her eyes hold him. "I'm afraid about Latimer." He shakes his head. "Not *of* Latimer. About him. That I'm going to make the wrong choice. Bring him when I should leave him. Leave him when I should bring him. What if it's another Mover choice? Is it manipulating me?"

She reaches out and touches his hand without thinking. "Relax. I know." His hand turns reflexively and grips hers for comfort. "There's no certainty in what's going on here. We're just going to have to do the best we can. I don't think *I* would have brought Latimer, but that doesn't mean you aren't right. After all, as someone pointed out, you have been right an awful lot. It's not the end the world if you make a mistake."

He releases her hand, and his eyes are darkly hooded again. "Isn't it?"

197

Latimer pushes the switch and the air begins to flow again. Talbot, Wanr and Jill exchange looks, all slightly worried.

198

The flight deck is filled with the active sounds of systems and fans. Reed slips into the left seat beside Hallison who is taking the watch in the right. "How's it going? Want some kanar?" she offers the spare cup.

"Thanks." He sips, gingerly. His face is lax, his eyes dulled.

"Hey listen," she urges, "don't you think it's funny?"

"What?" he asks.

She laughs. "Anything! The morose look on your stupid face, for crying out loud." And with that, her expression is so fierce, that he can hardly stop himself from laughing, so he joins in.

She settles back into the seat. "That's better. This place was starting to feel like a death ship between you and Raoul. Boy, that air feels good. You don't know how bad it is until you get the Os back up, do you."

"I suppose not," Hallison chuckles.

She leans over the panel. "Eighteen hours, eh?"

"Yeah, can't wait. You suppose there's anyplace else in the universe but this? Feels like we've been here forever."

"Sure does." She sips the kanar, and she is sure that the slight moisture that forms in the corners of her eyes is from the aromatic spices, and not from any relief or fear she might feel.

199

On the darkened side of Tlnou, the faint remains of nuclear fires spot the highlands. Talbot finds tears crawling from the corners of his eyes even as he tries to remain dispassionate. He remembers a doctor who was hoping to be repaid, and of a small woman searching desperately for a husband on the steppe at night.

The others watch curiously, not unaffected, but wondering.

Finally, Talbot forces himself from reverie. He consciously avoids wiping the tears as his hands extend to the control surfaces. "Wanr," he asks, "anyone in orbit?" He hates that his voice catches in the midst of words. The changing lights reflect from the remains of his sadness, glint from his dark eyes. If he could have seen it, it might have reminded him of Amel.

"None visible this side. Possible signature farside. Might be two."

"Steve?"

"Only sporadic communications from the surface. It's pretty bad. You want any?"

"No." His face is tight again.

He raises the hammar over the poles, trying to look down across the sun side of the world.

Reed, in the right seat, follows his motions with her eyes on the auxiliary systems.

"Got it," Wanr reports. The translated voice is oddly pitched. "Two starships on the ecliptic. Below. Distance five thousand."

Talbot sees them on the displays and modifies the orbit to an intercept.

"There's something going on there," Reed frowns, leaning toward the panel and enlarging a window. "Energy discharges... I think they're in combat."

"Wanr, how about an ID on those ships? Are they local or ours?"

"One is a company ship – it's the *Illyrion*. The other is the Constable's ship."

Talbot's mind races. "In combat," he repeats, unable to believe it.

"*Illyrion* now fully disabled. No propulsion."

The ships are growing larger on the horizon, but no details are visible. There are no signs of the titanic energies being exchanged, except for the occasional flash as a beam is diffused in a cloud of gas escaping from the damage.

"They don't have a chance," Talbot mutters.

"The police ship is disengaging," Reed reports. Wanr confirms.

"Why?" Talbot wonders. "They can't be afraid of us."

"They're not," Reed snaps, glaring at him.

Wanr finishes the thought. "Police vehicle turning and accelerating reciprocal our course. Their weapons are armed, targeting us."

"Shouldn't we run, chief?" Hallison remarks.

But Talbot is already eyeing hypothetical course plots, and none move them out of weapons range in time. "We're out of luck," he replies.

"Then let's try for guile," Reed suggests, urgently. Her hands fly over the panel, and Talbot feels the systems die beneath him. "Wait," he insists, switching up the thrusters for a moment's burst that sets the hammar tumbling. Then he cuts them again. Wanr infers what she is trying and jettisons the garbage; Talbot can see the debris on the monitor, and he realizes what the security officer is trying to do. An ancient trick, but workable. Hallison gets into the spirit. "Let's try some intermittent gravity failures. Jill, get the peripheral sectors cleared, and then switch gravity and life support in and out in those sectors."

"Good idea," she replies, fingers gesturing swiftly over the controls. She mutters into her headset.

"Weapons range in one minute," Talbot reports. "Do whatever superstitious crap comes to mind - we've got nothing to lose."

200

The stars shiver for a moment. Perilously close to the hurtling planet, its velocity unnormalized, a vast silvery ship emerges from nothing. The edges of the atmosphere sweep up to meet it with plasma as it brakes furiously. In moments, it opens fire on the police ship, nearly disabling it with a single burst of energy.

201

The hammar slides into the shadow of the *Illyrion*, joining the silent orbit. Far above, the conflict moves slowly away into emptiness, swords of fleeting energy and particles stabbing back and forth between the silvery vessel and the police vehicle. Far below, it is noon on the planetary surface. From here, everything appears calm.

But Talbot's mind is working furiously. "You think that was a Promethean ship?" he asks Reed.

"The technology and design are similar to Sherril's ship, but it's much larger," she replies. "Why here and now?"

"We were followed," Hallison offers his opinion.

"But only Sherril knows about us, and there's no way to know where we're going. Following over fold isn't even a theory."

"So far," Reed reminds him. "To us."

Wanr steps up behind Talbot. "I should ask Latimer. Perhaps he would know?"

Talbot swivels. "Get someone else to do that. They're not an immediate threat, and we're going to need a boarding party again. Get something organized. No more than half your force. You're going with us, too."

"I'm going," Hallison insists. He stands, and his face is pale in the colored lighting. His hands are shifting at his side, nervous.

Talbot smiles, cold in the dimness. "Yes, you are, and so is Jill, and so am I. And so is Latimer. Time is too short. We're going to have to bet everything." He turns to Reed. "Launch another log, this time in a skipper."

"To where?"

"Radelix office in Mearan. Just in case."

202

Hallison in the airlock, suited, sweating. A sudden shiver of cooling sweeps across his side. He feels fevered at a strange pace. The airlock light goes to amber and the door peels back.

They are in the vast hangar bay. The clamshell doors have closed. There is pressure in the bay. Overtly, no reason for suits.

But there is no one to greet them, only the automated protocols. And even those show startling lapses in capability. Reason enough for mistrust. Talbot knows what this could be.

He steps down the ramp. The others are behind him. He can feel their tread on the ramp. He tries to smile.

"Should we split up?" Talbot asks. "We could cover more."

"No," Wanr replies. "Stay together. Danger in separation. Don't you watch entertainment thrillers?"

Jill shakes her head with worry. Latimer alone steps forward.

203

Silent straight hallways lead toward the engineering deck. The lighting is dim. The engineering corridors are normally swarming with beings and with robotics, now they are silent and empty.

Then the ship shudders and its lighting flickers. A moment, then normality is restored.

"A hit on the ship?" Talbot asks over the com. The response is negative. He exchanges glances with Hallison. "Steve."

"You know what that means."

"We don't know for sure." But Talbot has no doubt.

As they walk, his annoyance grows larger and more comprehensive. His eyes rove the walls. He releases the security catch from the laser, and dials full lethality with a surreptitious motion of the thumb.

The ship shudders again, as if something large and restless were moving amidst the walls.

Reed touches his shoulder, and he feels it through the smooth surface of his suit. He whirls, weapon ready.

"Ho!" she cries, jumping back in surprise.

"What?" he snaps. She glares at him through the glass, then gestures to a dim corner, where a body lies, crumpled and in a pool of dried blood. A human body.

Talbot suddenly is overtaken by an anger that roars behind his eyes until he is nearly blind. His weaponed hand roves across the members of the team. "You bastards," he croaks. It is their fault, he realizes. They have been the killers all along, and they have tried to trap him at last. He sees their ugly faces as they are for the first time. The horrible pattern of tiny spots across the face of Gillian Reed; her thin, bloodless lips and eyelids - ghoulish. Wanr, a predator, adapted for the night, fangs tucked away in the folds of a crude approximation to a mouth, leering in triumph. Steve Hallison, always mocking, laughing behind his back, moving clumsily whenever he was needed most. "It's you," he whispers, mouth tight with hatred. He raises his weapon. To purify with the coherent fire.

But before he can bring the weapon to bear, he feels his biceps clasped in an unyielding grip, and the helmet is torn from his head. An icy touch on his scalp, on his brain. A voice whispers in his ears.

"I know what you are feeling," it says. "I know, because it is the Manganese t'la dirty little secret that they were cursed with emotions before they learned to think. That's part of why they sent me away. They had too much desire, too little control."

He feels cool breath on his cheek.

"But you are not so different from the ones around you and they are all better than the Manganese t'la. Think. Which of them trusted you?"

He remembers a tent on a far world, needing advice. A blond-haired man, young and irreverent. Hallison. The Director, a strange woman.

"Which of them saved your life and guided you through the dark?"

A night of fear as a force beyond their control crashed through the forest, pushing trees aside like sticks. A furry hand on his wrist. Huge eyes that saw more than he expected. Riding in the cabin, not at the controls, afraid.

A strange, blind metallic person with a precise accent, is talking smoothly and assuredly.

"Which cares for you and offers thoughts you need to hear?" A thin woman with tiny wrists, a smooth, tight jaw and a personal attitude like a drill. Asking him how he felt about Steve's ordeal. Her cold eyes on the consoles and her hands on his. Tears on her freckled cheeks, below copper hair. For a moment - Jill. Then the Director. Atrenn. He feels tears shudder into his eyes.

"It's not enough to feel, you have to know," the voice whispers. "There's only one universe. We are all looking at it. To live, we have to see what exists. And that one thing makes us all alike. Because our values come from the universe. Our thought. Our systems. Our lives. We just can't be that different, no matter how different we look or live.

More different as people than as species. More different across time than across space. Do you understand what I mean? I know you don't know how, but you have to know what I mean... You must know why you mustn't do this."

His rage dies like a tide running out under a receding moon.

"I do," he replies.

Latimer's extended fingers leave Talbot's face as Talbot collapses to his knees. Then those same fingers propagate like a fan of lightning to the wall and seem to slip through cracks like a metallic water.

Then the walls begin to steam with a dark, particulate smoke.

204

They step slowly through the ash, like refugees awakening after disaster. Talbot bends to pick up his helmet. He tips it over and shakes out the grey dust inside. He turns to look at Latimer, who stands quietly behind him, revealing a thin metallic smile.

His eyes travel to Jill, who looks stolid and unmoved. He touches her suited hand gently, and she stares at him from behind her faceplate as if she has been shocked with electricity. He smiles and steps away.

Wanr is crouched, weapon presented, black eyes narrow, focused mistrustfully on Talbot. Talbot touches him on the shoulder, and kneels beside him. "I think it's over," he says quietly. "At least, right here, right now."

"What happened, chief?" Hallison straightens, and brushes some of the fine black dust from his suit.

Talbot shakes his head. "I don't know. Maybe Latimer does."

"I'm not sure I know why it worked." The humanoid's gleaming surface reflects the irregular light. The chest shivers slightly, as if breathing. "I was trying to keep Raoul from killing everyone. I persuaded him. With philosophy. And then …"

Jill's eyes rove over the walls and ceiling. "Nonsense. Talking." She snorts skeptically.

Wanr walks over to Latimer and peers up at his metal face. "This... philosophy? - is quite powerful." It is impossible to tell if he is being sarcastic or amazed.

Latimer makes a strange gesture that, to Wanr, is affirmative. "It is, isn't it? Killed it. Dead as a stone."

"Backed up with some force," Talbot replies, gesturing to the walls. "You did something else, too."

"But how could Raoul and you affect it?" Jill asks. Talbot is uncomfortable in the glare of her harsh eyes – he has a fear of having any kind of relationship with the dank black dust that sifts across the tiles or any kind of kinship with the metallic cyber that stands shrouded in dimness from the damaged lights.

"Maybe because I started it?" he wonders out loud. But he is watching Latimer with a skeptical eye.

205

High above the ecliptic, the ancient game of parry and thrust between the constable's maddened ship and the interloper suddenly fades into a silence like exhaustion. The two drift slowly higher above the poles of Tlnou, facing at a distance, beams silent, scars open and cooling redly in the vacuum.

Healing proceeds across the surface of Prometheus spaceceraft, and there is a sudden silence on the chaotic broadcast channels, as if an age of screaming and violence has come to an end.

Then there are tentative voices, quiet, breaking the silence. Data links probe to reacquire networks across a void. Soon, the innocent chatter of machines is reestablished. There are losses, and partitions, but systems too long isolated begin to exchange information, compare their content, and decide about the real relationships of their objects to a world that has changed vastly since they were cut off.

And finally, the Constable's ship sends a standard protocol message to the others, asking what the hell is going on.

206

A war has ended, and the war-bound have regained their freedom with as little understanding as when they lost it.

In the distance, like a secret, an enormous fleet of spacecraft continue to shatter the remnants of a formerly inhabited system. Their origins are unknown. Their purpose is unknown.

The home of the Mover is as lost as ever.

207

Jane Sherril refocuses on the size of the ship, and various parts of it are withdrawn and stored. The ship slims swiftly to a more utilitarian size. Except for the party bubble. She smiles. That will come in handy.

208

On the *Illyrion*, the losses are beginning to be seen amidst the wreckage. In the still smoky atmosphere of the Defense Room, the Director sadly totals the deaths, the injuries, and sets in motion investigations to determine responsibility and initiate prosecution. Decontamination teams with sensors are walking the halls.

The Constable watches the activities of his crew with an even more weighty sense of responsibility. He thinks of his own self-decimated crew. Of the penalties he faces for attacking the *Illyrion*. Of the penalties for attacking a ship from a previously uncontacted society. Penalties his methodical personality must exact in full. He is only consoled by the presence of the Geodesic Counsel in his detention, and his story in the memory of his systems. His hatred of merchants abates as he watches them solemnly reckon their losses.

And in a conference room on the *Illyrion*…"But," Hallison protests, "they didn't know what they were doing."

The Director shrugs, a very human gesture. "The law isn't concerned with intentions, Steve, any more than business can be. Justice is about results, crimes are about effects. Besides, look at Raoul."

Talbot stands frowning in the corner. "Latimer showed me the truth. I didn't do anything." But he still watches Latimer with some level of suspicion.

Latimer lays his hand on Talbot's shoulder. "Truth is everywhere. You have to recognize it. Everyone who murdered, everyone who destroyed, they were as capable of recognizing it as you were. But they didn't, did they? You did. You stopped. Perhaps you at least had a part in stopping it."

Talbot sighs. If only he knew enough to know the truth.

"Come on," Talbot urges her. "I want you to go with me. You haven't seen it. It's a fantastic world. And I need the best help I can get on the sensors. This isn't going to be easy."

Reed stands in the shuttle bay gallery, looking down at the dimly lit graceful shapes, unsure of why she has agreed. Perhaps the odd eagerness of his expression, released after weeks of tension and pressure. Perhaps her own weariness of the smell of ships, the Mover and beings in close quarters. More likely an unaccountable willingness to follow someone who had brought her through what now seems like ages of fragile survival through one impending disaster after another. She wonders if she needs that thrill now, as she once needed order alone.

They quarter the planet in something that seems a hopeless search, tapping networks for transactions, using sensor traces on ancient steppes. Making an attempt that is important to Talbot.

Until, one afternoon, the shuttle settles with a buffeting blast of engines and anti-flame by the side of a lake. An old cabin of native wood shudders in the swiftly quenched wind. In the distance, snow crested mountains rise into a faintly turquoise sky. The ramp descends to the scorched ground.

Talbot stands in the doorway, as if afraid to step out. The strange smells of the world, mixed with smoke and chemical, join with the sounds of lifeforms in a sudden cacophony of sensation. He remembers the last time. Several last times. Reed stands behind him. She pushes briefly at his shoulder. "Come on, let's find out," she urges.

In the doorway of the small home stands Risha, a thin, woman with skin like coal. Behind her, a figure appears from the shadow. A shorter figure, with bluish flesh, and three bulging golden eyes, who rests a many fingered hand on her forearm, as if to restrain her. But she is not moving.

Talbot smiles. It should have been impossible.

Risha watches the stranger walk toward her. A feeling of familiarity grows to certainty. "It's him," she exclaims. Her husband touches her shoulder with his forehead. She smiles at him. "Make some oliatara. We have guests."

Phase 3

Norton and Prometheus

The events in this section of the book begin with a focus on the Prometheus habitat, located in the Galt system, near the southern portion of M4, just inside the edge of the cluster.

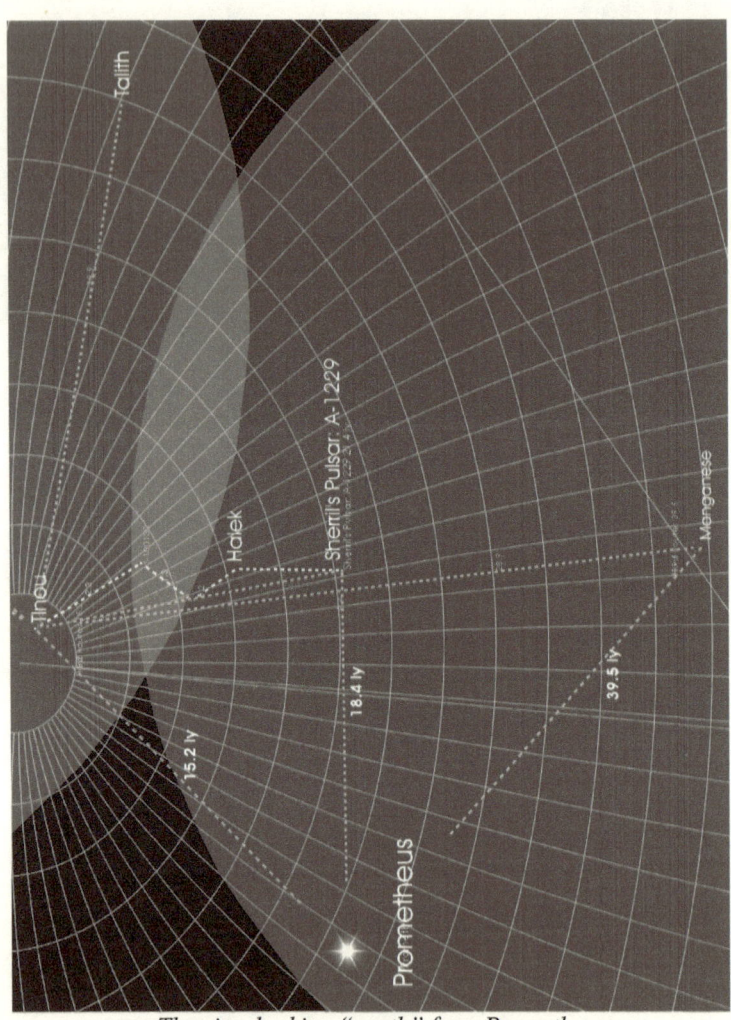

The view looking "north" from Prometheus

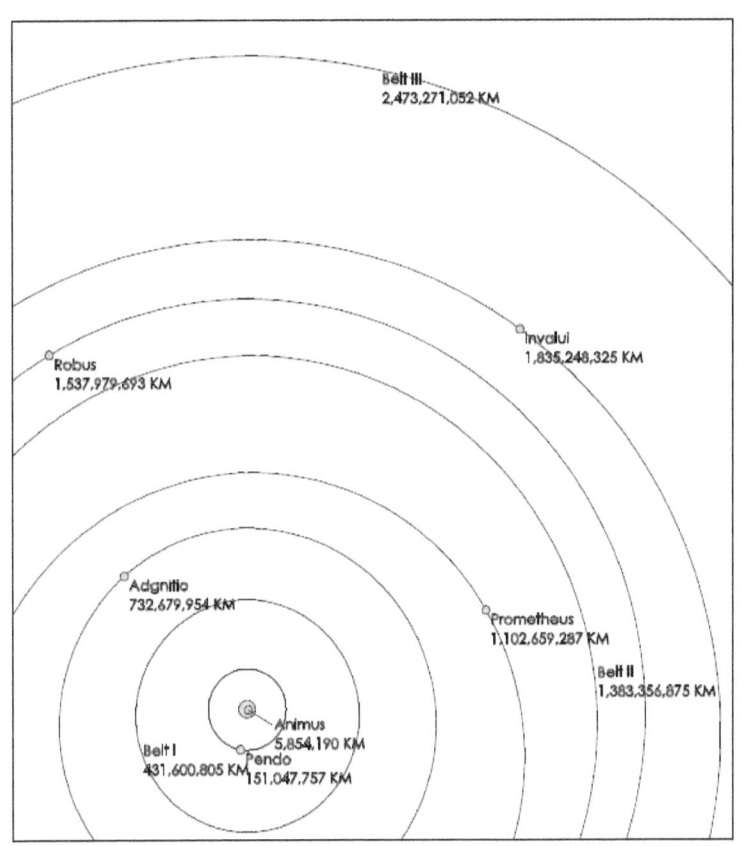

Galt System

Star Galt –
> Spectral Class: F9V, Mass: 1.674 sol, Radius: 1.51 sol, Luminosity: 6 sol

Star Animus –
> Spectral Class: A4, Mass: 0.67 sol, Radius: 0.73 sol, Luminosity: 0.2 sol

Planets:
> Pendo, Belt I, Adgnitio, Prometheus, Belt II, Robus, Invalui, Belt III

210

Behind the door of *Man Also Rises*, Raoul Talbot shifts his feet, scuffing the deck overlooking the ocean. Wanr squats at the railing, peering over into the water, waves reflected in his dark crystal eyes. Finally he looks up to follow Talbot's feet.

"In way how this is like a cage?"

Talbot stops and glares perplexity. "Cage?"

"You exhibit repeated behavior of one trapped in cage."

"Repeated behavior." He turns and leans back against the rail. "I suppose it feels like a cage. What's next? That's what I want to know, and that's what the Director won't tell me. m'Ilu Ram says it's going to be a military matter, and we'll be leaving. I can't blame the Director." He squints into the simulated sun. "There's no money to be made here. But what are we going to do?"

Gillian Reed leans in the doorway, her hair stranded by the artificial breeze, face glowing with the rich turquoise of near sunset light like the panes of glass beside her. "Looks like we're going on an adventure. Setting up a trade mission. And maybe helping to start an alliance."

Talbot sighs. "Let's hope the Geodesic can stand long enough to use an alliance."

Reed's smile hesitates and then slips to a guarded neutrality. "I can't think about that right now."

The door slips open and Wanr peers through. "The Director wants to see you, Raoul…"

211

In the end, the airlock door slides back, revealing a surprising number of beings standing at the brow, garments rustling, speech sibilants whispering from the walls. From the far side, the Manager, a Lipu mollusk, rolls forward in its cart, gentle sprays of salt water on its shell. The shell opens and a rack of blue eyes extends, followed by the glistening tentacle of its manipulator.

"Welcome, Raoul Talbot. Command access key. Of all future harmonies that which you may organize with the key will be the most blended." The metal tab passes from tentacle to hand.

Talbot does what he had practiced. "Supervisor. I am cooled by your trust in my song." He bends down to place his eyes only inches from the Lipu's. He can smell the salt. He waits, and finally the eyes snap into the shell. He stands and smiles. The eyes reemerge, rocking up and down in acceptance.

There is a round of applause from the humans.

Talbot grins. "Let's go see the Prometheans."

212

The flight deck door splits into the wall, and Talbot steps through with a recurring sense of awe.

The *Norton*'s flight deck is an enormous arched volume, softly paneled with stone, wood, displays and smooth expanses of richly figured fractal relief. The consoles are holographic spheres, spaced evenly across the floor, and their operators are seated or standing within them, swiveling, gesturing the programming of control in the symbolism each prefers, muttering meta commands to ensure the proper interpretation of gestures. There is no sense of travel. But in some of the holographic spheres, Talbot can see representations of the stars. It is as close as he may ever come to piloting a full-scale starship.

Sherril's pulsar winks periodically from the walls, spilling its energy into invisible orbiting crystals.

Talbot steps down into the pit and wanders between the posts, to where he can watch the management pilot, as he often does. That pilot, RnaTneya, is a whipcord creature of pale gristle, trilaterally symmetric. Black bulbs hang by wire from bony ridges and shield its triad of eyes from the UV brightness of the dimly lit room. Its extended fingers rise, fall and swirl as it composes and tests.

Talbot remains envious. He barely understands the systems, though his hours during the last few days have been crowded with charts, graphs, text and animations so he can know the capabilities of the *Norton*. The details of the local gestural languages are still largely beyond him, though he can use some of the more basic positions to access food and transport. His eyes rove the room and he lets his breath free.

As a child on Clotinus, he had watched programs about star pilots, and he had played endless games in his home to mimic what he saw. When he became older and more rootless, he had turned back to his childhood for the strength to apply for training.

How many places I've been since then...

He remembers Dynareal training, and then his first trip out. Finally Govault. Tlnou. Most of it so many years ago. His head turns away involuntarily. Years ago for some events, days like centuries ago for others.

RnaTneya swivels in a near copy of the motion.

"Better watch out," Talbot grins, pushing away worrying memory. "Crash us all."

The bony tapered head, two eyes on this side facing, cants at a slight angle and then returns to the vertical.

"Copying me," Talbot finishes. RnaTneya wriggles its fine manipulators in the safe zone, expressing laughter.

I'm actually communicating tersely with it. I think.

RnaTneya gestures, and its own sphere swings up the stars, the remnant and the glowing trajectories of the crystal stations.

213

In the deep rooms of the *Norton,* Latimer, Jane Sherril and a team of Radelix mathematicians try to resolve two disparate coordinate systems so that a curvespace transition to Prometheus will be possible. Hallison stands in a corner of the room, looking on. His translator is making noises, but it might as well be an untranslated alien language for all he understands. Still, he watches, and listens.

"I think a lower operator transform on delta tri epsilon, with a total division under the sigma..."

One of the Tereniades starts clicking raucously. "Look where that ends up!"

Latimer turns a metal gaze on the chart display. "Of course." He pauses in an almost laughable mimic of a thoughtful pose. Then he points at an equation on the panel, and in moments they are again deep in discussion. Hallison sighs and wanders out.

214

"Our society is more highly individual than your own, if you'll pardon my saying so," Latimer replies. Jane Sherril smothers a smile behind her hand. "This means in general that any of the specific oddities of your various peoples are likely to be ignored."

Sherril swivels her chair away from the video wall. Her face is painted pale white today, with a black diamond centered on her left eye. A tall black ponytail rises from the top of her head and spills down her shoulders. "Doesn't mean we don't have a shared core philosophy.

We do. Everyone in Prometheus chose to come there, chooses to stay there, and will be removed if they violate certain fundamental laws. We offer refuge from every kind of oppression. Which means we don't think much of authoritarians. But we behave under the law out of respect for each other. It could be confusing, I suppose."

Reed mocks, "What could be confusing about a population of law-abiding anarchists?"

"Strictly speaking, we are not anarchists," Latimer replies. "We have a government. Just not much of one. After all, there isn't that much for it to do."

Talbot smiles thinly. Worried. *Who will help us, then?*

Hours later, Talbot sits under the desk glow, the room shadowed around him. One wall reflects the estimated image of the space outside the fold, stars shifting very slowly. The panels ranged before him show much more; shifting scenes from a 2D translation of an immersive Promethean entertainment program, a page of text describing cultural trends since the Shutdown.

I'm not a trader, he thinks. For that matter, he feels completely lost. *I've barely got a light knowledge of my own culture, much less trying to understand this.*

He pauses the program, leans back and sighs, hands rough on his neck and shoulders.

I should call Hallison. Maybe he could help.

But some sort of stubborn impulse pushes his hand to gesture the recording to proceed.

"Are you suggesting I have an agenda outside the League?" the older woman asks, lounging on a windowsill that overlooks a strangely curved landscape...

He sighs and calls Steve.

...Watching, Hallison crosses his legs. "Entertainment doesn't travel well, Raoul. Too many implicit concepts, too much fashion. Oh, we can make something of it on novelty, and one of the subsidiaries can try to develop a market for it wherever, but science and tech are the real opportunities."

Talbot shifts uncomfortably in the doorway. "Steve, I need to understand this stuff. How am I going to talk to them? I'm drowning in charts and tables and flows, but somehow I'm missing it."

Hallison picks up a small glass object from the table beside him. "What we're really missing is what the hell is going to happen to home by the time we get back." He pauses, as if wondering whether to broach the subject. "Talked to Jill, lately?"

"No. I told you, I've been studying. You?"

"Yeah. She's doing her job. She's not real happy. But then, she wasn't before we left *Illyrion*, either. Maybe you remember."

Talbot flinches.

"Well, I don't see why not. Everything was fine. We can't do everything, can we? Hell, we did more than anyone can expect to and live. Aren't you just happy to be sitting here right now?"

"I don't know, chief. I've got some bad dreams. I look around corridors a lot more before I go in or out." Beyond simulated windows, two simulated suns slip behind simulated clouds for a moment, dimming the room to a grey tone.

Talbot slaps the doorframe. "Let's give it a rest. We nearly all cracked back there. Let's take the job we have, for a change, and do what we can. If we do this right, and get Prometheus to help, maybe we can be contributing. Right now, I need to get my hands around this one problem that maybe I can handle. And I need you to give me a hand. Listen, let's get together tomorrow and watch this thing end to end. Work on it. See if you can tell me why it's funny. Jane swears it's funny."

215

They break out of fold on the boundary of the system's Oort cloud remnant. Twin stars glint against the barely visible wall of a gently fluorescing nebula a half light year beyond. As Talbot gestures increased magnification, the star grows brighter, but not larger. The companion star begins to resolve at its side. Then a vague trail slides into visibility, ripped tidally from the main star's outer atmosphere into a vast but faint equatorial spiral by its companion's gravity, spreading out through the system toward the *Norton*.

The *Norton* moves slowly into the system from above the ecliptic, watching for comets, asteroids and small planets. Talbot is resentful, watching RnaTneya gesture the vehicle through the outer system. Far ahead, the spark of Jane Sherril's vehicle glints as it moves effortlessly through the complexities of the outer system.

216

Close in to the suns, swimming in the currents of turbulent hydrogen, a more complex object catches the light. It swells slowly into a shape that is very difficult to recognize.

Think of a string of very irregular dark pearls lying on the top of a dresser, dark against the starfield. Pearls which resolve into thousand mile diameter planetoids, linked by massive segmented metal collars hundreds of miles long.

So this is Prometheus.

217

The spaceport, with its vast, windowed caverns, lacking all orientation, filled with massive moving structures, lights, mists and radiations in many frequencies, is bad enough. The first step into Prometheus, however is perhaps even more disorienting... The path beyond is cunningly set stone, lined with hedges and trees. The ground swirls up on all sides like a vast gentle valley, but it never stops. Eventually, the eye follows fields, roads and towns up the distant curve of the world to lose sight of it in the haze behind the sun tube. The tube sheds light on sections of the world - the remaining segments are darkened by slowly passing shadow swaths.

A ground vehicle is waiting a little way down the wooded path. It is wheeled, sleek, complex and gleaming with crisp and tasteful colors, canopied with carefully formed tinted plastics. Talbot thinks of how far he has come, to a place no one he knows has ever seen, and how mundane to admire this lovely and probably simple object of technology in such a context.

218

The porch overlooks a vast curving ocean. Sails shift ever so slowly on the distant rising wall of the world, and there is the cry of seabirds. Distant clouds are forming under the perpetual noon.

The statuesque woman is steel-haired, with a profile that would be classic if it were not slightly gaunt. She smokes a slim cigar. Her chair is drawn back into the shadows of the porch and its vines. Smoke spirals slowly from shadow to sun and back again.

"This is my ancestor Clu, and this is her vacation place," Jane Sherril remarks. Talbot glances between them, and he can see a resemblance. The older woman turns slowly, and the light slices suddenly across her face, etching crisp features that had been lovely in youth and had since been layered with complex experience.

Talbot stares at her, his mouth shifting slowly. Finally he speaks quietly. "I'm sorry, but didn't you say that she established the crystals several hundred years ago?"

Jane Sherril turns to the older woman for the answer. "Well, gran, what was it, four hundred?"

"Jane, you know I don't keep track like that." The older woman's voice is surprisingly melodious, and her brows kink in a normal way as she retrieves the recollection. "Let's see, it was back in forty-nine, wasn't it, so that would make it, oh, three seventy, three seventy five, I guess. Lan would know." She takes a smooth draw on the cigar and breathes it out into the gentle breeze. She stands and stretches out a hand to Talbot in a gesture used among humans for millennia. "I'm Clu Sherril. And you are?"

"Raoul Talbot."

"Jill Reed."

"Wanr." Wanr accepts the hand with small furry fingers, though his custom is a hug.

"I've never met anyone like you, Wanr," Clu replies. "Where are you from?"

"I don't know your referents, Clu Sherril. I come from a red giant system a little further in toward the center of the cluster, born on the colonized third planet."

"A cold world?" She asks, squatting down to match his height, eyeing his fur.

"Yes, sometimes."

She smiles. "I think Atlantis is running winter right now, perhaps you'd enjoy that."

"Atlantis?" Talbot asks.

Clu looks up at him. "One of our worlds. Planetoids, you might say? I think Jane has been using that word, am I right? They each have names. I came originally to Haven, one of the first two, although I wasn't born there, but now I live in Rand's Hope."

"Gran, I'm afraid we won't have too much time for travel. These people are here to establish a trade deal, and maybe an alliance."

Clu stands with a sudden rush, and eyes them narrowly. "A military alliance, is that what you're saying, Jane?"

"Can't we wait for the formal session on this? It's not exactly courteous to be having this conversation when our guests have only just arrived."

Clu frowns slowly. "Of course." She draws on the cigar. Her exhalation travels out over the edge of the deck as she looks away down the vast cylinder of her world. "Perhaps we need to get the flyer and go home for dinner."

219

Below, the shell of Rand's Hope is largely ragged conifer forest and mountains, just beginning to be developed with scattered roads and settlements. Through the distant opening to the next world, the suntube is scaffolded and dark. There is a cool wind gusting from that opening, streaking the clouds into fine feathery cirrus in the blue haze below.

"Someone is always trying to keep two worlds ahead of the current development. We have to have wild places where no one can go easily. We need mountains and forests and waterfalls that no one's ever seen.

There's a big market for the new world when an old one starts getting urban." Jane Sherril pauses to smile at him. "This seems a little odd to you."

"I've never imagined anything like this place," Talbot replies. "How old is it?"

Sherril relaxes. It is the right kind of question. "Over five thousand years, probably. No one's sure, really – there's a lot we still don't know. The first four worlds were the originals, found derelict. That was about six hundred years before Clu came. They were heroes back in those days. Ice cold atmosphere, what there was of it. No life. Systems wrecked or ripped out. Hard to believe how much we've built since." Her dark hair shifts with the breeze of the ventilator. "But Rand's Hope is a lot younger than that. Of course, Crystal Energy has a lot to do with the new worlds."

220

The ornithopter backwings gently, pinions swirling dust and dead leaves from the pad as it settles in the yard of the Sherril home.

Talbot finds his legs still weak as he steps from glossy streamlined cabin to stable ground. Powered wing travel had been beyond his experience until today. Now he has experienced it twice. Reed looks on as he joins her.

"I'm OK," he replies to her unanswered question. "I just never did this before."

She shrugs, flippant. "So who has?"

They walk away together into an arbor of tall woody funnel plants that leads to the house. The sound of the ornithopter engines whines into muffled silence behind them.

"What do you think?" Reed asks, eyes ahead.

"What do I think? Hardly matters. What's Steve think, that's what I want to know. He's more qualified to judge this than I am."

"Raoul," she cautions, shortening the vowel to Rawl, as she always does when she is warning him.

He looks around, but he knows the action is meaningless. These people have a technology that makes eavesdropping undetectable.

"It's a little scary," he replies, finally. "This place. Well, you saw everything I did. They might be able to help."

"Yeah."

"But?"

"But the place looks like a resort. These people don't look like warriors to me."

"Remember the Constable? Maybe he made the same mistake about us."

There is only the sound of their feet on the glossy stone of the path.

221

Dinner is held in a large wood-and-glass walled room that looks back into the forest. They file in quietly, taken with the view and the strange but attractive smells of food.

The table is low to the floor, accommodating almost any species. It is oval, ensuring the absence of precedence conflicts. The hosts are asymmetrically spaced, offering no clue as to relationship. But they both smile and stand, almost like sisters, close to the grace of dancers.

"Is the table suitable, Raoul?" Clu asks in her slightly raspy tones. Behind her, a poster plays a long vid of strange streamlined creatures wheeling and distancing in the texture of a supernova remnant. "Wanr?"

Talbot nods. Wanr bows deeply. "It is more than acceptable, it is home."

"You do us great honor," Jane responds quickly. "Keep us in your eyes."

Talbot is unnerved by an involuntary shudder – the comment reminds him of how much these people know about the Geodesic. *They have been watching us for a long time and in great detail. But from where? By what means?*

Hallison takes the lead, asking, "Do you have any special structure to your meals? Any practices we should observe?" He has seen no sign they are deeply ritualized in this society. They seem to take on characters and forms like actors wear roles. He is uneasy, as he often is with sophisticated societies.

"Eating everything unless you don't like it?" Jane replies impishly.

"Good thing you're human," Hallison replies, trying to ride the spirit of the thing. "Otherwise I might have to ask if you meant it."

222

Hallison knocks softly on the door. Talbot thrashes violently in his bed at the sound, dreams leaping from silence to horrifying lucidity.

The door opens a crack, letting soft warm light flow across the floor and paint the walls beyond. Talbot starts up; his blankets slip away into the bed. His eyes are wide and white in the dimness. Hallison is silent, waiting for Talbot to fully awaken.

"You okay, Raoul?" he asks, quiet. His eyes are sleepy, but his mouth is alert.

"What do you mean?" Talbot complains. "Of course. Or at least, I was until you woke me up. Damn, what a nightmare."

"I could hear you through the wall. What the hell are you dreaming about?"

Talbot shakes his head, eyes heavy lidded with regret. "Same stuff. Atrenn's lost in some ship, I'm hunting for him, the planet killers are on their way. I find him, he's dead." He rubs his eyes. They feel hot and tired. His arms and legs feel unsteady, as if they are shaking to a tiny but violent rhythm he cannot hear. "Oh, Steve, I'm sick of this."

Hallison squats beside the bed. The door slides softly almost closed. "What are you sick of?"

" Do you know if the Geodesic is still there? Tlnou?"

Hallison glances down at the floor for a moment, and then back up. "Do you suppose you're the only one who wonders, chief? I never told you, but Jill's been having me call through fold every twelve hours, relay through the *Norton*. Making sure everything's still there."

Talbot feels less trembling, but it is not gone. His throat is tight, and he wishes he could cry. "And is it, Steve? Is it?"

"Yeah, it's still there, for now. Let's hope we get this negotiation right tomorrow so that's still going to be true, chief. What do you think?"

Talbot wipes an eye with the back of his hand. "I don't know. You're the cultural guy. What the hell I'm doing being point for this, I just don't know. Can we get a military alliance with these people? We're not even negotiating with their government, if they have one."

"Oh, they have one." Hallison sits back on the floor, eyeing Talbot, arms crossed, legs folded.

Talbot leans up, interested. "What's it like?"

"Loose, federated. Multi-layer. There's a Promethean government, which doesn't do much except mediate legal issues between the worlds, and set up a uniform external policy that the members have to follow. The world governments have responsibility for the relations between the urbs, and the urbs do most of their lawmaking with reference to the common code for the world they're in. But, I'll tell you, there isn't much law, no matter how you look at it. No regulation. It's all retributive. The retributions are damn harsh, though, chief."

215

"Who does self-defense?"

"I can't tell. They all seem to be involved in self-defense. There are weapons everywhere. For sale, even. But not to us. Members only."

"What are we going to do?" Talbot groans.

Hallison stands awkwardly, and lays a hand on Talbot's arm. "Take what we've got, and let's see how far we can get it to go. Look, the Geodesic sends in government people to negotiate - and believe me, they will be planning that if they have time - these people are going to recoil. They do not want to deal with authorities. And for reasons I don't have to bring up, it's better this way. We have their trust, they like merchants, businesspeople. Let's make the most of that, and see if they'll accept us by that route."

"It'd help if I knew who I was going to negotiate with."

"They aren't getting explicit with it yet, so let's not push. We'll find out soon enough. Tomorrow. Or is it today?"

Talbot glances at his watch patch. "Today," he sighs. "OK, Steve."

223

Talbot isn't sure, but when he steps into the hallway, it seems that the layout has changed. Then he realizes. Hallison's room had been across the hall. But where the door had been, the wall is blank wood slats. He raises an eyebrow in surprise. Then a door down the hall slides back.

"I could have sworn that was a swing door," Hallison mutters.

"I could have sworn you were across from me," Talbot replies.

"I was."

Their eyes meet, but there is nothing safe to say.

224

They eventually find the breakfast room. Wanr is already gnawing on something where he sits cross-legged by the wall of windows. He glances up and waves a set of fingers in a gesture of negation. He hasn't seen their hosts.

A variety of foods are on a waist high buffet opposite the window, human food carefully separated from that which Wanr prefers. Talbot wanders past, looking over the breakfast. "Hmm," Gillian Reed is suddenly looking over his shoulder. Very close.

"Hi Jill," Talbot is surprised. She seems relaxed and comfortable. Her smell is clean and he wonders if she has been able to bathe here somehow.

"Ready for the day's work?" she asks.

He sighs and looks back along the table. "Yeah. Sure. You?"

"You bet."

He recognizes her enthusiasm.

"Good," he replies. "I need you to handle as much as you can."

Her eyes are level and she isn't smiling any more. "I know. You'll do fine. Just stick with me. Here, try some of this, it's wonderful."

225

The platform is at the edge of a cliff that overlooks the ocean. Its glossy squares reflect the lowering clouds, and click or whisper with their footsteps. They take seats, and small tables unfold from the side of the comfortable chairs.

Finally, Clu and Jane arrive down the path from the house. They take chairs and Jane smiles at the group. "Hope you won't mind our informal negotiation style. I know it's a little different from your society's 'table dominated' way of negotiating, but we find this to be very productive."

"It's not a problem, Jane," Talbot replies. Reed glances encouragement at him, her face unreadable to anyone else.

"OK. Well, first, I will be negotiating for Sherril Externality; Clu is here as the representative of the Prometheus level government to make sure we meet the legalities required by that law, and the marshal over there is watching Clu to make sure she does that."

Talbot relaxes.

"Also, I'm required to ask if you would have any problem with recording or broadcast of this session."

Talbot glances at Hallison, thinking, So much for relaxation. "Any comments, Steve?"

"Normally we consider negotiations to be private, so that all views can be aired, and mistakes made."

Jane nods. "We prefer to negotiate in public so that people say what they mean, and so that everyone's careful. What do you think?"

Talbot thinks they have just been placed in an extremely difficult position. But, at the same time, he is feeling some of the same bravado that powered him diving toward the planet destroyer in the wake of a meteor.

"I don't see why not," he replies. Jill and Steve are both trying to be stone-faced, but he can feel the pressure of their restrained glares.

"But," he continues, "what can you offer me in return?"

There is a pause. Clu Sherril raises a hand. "Perhaps before we begin to negotiate, you would like to allow your systems to complete their integration with ours, in case we need to record any agreements."

Talbot glances at Reed, who nods. Hallison transmits with a private code to verify, but Talbot knows well enough that there may be no secure transmission mode anywhere in Prometheus. And he knows that he has no idea of what may happen to their systems as a result of this interface. He nods. "We have our private net."

Reed continues. "And the gateway seems to be working properly. We can start."

Jane continues. "So what can we offer you in return for what should be a normal negotiating process?"

Talbot glances at the others, but they are blank faced. "Rights to the recording. After all, there will be some amount of interest in the Geodesic, and this might be one of the few entertainments you have that can be an immediate export. What do you say?"

Jane glances up from her tablet, frowning. "You split Geodesic royalties with us."

"Deal, if you split yours with us."

Jane taps her pad with a stylus. Talbot watches the contract appear from the gateway onto his pad. He forwards it to Wanr, who is holding watch on the *Norton*, working on the legal equivalency database. "I'll have our staff look it over."

"Do you want to wait?"

Steve leans over to Talbot. "Let's take it as an agreement in principle, and if there's any negotiation, we can take it up later. I think they admire directness and willingness to work on faith within limits."

"We'll hash out the details later," Talbot replies to Jane. Jill raises a hand. "But the agreement will be retroactive if the negotiations are broadcast."

He worries again that he has to negotiate. His training is incomplete. He has no real experience. But he is trusted to do a First Contact negotiation. Reed had outlined it earlier. "They trust you already. Changing trust in midstream is not a good idea. You have plenty of experienced backup to help keep you in line. The Director knows that. Remember, it's her career if you screw up. Don't screw up."

Her career! he thinks.

His hands are feeling a little unsteady, but he grips the pad a little more tightly and presses the hand more firmly into the top of his leg.

*It's a beautiful day, I'm having an adventure with a lot of responsibility.
I can handle it.*

226

Talbot stands at the mirror wall, dressing formally. As his hands seal
the seams of the complex dark garment up to the high, angular collar,
he is looking at his own eyes. His hands draw the depilator across his
jaw, but he is still looking occasionally for some mark, or wrinkle, or
narrowing, or color change.

But everything seems to be the same.

He stands back, turns to the side, and considers the profile of the
suit. He pins a gold insignia to his lapel.

*Everything fine, dressed in a suit, civilization being destroyed... just
another night in the far reaches of the galaxy. What am I doing?*

The door closes behind him. Unfortunately, the layout of the house
has changed again and the door has moved, so it takes him a while to
find his way out.

227

Talbot waits at the ornithopter pad, looking out over the vast core of
the world as night sweeps toward him. The lights of cities and towns
glitter into grids of stars on the leading edge of the shadow. A strange
illusion, but a saving one, providing a diurnal schedule, but on its own
time scale.

"Talbot, come on, are you ready?" The voice is Jill's. He holds up a
hand but doesn't turn to look. "I want to see the sunset," he replies.

There is a breeze, and in a moment, the clouds are etched with a
sienna flash. Then it is twilight, as the shadow races on, pushing away
the sunlit band on the wall of the world. Above, the cities are the stars.
There is a touch on his arm, and he turns to see a woman he doesn't
recognize.

Her face is limned with the sienna and the faint light of the distant
wall, mixed with the cool blue emitted by the far side of the world.
Eyes might be blue, and there are delicate suggestions of freckles. Her
hair is an indeterminate color, but not as dark as brown. She is smiling
quietly. It is the smile that triggers his memory and connects this face
with Gillian Reed.

But she is dressed in a soft black dress that clings carefully to every contour, ending on her mid-thigh. A small diamond glitters on her forehead, its light changing with every breath, and every expression.

"Come on, chief, we're going to be late!" Hallison shouts from the door to the ornithopter. The engines start spinning up.

228

The ornithopter flaps slowly above the towns and cities. It is not much different from being in space, except for the faint signs of a ground illuminated with the bluish light of the lighted surfaces, and the obvious geometry of the world shown by the way the lines of buildings and roads line its cylinder.

The wall of the ornithopter is glass, looking from dimness to darkness. Talbot watches the flow of the clouds, the ground, and the vast structure of the suntube, somehow never tiring of the scene. Wanr sits beside him, conversing with Hallison across the aisle about some point of legality. Jane smiles from the left seat.

The wings form into a gliding configuration, and the ornithopter descends toward the distant clouds and the ground beyond.

There is a brief rain shower as they step to the platform. But the drops only deliver their sound to the travelers – their wetness is spent somewhere above. In a plaza studded with sculptures representing the physical optimum of many species, ringed with trees and sleek buildings, they walk with Jane and Clu to a large low table.

The chef is a mass of bluish tentacles moving with a startling swiftness and stopping into an equally startling rigidity. Its kitchen looks like a fantasy of some kind of foundry, with spurting flames and hissing oils.

They are perched on the wall of a cup fifteen miles across, a vast indentation in the fabric of the world, and a sign of the sophistication of Promethean gravitational engineering. The cavity opens before them, above the thinning clouds into the world, and the cities beyond are even more an illusion of stars. A breeze stirs trees around the plaza. Talbot can feel the cool moisture.

The food, though strange, is excellent, a combination of various unfamiliar meats and vegetables quick seared in the flames on rods. As each course arrives, Wanr's assistant, a lean D*Azar, leans its blind metallic snout over the food, and manipulates a sensor over its radome to determine its safety for each species' metabolism. So far, only Wanr has had to reject food. A single spear of bluish cabbage-like vegetables was unsafe.

A small circle of musicians play unfamiliar instruments in complex intertwined melodies. The sounds are strangely attractive, though sometimes they seem to be no more than a windy, chaotic noise. Talbot finds himself tapping his fingers in time to the odd time signatures. And his eyes keep finding Jill across the table. Her eyes catch the candlelight and reflect it back toward him, whenever she glances toward him, which is not often.

"This is great, Jane," Hallison comments. She smiles. Clu is half swiveled in her chair watching the band. She glances over with an unreadable expression, then returns her attention to the players.

"By the way, Jane," Talbot asks, "I've been wondering about Latimer."

She is surprised, and she leans away from the table to gesture at the band. "Didn't you see him?" she replies.

His eyes follow her gesture, and then he notices the metallic figure playing a wood breath instrument, swaying with the surge of the music in a counter-rhythm. "Latimer," he whispers. "So where's he been?"

"He's been away from the band for months, and he knew we'd ask them to play this party, so he wanted to be able to rehearse a little first."

The current music sweeps into a devastating silence, and then Clu and Jane slap their fingers on the edge of the table. Applause, Talbot realizes, joining in. It hurts a little.

Then Latimer is gesturing, and Clu is standing, and the band is applauding. The percussionist, a blue tentacled sphere of the same genera as the chef, rattles its drum, and a strange dark creature with a ring of brassy eyes appears with a large, glossy white stringed instrument. A cello, Talbot remembers being told. Clu takes the cello and bow from the creature and lowers her head. He nods in return, and backs away.

There is silence as she takes a stool at the front of the small orchestra. The silence is utter, except for the distant sound of the rain. She raises the bow, and the light of the cooking fires flickers against her as she attacks the instrument. Sudden, urgent sounds resonate. The other musicians sway, but resist the tug of the music for as long as they can. Finally they one by one slip into the thread of the theme.

Jane laughs. "They're improvising. She loves doing it to them."

Talbot stares, shocked. "You mean, they're making it up? Right now?"

"Yeah!"

He laughs. "As if I could tell, of course."

221

"You don't have music?"

"Not like this."

"Come on, you dance?"

"No," he replies, shocked.

"Good," and she reaches over the table and grabs his hand, tugging him around to the plaza.

229

The dinner winds down, and they walk back to the ornithopter. Talbot is sipping at an invigorating drink in a slim crystal glass when Reed touches his arm. A little of the drink skitters out of the glass and falls to the ground.

Talbot looks to her, and he sees that she is angry. He wonders why. But it is only a moment before he finds out.

"This is taking too long. When are you going to get to the military aspects of the alliance? They know we need it. They have to. Every day we play around here getting to know each other, is one more day for that thing to get closer to Tlnou and the rest of everything."

"Jill, these people hardly know us. We need their trust. Not just Jane and Clu, but all of the worlds, here. We're asking these people to fight alongside us. Why should they fight and die for people they don't know? Or care about."

"So when are you going to ask?"

"Why the hell are you riding me? What the hell is it you hate so much? Is it that I have this team? That this is my mission? What?"

"You used to run by the seat of your pants. Now you're timid. You're spending time dancing with that damn woman when three million people are dead and more are on the butcher block. That's what I can't deal with." She reaches up toward his face, open hand, and he flinches, thinking she's about to slap him, but her hand stops, and gently runs over his cheek, and Jill is looking suddenly very sad. She steps past him into the ornithopter, and takes a seat beside the pilot and stares fixedly into space.

230

Talbot looks past the window wall at the wind-shivering trees beyond, waiting. A breeze drifts through the screen. He reaches out and presses a hand on the glass beside the chair. Sun from the endless noon pools on the porch beyond, dappled by the shadow of leaves. Finally, Clu Sherril replies.

"Raoul, I can tell you that I'm impressed to see the Geodesic businesspeople asking for an alliance. It shows you have spirit and self-reliance. I like that."

He turns to her. "I won't lie to you, Clu. I might want to, but I can't. One reason is that we're not entirely sure our government will back us up. There's some evidence that part of our government may actually be dealing with the xenophobes for reasons of their own."

Her expression becomes still and silent. "I see."

Finally she continues. "No promise of cooperation, and they might fight us."

Now it is Talbot's turn to weigh a response. He elects to stick with the truth. Trust is going to be important. But he feels a sinking in his chest as he answers. "Yeah."

"Or are you trying to get us involved in your civil war?"

"I hope not," Talbot replies.

"This should be dealt with in public." She sighs. "We'll have to do all this again out on the platform, you know." Her face creases at the corners of the eyes, and her lips purse as if slightly dry. "You need to understand how we do defense here. It's not so much a function of Prometheus. There are three companies that compete to provide defense to Prometheus under contract. They handle deployment. They're the experts. But every world has its militias, and then there are the spaceborne militias under contract to guard the transports." She takes a draw from her cigar and exhales the aromatic smoke into the sunlight where it wheels and disperses. "When some governments talk about defense, they're just making a euphemism for war - but here, we take the meaning of words to be what they are. And we only do defense. We may stretch the idea sometimes, but the idea that we might deploy in your systems, that we might attack without provocation, I'm afraid, is misguided. I may or may not agree, but that's the law."

His smile is bitter. "I think I'm hoping your law is on our side."

"We get involved when we have to. We're not altruists. It's why we never lose."

"I'm afraid you're not going to have that luxury this time," Talbot mutters. He stands. "You'd better think it over. And talk to Jane. I would have thought she would have told you what we've seen."

231

They meet on the platform under lowering clouds. There is the distant sound of a transport vehicle like the sound of a long, drawn-out scratch against the sky.

Clu's place is taken by something like a stump with two large stalked eyes. The tips of its roots lash occasionally, as if driven by some demon. "I extend explanation," it speaks in a resonant baritone, "but Clu Sherril is not attending. I have been briefed sufficient to the day."

Talbot smiles over at Steve. Promethean translation technology is better, but the semantic problems are still sufficient as well. He glances at Reed, but she is stony faced. "At least you asked," she whispers. He shrugs. "Today's when it counts. Besides, she said no."

"Try again. We have to get them to agree."

So he begins the argument again, leveraging Steve's presentation materials. Jane listens, stony faced, and the alien is unreadable.

232

Wanr meets them on the walkway, pelt fluffed with fear, posture straight with worry. "There's been a failure in the link to Tlnou," he whispers to the translator.

"Fold collapse?" Reed asks past Talbot's shoulder.

"Pinched to reflect," Wanr replies. His eyes glint and flicker as they shift rapidly from side to side. "Completely snapped back."

"What does that mean?" Talbot asks.

Wanr pushes his head uncomfortably close to Talbot's face. "It means that the receiver has been moved, disabled or destroyed."

233

"So what does this mean," Talbot shouts, confronting Jane Sherril in the garden. Jane strips off the gloves and looks regretfully down at her plants. Her eyes are slightly metallic with reflections, and Talbot wonders if it is just a trick of the light, or some effect from something on her eyes.

"I have no idea," she replies. She looks off toward the distant curvature of the world, eyes narrowed with the distance. "Remember, my grandmother's out there, too."

"I noticed she wasn't here. What's she doing?"

"Checking out your story."

He wants to cry, but a sigh is the best his exhaustion can manage. "Well, maybe she found out we were telling the truth. But a little late. Are you in touch with her? Can you call her?"

Jane rubs her forearm, once. "Yeah." She looks up at the house. "We have a signal rendezvous this evening. I'll come get you when it's time."

He nods and turns back to the house. He doesn't see how Jane's eyes watch him up the path.

234

"We're about a light day outside the system now, and we're going into fold at the slightest sign of aggression from them."

The location is a darkened basement room walled with what seem like openings. One is a window on Clu Sherril, sprawling on a recliner, her face younger than its nearly five hundred years in the sourceless lighting of her control center. Another is a plot of a solar system, neon lines and unreadable symbols against the dark. Last is a crisp fold telescope view of the inner system.

Jane whispers at his side and he smells a faint fresh perfume. "She's talking about Tlnou."

He looks over to her. His voice shakes a little. "You didn't tell me she was going there."

Jane frowns apologetically in the dimness. "It's the only place we knew how to go to on short notice."

Reed is standing with Wanr by the screen, peering at the diagrams that show the Tlnou system. She looks back at the others. "Am I right? There are things that shouldn't be there, near the Oort ring."

Apparently, Clu can hear her. "Yeah, you can see better, this way, but it's a little blurrier." She lights a cigar, gestures, and the image of the system grows more magnified in the other window. A set of specks appear on the schematic, orange. In the image window, there are blurry faint tiny spheres against the images of stars and nebulae. Their motion, if any, is so small as to be invisible. They are the size of giant planets.

"We're seeing some gravitational effects already, disruptions in the comet reservoir. It'll be centuries though, before anybody insystem sees any of that. We're getting ready to trip fold a probe into the formation, with a double link to you and to us, in case anything does go wrong. Have you folks met :Listarof: ?"

A suited figure with a bug-like helmet leans into the image background and waves.

"Anyway, :Listarof: is programming the probe right now for me, it's the best there is for that. We should know more soon."

Reed stands in front of the screen facing Clu. Her hands are on her hips and her eyes reflect Clu's image. "What more is there to know? How many more have to die for you to make up your mind?"

Hallison is looking away, slumped, leaning on the wall beside the door.

"My mind's made up, girl, but you're just a little impatient. I'm not the only one you have to convince. There are four hundred million people in Prometheus, and you have to convince every one of them, not just me. So do I. Give us the chance."

Wanr steps up beside Reed and takes her arm. "We want to give you time, Clu Sherril," he announces. "But hurry you must."

A voice makes a strange sound in the background. Clu smiles. "That's :Listarof:, the probe's away, folks. :Listarof:'s translator doesn't do Basal yet, so I'll have to do the intermediate stuff for you for now."

A fourth panel lights with distorted images from the speeding probe.

Talbot stirs uncomfortably. The images remind him of his own flight into the depth of the fleet. He has a night feeling about the probe. He doesn't want to see what it is about to show. He doesn't want to be standing in this room amidst the pleasant scent of Jane Sherril, the odd must of Wanr, with the sweaty fear of Hallison at his back. The immobility is suddenly terrifying, as if the xenophobes could race down the link to where he waits so silently.

Gradually, the blurred specks are resolving at the end of the tunnel. They are taking on dimension and shadow. And they are, finally, walls like planets, fragmentary atmospheres from ancient leakages clinging in the cold dawn of their approach to Tlnou. Strange symbols and bumps contour their vast sides. Energy lances out from them, randomly disintegrating thinly swarming condensations in the Oort ring as the probe begins its flyby.

Chambers light all along the basement walls to display the images in various wavelengths and modalities. The radio noise of the fleet is played in various soft fractal melodies, whose voices are subtly menacing.

In the distance is a sound of Basal, distorted and noisy. "...ighter 697, ice freighter 697 declaring emergency .... ostile ... fire" Then the transmission is silent. A window overlays another, showing a blurry slow motion replay of the destruction of a far outsystem ice freighter by a directed energy beam from the fleet.

226

"It looks like some kind of automatic response," Clu is saying.

"So how much attention do they have to pay to get rid of a tiny thing like that?" Hallison speaks up. "It's like killing a mite. But they won't stop there."

A sibilant sound. ":Listarof: reports activity is not entirely random, but there is no complete pattern. Not all items are being interdicted. Small amounts of damage are being done to the fleet by comet impact."

Jane turns to Talbot and lays a hand on his arm. "It's going to be hours before anything changes. Maybe you folks want some rest." She glances at Reed and Wanr. "Or a ride back to the *Norton*? We can relay the transmission and also bring you up to date with the recordings we've been making."

"We should go back," Reed insists. "Who knows what's going on with the team?"

Talbot is torn. The data is addictive. There will be negotiations in seven hours. Everyone in the room is distressed, and no one on the *Norton* has the slightest idea about this new data. But the negotiations…

"Clu, what's going to happen?" Jane asks. "Are you coming back for tomorrow?"

A brief lag as the signal passes the fold. Clu stirs and draws on her cigar. "Yeah," she replies. "I'm coming back in time."

235

The car sweeps down the road with a faint rushing. The trees and crisp glowing images of signs and billboards, mostly incomprehensible, grow, slide and flash past. Talbot rests his head against the clear dome, feeling its coolness on his temple. The darkness rests his eyes. But his heart is pounding helplessly, and he feels as if his lungs are exhausted, taking the merest sips of air.

Jill stirs, half asleep, on the seat beside him, leaning against the far window. In the front, Wanr and Jane keep up a quiet conversation, but he finds himself unable to muster the attention to follow their words.

At the end of the curve, they move quietly to a stop under a circle of lights. The airlock admits them into the hallway, and Talbot waves tiredly at Jane. He can't stop the recurring images of Clu watching Tlnou.

236

Sleep is difficult, wrestling with the fear and the pressure to actually do something. So he shakes and writhes and sweats with anger. And the images crowd his mind, until he is finally dreaming, but the dream is a nightmare of energy boiling a city away into vapor, the ground glowing away into whispers of screams in vacuum. Then he is awake again, hand hammered briefly against the wall.

237

After a dreamless silent period, Talbot suddenly awakens. For a few moments he wonders why. Then, he hears the sound of things being broken, some shouting from the other side of the door.

In an instant, he is on his feet and standing by the door, listening. There are strange, untranslated words and screams. He steps quickly back to the bed and unholsters his laser. He slaps the power pack into place at his waist, and watches the quick self-test complete to blue. Then he is at the door again, weapon raised as it slips aside.

He is in the hallway and the noise is louder there, but in the complex light and shade, there is nothing but volume to tell the direction of the source. He turns right and races down the narrow hall.

At the turn, he can see the melee spilling out of a room into the hall. Wanr's security staff is tight against the walls, out of the line of sight of the door, through which objects are being thrown. Hallison notices Talbot, and gestures Talbot's weapon down before walking over.

"It's not that kind of problem," he states. "Wanr's lost it in there. He's breaking up his room."

"What?"

Hallison nods. "Yeah, chief, it's a ritual with them. When death is near, they destroy their possessions."

"Wanr's dying?" Talbot asks, shocked.

"No, no. It's the situation. He's lost hope we can solve the problem."

"Damn it, he's spent too much time with m'Ilu Ram."

Hallison is looking back at the room, but Talbot's comment catches his attention. "Oh. Yeah, the fatalism thing. No, this is Pandalin."

"But bad security."

"Bad security?"

"What the hell is it about the security profession... Will he talk to me?"

Hallison spreads his hands. "Maybe."

Talbot steps to the door, and instantly flinches as a flying object flies just past his face. "Wanr," he yells. "Come on, it's me!"

The furry creature stands at the far side of the room, by a case of elaborate fiber and glass. To Talbot, his expression is completely blank and alien. Suddenly, Wanr whirls like a dervish, and slams himself into the wall. Frightened of Wanr's unknown manic strength, Talbot still forces himself to walk forward to where the Pandalin is standing straight, legs slightly buckled, face to the wall, huge eyes lidded under thin fur. He can see Wanr's chest rippling with oddly distributed breaths. And then his hands are moving slowly out, in a human comforting gesture, to clasp the upper section of Wanr's arm. He almost stops. Then he touches the fever hot fur and his fingers close. He feels a muscle twitch under his fingers. "Wanr, please. It's not over yet. Don't let go too soon. Stay with me on this. I need your help."

Wanr speaks softly and the translator informs Talbot. "I am like you and doomed. What to believe in is left? Prometheus will not help, Tlnou will be gone in days, and soon the rest of our homes, our traditions, our ... everything." His voice trails into a faint gasp.

Talbot sighs. He wants to not think about these issues, because considering them will only cloud any chance of surmounting them. "I hear you," he whispers. "I know. It seems true. Maybe we should give up. We thought we killed them with ideas, but the physical threat... I don't know what we're going to do. No one is ready for this. Not me, not you, not Jane, not Jill, not Clu. But we haven't even started yet, and I know you have good ideas. Ideas we'll need if we're going to win." He pauses. Wanr never moves. Talbot tugs at his arm. "Come on, we need to do some brainstorming. Steve's waiting for us." Wanr allows the pressure to shift him stiffly from the wall. His eyes open and their surface ripples as they focus and regain hard reflectivity. Wanr's white lips stretch and curl down at the corners. So he is strengthening, Talbot remembers.

Outside the door, Hallison, gestures the security staff away, and then takes a cocky stance across the hall.

"Can't leave during ritual. No additional hope given can be, must complete." Wanr's eyelids seem to be flickering in pulses across his glossy eyes. "What hope when everything dies in the end?"

Talbot stops, hands in mid gesture. Finally, he finds words. "Wanr, I don't have all of the answers. But I know giving up is wrong. Being alive is not giving up. Everything's trying to kill you. The gravity, the germs, the air, the vacuum, the entropy. The second you give up, you die. And if you give up this time, everything's going to die. Everything you care about. What are you going to do, stand in the ruins and complain that there was nothing you could do about it? Or if it comes to that, are you going to be able to say - 'at least I tried'?"

Wanr whirls, first one way, then another. Then he looks up at Talbot's hard eyes. "I want to, Raoul. If I could. I can't, no, can I? How?"

Talbot leans forward, earnest. "Come with me," he replies, slowly. "Come with me, and help me brainstorm. Work with me and help me figure out what we can do."

"You will not mind? You will trust me still?"

Talbot smiles carefully. "Of course. Come on, let's get to the conference room."

As they walk out, Hallison steps next to Talbot and whispers. "Good job chief. But don't touch them when they're depressed. You almost blew the whole thing."

Talbot shakes his head. "Thanks, Steve. I can see we're going to have spend more time together. You suppose we could work out a deal on a cross-brain transplant?"

238

He slips quietly into the strange bed. Darkness seems close and comforting. And though the tug and play of ideas had not led to a closure, he knows that Wanr is reengaged. Unfortunately, the thrill of his heart will not let him rest or sleep. He tries to think of a song, but what he hears is Wanr's voice.

239

They step back into Prometheus, and it is raining under a cold grey sky. Reed touches Talbot's arm. "Where are they?"

There are vehicles, parked, drops glistening as they run down the glossy bright surfaces. But Jane Sherril is nowhere to be seen.

There is a distant sound of thunder. The rain falls with slightly greater intensity.

Talbot steps to the kiosk beside the door. "Jane Sherril," he requests. A golden hoop lights with an image, distorted in angle, looking toward Jane, who is pacing in the cellar room at her home. She wheels toward them.

"Oh, I'm sorry, Raoul. I've been trying to reach Clu; we've had a communications fault. I lost track of time. I'll send someone out for you right away."

240

Latimer steps out of his vehicle into the slackening rain. "So good to see you all."

"What's the news?" Talbot asks.

"Nothing yet."

241

Shafts of sun slip into the room through a side window as they sneak past the edges of cloud. The surfaces of the walls are still dark, except for processions of numbers, and Jane is slumped in a wide chair, staring, until, at a sound, she turns and sees the group of them silhouetted in the doorway.

"No luck?" Talbot asks.

"Not so far," she replies, quietly. "We're just retrying. It's probably the gravitational distortion caused by those things affecting the coordinate system." Her eyes are heavy lidded, as if she hasn't slept.

Latimer steps past them, and the scene through the door is reflected softly on his back. He holds out a hand. "Jane, let's walk in the garden. Raoul can watch the displays for a while."

242

Talbot leans in the doorway and watches the metal man and the young woman walking slowly in the new sun of the garden. Reed steps to Talbot's side, her light Promethean dress making a soft sound of movement.

"A strange pair," she remarks. He glances over, and then back out.

"I'm not sure how you can say that," he replies. "They seem good friends to me."

"To each other or to you?" she asks.

He makes a musing face. "Both, I guess. I hope." He looks back toward the screen walls. Except for the retry traces, they remain blank. "Damn Clu. What's happened?"

"I think waiting's part of the trial," Reed mutters bitterly.

Talbot watches her face below his carefully. As always, her hair is tied off severely, and her pale skin seems even paler by the side light from the axis, extending down into the soft hollows of her throat, and then disappearing beneath the collar of her dress. He finds himself wanting to run a hand down that smooth shape, but his hands are unmoving. He finds himself sensing the shape beneath her dress, but his thoughts are still. He realizes that her eyes are on his, and he is afraid she will see his feeling. But she looks only a little more intently, and then her eyes are gone as she steps beside him to the door, to where the light can pour down over her shoulders. Then, he is sure that his heart has hammered - hard - once. The small pressure of her hand had crawled into his, now enfolds it. She looks carefully at him, telling him she knows exactly what she has done. After a moment she glances down and releases. She lays a hand briefly on his forearm. Her gaze follows Latimer and Jane in the garden. Finally, she says, "We should go back to Tlnou, and get Clu."

"I know," he replies. He pushes away from the door to join her in the light. He looks at her carefully, telling her he knows exactly what he is about to do. "We've been in debt to them long enough. Let's talk to Jane."

243

Jane stands silent in the basement room, staring at the screens, watching the continual retry. Finally she sighs, picks up her duffel, and as she turns to leave, the lights wink out behind her. The door closes and locks, leaving only the faint whisper of a hundred years of cigar smoke.

244

The flight deck is its usual pre-departure day chaos. "Are we synching?" he asks the relief pilot. Whispers at various frequencies fill the room. "No, not yet," it replies, lenses glittering with the movement.

Talbot frowns impatiently. "I thought we had this down. Jane? Jane? What's the problem? We can't integrate if we can't synch the protocols."

"System's decided to use a different frequency for some reason. I'm working on it. But if I can't get it done, you'll just have to stay behind."

"Don't try that crap with me, Sherril. Fix the problem, or *I'm* going with or without you in ten hours. *And* we're starting the planning sims in ten minutes." He grins over at the chunky Tereniade systems manager, meaning it their way. It frowns back at him, knowing the bluff.

Talbot leans toward the pilot. "Can you direct fold for Clu's last position, if Jane runs on us?" he whispers.

It spirals three tentacles. Talbot thinks that means yes.

"Protocol join," the systems manager announces.

"OK, let's get started now." He is relieved. If Jane cooperates this time, the next will be easier.

He doesn't notice Jill Reed standing at the back of the room, watching.

245

Talbot stands and steps back from the panels into the darkened room. His eyes are teary from exhaustion. Wanr enters through the door at his back, carrying refreshments. The room is Wanr's, and it is cold, so Talbot's kanar steams into the air. For a moment he finds himself wishing for a harsher drink. He chuckles, thinking of how long it has been since he has even thought of that, and knowing how tired he must be for it to break through the guard of the constant stress.

"So let's go through it again."

Wanr whimpers and steps past him to consider the display. Talbot sips the kanar and makes a face at the bitterness. "Remind me to make the kanar next time," he mutters.

Wanr's stubby fingers flare at the panel. "This contingency, here. Acceptable probability is lower. But if this course, and fleet deploys energy weapons, only concealment past limb is sufficient to ablate. But time under reaction drive sufficient not is."

Talbot gestures, hand cupped toward the ceiling. "Come on, what about the edge of the moon. If their beam spread is this, then the edge of the moon reflects an interference pattern into the energy stream. The program says it attenuates." He waves the cup slightly, and a faint slip of coffee moistens the rim and his hand.

"Program insufficient is. Observe ignorance of albedo of atmosphere of gas giant given range of Daltons possible, nonlinear? Try value in plug of yours, OK, try these from extrapolation of gravity mixing from masses of fleet, and reflection is different, moon is elsewhere." Wanr's white lips form unheard sounds, and stop moving before the sentences end.

Talbot knows he has been trying to argue Wanr down with no basis available, but he has been learning. "All right, what about Promethean assets?"

"Not very forthcoming, they are. Sherril, we know, her capabilities discussion occurs on some level, unverifiable due to morphics. Two other vehicles, older, perhaps, not using morphic technologies. Latimer with Sherril. Militia crew unknown, heads say Ormic Ritcalin Voyjay, and Michael Haggis." Wanr leans back against a stand chair, and waves his hands about. "Still think of age of craft making scans more... informative? Indeed true is. Weaponry of energics and propulsives, compliment detailed... here."

Talbot remembers his conversation with Jane.

..."*You know what you've gotten us to do. Now some of us have to take a run at this war of yours.*" *Her voice over the comlink is bitter in the dark...*

...and then..."*That's why we have to go with them,*" *Talbot insists to the irate Ship's Manager.* "*They don't need us, but we have to be willing to lay it on the line with them.*"

"*But our function is diplomatic, our weapons are minimal. How cannot the rumination portend the vehicle at risk?*" *The Lipu molluscan extends eyestalks, and excess water sloshes in its mobile bowl from the sprays.*

"*We are at risk, Manager. We'll minimize it, but without taking the risk, we won't get their support.*"...

"OK, Wanr, let's hear it. I don't know how to do this and I shouldn't keep spying over your shoulder."

"Enough, is it not, to have started the motion and to watch? More unattended than this plan, and my staff tactical can help elaboration. As you say."

Talbot shakes his head, but he only feels a slight flush of blood to his face. He remembers when Reed had first inspected his mission, his feelings about her scathing but silent observation. "All right," he replies, finally. "I... yeah. Listen, let me know when you need to talk to Jane. I want to make sure we handle asking for integration as best we can. She seemed a little unwilling to let us link at prelaunch, and we have to get our plans in sync before fold."

Wanr taps hands to his forehead. Talbot raises his cup and then walks out into the warm corridor, a little sad.

246

Reed turns into the wide dorsal corridor from a doorway far ahead, reading a display as she walks through dappled light.

"Hey, Jill," he calls as she approaches. She looks up and frowns for a moment, then smiles.

"Hi, Raoul." She glances one last time at the display and tucks it under her arm. "I've been helping the Manager with some pre-fold activities, hope you don't mind." Other beings pass them, hurrying or slowly moving on their own missions.

His eyes narrow slightly. "Of course not. But I'll need you for some planning sessions before we go downcurve. We have to finalize how we work with Jane and her people as soon as we pop out."

She pulls out her display again and manipulates the surface. "We're about seven hours from fold, how about at three?"

He watches her eyes, and she is all business. But for a moment, at the end of her sentence, her eyes flash out blue from under her thin brows, and even though her mouth only changes a little, he sees a smile. Or did he imagine it, and dream yesterday?

"That would be fine," he replies, pulling out his pad. "... How about conference 16, at three plus thirty?"

"Great." She squeezes his arm briefly as she walks past, and, even as he worries about issues of authority, and marks an appointment into his calendar, he feels that strange acceleration.

247

On the morning they fold to Tlnou, Talbot wakes to the sudden darkness out of dream. He swings suddenly to sit, and then bows his head to his hands. The faint light of displays glistens on his sweaty pinkish palm.

He washes carefully and looks at his face in the mirror, water beaded on his forehead and at the edge of his hair. He rubs his cheeks and looks in his eyes, and wonders at his normal appearance.

He slips his naked legs carefully into his bright blue vacsuit and fits the plumbing. With a quiet gesture, he seals the suit to his throat ring. He picks up his helmet from the table, and reaches over his head to hook it to the ring. Both helmet and suit are blazoned with large symbols that signify his role. He runs a hand along the arm blazon and remembers how it had felt to see that for the first time, when his suit had been delivered from the *Illyrion*. Today it makes him feel a little afraid, a little excited.

He walks to the flight deck, exhausted by three hours of sleep after endless planning sessions. His step is slow, and he pauses for a moment to rub thick eyes one last time before going in.

If only I could have had more sleep.

The door slips aside to the large space of the control center, a barely ordered chaos. Beside the door and along the wall are a variety of refreshment dispensers. The odors of coffee and various other beverages and foods mingle as everyone tries to attain full readiness. A caterer hands him a cup of coffee, knowing his needs from long habit. Talbot realizes he has never asked the young Tereniade's name. "Hey, what do they call you?" he asks. "Gennead," the youth replies, with the tight Tereniade smile. This is a scene being repeated everywhere on the ship as isolated people awaken to each other in a time of extremity.

Reed greets him with a gesture from the management platform. He joins her and settles gratefully into a comfortable chair at the situation table. Behind, above and around are the stars.

Lights are settling to a quiet blue. He sips his coffee and worries about all of the things none of them may have remembered to worry about, while he watches the flight crew taking their places amidst their interfaces. Finally, he watches the checklists mounting on the smoked table between the team and the bridge.

"Almost there," he whispers to Reed. She nods, and the stiffness of the movement, the concealment of her eyes, all speak of her tension. He tries to smile. "OK, we're going to do it."

Wanr calls on the link. "Where Hallison is? Late is why?"

Talbot senses the first defect that could unravel everything. Reed shakes her head. "Steve's offline."

He has to decide fast. "Wanr, prep somebody else. Ship Manager, find out where Hallison is, if you have to get search teams out. Make sure all the inner links are running."

"m*Karanad is being slotted for consultant," Wanr notifies, identifying a young D*Azar from another FC team.

The org chart on the table shifts to reflect the change.

"Fold preparations completed," the Ship Manager announces.

"What about Hallison?" Talbot demands.

"No results have been reported to us. Faults not observed in system. Teams are in the corridors looking right now."

"Sherril's leaving, Latimer's with her. Hey, look at that," the sensor op calls out. Sherril's vehicle is changing shape like a silvery balloon wavering in a wind; then the fold winks up around it and she is gone.

"Go, go, go!" Talbot yells. The ship shudders briefly and the stars wink away. There is only the faint hum of the passing fold. He stands and paces, staring at the timer on the table. "Three days," he mutters. Then he looks at the Ship Manager's shell. "Manager, where the hell is Steve Hallison?"

248

At that exact moment, Hallison is sleeping, lying sprawled on his back across his bed, snoring in the dark. The call alert is sounding bell tones, but he doesn't move.

The door slides away, and the search team steps into the light fan, long shadows slashing across the floor and the low bed. "We found him," a woman reports, leaning over the bed as he stirs. "He's out of it."

249

"You're buzzed!" Talbot shouts, right next to Hallison's crestfallen face. "Right before we're going on a rescue and you're a drop consultant. You idiot! You're out of the game this round. I'll talk to you later. I don't have time now." He storms from the room.

Reed shakes her head, looking carefully at Hallison with an expression of disgust.

From the hallway, he hears Talbot. "Get him in his suit and make sure he's out of here into the non-participant center in fifteen minutes."

Hallison sits on the edge of his bed, head in his hands. Reed steps into the hallway and then hurries after the receding Talbot. "Hey," she calls. He slows down and stops at an intersection. Almost by itself, it seems, his fist slaps the wall. She catches up to him.

"Listen, Raoul, he hasn't been the same since his team died."

"Don't try to make me soft on this. You know damn well I want to forgive him. I've done worse myself. But I can't right now." His eyes are darkly gleaming in the dappled hall light. "And you wouldn't, either, if you were in charge."

She frowns.

"Let's go," he orders, and walks away.

250

The timer winds to zero, fold unwraps, and the dome blazes with imagery and diagrams of the situation around them. It takes a moment for Talbot to realize where they are. Reed is slightly faster. She leaps to her feet, screaming, "Pull out, pull out!"

But the pilot is on it, and the ship is slowing its terminal plunge from fold. Ahead, the wall of the planet destroyer is already too large for comprehension, its features complex yet meaningless, growing too fast.

On the distant horizon, a brief rod of energy lances upward, and something is destroyed.

"Stay in," Talbot orders, "Don't pull away. We must be inside the defense perimeter. Man are we lucky!" he laughs. "Where's Jane?"

"No idea," Reed snaps, dragging things around the situation table. "Maybe she's not out yet. You know how it is; just 'cause she went in first doesn't mean she's here first."

"She's here." Talbot mutters. "Maybe that's what they're shooting at."

"Clu detection," the sensor op calls.

"Where?"

"Twenty million sunward." Jill takes up the flow. "I don't think they know she's here."

"Damage?"

"Not that anyone can tell, but this morphic technology is making it difficult."

Talbot is pacing. "So we can't get out of here, can we?"

"Why not?"

"Well, we're inside the defenses, right, so we're not being attacked. If we go out..."

"Well, maybe." Her eyes are alert, and suddenly flick up to the dome, and then back again. "But maybe not. Maybe the defense perimeter only attacks incoming?"

He considers it. "No, remember before, the meteor defenses handle incoming, don't care too much, but the cometary debris is being destroyed; it's not incoming. They check."

Typical brainstorming, but she is disturbed. "Then we're stuck."

"We're not only stuck, but the distortion has changed the coordinate system, so we can't even fold out to any place we want to go. We're too close."

Unfortunately, everyone is looking and listening. Reed stands and walks around the table. She stands next to him and leans up. "Raoul, that doesn't leave any alternative."

He is furious, but it only shows in a slight stiffening in his face. "There's always an alternative." Things are coming apart around him. "All right, can we communicate with Jane? She's got to handle getting Clu, while we figure out how to get out of here." *I wanted to come to help; to show how much we could help, now all I'm showing is how serious the problem is, and doing that by getting everyone I know incinerated.*

Suddenly Reed grabs his arm. "We can't get out. But we can get in."

"What?"

"We did it before."

"What, crash into the destroyer?"

"Sure! On purpose."

"Then what?"

Intuition runs away and she is suddenly silent. "I don't know," she whispers.

There is a tremendous sound, and some reflex causes Talbot to reach for Jill and her helmet, slapping it into her hands to put over her head. The deck shudders as she stares at him through the glass, and he fumbles with his own. Another sound and there are myriads of patterns across every panel screaming errors and disaster. And a last sound rips away the other side of the flight deck, and the tens of levels above it. All of the air goes roaring into silence, carrying bodies and consoles and fluttering scraps of unknown fabric out into the sunlight. The railing slams Talbot in the side, and he is clutching Jill by the arm and then the waist as the wind dies to silence. Lights flicker and go out, but gravity is still on, and some of the panels look active. The ship is spinning slowly, and the sun crawls through the vast layered pit in the hull, harsh pools on the floor beside him moving away.

Some icy feeling is clutching his skin, not just the cold of space, and he feels as if he is watching from far away. He feels a motion in his arms and it is Jill, but something is strange about her face. Finally, he realizes she is screaming. "Stop it," he yells, but she can't hear him. He pushes his helmet against hers, and the very faint sound comes through. "Stop it!" he yells again. He feels her shudder and then she is crying.

Intersuit com comes up, and then he can hear a cacophony from all over the ship. The problem is too big. He can't think.

Then, a moment later, he remembers, and he tunes his com to local and directional. Now he can hear Jill panting as she recovers. "Are you all right?" he demands. "Jill!"

She gestures assent, and, releasing him, clutches the rail just as the gravity fluctuates. Talbot looks over at the pilot area, but there is no one there, and the imagery is gone. He looks out the vast tear in the hull, and sees the bright surface of the destroyer moving slowly beyond. He senses it is closer, but he cannot be sure. Did RnaTneya establish a stable orbit?

He starts down to the pilot area, past a strange rusty streak that may once have been the blood of the gaunt grey creature he had joked with not so long ago. The gravity bobbles, and he nearly loses the floor in panic. He flattens himself down on the darkened surface and crawls to the pilot station. Then, he has to stand up. It may not even respond. He knows that. His familiarity with this level of controller is not what it needs to be. He knows that. But he needs information. Cautiously, he stands and the imagery snaps up around him. The gravity is steady. Swiftly, he switches the system to impersonal. A gesture envelops him in the orbital plot. It is as he was afraid - the orbit was not established and the path is decaying. He begins the struggle to control the chaotic deterioration.

Reed watches from the railing, her breath so loud in her ears that she can hear nothing else. Talbot is moving like a magician, gesturing and tugging at virtual objects that seem to be fighting his will. And in a corner of the room, she sees the suit-shrouded shell of the Ship Manager struggling slowly from some wreckage by the motion of its prosthetics. Finally, a gesture of disgust from Talbot dismisses the piloting globe. He hurries back to her. "I can't get this thing flying, the control runs are only partial, even with the auto reroute. We've got twelve hours, now, that's it. I tried to call Jane, or Clu, but they're on the far side, and fold com doesn't work with local gravity and no coordinates."

Reed grabs his shoulder. "Then we have to abandon ship. And there's only one place to go. The destroyer."

Talbot feels a wave of hopelessness. Everyone will think they have been destroyed. There may be no rescue. They may all die. But there is no time for that fear. "I'll try to raise Wanr, get him to shift agenda from drop to evac. See if anyone's left here. Twelve hours, we get enough on the job, maybe we can get everyone off. If the destroyer doesn't decide to swat us again..."

251

Talbot locks the hatch shut. Half a hundred beings are sealed into this hammar. Seals hiss closed and they are on their own. Should they have spent the time on trying to jury rig control systems for the *Norton*? Could there have been any other solution? He pushes his way through the crowd toward the flight deck. The new yet familiar door slides back and then he is in the hushed darkness and light that is his first and still favorite home.

"Hi, Jill," he slides into the left seat.

"You're on time."

He opens the helmet and the scent of a new flight deck envelops him. His eyes travel the virtual window for an idea of where the vehicle stands. The checklists are almost complete. He nods in the dimness, and announces to all compartments, "All personnel to acceleration stations. Five minutes to departure."

Except for the sound of the machines, it is silent, even though the *Norton* has been rocked by occasional fire from the destroyer for the past ten and a half hours. Talbot punches through a few independent checks for his side of the board. Finally, Reed looks over, and her eyes glint with the displays. "We're ready."

Talbot's throat tightens. They are abandoning the *Norton*. In a moment, they will be a very threatened lifeboat, and he doesn't like it.

Reed touches his arm. "I don't like this either."

He frowns. "Yeah, let's do it."

He makes the final announcement and they are at the launch time. The stars flash into presence as the *Norton* slips behind, and then the destroyer is below and ahead. Talbot yaws the vehicle and the slowly rolling carcass of the *Norton* swings into view. Both he and Reed gasp at the sight. Hideous gaping holes have shattered the hull, and various structural elements are ripped out and drifting with it. The venting of various gases and atmosphere has formed continuous faint clouds, some of which are still crackling with distant tiny flames.

As the *Norton* passes them and recedes against the vast landscape of the destroyer, and its sky of stars, he can see the other hammars following. Talbot can hear the tinny chatter of the other pilots over the links.

"Look at that."

"Man oh man, that is bad. We're lucky."

"Plasma fires near the fold room are, back. What's going to happen when that goes, I see do not want to." That one is Wanr's voice.

"So where are we going, then?" a closer voice wakens him from reverie.

"There's only one way to be sure of getting out, and that's getting in," he replies grimly.

"Impact?"

"Impact."

252

The *Norton* slowly gets further ahead of them, and drops below their course. The flames are more violent now, and their venting is causing the hulk to spin in unpredictable ways. They can still see the other vehicles in the sunlight, but the terminator is not far ahead, and the others are hundreds of miles away to each side. A bolt from the horizon strikes the *Norton*, and it reels with the explosion of an entire side. Then the destroyer is silent for a long time.

Until one of the boats turns upward as if trying to depart, and they are never to know if it was some secret consensus or a malfunction, because a sword of energy disintegrates it a thousand miles above.

Talbot and Reed trade glances. They are too numb to feel anything for those who just died. "Maybe later," Talbot mutters.

Just then, near the horizon, the *Norton* smashes into the destroyer.

There is a small initial reaction. The light spreads slowly, and then there is a flattened disk of gases that bursts into flames. A moment later, the *Norton's* fold generator implodes and the entire explosion is first sucked back to invisibility in a strange inverted reaction, and then the window wall dims to near black to contain the brilliance of the release. Ten minutes later, the shock gases roil past below at hundreds of miles an hour.

Talbot is watching, heart pounding, as the heavy energy facilities of the destroyer begin firing on the rising plume from the impact. They may be doing additional damage to the site, but it is hard to tell. The worst part is that his craft and the others are sailing relentlessly toward the damaged area. And the blasts. As they must.

253

Talbot sips at a coffee in the darkened left seat. He offers the cup to Jill. She shakes her head and resumes staring out at the surface, now much closer.

As they approach the terminator, they can see the glowing edges of the *Norton's* grave just beyond. The plume has long since escaped into space, and the weapons are quiescent.

"We're getting close," Talbot mutters into the com. "Remember, stick with us until we find a safe zone inside."

"This is crazy, Talbot. What about the radiation? And the crew? And the weapons? I mean..."

"You see a choice for us?" he snaps. "Head for high orbit, and you'll be roasted. This is the chance we've got. Pass, and we're dead." He shakes his head and turns to Jill, switching to personal com. "They spend too much damn time flying taxi service. Take it for granted. Idiots! Looking to die."

"They're just afraid," she replies gently, staring out to the horizon.

"Yeah." He feels his voice crack. She looks over. "Please Raoul, we need your expertise, or we're all dead. Stay with us."

He knows that if he unleashes his fear, he may never come back. So he reins it in tightly. "All right, let's get to work. We need a systems check, get everyone back into helmets, and figure we have... ten more minutes before we start braking."

She nods grimly.

254

They are falling past endless scorched and broken levels like a ship sinking into an oceanic trench. Talbot stares downward in awe at the depth of the destruction. He scratches absently at his arm, thinking of the billions of tons of material that had vaporized in the flash that ended the *Norton*.

The slanting light vanishes as the terminator sweeps over the last of the blast canyon. Then only the sensors show the walls, limned with radiation remnants.

255

A grandmother and her granddaughter meet in the linkway between liquid metal ships, clothed in liquid metal. Beyond the walkway, Clu's ship has lost some of its fluidity, where the energy of the destroyer has crisped the morphic substance and healing has not succeeded.

The two embrace in their smooth metal suits, faces hidden behind their hoods, and their love is in the extra pressure and its nuances. Clu is alone, and they walk embraced to where Latimer waits in the opening.

"Thanks for coming," Clu says to the metal man.

"I couldn't stay behind. What about :Listarof:?"

Clu shakes her head, eyes a little wide. "The outside looks a lot better than it was inside."

Latimer nods. "Morphics heal better than flesh."

Her face is invisible, but a shudder is not. They step inside and the hull heals behind them.

The women strip off their hoods. "Anything else from the *Norton*?" Jane asks as they walk.

Latimer's hood dissolves. His face is cold and his expression doesn't change. "Nothing since the explosion on the far side. It's possible they unfolded too close. We won't know unless we go over there. I wouldn't advise it."

"Who's the *Norton*?" Clu asks, slipping a cigar from a seam in her suit.

"The Geodesic team insisted on coming. They wanted to help, but..."

"Oh, no..." Clu turns the cigar over and over in her hand as if she is unable to recognize it.

256

There are cold blue lights, hot with ultraviolet.

There are endless hexagonal rooms, separated by more or less open spaces. The dust is thick and there are places where strange vermin have died in heaps. Talbot pokes at them with the toe of his boot.

There is atmosphere here, past the first intact airbreak, but it is the wrong type for humans, so Talbot wears his suit.

He walks slowly through a place where no human foot has ever trod. He can almost feel the knowledge of billions of dead like a cold moisture. The ranks of cells diminish into the distance without a clue as to their content.

There is nothing here to see; nowhere to go. And he is again afraid. The air in their small craft will not last forever, nor will the power. Yet there is nowhere within the destroyer for sanctuary, and he realizes how desperate he had been. The vehicle is the size of a planet, and even this monotonous floorscape can be seen to run for miles toward the curvature.

He turns and starts back to the portaseal that membranes over the hole in the airbreak.

Hallison is waiting for him.

"Be nice to find a control room or something, eh, chief?"

"I'd be satisfied with some plain nitrogen/oxygen mix." Talbot sighs, looking at Hallison carefully. "You feeling all right?"

Hallison's eyes close for a moment. "Yeah. Sorry."

"Yeah." Talbot still feels bitter.

Hallison looks around. "You know, this thing is too enormous. We're not likely to find anything close or useful."

"Any ideas?"

"I reviewed the sensor logs."

"And?"

Hallison gestures helplessly. "There's not much to work with. But the upper levels are out. There's too much radiation from the fold inversion, and even if there weren't, with the attitude they seem to have about repairs, the outer surface has probably been holed a million times. If we head along the equator, that leads toward the hollow on the outer face. Best guess is that probably represents the focus of whatever they use to destroy planets. Likely to be mostly machinery, and who knows how much residual radiation of who knows what kind."

"So, the other way? North?"

"Down. To the center."

"Sure! The same as we put our control rooms at the center of our ships to avoid damage." Suddenly there's something to do.

"Raoul, it's possible they don't think anything like us. Or there might be other design constraints. This might not mean anything. And, don't forget, this pit doesn't go all the way. And even if we get there, they may be nothing of any use to us."

"Steve, if we go out the way we came in, the weapons will wipe us out. We still have a couple of days of resources. There's nothing better to try." He steps through the membrane, and it seals behind him.

257

In the light cast by the ship, a million shadows move like ants across the base of the pit. Repair systems like nothing they have ever seen, bulking large and hideous in their alien movement. Cybers and other autonomous things, crudely shaped, reforming walls, laying conduit. But the lifeboats are ignored. For now.

"Within new repairs, trapped we be can," Wanr offers. Jill, leaning over Talbot's shoulder, nods. Talbot shrugs. The other craft are a mile above, safe at least from the current repairs. "We have to find out," he replies, though he knows he is unsure of exactly what he is looking for.

Reed sighs and turns away. She looks over her shoulder, then, at the back of his chair. "I should go."

Wearily, Talbot pushes himself from his seat. "I can't leave these people without a pilot. And I have to have Steve, and r*Zaranil, if I'm going to make any sense out of what's down there."

"Of course," she replies, bitterness quiet, harnessed to a hopeless fear.

He pushes past her into the hallway, and she finally follows him, past the doorways open on crowded cabins. She stops him at the tiny galley. The light from above casts shadows to hood his eyes, but she can see the corners netted with blood, and the faint stubble filming his chin. Worst though, are the eyelids, slow to respond to his eye movements, as if they are thick and sluggish. "I can't have any more coffee," he mutters.

"Why don't you get some sleep?" she replies. For a moment, her anger is stilled. "There's time."

He tries to shake his head, but he moves clumsily and almost staggers. "Yeah, I guess..." As he walks away, his head is low, and his gait shuffles. But Reed looks after him with concern, hoping he *can* sleep.

258

She falls endlessly toward the busy machines.

Her private channel opens. "Jill," comes Talbot's hissing whisper. "What are you doing?"

"Steve, r*Zaranil, and I are investigating. I decided you needed your rest. Besides," her voice cracks a bit, "it's easier to go yourself than send someone else, isn't it? Well, it's your turn to see how that feels. You be the pilot. That's your job. Or at least the one you really like, isn't it?"

Her personal music is soft in her helmet, but it is comforting in the digital silence.

"All right, Jill. I suppose you told them I wanted this? Or did you tell them you knocked me on the head and tied me up and would they please join you for a quick recon?"

She sighs. "I told them you needed to sleep. Funny, they believed me."

His chuckle is warmer for being so close to her ear. "Good thing I slept, or I'd be so stressed I'd be yelling. The problem is, I have no idea what you're going into, and I don't like the idea of sitting up here waiting."

"Yeah, well, remember Tlnou," she snaps.

More silence underlined with soft music as the floor and its busy hordes grow closer.

"I remember," he finally replies.

"Then get out of my ear and let me do my job."
More silence. Then, "OK."

259

The gravity at the center of a massive body is near to zero, as the mass above and below tugs equally. But there are gravity generators here, and the team hits the floor running. Then, from a corner, they peer out onto the activity, like children watching the inexplicable activities of adults.

There are machines of every size, but mostly large. Extruding, manipulating, gradually creating a ceiling. Reed tries to restrain her feeling of slowly being trapped.

The world is creaking and moaning in silence, but the sense of the stresses is transmitted as vibration into their suits. Every once in a while, there is a shuddering, like an earthquake, which could be from anything - perhaps the disintegration of the structure, perhaps nothing more than the complaining of buttresses that support the mass of an injured planet.

Below their feet, the surface is more complex than a flat floor. It slopes in various directions, with sharp angles and curves. The machines carry harsh lights of various wavelengths, which cast wildly shifting shadows of chaotic color.

Hallison and r*Zaranil are recording the scene in their accessible spectra, but Reed collects them with a gesture. "Let's go."

They hasten down a vast corridor, its roof a mile above them, with a variety of vast machines lined up and moving past on wheels and jointed legs. The team stays close to the walls, afraid to be crushed, afraid to be noticed.

"OK, let's get out of this area, and see what we can find. If we can just find someplace where the crew lives, or works."

"Machines, unless," r*Zaranil offers. "Crew not beings?"

"That's what Raoul always thought," Hallison offers. "Maybe he's right. Look at this stuff." He shakes his head as he stares up the flank of a slowly moving machine the size of a cliff. "Can people really manage this?"

"Some variant, paradigm of decentralized authority, may."

They seek quieter and quieter byways, avoiding the smaller robotics that are still racing toward the damage.

Until they arrive at an airbreak that walls off the corridor from the rest of the core.

"Is a new construct," r*Zaranil announces. "Within hours."

"So," Reed finishes, "it must be between us and some work area of importance. Some place that requires an atmosphere."

"Maybe," Hallison replies, standing beside the wall. He slips out a pad of membrane and smoothes it over the oddly textured metal. When he is satisfied, he shines a laser through it, tuned to metal, and a pinprick hole appears behind the membrane. r*Zaranil produces a fiber, and Hallison slips it through the center of the membrane and into the hole. Then, r*Zaranil clamps a lead to it, and an image leaps onto a screen at his feet. r*Zaranil listens to the screen's radar translation, head tilted to the side.

260

Talbot suddenly awakens from a nightmare in the left seat of the hammar. The young D*Azar is leaning over him, concerned, perhaps, or perhaps just checking, and at the sight of the metallically scaled visage, Talbot's heart thumps quickly and then resumes its normal operation.

The nightmare floods back - *Latimer throwing a spear that knocks Gillian Reed to the ground in a gout of blood and a welter of screaming that Talbot now recognizes as his own.*

"I'm all right," he gasps. He punches up a channel to the team, and watches the repairs below on the window wall as he waits for the answer.

"What is it?" Reed snaps irritably from the other end.

"I... how are... well, what's going on? Are you finding anything?"

"Steve's just getting an optic through a wall. We'll call you in a little while."

"All right." He sighs and stares ruefully at the closed connection icon.

261

"Nothing," r*Zaranil comments.

"Not nothing," Hallison disagrees. "No one, but not nothing."

"Can we get in, then?" Jill demands.

"Let's try," Hallison replies. "What's the chief got to say?"

"He's waiting on us. Let's get to work."

262

Reed stares at the tiny display, suspicious. "I think... it's something that lives there, but..."

"But not civilized, or perhaps sentient," r*Zaranil remarks.

Hallison has been sealing a membrane to the wall, but stops at their comment. "What have you got?"

r*Zaranil bobs his head. The sightless muzzle points at Hallison. "Hard to say."

Hallison grimaces behind his faceplate and then turns back to finish his work.

r*Zaranil places a suited hand beside his. "My attention. Structural matters are in my domain. Are these sentients?"

Hallison squats beside Reed and looks at the vague images of movement. "Terrible imaging," he remarks. She twists a hand in the air. "It's dim. There's not enough IR to use for feature enhancement. And the aperture is too narrow for good radar."

He shrugs. "Well, about all I can tell from this is that they don't care much about orientation, and they move at moderate speeds, and they have limbs. But you probably figured that out."

"Well maybe we'll see more inside." She packs the display, just as r*Zaranil begins with the laser.

263

As they step through the membrane, the half-seen creatures scatter into the webwork of girders, but the radar band gets a good view. "Tripedal, heavy skeletal, partly endo, partly exo. No visible metallic tools. That's about it, " Hallison reports.

"Atmosphere's like the higher levels, about the same temperature and pressure," Reed comments. The frustration hits her like a wave. "This place is too damn big. We don't have time for a survey."

r*Zaranil is dropping his heavy pack, and unlimbering some device from within it. "Thought we might need this."

"What the hell is it?" Hallison asks, peering nervously at the ceiling, watching for the hidden residents.

"Radar inducer," r*Zaranil replies, the voice coming more slowly. "It induces the material within a radius to emit radar, depending on properties. It will make the area appear more transparent at my wavelengths."

"What are you looking for?" Reed asks.

"A conduit. You see, we are near the center of the ship. The control conduits, ventilation systems, everything, still have to reach here, especially if there is a control center. So we look for one, and follow it."

Reed is shaking her head. "Brilliant. But I'm afraid I've lost contact with Raoul, so make it fast. I'm going to step out and let him know what we're trying."

Hallison grabs her arm. "Tell him to wait. He's got to wait."

She carefully uncurls his fingers from her suit. "He'll wait, Steve. What else is there to do?"

264

"That damage is incredible," Jane Sherril mutters.

Latimer steps up beside her, staring at the enormous view. "It's more than the damage that's incredible. It's incredible that the object has remained intact this long."

"This long?" Jane asks.

"It's collapsing. Slowly, but in a few days, it will be debris, unless their repair capabilities are far in excess of what we've seen. Look at what I've been able to measure of the stresses. The support members radiating outward and forming these polygonal volumes depend on whole structure integrity, like an arch. We would never use this in Prometheus, because of how precarious the construction environment would be, and the lack of modularity... still, there might be some innovations that could come from looking at it. This is orders of magnitude larger than the largest thing we've ever built, anyway. Look at the critical stresses caused by the members destroyed in the fold implosion. These supports have already moved two miles from their normal location. They are making some kind of repairs, I think, but they don't seem to be acting quickly enough."

"What about the *Norton*?"

"They could not have survived the impact. The fold generator ruptured, and the damage was done. Most likely, they folded into congruence with some part of that thing, and that was the end."

Clu sits in a chair at the far side of the bridge, staring up at the spectacle, and a wisp of smoke trails from her thin cigar.

265

The segment of a vehicle drifts tumbling amidst the confetti of shredded metal, optics, and crystallized liquids. Clu gestures.

"I wonder how you missed that, Latimer," she muses.

"I don't know," he replies, neutrally, standing away across the flight deck.

"It's not a piece of the *Norton*. It's one of the sub-vehicles. The volatiles, of course, wouldn't be here if this was debris from the fold implosion. I doubt even the piece would be. Am I right?"

Jane grins at her. "Always." Her expression is muted at a thought. "But they did escape, so where are they?"

Latimer examines the displays carefully. Tendrils lash out from his wrists into sockets in the panels. "They could have been destroyed by the point defense. Scarring on the hull indicates energy weapons. If this was the only vehicle..."

Jane is looking over his shoulder. "Let's assume it wasn't. Where could they be?"

266

Reed, r*Zaranil, and Hallison are standing on the darkened edge of a pit a half mile across that falls away into intricate dimness away from their light. A stream of warm atmosphere that they are not allowed to feel is whistling softly upward over the intertwined piping and supports.

"To the left, another, three miles."

The floor shivers, and there is an odd tug of gravity, like a sudden sea change.

"Behind us, six miles, open to space."

"Never mind," Reed snaps, staring unnerved into the hideously complex opening below. Hallison leans against a support and stares uncomfortably away. Finally, Reed looks over at r*Zaranil.

"One of us can get out from here. But anyone who goes down there... might need help. Two go down, one waits. And not for too long," her eyes rove the ceiling, "or the place is going to shake out around us."

Hallison turns to look at her. "I'll go," he whispers, but his voice nearly cracks.

"No, Steve, I'm going. I need you here to watch our back - and maybe you'll have to negotiate with the things in the rafters. I need r*Zaranil's radar with me. OK, snoutface?"

r*Zaranil bows his sinister black helmet.

267

Talbot stalks the corridor. From flight deck to galley, to stern, he paces his shadow down the narrow hall, and the refugees watch him. For once, he feels as powerless as they.

268

Reed and r*Zaranil climb carefully down into the wind.

"How long have we been in here?" Jill asks.

"Five hours."

She hangs from a bar and watches the graceful movements of r*Zaranil.

"No wonder I'm starving."

269

They descend mile after mile into the core of the ship, and Hallison waits, staring down from far above at the tiny points representing their beacons.

Suddenly, the points are gone.

270

Jill Reed leaves a beacon and drifts free past the lip into a dimly lit vastness, walled with conduits and beams. Thousands of chittering beings wandering along the surfaces of the core pause to stare as she falls deeper and deeper in the weightlessness. r*Zaranil follows as slowly.

Other apertures let into the core, and the flow of the air tugs Reed and r*Zaranil slowly along the length.

r*Zaranil analyzes the movements of the creatures and can find no organization to it. Yet he is aware that analysis of purpose requires more information than may yet be available. He senses the flow of power and data through conduits as humans sense light. There is no special concentration of those below around concentrations where conduits join nodes. This is difficult to understand if the core is a control center, and the signs of signals received and distributed are unmistakable.

Reed has used a series of complex body motions to bleed momentum until she hangs in the air. r*Zaranil executes a similar series of movements and comes nearly to rest. "We must look at a control node. Can you identify the location I am indicating?"

"Yeah," she replies. She fires off a thruster and they descend to the wall of the core. The creatures scuttle away, staring with gleaming eyes behind each pipe and box.

"They can see," Reed remarks.

"Is that so?" r*Zaranil asks, curious. "Human wavelengths?"

"I don't know. But they have visible eyes, reflective. But why are there no indicators on the node? In fact, there are no signs of interface at all."

r*Zaranil bends down beside the box. "This is newer than the rest. It actually appears to be a different design." He swivels his blind helmet toward her. "It seems to be morphic."

Reed looks around. "The conduits, feeders, the substrate - all of that is more primitive than the controller. Design? Convention? Optimization?"

"Possibly. However, solutions can wait. Check stress sensors, and observe the controller activity."

She looks around and muses over the heads-up on her visor. "Connectivity is deteriorating and stress is increasing."

"This vehicle is suffering from multiple cascading failures - physical and control. We should leave. Now."

271

There is an enormous bell-like clang that Hallison can hear even though the suit. Thousands of tons of debris cascade down the conduit, drifting and tangling slowly toward the core. A strut is swatted by the flow, and smashes chaos across the floor a half mile away.

272

"It's getting worse," Talbot mutters, sitting uncomfortably at the front of the seat. He looks around, but there is no one to answer him.

273

"See that?" Jane points to the highly magnified display of the tear in the distant destroyer surface. There is a small speck against the dim and distorted shelves of the tens of thousands of floors.

"It could be anything," Latimer mutters. Clu leans hands down on the console and watches the sensor profiles on her contacts.

"But it isn't debris, and it *is* different from every repair system in the damage." She sighs and paces. Finally she stops, still turned. "It could be Talbot. The active defenses are getting more and more inaccurate. There's going to be a window during which it will be safe before the collapse of the ship." She turns and points at Latimer. "Get me that window, Latimer. Jane, I want my dinner."

274

"Something's wrong with Latimer," Clu says quietly over the sound of fork on plate in the glossy room.

Jane settles down at the low table with a plate and stares at the wall-sized image of the destroyer. "Wrong?"

"He's balky. Moody. I don't know." Clu's eyes are clear, but the corners are webbed with tiny wrinkles. "It's almost like he knows something he's not telling us. I know him better than anyone. You know how many years it's been?"

"Centuries, grandma? More?" she replies gently.

"Keep an eye on him when I'm not looking." Clu pauses for a moment as if thinking about adding more, but then she returns her attention to the meal.

275

A vagrant breeze starts to tug at their suits as they lift above the surface, heading for the beaconed conduit. Vast banging and popping sounds echo with distant reverberation from the far side of the core. Their external audio pickups hear the thin sounds of wailing, screaming, and fear from the hidden population below.

Then the wind becomes a gale.

276

A hidden thousand feet above them, a structural member damaged by the titanic forces the *Norton's* fold implosion disconnects from its massive socket, and the stress which it had contained is freed to run madly through all of the floors below. The first level below the gash, newly laid, tears apart piece by piece, and the trapped atmosphere below begins to react with the icy cold of the void. The temperature changes, and the materials react to the differential with fractures that split even wider - until the flow of air from the core begins to blow away the plates and the repair machinery with a shock of atmospheric snow.

277

Talbot stares at the debris flowing slowly up toward the hammar. The radar systems indicate the mass and the density of the objects, and they are dangerous. He knows he should move the vehicle. There are people in the back who are depending on him. But Reed and Hallison and r*Zaranil are also depending on him.

If he fails...

He looks down at his chest and hands, suited and glistening. It is the illusion of an exoskeleton - an armor. But those machines drifting up toward him will smash that armor, and him, to bloody frozen ruin as easily as they can crumple the skin of his vehicle.

And they could just as well be the markers of the destruction of his friends.

He checks the comlink indicators - they are still zeroed. No information.

He waits, tapping his thumb hard on the seat rest.

"All vessels," he calls.

They acknowledge the call.

"I'm going lower to try to retrieve my team. I can't leave them. But the rest of you have to be ready to get out. Move up toward the rim.

When things really start to break down, you can get out, no matter what happens."

Wanr connects from his hammar on a private channel. "Passengers, Raoul?"

"Yeah, I know, but I'm not leaving anyone."

"Not understood."

"I know the passengers could be killed and so could I. But I'm not leaving Jill. Do you hear me? Do you understand now, damn it?"

A long pause. "Understood. Stay safe, or I will have to sing your song at the Fields."

Talbot punches out of the circuit and triggers alert status. Then he drops the nose of the vehicle and slowly descends toward the shifting metal below.

278

Hallison stands by the membrane as more material shakes free of the conduit and spills clanging across the floor in the microgravity. The noises are louder and he senses worse damage is occurring elsewhere. If Reed and r*Zaranil are in the conduit, he will stay. But he feels achingly hot and sweating, as if he is fevered. *Sick,* he thinks. *Maybe I am.*

279

The wind does not allow them to reach the beaconed conduit. They are torn across the sky at a swift pace, and the turbulence near the conduit that leads to the break smashes them unforgivingly across machines, pipes and cabling. Reed's hands clutch helplessly at each possibility, and occasionally catch for a moment, but the unaided strength of her muscles cannot hold. For a moment she sees r*Zaranil being bounced along behind her, illuminated for an interval by her helmet light, in the chaos of machines and dying, screaming ship creatures. She knows she should be afraid, but the forces that are pulling at her are so strong that all she can do is huddle within herself, and wait.

Then she is sucked over the edge, and blown out toward space.

280

Hallison nearly jumps at the sound of the hailing chime.

"Raoul! Raoul! I'm here!" he cries whirling nearly off his feet to face the membrane.

The transmission is distorted, but he can hear Talbot's voice.

"... your location. ... n't get too close, Steve. But I only get you... Jill? r*Zaranil."

"They went down into the core," Hallison shouts. "They're in the damn core somewhere."

"Get out on the floor, and try to use thrust... get up here.... get them out if we can."

"But what if they come up here?"

"... out now, you can't wait.. The place is coming apart."

Hallison pushes through the membrane, and he starts to tumble in his haste, but the suit stabilizes, and he is flying swiftly through the maze of shifting machinery. He stops at the edge of the broken ceiling and stares upward at objects slowly receding toward the distant stars. There are tiny flashing lights an indeterminate distance above. He knows it is Talbot, and he feels a sudden, shaming stream of relief. He can leave. No one will blame him. Talbot wants him to leave.

"Any sign of them, yet, Chief?" he calls.

"A couple of signals that might have been beacons, but transient."

"I want to come back, Raoul. I do. But I can't. I won't leave them." He can feel his cheeks are wet, his voice is ragged and almost seems to belong to someone else. Someone out of control.

He turns and steps back under the roof, heading for the membrane.

281

A silently tumbling object coasts slowly upward into a gravity gradient. At its edge, a suited hand. Then another, and a helmet. The woman's face within is pale, and her eyes are rolling slightly, involuntarily following the motion of her surroundings. Her thrusters are spasming, not realizing the tumbling is a property of the object, but she clings to the object desperately, afraid of the other shards and blocks of metal, and unable to neutralize the reflexive actions of her suit systems.

"r*Zaranil," she gasps, clutching at a sloping knob, trying to work her way to a more stable position.

"Almost arrived I am," he replies.

r*Zaranil drifts upward toward the object and latches the edge. he can sense Reed dimly through the material.

"Jill!" Talbot calls. "Can you hear me?"

"Raoul, I'm here. We're on a machine. It's broken free... heading up. For now. Where in space are you, damn it?"

"I'm not far. You stay there, you understand? I'm on my way. It's going to take a few minutes, though."

Reed's thrusts, with the addition of r*Zaranil's, have damped the rotation of the object to near stillness. She amplifies the stickiness of her suit and crawls toward the edge. Down into the dizzying pit, she stares at an avalanche of material vomited toward space from below. But the objects are tiny with extended distance, and slow with relative velocity. Not far from her, r*Zaranil crawls slowly over an edge, a dark outline against the only slightly brighter backdrop of thousands of shattered floors and hundreds of free-falling objects.

She swivels her head carefully, waiting for Talbot.

282

It is like flying a tight asteroid cluster. Some of the blizzard of particles are nothing to disturb the skin of the vehicle. Others are sections of machines or deck plates sufficient in mass or kinetics to puncture the hull. It is all approaching, and Talbot has no choice but to set a course that allows it to approach him at a potentially dangerous speed.

It is not enough to be engaged by this - he also is terrified by the thought of what may be happening to Hallison. Talbot knows that the destroyer will not cease disintegrating.

But Hallison is out of reach now, and Talbot is entering the debris.

283

She watches the vehicle descend slowly from above, its edges glinting as the visibility lights flash. It is almost time to jump.

284

Hallison stares in horror as the supports crumple like paper above him. The pain is sudden and complete.

285

"OK, use the jack, come on, it's not that far."
"We need a brace."
"This to push, to lever."
The cacophony of voices and movement returns to haunt his agony.
"Cutter. Use the strut; shorter."
Hallison is screaming with pain, but hears no sound.
"Oh no!" someone gasps.
Then he can't see or feel, no matter how hard he tries.

286

The flight of small vehicles flees the heart of destruction, thousands of miles unreeling invisibly. Behind them, in a sudden bifurcation of catastrophe, the vast ship is crumpling into a final debris.

An intricate morphic object accomplishes a sudden fold to the brink of the canyon. In a moment, Talbot recognizes what he hopes it could be. Sherril.

As the vehicles pop out, the planet destroyer point defenses are firing randomly into the debris, their beams flickering as the power sources die. The energy casts a shattering light through the flight deck. Reed, in the right seat, eyes opaque behind darkened visor, smiles with a fierce competence. "Gonna make it Raoul. Gonna make it if that's who I think it is."

"We'll make it," he snaps. But there are thousands of miles to go.

Fissures are crawling slowly outward from the canyon behind them, venting plasma, volatiles, and flames.

There is a sudden light which slaps them in the back. They are tumbling, and the systems are crashing and restarting and crashing again. The morphic vehicle ahead lurches closer and expands like a parasol to envelop the tiny ships and then winks a billion miles in a second. The lights snap back on and the systems come back awake, checking to determine what has happened while they were sleeping. Talbot leans back in the seat, choking on a sudden breeze of smoke.

287

The death of the destroyer plays its way across the Oort field. The twelve hundred remaining crew of the *Norton,* excepting Hallison, stand in silence in a large bubble on the surface of the vessel as the quiet event occurs. The vast destroyer sheds its mass into space like a glacier collapsing, with barely visible flashes of energy at locations that slowly separate into faintly shifting plates. Point defenses still fire randomly at the debris, but the quantity of fire is decreasing.

288

Hallison lies without pain or sensation; silent, unmoving, eyes narrowed to slits. r*Zaranil steps into the dim room, and crosses the pool of golden light and shadow cast by the bedside lamp. Hallison feels its presence.

"Zar'," he mutters, eyes shifting under the lids. Miniscule cybers creep up to his neck and tap it gently with their tentacles. His skin is clouded with vacuum burns and bruises. He twitches at the movement of a rib. "They do medicine a little differently here..." he whispers.

"In what way different is?"

Hallison's eyes squeeze shut, and a tear slips from between the lids. "They have machines. Tiny. They crawl inside." He gasps as he feels his lung expand and reattach behind the rib. "You can't feel them. Much. You can't even see some of them." Carefully, tiredly, he raises an arm, and his bloodshot eyes peer at it. "They're there, on the skin, working; under the skin, cleaning the bruises. I don't know if I like it. But I don't have much choice. It was the only facility they had." The arm falls away. "I think there's even some in my eyes." He brushes weakly at the blanket. "Sometimes they crawl out and... I don't know... die, I suppose."

"I can sense them," r*Zaranil replies. "Soon you will be better? There are things of many to discuss. Core recordings need analysis."

Hallison is coughing suddenly, and a streamer of silvery specks boils swiftly from his mouth, running away into the covers and vanishing. He smiles, wanly. "Yeah, soon."

"I am... with you. You are my associate. I will stay."

289

Reed wanders the long looping hallways of the Promethean ship, wondering where Talbot might be. Her joints are stiff from the aftermath of their ejection through the conduit, but some painkillers from the ship's pharmacopoeia loosen her step. She nibbles on a food bar as she looks around.

The corridors are lined with paintings and animations. She pauses to look at one, chewing slowly as she tries and fails, to make sense of it. Finally, she gives up and moves on, tucking the wrapper into a pocket.

There are doors at odd intervals, many of them open on rooms, revealing difficult to understand systems and objects. Some of the rooms seem slightly messy, with tiny cybers laboriously collaborating to shift large objects slowly across the room to proper receptacles.

She pauses at a junction and, glancing around, sees a dark limb hanging over the edge of recliner in a nearby room. She walks quietly to the door.

Talbot lies asleep in the dimly lit space. His entire body has loosened its normal tension to a complete relaxation. She assesses the gentle movement of his eyes beneath their lids, the occasional twitch of a finger, and concludes that he is dreaming. His vulnerability reaches her for a moment with an unusual impulse to protect. Her hand moves slowly and traces a line in the air just above his arm. She turns to leave and then she hears him stir and mutter in a throaty whisper: "Jill?"

He is looking at her, and his eyes are still exhausted, but he sees her clearly. She smiles. "Hi."

"Oh," he says, as if suddenly everything has rushed back into his mind. He reaches out and catches at her hand. "I'm so glad you're here." He straightens, without letting go. She smiles down at him, uncomfortable at the directness of his gaze. "I'm glad you're all right."

He releases her hand and pushes forward on the chair. He rubs his face and looks up at her. The barriers are suddenly close to normal. "I had to get some rest. I didn't really sleep while you guys were in there. But there's a lot to do, isn't there?"

She leans against the doorframe. "There's a lot to do. But Steve's recovering, r*Zaranil is with him, and you need a little recovery yourself."

"What about you?"

"I slept. I had something to eat. I'm in no rush right now; the crisis, I think, is a little further away than that."

"I'm glad." He pushes to a less reclined position. "But there's some things to hear about, and start thinking about – aren't there?"

"I know some things. Remember, I can give you some idea of what I saw, and what it might mean, but r*Zaranil and Steve will have better perspectives. I'll tell you, Raoul, I wish Steve had been at the core with me. I'm not incompetent at cultural analysis, but it's not my field, and there was a lot there that needs interpretation."

Talbot gestures at the wall. "I was watching some of it. The things that were living there. All dead now, I suppose."

"Am I getting callous?" she asks, staring at the blank surface. "They were people, I suppose, in some way."

Talbot frowns. "I suppose. But there was nothing we could do."

"No. There wasn't. You know, on the upper levels, we thought they were vermin, but toward the core, they seemed at home in a different way. Like they worked there, or belonged there. I don't know how else to put it." Her hands shift in an ambiguous pattern.

He paces the room and turns toward her. "You think they were crew?"

She considers. "I think they might have been crew... once. A long time ago. I think they forgot how to run things. Everything seemed automated. They didn't seem to care about what was happening." On some unnamed impulse, she steps forward and touches his cheek, but he leans into the gesture and kisses her. She is surprised, but there is a hidden reason that she doesn't release. Their lips press and move in a sensation that seems almost alien and yet impossibly desirable to her. And Talbot feels a sudden outpouring of his feelings for her, feelings that clamor to be closed away before something irrevocable occurs. They separate, and he sees her looking at him with new eyes. He doesn't realize the tears of relief in his own eyes, and he doesn't yet admit that the irrevocable occurred long ago.

"I...." he starts. But she holds up a hand to his lips.

"Listen," she says. She pulls his ear down next to her, and whispers. "The controllers were morphic." Then, as if in apology for the business, she kisses just in front of his ear. "You keep quiet about this, OK?" Her voice is almost silent.

He looks worried for a moment. "The controllers... or..."

"Both," she snaps. She squeezes his hand. "...both, OK? For now."

"OK." He squeezes back and a host of unaccustomed emotions fight for his face. "Let's go see how Steve's doing."

290

Talbot sits by the door and watches the dust-like cybers come and go from his friend. r*Zaranil squats immobile in a corner. The soft glow of the door gleams from his scales and casts a faint reflected light on the walls.

291

"I sense some vehicles coming upsystem," Latimer notes from his position reclined at the head of the flight deck. "Inertialess drives of about eighty three percent."

"They were bound to notice," Clu replies. "Good thing is that they had something to send out."

"Diplomacy is going to take time," Jane remarks.

"What kind of diplomacy are we going to do?" Latimer continues the thought. "Are we going to agree to help them?"

"Against what?" Jane asks. "The threat is over. We know what works, now."

Clu stands silent. She draws out a slim cigar from her pocket and inspects it. She thrusts it into the side of her mouth and puffs it to ignition. The cloud drifts away on the faint breeze of ventilation. Clu stares levelly at Jane through the tendrils. She takes the cigar from her mouth and sighs smoke.

"This instance of the threat is over," she replies finally. "Let's talk to Talbot."

292

The vast bubble room overlooks the stern of the Promethean vehicle and the slowly expanding debris field that used to be the destroyer. Beyond are the other members of the destroyer fleet, still engaging in random destruction. Talbot looks around, uncomfortable. He turns to watch Hallison walking slowly up the ramp to join him. Hallison's face is pale, and one eyelid droops. But he smiles wanly at Talbot.

Reed is kneeling on the couches that edge the dome, deliberately turned away from the destroyer fleet, staring out at the starfields and the slightly brighter star that is Tlnou's sun. She turns back to face them, and at the sight of Hallison, her smile gets wide. She hurries over and embraces him. "You bastard," she cries. "You're OK." He tries to chuckle, but it is a weak effort that almost makes him double over, and he avoids her eyes. But she won't let him go, and she continues. "I know you went in for us. You can't know what I think about that, but I owe you."

He meets her eyes, but he says: "I didn't do anything except get trapped."

Talbot grips Hallison's arm. "This time it's the intent, not the result, Steve. Come on, sit down. Let's see what they want to negotiate now."

r*Zaranil and Wanr enter the room, in a quiet but heated debate.

"r*Zaranil!" Reed calls. She steps from Steve to the stooped D*Azar and waves her hands in an intricate pattern before his blind head. His small pursed mouth works in reply. Reed whispers to it... "You look none the worse for wear, now do you?" r*Zaranil's translator emits a cackling laugh. "It is required that I wear clothing or many disarrangements in integument visible. I *have* fallen down many holes before. Though as child."

She grins. "I just bet you did."

Talbot stands looking out at the sun, and thinking of a small woman who had found her husband. Suddenly, as he watches, a portion of the silvery surface below balloons to a large size and then reforms into a complex artifact that fissions from the surface and, now clearly a spacecraft, moves away from them toward the sun. "What's going on!" he yells. Reed hurries to join him, and the others turn in shock, watching the object accelerating into the distance.

"It's simple," Jane's voice replies from the doorway. He stares at her, eyes narrowed.

"How simple?" he asks.

"That's the shuttle taking the survivors of the *Norton* to rendezvous with vehicles approaching from Tlnou. It will return if they are accepted by the vehicles. If they are not, it will continue to Tlnou, release them at a space station or port, and return. Latimer is piloting, so they are completely safe."

Reed seems about to speak, but Talbot steps forward, and his face is ominously still. "And why are *we* still here?"

"Because we still have things to discuss," Clu answers, stepping up the ramp behind Jane.

"Things you would perhaps prefer not discussed before Latimer?" r*Zaranil suggests.

There is a sudden stillness in the room, and Talbot senses that r*Zaranil has successfully taken the initiative. And he remembers... *But the controllers were morphic.*

264

"Direct," Clu replies at last.

Talbot seems to Reed to have suddenly transformed; his expression is completely opaque to her, and she sees no reaction except a small, satisfied smile, which, for some unknown reason, she does not think is genuine.

"I wondered when you would decide to get this into the open," he says calmly, walking slowly across the room, deliberately not looking at the Sherril women. He knows that his problem now is to not trip over his lack of information until he has enough to provide a better focus. "But you've taken long enough about it. We know about the link between the destroyers and the morphics."

Clu lights a cigar and Talbot thinks she is playing for time.

"We're traders, Talbot. Let's exchange some information. What do you know about morphics? You don't have them."

Talbot knows he can't bluff this part. But there is a little more to do before he lets them know anything. "What exactly are you going to tell me in exchange?"

"Something that may fill in the details. Why all this dancing? - we're on the same side, you know." Her eyes are experienced, and the faint wrinkling at their corners deepens slightly.

Talbot glances over at Reed. He knows that she is the only one who can handle this part of the negotiation. He nods slightly, and she purses her lips, thinking furiously. Finally she opts, as they would, for candor... carefully.

"I'm not entirely sure that's true," he replies, looking to Reed with a slight nod.

"The xenophobes use morphic technology. In fact, except for you," she points, "they're the only ones we know who do."

Clu smiles and settles into a chair. Jane stands behind her, hand resting on its back. "Yes, that's almost true."

Wanr stirs beside Reed. His eyes open and it mutters. "Except for Latimer. Who gave morphics to you."

"And," Talbot murmurs, realizing, "who isn't here."

"Who isn't here," Reed meets his eyes, then looks back to Jane and Clu, "because you're starting to get worried too."

But they are stolid and unrevealing. Reluctantly, Jane speaks. "Clu has her reasons for this."

Talbot raises a eyebrow. He wonders what Hallison makes of this. But Hallison makes it clear after a faint pause. "Reasons she isn't discussing. Is that it, Clu?"

Talbot leans forward. "We've given you some of what we know, now it's time for payment." That much he feels comfortable that he understands. And so he waits, and the others wait with him.

Clu steps to the window and rests a hand on the arcuate support, looking outward at the receding vehicle. She stops and looks at them with slightly widened eyes. "I brought Latimer to Prometheus a long time ago. He's been my friend and a friend to my daughters and sons and their descendants. Now he works with Jane. I know him as well as I know anyone." Her eyes narrow. "Better than I know you." She draws on her cigar carefully, inspecting the ash. Then she sighs smoke that swirls away in the ventilation. "On the other hand, he came to me in a very strange way, and even I know only a small amount about where he came from, and how he used to live."

"He told us a small piece of his history," Talbot acknowledges.

Clu holds up her cigar. "You see this?" she asks. "I can afford to indulge in this because I have morphic bugs infesting my lungs, fixing any damage done. They're cleaning my skin and arranging my hair. They form the fabric of *Zadar 47*. The most advanced technologies of Prometheus are derived from them, and they are derived from Latimer."

"So what does this mean?" Wanr asks. "Latimer has power over you?"

"Latimer licenses the technology," Jane replies, head tossing thick dark hair from her shoulders. "It's made him the richest being in Prometheus, but five hundred years won't give even him a monopoly. There are several competing concepts now. There's no special power involved."

"But," Clu continues, "Latimer has been getting more and more... uncomfortable as we pursued the problem you brought to us. I think he was avoiding a conclusion that would have made things easier when we wanted to rescue you."

Jane frowns. "So that's what you were talking about!"

Talbot tries to resist the gratitude that starts to warm him. He has to remain clear.

"It's the first time I ever mistrusted him. I don't like it. But I've seen this fleet you were talking about, now. There are more of them, aren't there? Jane showed me recordings."

"There are more," Talbot replies. "Probably any one of them could turn even Prometheus or Tlnou into dust, given a week or so."

Clu smiles thinly. "I doubt it would be so clear cut."

Hallison has been watching it all, and his interest has started to rise. Finally he leans forward, but Reed is worried by the blotches on his face and the hoarseness of his voice. "I'm surprised you don't confront him."

"I intend to," Clu replies, annoyed. "But I want to know more about what you found on the destroyer before I start. I think you have information I need if I'm going after one of the best friends I've had in half a millennium."

Talbot nods to Reed, and Reed gestures for r*Zaranil. "Tell her about the controllers. I'll tell about the crew."

293

Latimer daydreams about less complicated centuries of gradually changing grasslands, forests and mountains. Of a civilization risen from near animals under his guidance. Of a fatal mistake that nearly left him alone again. He can feel his metallic hands vibrating slightly, as if the stress is close to making them disintegrate. He knows that his friends regard him as imperturbable, because of his robotic appearance - even those who know him the most closely, like Jane and Clu. But he is really worried this time. For the first time, perhaps, in millenia.

The oncoming ships are ranged across his mind as he shares part of his capacity with his vehicle. There are hours of time and billions of miles remaining before they come together.

As he waits, he tries to avoid the fear that is not the only thing returning to his life.

294

The Director steps into her office and looks across the red lit room at Latimer, who is peering curiously around at the artwork and the furniture from his capacious seat. "Welcome to the *Illyrion*," she greets him.

"I appreciate it."

"May I ask where the rest of my people are?"

Latimer is strangely still. "I am not sure what you mean."

"The *Norton*. Are they still in Prometheus?"

"No."

The Director analyzes Latimer's motions and expressions as being largely human. But she is suspicious of Latimer's apparently cybernetic nature.

"Do you intend to tell me what's happened?"

"Yes. I hope you're ready."

Her fingers twitch on the arm of the chair. "Oh?"

"It's an amazing story."

The dark metallic eyes Latimer shifts slowly reveal nothing. The Director waits. "The *Norton* has been destroyed," Latimer continues, and she lurches forward with a wicked smile.

295

Talbot lies asleep in a spare room, exhausted. His dreams twitch his skin. Suddenly he is awake, and his sweat is sour and afraid in the room. Then he is shaking and his muscles swing his legs off the shallow bed to the floor. A sob is torn out of him, and then the tears start coursing down his face. He cries and the sound is damped by the hidden walls.

But the door opens, somehow, and Reed stands silhouetted against the hall light. The interior light start to glow dimly, and through his tears, he can see some of her face.

"I thought," he sobs," I thought I was OK."

She kneels beside him, and her hand is pale on his cheek. "I know."

"But I... I haven't quite been paying attention, I guess." His shaking is subsiding. He is ashamed at his weakness.

"I know." Her voice is low and hoarse. Her hands reach up and clasp his shoulders. She draws his head down to rest on her shoulder, feeling strangely helpless and sick. At the same time, she knows his feelings, because they have been her own, and she once had to bear them silently. "It's the way things are for us. Here and now more than ever. But we're always on the edge of the unknown, Raoul, it's always this way. Don't worry."

He lifts his head and smiles at her. "Thanks," he whispers. His eyes are swollen and red; his cheek glistens in the dim light. Her face is close, and she feels an unnamed emotion that tips her forward to kiss him gently. The taste is briefly salty, and she is afraid of what she has just unleashed within herself. But at the same time, it feels like a correct step on a long path. "Go to sleep," she says quietly. "I'm across the alcove. Call me if you need me."

He nods. "I will." He wants to reach out and catch at her hand, but he is afraid to reach for her in a moment of weakness. He wants to be able to care for her in strength, not fear or sadness. So he watches her walk away, and he remembers a time, not so long ago, or maybe it is a century ago, where he watched her walking away down the hall and dismissed his attraction to her. Now, he is unable to. So he curls up and lies at the edge of the bed, hands heavy on his wrists.

296

Breakfast is a strange meal of odd bitter and sweet foods, and some coffee rescued from the hammar. It bothers Talbot slightly that they eat sitting on the floor of a hallway, with one side and end transparent. But that is no stranger than Jane Sherril sitting down the hall with a holographic panel projected in front of her as she manipulates its symbology for some unstated reason. Finally she looks up, using a pair of sticks to scoop some food from plate to mouth. "Better eat up," she warns. "Latimer's on the way. I think he's bringing someone from the incoming ships close behind."

297

Talbot is surprised at how strange the Director's face has become. She stands small of figure, large of presence, in the doorway from the *Zadar 47* hangar. He controls his smile and greets her. She nods gracefully. "So, I see you are improving and remembering, or is it just a bad mood?"

Now he laughs. "This is humor. From you."

Her tiny face is lowered and she says, "After the epic you have experienced, you deserve the effort. Latimer has told me about this. I wondered if it was the same Raoul Talbot so well known for misadventures. Perhaps many of the changes Atrenn predicted have come to pass." She eyes him from under lowered brows and then pulls him down to where she can inspect his eyes with her slit golden pupils. She releases him, and for a moment he remembers a rash suggestion by someone who must have been ages younger, and a similar response.

"Maybe," he replies. "Feels like I've still got a long way to go."

She wags her head briefly and he has forgotten what that means. "We'll talk more. There's a lot to do. I've brought you a hammar – the *Aeolo*, and some of your things from the *Illyrion*. We're not done traveling yet. There are some things to finalize with the Promethean representatives, and then we need to talk about the next step. Meet me on the hammar, would you?"

He feels a typical annoyance at the passing of command. "Sure. I have some things to pick up. What about Jill, Steve and Wanr?"

"Yes. I won't be long." She walks away down the unknown hall with the possession of someone completely at home, stored in a tiny angular figure.

298

Talbot leans through the door to find Reed. "Director's here," he tells her. "I'm to meet you all on the new hammar, its called the *Aeolo*. Get your stuff."

She sees a surprising pain on his face before he ducks back out the door.

299

Talbot is wandering the *Aeolo*, getting an idea of its status. He hears the lock chime and pauses. He shrugs and stalks toward the flight deck. But almost there, he encounters the Director, who is pacing in a narrow circle, teeth bared. He stops and watches for a moment until the Director notices him.

"Director?" he asks, puzzled. "Are you all right?"

"I don't like being compressed, Talbot." she hisses.

He is taken aback. "Compressed? Oh, pressured."

"Yes, compressed."

"By who?"

Another voice sounds over the lock chime. "By me," replies Jane Sherril, stepping through the door, clothed in a flowing garment flickering with animations.

300

"Something's happened with Latimer," Wanr mutters to Reed from his console at the rear of the hammar's flight deck.

"What do you mean?" she asks, swiveling to face him in the familiar dimness.

"Leaving he is," Wanr replies, head looking away in surprise. His voice is abstracted. He drops the window into her workspace, and she watches plot and projections. "That doesn't look like a vector to Prometheus space. Where's he going? Raoul?!" she calls, "come here!"

Finally, Talbot leans through the open door into the red light. "What?"

"Latimer's leaving, you know anything about that?"

He considers. "No, but Jane's right down the hall, let me ask."

Wanr picks up the thread. "Destination Prometheus is not. Very unlikely. Soon depart or catch never."

Talbot knows what they are thinking. "Get Steve on board, unlatch, and pursue. Make sure the recorders are at the highest resolution. Watch the fold open, too. He may or may not use the Promethean coordinate systems, and we may have to figure out what he used after the fact."

"But we'd need a mathematician for that," Reed protests.

"You'll have to do for now, Jill. I have to tell Jane and the Director. You guys run the show until I get back."

301

The *Aeolo's* flight deck is crowded as the Director and Jane Sherril stand in the space by the door, watching.

Talbot's hands fly over the control surfaces, and he finds himself comparing the crudity of these systems with the polish of the *Norton*. He remembers the pilot of the *Norton*, and its frightening death. But the hammar systems come alive with his intuitive movement - once again the vehicle is an extension of his mind, and they are moving.

302

Clu Sherril stands at the center of a drastically altered flightdeck, watching fisheye views of Talbot's hammar and Latimer's vehicle on the air in front of her. The smoke curls softly from her thin cigar and her teeth are bared as her ship swings out of solar orbit to follow the two ahead. Once again, she tries to reach Latimer, but he is not responding, no matter how hard she concentrates on the tiny nanocommunicators that sift slowly through her brain.

303

Latimer lies amidst stars in null gravity, silver eyes unblinking, controlling the vehicle slowly as he tries to recall the coordinates which he had spent so much time blocking from his mind. He must be sure, and he must translate properly, and there is very little time. He can feel the others following him.

304

Talbot is thinking furiously. There is no question that Latimer has lied to them. For all he knows, Jane and Clu have lied deeply as well. But they seem equally shocked by Latimer's desertion. Why? Had Latimer lied to them, as well?

And as he watches, the morphic vehicle ahead vanishes. From behind, Clu Sherril overtakes them, flashing in a lengthy complex of silver overhead and then diminishing with distance to a point. The magnification tracks as her vehicle folds away.

"Same orientation," Wanr reports.

"Field strength converted for size, mass and geometry seems to make sense as heading to the same destination. She figured it out a lot faster than our systems," Reed remarks to Talbot.

Jane snorts. "Sure, she's got those Gomeac neuronal parasynths smoking away. She sent the coordinates to me, though, pre-translated into your system, so don't strain."

Hallison watches her from a face pale with mistrust. "Why should we - "

"Believe me? You think I want to be stranded somewhere in this tiny thing? You think my gran wants that? Come on." She leans over Wanr's shoulder and studies the displays for a few moments. Wanr calls up a coordinate pad, and she enters the information with a swift patter of fingers across the matrices.

Talbot pushes the vehicle to the limits of the dampers and slightly beyond. He can feel faint strings of acceleration tugging through the fields. He reads the coordinates and sets a direction and velocity that will achieve the proper fold orientation.

"Here we go!" he cries. His hand comes down on the panel. Hard.

Then they are gone, too.

Phase 4

Aeolo and the Web

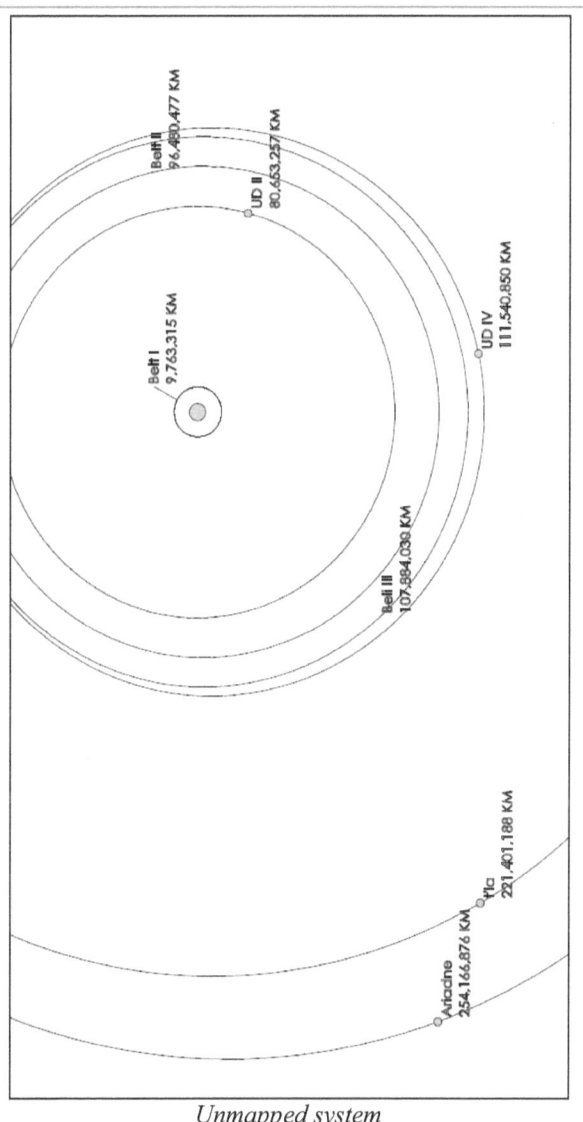

Belt II
96,480,477 KM

UD III
80,653,257 KM

Belt I
9,763,315 KM

UD IV
111,540,850 KM

Belt III
107,884,039 KM

Pla
221,401,188 KM

Ariadne
254,166,876 KM

Unmapped system

305

Three space vehicles wink into existence at slightly different distances from the star. Latimer's vehicle accelerates inertialess toward a planet near the margins of the humanly habitable zone, and the others follow.

"He won't answer," Wanr replies.

"Won't, or isn't listening," Jane mutters from the back.

"You've got some insights you want to share with us?" Reed snaps.

Jane sighs. "Look, he knows something he doesn't want us to know and it made him desperate enough to come here. We're pretty far toward the cluster core, if my guess on the coordinates and the constellations is right. Nobody knows anything about this area, other than that there are some very old planets here, but Clu met Latimer somewhere on the fringes of this concentration. What I think we should do is contact Clu and get her to hangar our ship, so we can work together from *Zadar 47* and find out what's happened to Latimer."

Talbot turns in his seat to face the window wall, and his face is furious. Finally he looks at Reed. "Do it." He stands and walks to the door, pausing beside Jane. His mouth shifts slowly, and finally he says: "I have been lied to, set on fire, blown up, and watched friend after friend die because people are not telling the truth about the xenophobes. If you ever want a relationship with the Geodesic, don't lie to me this time." He walks out before she can react, but the Director is frowning madly.

306

The wind howls along the crawling surface of billions of fractal sized machines. Sometimes the wind forms tiny whirlpools in the lee of larger, more stationary machines, and dusty little systems are lofted into the air to join glistening clouds in the turquoise noon sky, and then rain down in glittering streamers against the horizon.

The travelers tear at the fabric of the larger constructions, infecting them with dissociation. No feature larger than an inch high survives the vicious winnowing. But the plain is constantly changing.

307

As he travels inward from the fold point, Latimer finds his substance gradually merging with the vehicle. He wonders if it merely represents the relaxation of ancient constraints, or if his destination is raising a fear.

He feels the slow protons like a fresh breeze on his skin, and he turns down his reflectivity so that the cascade of radiation seeps down into his core for storage. The worlds are like small pebbles in his brain, and the double suns are dancing a texture of radiation and particles that he can feel as three-dimensional currents. He swims those currents, inertialess, driving inward against them with all of his strength. Because, upstream, he can feel the hard surface of his homeworld.

He never notices the vehicles behind him, so fixed is his attention and his hope.

The worlds are silent, and their orbits are empty of the Manganese-t'la and the Companions. The Webs are missing, and if he had human eyes, the sadness of that destruction would make him cry.

He orbits the world, and it seems strange - clouds, earth, and sea, all the same shifting grayness. He calls and nothing is answering, except a faint echo from somewhere behind him, but he ignores that, listening with every quantum for any response from below. Yet all he hears is a faint hissing, as if thousands of insects have been given voices that can only whisper a single thought each. And in frustration, outside awareness and a carefully grown consciousness, Latimer plunges into the atmosphere, like a swimmer, arms outstretched.

308

As the clouds wisp across his skin, Latimer starts to scream.

309

Clu watches the projections and her face is still while her eyes burn. The screaming is faint in the background of the flight deck.

"Can't we do something?" Jane demands. "Gran, we've got to help him."

"We can't," Clu snaps. "We can't." It is almost a cry.

"Why not?" Talbot demands. "What do you know?"

Clu turns to face him, and for the first time Talbot sees her age. An incipient tear glints at the corner of her eye. "I know that my best friend is going to smash into the surface of that planet in about ten minutes at a speed that's going to kill him. That's what I know. Ten minutes is too short to do anything."

Talbot turns to Reed. She nods and sets off at a run for the hangar, gathering Steve and Wanr with a glance and a gesture. The Director watches, mystified, as Talbot leans toward Clu. "Ten minutes is plenty of time. At least, the way I fly. If your ship can't do it, I will."

"I.... I can't."

"When I come back, you're going to explain why." Talbot's voice and eyes are cold. His eyes break contact as he turns.

"But I can't let you come back," she cries.

He ignores her as he takes flight into shadow.

310

The plasma lights the underside of Talbot's face as it forms under the belly of the hammar. He watches the graphs carefully and inches the nose slightly higher.

"Seven minutes," Wanr glances over at Talbot with eyes that reflect the hellish external scene.

"What's Jill saying?" Talbot demands. "Is she on schedule?"

"So far." Wanr replies. A brief transient sound slips into Talbot's supersonic.

"So are we," Talbot mutters, wrestling with the controls in a space of turbulence.

311

A huge robotic arm lifts the brace into position near the stern of the *Aeolo*, pushing hard against acceleration. Six welders fly into position and sheaves of sparks fly momentarily as they fuse the glues into the fabric of beam and sheet.

Reed whirls her hands, and the testers replace the welders, checking for seams and weakness. Her eyes flick rapidly across the remote displays. She compares the stress factors and calls to Steve. "Get me a three gauge up there, point two seven to the stern. Hurry! Not long now. We've got to get this braced!"

312

One minute

Latimer appears ahead and below. Talbot has long since stopped listening to the transmissions. But he can see the chaotic plasma tail stretching for miles against the misty darkness of the clouded grey world. He pitches the nose slightly downward, and angrily slaps the alarms to silence.

Thirty seconds

Latimer's plasma tail sweeps erratically across the hammer, and the currents toss the nose briefly. Talbot shoves the nose down and the *Aeolo* dips under the plummeting vehicle. He stares upward, watching the docking mark, shaking with the effort it takes to ignore the closeness of the ground and the turbulence of the Promethean ship. Finally, the reticule matches, the routines link, and the engines push the hammer up against Latimer. The configuration shudders under a load never intended. Wanr extends their inertialess field to include Latimer, and for the two vehicles, inertia reduced, the power of the engines is almost sufficient. The friction of the two bodies is almost enough to keep them together long enough. Almost.

313

The first hint of failure manifests itself as a sudden and wicked roll counter-clockwise. Talbot drags the controller, but without effect. He can see the shape of Latimer's vessel shifting and then slipping past the edges of the window wall. Alarms scream as section after section of the hammer is violated by a never-intended pressure. He hears the doors slamming behind him as areas seal and he can only spare a moment for the terrifying thought of what might happen to Jill. He tries to reach down for the helmet between the seat, but the hammer lurches and he refocuses on the balance problem. More alarms sound, and Talbot suddenly knows he has an altitude problem. Outside, the horizon bucks wildly, and suddenly he is staring down at a strange heaving sea of silvery dust, crumpling and smoothing under the winds, then again at the turquoise sky.

For a moment he realizes the feeling that makes a pilot ride his vehicle into the ground. The conflicting alarms, the skewed handling, the uprushing ground - an irresistible problem; a problem he knows he can solve. If only he has enough time. It is so terribly seductive that for a moment he allows himself to be deluded into thinking that there is time. But he can wait no longer, and with a sob from tightly compressed lips, he yanks the hammar into an opposite roll, casting Latimer to the wind, and the ground below.

Gravity and acceleration leap through the dampers as the *Aeolo* springs free. The world below rotates swiftly and unstably past the window wall as the pale echoes of deadly forces slap blood from his brain and tug at the skin of his face and belly.

Time stands still and the hammar splashes into the sea of dust, casting microscopic machines hundreds of feet into the air. Talbot stares in helplessness as the hammar slides and rolls across the surface, plowing the thicker layers of machine into a wake. Then his hands move to anticipate the auto systems and shut down anything that might be damaged by the crash.

The *Aeolo* gives a final shudder and halts under the late day sun.

314

"You know, Raoul, if the Director ever decides to charge you for the vehicles you've wrecked, you'll be working for the rest of your life to pay it off." Gillian Reed leans through the flight deck door, grinning broadly with relief.

He laughs. "I've never lost a ship. I know right where they all are, including this one."

"Yeah, chief," Hallison chimes in from behind Reed. "Right in the middle of a metal desert on a planet no one's ever heard of at coordinates in a system we don't know, following a runaway alien cyber, who's skipped out for no apparent reason."

"Seems reasonable to me," Wanr intones quietly from his console. Talbot stares, wondering if this is his humor.

He stands slowly and stares at the slanted landscape. The hammar is nearly on its side in the granular metal sea.

"What *is* that stuff?" he wonders.

Wanr glances at the console and back up. "Morphic quanta. In nearly an isolated state."

Reed calls up a display to confirm. "I wonder if this is something like Latimer's homeworld."

"Where's Latimer?" Hallison asks.

"Planetary south extension one quarter mile leading to site of crash." Wanr replies.

Talbot drops back into the left seat and attempts to open communication. The screaming has stopped, replaced by static. "Can Latimer die?" he wonders out loud.

315

Shadows thrust millions of fingers across the landscape toward them as towers rise and erode like a time lapse. The suns are noticeably settled toward the horizon, and the clouds are dissipating as the temperature diminishes. Talbot steps from the lock and the dust puffs up around him, then resumes its ceaseless building and destruction. He stands terrified, up to his calves in rustling movement, but the constructions are fragile, and he is not trapped. His anxiety eases, and he sets out toward the wreck.

316

The vehicle looks pitted and melted. It seems as if a smoke is rising from where it meets the ground. Reed bends to inspect, and then remarks, "It's dissolving."

Talbot runs his hands over his skinsuit, but the suit is not affected.

"No," she shakes her head, "it's more like the quanta of the ship are splitting away. Walking away. I've never seen anything like it."

Talbot is running his hands along the hull. "How do we get in? Does Latimer have to let us in? I wish we had Clu here." He slams his hands on the corroded metal.

Wanr approaches from the shadowed tail of the huge spindle. "Perhaps, entrance can be gained with correct persuasion?"

"Persuasion?" Talbot asks.

"Quanta move if asked nicely with certain radiative combinations – a key. I rigged from communications something." A camera pod is drifting above his suited head.

"What the hell is that?" Hallison asks, pointing at the camera pod.

"It's a hobby," Talbot interjects. "All right, see if you can convince the quanta to get out of the way and let us in."

"Process actually more of an absorption, so stand close please."

The surface suddenly bulges inward like a vast pocket; it glows with rushing colors. Talbot steps up into the formation and as they walk forward, it irises away into an opening. He bends through into the

280

darkness of a chamber. After the iris seals behind them, the chamber opens into a large open space.

And hanging in the space, webbed with quanta extending from every part of his body, is Latimer, sobbing with pain.

317

Talbot signals to Wanr. "Can you use your 'device' to cut him down?"

Wanr stands on his toes to peer at the webs. He looks along to Latimer's contorted face, and Talbot wonders what Wanr feels about Latimer's agony.

"Perhaps." He steps to a web and adjusts the stick. A few more adjustments, and the web falls away. Wanr shifts his head to one side, staring at the floor near Talbot. Talbot remembers and shuffles his feet. Wanr quickly turns and waves the wand across the webs nearby and then moves around the room. Latimer rolls under the unequal stresses, and then, as the last web parts, falls to the floor.

Reed holds up a skinsuit. "I think we should put him in this."

"Why?"

Hallison responds, "The stuff outside. The hull. Remember chief? The stuff was eating away at it. Maybe it could do the same to him."

"Maybe it was," Talbot muses. "OK. Let's do it."

Latimer moans and writhes on the floor.

318

They stumble across the twilit plain to the *Aeolo*, and the airlock seals behind them. "Clean us up," he instructs Wanr.

Talbot slides gratefully into the left seat. The smell and sound is like a homecoming. Systems come up at a gesture but there are numerous failure indicators and risk lights. Suddenly there are hands on his shoulders. Jill. He smiles at her as she settles into the other seat.

"Think we'll find out what's going on?" she asks.

"Yeah," he replies. "We'll find out."

He readies the hammer to launch.

319

"I can't see them," Reed replies.

Talbot swallows the last of a hot cheese sandwich and takes a sip from the soda to clear his throat. "Why not?"

She looks at him with mock exasperation tinged with worry. "Because they're not there."

He waves up her window and sees that, indeed, the *Zadar 47* seems to be gone. "The question then is whether we have good enough coordinates to get back to Tlnou ourselves." He calls up equations and constraints in another window and stares at them, frowning.

"I have to go help Wanr with Latimer," Reed reminds him.

He sighs and looks up. "I know. I wish you could help me. Do what you can, and then come on back."

She smiles, and for a moment, he notices that some of her hair has escaped into thin tiny curls from her severe ponytail and that the skin around her eyes is faintly darkened with tiredness.

"Get some rest," she replies, ignoring her own state. "We don't have to get out of here that fast."

He nods. "You're right." He pushes to a stand. "But since we don't have to leave so fast, let's both take a break."

320

Latimer lies in a large tub, and some parts of his body have become softer or have changed shape. Latimer's eyes have become pure black, glossy and round, and Talbot wonders if Latimer can still see.

A variety of sensor arrays, many obviously ad hoc, hang over the tub or touch the surfaces of Latimer's body. Some shreds of Latimer's webs remain at the tips of his fingers and the base of his neck.

In the corner, Wanr is musing over a variety of hastily erected displays, occasionally correcting a program with a finger motion or soft reconnect. He looks up with huge dark glass eyes. "Latimer was looking at my eyes too long. Changing to match. Some kind of degeneration. Working on it."

Suddenly, there is a motion from the tub. A gasp and shift. Talbot grabs Reed's arm to keep her from tripping into him.

"Clu...erandc sksl tradis..."

Talbot leans over the tub, worried and slightly afraid. "Clu's not here right now, Latimer." And he is slightly angry for her abandoning her friend.

"Oh. Raoul." Latimer recognizes. His voice is slurred, but otherwise normal, and Talbot is reminded once again that Latimer is not biological. "What a horrible sight."

Talbot has to smile when Reed remarks, "Hey, Latimer, sure he looks tired, but it's not that bad."

"No, not Raoul. Hlshetni. My home. Oh, it's so awful, what they've done." Latimer's fingers tremble slightly, and Talbot wonders if he is crying.

"But what did you expect?" Reed asks.

Latimer's eyes slip shut and then open again, and they are silver. "A civilization."

Suddenly he writhes, and then steadies. "Shape Wars. Wiped out everything. The Webs are gone. The Companions are gone." For some reason that seems to sadden him more than anything.

He looks at Talbot. "Do you see what's wrong with me? You brought me back... you know what it's like down there. The whole planet used to be the morphics and the Companions. Now there's nothing, because the virus is telling every quantum to break away, to destroy any organized construction."

Latimer shivers again.

"What can we do?" Wanr asks, leaning down beside Latimer's head.

Latimer whispers. "Nothing. I'm doing what I can. So far, its working. All right."

"Why did you come here?" Reed asks.

"I thought this was where the vehicles came from. I was right."

"Vehicles?"

"The destroyers. The life forms, they are much like the Makers, the Manganese-t'la, but not identical. I think they have devolved. Or perhaps they were... related. But I knew what they were. And I was afraid."

"Of what?" Her face is lit coldly by the reflection from his metallic body.

"The Shape Wars."

"I don't understand."

"We were made by the Companions. They were... they needed us. They wanted us to look like them. Flat... I was riding to the transitage, and my parent was with me, and I saw an alien in the next vehicle. Pointy. I tried it, but shoan punished me."

Talbot and Reed exchange glances. "Why?"

"Because we have to look like the Companions. But the Companions were meeting more and more strangers, and the strangers were coming down and we started trying to look like them sometimes. There were campaigns to fix our shapes and some Companions tried drastic measures to freeze shapes. It became political. I had to leave."

"Why?"

Latimer began to lose some cohesion. "By then, I was ... a leader. They exiled me. I was afraid it would come to this, so I didn't fight them. I was so afraid." He trembles, and Wanr leans back to look at the displays for a moment. Wanr's large eyes close for a brief but extended moment. "I should have. I was right. It couldn't have been worse."

Though Latimer's lips continue to move, there is no sound for a while, except an occasional high tone. Finally, the tones return to the translator range.

"The Kleztharn faction... started the hating of different shapes. They wanted the Manganese-t'la to band together and keep out all aliens, so that we wouldn't be tempted by anything.. we would be loyal, they called it, to the Makers." His eyes close again. "It didn't work, and the Kleztharn...We had a war. I left. It was exile, but it was better... than what was coming."

Talbot leans against the side of the tub, suddenly drained. "But where is everyone?"

Latimer looks at him with a sudden lucidity. "They are still present. The machines, the devolved and the morphic pools on the surface. And me. That's all we've got."

Talbot looks at Reed. "Do what you can. I'm going to get some sleep. Call me. Get some rest too if you can."

She nods.

"He's right about one thing," she says quietly.

"What?"

"I checked the fold line. This is a potential terminus of the signal from the Mover on Tlnou. It may have sent it to tell them it had... well, whatever you want to call it – metastasized?"

Then, suddenly, she leans up and kisses his cheek lightly. "Maybe it's over, Raoul."

"Maybe."

321

The Director's anger is coldly directed at Clu Sherril. "You must return for the others."

Sherril is in a weary, sad mood, anger returned, and she stands legs apart with the stars sprawled behind her. "I will not. You don't understand. I know what's down there, and it's the end of Prometheus if it gets back. I wish I could shoot their ship out of space."

"I thought you were Latimer's friend," Jane shouts, "How can you just leave him there to die?"

"He was dead the moment he touched atmosphere," Clu replies. "Didn't you understand what you were seeing and hearing? There's something about that place that kills morphics. We would have been riding air as soon as we entered the atmosphere, and if we lived through the impact, we'd be still there, because our ship would be gone. Just like every piece of morphic technology in Prometheus will be if they get back, damn it. And," she turns to the Director, "this is the end of the relationship between the Geodesic and Prometheus, if they get out and go home. We could never have contact again. It wouldn't be safe for Prometheus."

322

Talbot crawls into the bed, every muscle tired and his eyes feeling like they are splashed with sand. But as he falls asleep he remembers something that startles him to wakefulness.

The Geodesic government was negotiating with the xenophobes. They can't all be dead.

And who actually sent the destroyers?

323

r*Zaranil stands over the tub where Latimer gleams in the cold light. Wanr sits in the corner, fur flat with anxiety, trying to assess the displays, which r*Zaranil listens to as a radar whisper that fills the room. He listens to the faint suggestion of chatter between the quanta, on a band close to the D*Azar verbal speech pattern, and knows that they are somehow forcing themselves away from each other, as if it were an appropriate stage of their development. But it is the effect of a conceptual virus.

r*Zaranil links a thin waveguide to a support over the tub. Latimer stares sightlessly up and does not respond, and r*Zaranil knows as well as Wanr that it is impossible to know if Latimer is surviving or dying. But it is fascinating to finally have an unrestricted access to morphic technology. r*Zaranil muses slowly over the similarity to other forms of life, hoping that somewhere in this relationship he will find a cure.

324

Talbot starts awake at the sense of someone sitting on the edge of his bed. Blearily he stares into the darkness and recognizes Reed. "Jill?"

"Hi, Raoul. Sorry, but I need you."

"What's going on?" His voice is thick and cracks briefly.

"I think r*Zaranil is trying to cure Latimer."

He is fully awake. "Really?"

"I'm not sure. It's just that ... he's making equipment over the bed, and.. he wants to take a sample. I think you should come with me when I ask him about it."

He sits up and as she starts to stand, he tugs at her arm, bringing her close, and he scents the faint sweat of her long shift just before he kisses her. For a moment, their eyes close.

325

The piece of morphic web glints in the bowl, and tiny dusts are being shed from its edge. r*Zaranil focuses a waveguide and then places a wand into the energy stream. The dust seems to swarm back toward the web, and the web itself trembles. r*Zaranil closes the waveguide. The web seems more reflective, and the dust no longer leaves it.

r*Zaranil's blind snout quests the air above the dish.

"Is it permanent?" Talbot asks.

r*Zaranil makes a spiral gesture in the air.

Wanr, hovering over Reed's shoulder, comments, "Does it matter?" Talbot eyes his flattened fur.

"Yes, I think so."

Reed glances over at the tub in which Latimer lies slowly dissolving. But r*Zaranil is already shifting equipment.

Energy scans over Latimer's silvery surface, and the liquid quanta begin to reform.

326

In the quiet light of the small cafeteria, they lean back against seats that reshape to fit them. "It is an interesting problem," r*Zaranil sips a pungent hot oil through his orifice, but his speech continues. "A strange virus, thought I, like the Mover it is. Defects in messages between the quanta, telling them to leave when they should work together, telling them to clump when they should be independent. Listening to the Mover, to you, to Latimer, and to my little listeners - heard I the messages, and once corrected, the damage is almost self repairing."

He reaches up to groom scales on his head with a thin metal tool.

327

Talbot leans over Wanr to watch the stubby whitish finger point to an element of the display, in orbit around an outer system gas giant. "So maybe Sherril didn't really leave."

"Yes, but realize they must prevent us. From leaving. If this is contagious, or they think so… We are… quarantined like plague bearers."

The isolation strikes Talbot hard, and he rocks back against the wall at the back of the flight deck. "They wouldn't..."

But Wanr does not finish Talbot's statement, and simply stares with huge black eyes, pursed white lips, and an expressionless furry face.

"We're clean, aren't we?"

"As best as instruments show, assuming r*Zaranil's technique maintains."

"Then we'll convince them not to destroy us." Talbot steps forward to the left seat.

"How?" Wanr asks.

"Damned if I know." He sits and stares at the window wall as the panes fly toward his field of view, anticipating commands. "Check Latimer if you can. We need to make sure there's no more infection. Get r*Zaranil to use that waveform thing to make sure every crevice of the ship is clean. And ask Jill to come up. I need a shower before we get out to them. Wish we could just air out the ship and know we were safe…"

328

Wanr in the right seat looks suddenly to Reed. "It isn't what it appeared. Not Sherril. Someone else."

The magnification shows vaguely a strangely appendaged object, covered with antennae like hairs, crusted with lights that shift slowly. "Five hundred miles long," she whispers. "And nothing I've ever seen."

329

Hallison peers down the flight deck to where Wanr and Reed are working. He gnaws on a thumbnail as he watches them, envying their composure. He feels as if the air is always cold, and a faint shiver seems to be symptomatic of his body in repose.

Talbot steps up beside him. "Steve, you're looking better. I'm really glad." Talbot's dark eyes are searching Hallison seriously from behind the smile.

"Hi, chief." The answer is the faint echo of a phrase Talbot has heard many times now. But Hallison's demeanor is... withdrawn?

Talbot looks down between the seats to the image on the window wall. "What the hell?" Suddenly his face hardens with attention. "I'd better get a report. Talk to you later, Steve." And he steps down into the pit, to engage in a low voiced conversation with Wanr and Reed. Hallison feels the cold increasing as he looks at the alien station imaged on the window wall. He turns from the room.

The hallway seems longer and quieter than he remembers. His steps ring on the floor metal, and he feels like he should be asleep.

330

"Additional sensor passive receipts," Wanr reports from his usual console at the back of the flight deck.

Reed glances at his image on the sensor wing of the window wall. "Like what?"

"IR sufficient, electrostatic, emissions some short wavelength."

"They don't seem to be scanning us, except passively. What do they see, Wanr?" Talbot asks. Wanr puts a simulation up on the window wall for Talbot. He glances over at Reed. "They can't see much, but if they get lucky and look over here..."

288

Wanr presents a rectangle with a modified course. "Acceptance modifies visibility keeping stranger largely planetary shadowed. Like it?"

Talbot processes the syntax for a second or two and then raises his eyebrows and his lips curl slightly into a self-mocking frown. "Yeah, I like it. Thanks." He adjusts the path to intercept the modified course, and triggers internal communication. "Steve, are you feeling up to trying some work here?"

"Anything but sitting around."

"Come on, then. We need you. Bring r*Zaranil with you if he's not...asleep."

He turns his attention back to the views. The image of the distant station is slowly blurring in the atmospheric limb of the gas giant.

Hallison slips in through the door and takes a seat at the rear. "What do you need me for, chief?"

"Some analysis of that station would be nice. Wanr's tanked the images. What is it? Who makes it? How alive is it? What can we expect from it when we pop around that gas giant? You know, the basic guesses."

Hallison sounds better, but still a little unsteady. "Okay. I'm on it."

"This could be the xenophobes. Latimer's 'Makers'. Get everything you can."

331

Reed leans toward him, and frowning thinly, she mutters, "Have you thought about the real issue?"

Talbot looks over, puzzled. "What are you talking about?"

"What we do when we get there?"

"Such as?"

"What are we going to do? Talk to them, or kill them?"

He sighs. "I wasn't aware that was one of our choices. In fact, I'm not clear we're wise to even go over there. We've got the chance to get out. Go back. I'm thinking that's the better choice."

Her eyes glint with the instruments. "So why is Steve working?"

"Because he needs to be."

She settles back in the seat and shakes her head slowly. He wonders for a moment what she feels for him. But then her face convulses with anger and she thrusts herself forward out of the seat. "Well, damn it," she cries, "I'm sick of this. Back and forth, back and forth across half the universe, and we're going to do it again? Sure, go ahead. But do it without me helping." And she stalks out of the room, back arrow straight, but head lowered. Talbot stares after her in shock.

332

Latimer struggles over the edge of the bowl. r*Zaranil tries to help him, and their two humanoid forms of silver, slick with cool backlighting, shift to a standing position - one scaled, one smooth.

Latimer's hand lingers on r*Zaranil's upper torso joint for a moment, as if for support. There might have been a moment when Latimer was tempted to shape shift and overwhelm r*Zaranil. Perhaps then he would have done something to regain freedom. But Wanr is standing in the doorway and he gestures with a bluish hoop; suddenly the portion of Latimer which senses and changes configurations is gone. Or hidden.

"A small imposition on your freedoms accept you must. There are questions of essence which answers are required."

r*Zaranil bobs his snout, and asks, "Where?"

"Flight deck conference 3. Talbot will access information directly."

"I suppose I deserve this," Latimer mutters.

Wanr waves his hands, and his fur fluffs; he then pushes at Latimer's shoulder so that the artificial gravity impels movement into the hallway.

333

The atmosphere of the world designated Ariadne rushes below them, with the cloud tops so well defined that Talbot feels as if he can reach down and touch them. Yet that layer is thousands of miles below. They are mutable canyons, heaving under winds unfelt, trapped within an atmosphere unbreathable. But they are still beautiful, and Talbot realizes how much he loves these sights. How much he always loved these sights and his life, even as he fought with himself and everyone else, even as he sank into self-destruction.

And at this moment, he is racing toward something which might destroy him. Yet this is so much different from self-destruction that he feels as if the air around him is cool and cleaner than anything he has ever breathed, even as he scents Jill's faint perfume, which she put on an hour ago, and even as the myriad odd scents of his team awaken many memories of the past months. Months which he realizes represent something so large that they will never be repeated.

"Two minutes to horizon," Reed remarks.

"No sign of active sensors," Wanr's voice is crisp from behind Talbot. Talbot looks at the image of Wanr in his window wall, and for a moment sees Amel. His vision blurs for a second as he realizes that he wishes Amel, x*Rkar, Schacther, and most of all, Atrenn, could be here to see how far he has come.

Talbot looks over his shoulder at Latimer. "Any last words?" he asks.

"I hope that you are not planning on dying. I've already been brought back once."

Talbot looks back at the window wall to see the faint speck of their destination targeted just below the cloud line by light amplifiers. The terminator is moving toward them like a wall of darkness across the rumpled endless sheet below. Then it is on them, and the light of the cloudscape is a pale and amplified blue lit by one of the moons.

Reed reaches over and touches his hand. "It's up."

"Any ping, Wanr?"

"Please?"

"Active sensors?"

"No."

The tiny star crawls up from the horizon.

"I hope we're good at this." Jill grins at him, and he wants more than anything to take her away to a quiet spot with nothing to worry about.

"Yeah, we are."

Talbot gestures and starts the hammar up to intercept. Then he flickers his hands across the touchpoints on the armrest, and the window wall goes to visual. A tiny countdown clock flickers in the corner. *Waiting...*

334

"Still no active sensors," Wanr remarks. "Derelict I might suggest except for various outflows energic."

The object is now a small darkened blot against the crust of stars, one edge just beginning to catch the light of the sun.

Talbot can feel his heart pounding, and he wonders if he is afraid, or just in suspense. He takes a last sip of steaming soup and seals the container. "OK, they're not looking for us – maybe they don't expect us, maybe they don't care. We'll reorient at the orbital stern of the vehicle and then accelerate to catch up with them. Wanr, give r*Zaranil your console and do what you can to protect the docking port in case we make contact or they send something after us."

He lifts his helmet from the rack and stares at it for a moment. Then he pulls it over his head and locks it against the metal collar. The stiff armored gloves over his hands, collared and locked. He thinks about a long ago shuttle drop, with no premonition of trouble, with death at its end. He wishes worrying about the present would protect him. But he knows it won't.

335

The *Aeolo* comes to life and the displays flicker into existence around the edges of the window wall. Talbot takes control and the hammar wheels under the impetus of thrusts to face the ancient object and the sun beyond. The thousands of antennae are now seen as a forest of vast but irregular towers, glittering with bands of light, silhouetted against the distant sun.

"The center is more open, there may be a platform," r*Zaranil suggests.

The towers sweep slowly past them, and they can see beings moving behind the vast windows that cover the towers. "They look like the Manganese-t'la," a voice comes from behind them. It is Latimer, and Hallison stands behind him.

The beings are flat and multilateral. Tendrils pop up from their surfaces, but it is impossible to tell their meaning.

"But they are not," Latimer continues.

Talbot nods to Reed who takes the controls. "What are you talking about?"

"They are morphic, as I am. They are Companions who have taken the form of the Manganese-t'la. They think we are representatives of the Geodesic who have come to complete negotiations with them. I have not disabused them of the notion."

"How can you know that?" Reed snaps derisively, staring ahead as she controls their course.

"They are communicating with me," Latimer replies.

336

"This is the location. Lower to there," Latimer recommends. "Observe the markings in the ultraviolet."

Talbot turns to the others. "Fine, we're locked into a slow descent, and we need the five minutes or so to figure out how to handle this."

Reed's face is largely hidden by her focus on the landing, so he wonders at her expression when she snaps: "We should get out of here, now, and let the Geodesic government or Prometheus handle it. This is out of our league."

Latimer crouches into the aisle, level with them. His voice is low and melodic. "We can do this. They assume that I am one of their interpreters, damaged and resignatured by my crash on the planet. I have explained it as an accident caused by your curiosity."

Talbot sighs. "The question in my mind right now, Latimer, is why you want to do this."

Latimer looks at Talbot in a way that is very hard to read because of the blankness of his eyes. "I want to find out why they are willing to let this plague run free. They are morphic, they are not the Manganese-t'la. They live in a broken remnant of the Web. Why do they want to negotiate to destroy other forms of life? I had hoped that the survivors would be followers of mine, but they no longer even remember me. What happened to my legacy, Talbot? Why did they squander it?"

r*Zaranil states, "The vehicle is not diamir. It is morphic. I am confused as to the connections with the other xenophobe technologies."

Latimer looks on sightlessly. "Morphics can synthesize diamir easily."

Talbot asks. "Will they accept the shapes of the various species in the Geodesic?"

"They know of humans and Tereniades. I do not know regarding others. If they are the remnants of the Kleztharn, then they may be hostile to variety only in the Vantmar. Suits may hide your differences. I am not under the impression that you are expected to be naked, and your bipedal forms are similar enough that any might pass as the same."

Talbot is staggered by a realization. "But I thought the Kleztharn were Makers... a Manganese-t'la faction."

Latimer seems surprised. "Oh, no, Vantmar were the Kleztharn. That is, some of us, the Companions. I'm sorry. I would have told you if I thought you didn't understand."

Talbot turns to Reed. "I'm a lot less comfortable discovering something like this just before we go in."

Her hands twist up in a human spacer shrug. "I don't see how it changes anything. I wasn't assuming they'd be friendly." She turns to Latimer. "Will they allow us to carry side arms?"

"Morphics are not endangered by energy weapons, so I am sure they will not care."

"I don't give a damn about harming them. I just want to be able to cut my way out through the hull. As far as protecting ourselves, my guess is that Wanr and r*Zaranil have been working on that issue."

Wanr's pelt is soft and fluffy and then subsides to a flat shape. "You are quite wise," r*Zaranil replies.

Wanr picks up the thought, "You I am sure knew that I would not fail to be prepared. Indeed working we have been, and successfully we hope. I think, however, there is no need to discuss this further, am I right?"

"Of this I am sure," she mocks gently.

"Latimer, come with us you must, for your protection," Wanr states. He leads Latimer away toward the medical area.

337

They step out into the golden sunlit vacuum, and the shadows it casts from them across the deck are long and autumnal. The metal is oddly dark, yet iridescent, and there are tiny lights irregularly embedded it like seeds, leading across to a low oval portal at the edge of the landing deck. There is no sign of where the opening leads, because it is dark with unmoving shadows, even with the enhancement of their contrast enhancers.

Wild towers, crusted with windows, stand against stars and sun alike. There is movement behind the windows, figures in amber light, and occasional flashes.

As they step across the platform, Talbot feels the metal sucking gently at his feet, and there is now no question in his mind that he is afraid. His jaw is held tetanic to prevent his teeth from grinding, or a moan from escaping. Somehow, he wishes he could turn back, leap into the *Aeolo*, and escape. But he does not even turn for a look. He cannot. *The answers*, he tells himself, *are here. And I deserve those answers. I need a way to end this for Atrenn, for Amel, for x*Rkar, and Schacther.* And for that man left quaking at the rear of a shuttle on a world the color of blood - whom he tries not to remember.

Reed watches them from the window wall, their tiny procession against the myriad towers arcing into the sun. Her eyes are cold, but somehow faintly sad.

They step into the portal, one by one, and are swallowed by shadows.

338

The tunnels are low and wide, and ahead of them, Latimer has changed form to match the Manganese-t'la. But he has retained an additional backward facing human head, with which he communicates with Talbot and the others. Talbot wonders if Latimer has such a dreadful sense of humor that he thinks this is a joke, or if he is simply humorless and doesn't recognize the ridiculous.

"I don't like this," Talbot gripes. "I hate tunnels."

"Good thing you didn't go down into the destroyer, then," Reed replies over the link.

"Those were tall," Wanr mutters, ducking under yet another narrow segment. Talbot peers up into the join, but sees no mechanism to seal the tunnel. So the narrows are yet another mystery. As is the general filthiness. "And clean," Talbot remarks.

"This station has been in use for ten thousand years," Latimer replies. "And with the population recycling every spare quantum, there isn't much for housekeeping. This isn't like Prometheus. These people have been here for a long time, and haven't expanded."

"Why?" Talbot asks.

Latimer materializes a set of shoulders beside his head, and shrugs. The shoulders disappear and the head resorbs except for a ripple of features. Talbot wonders if Latimer is worried that the inhabitants might scavenge for his quanta. Wanr seems to have read the thought, and hefts his modified laser casing. Talbot sighs. All of the options seem to lead to death. He hopes he will do better with this blind negotiating that he was able to in Prometheus. This time, a mistake might literally be the end of the world. He wonders if he is getting used to the idea.

They step through a last narrow into a vast, low-ceilinged, gunmetal dish. Faint cold lights, bright in the ultraviolet, line the upper segments. And thousands of the huge starfish glitter in the bowl, shifting restlessly, with a sound that Talbot's sensors translate like a rustle of foliage. And in that instant he is horribly sick for the sight of a tree or some grass, of any color. He coughs to drive away the nausea.

"Now what?" he asks.

Latimer has paused at the edge of the bowl. "Spectators, I think. This way." He leads them along the edge.

"Steve, why spectators?" he asks.

"Could be we're local heroes, chief. Economic emancipators. Get the drift?"

"Odd, considering the product." It is a small strain to keep the conversation cryptic, but Talbot is banking on these creatures' lack of experience and need for Latimer as a translator. If all of this is not a reverse deception.

The shelf slips through the narrows again and into the constantly wavering tunnels. Behind them is sudden sound and a flashing. Talbot watches the display of the route recording on the inside of his helmet, and hopes it won't get too complicated. They ramp down underneath some other openings, heading deeper.

Talbot brings up a recording of the bowl onto his visor as he walks, and he sees what he thought. His gloves gesture markings and he shares the result with Hallison - who stops and turns. "You're right. What the - " but Talbot silences him with a gesture. "Just remember," he replies.

The shapes had been forming replicas of their suits. Even the visible light colors had been correct. Talbot forwards the image to Reed. After a few minutes he hears a whisper from the hammar, "Don't forget Rosebud, Raoul."

"You too," he replies. But he is ashamed that his voice cracks slightly.

339

Three of the Companions lie on the floor, their surfaces gently undulating with stalks that grow, fall and resurge in the cold dimness. Talbot stares at them, and thinks of how weak they appear, and how dangerous they are. He can hardly speak, but he gestures to the others, and they assume seats on the floor, the humans cross-legged, Wanr on his haunches.

"Latimer?" he prompts.

"They would like to know your response to the result of the second test."

Talbot thinks of all the things he wants to know. *The locations of the tests. The timing. Who performed them. But how to ask?* His mind races through alternatives. He starts with indirection.

"Tell them that the second test was extended in a way we didn't expect."

The creatures seem to stir slightly.

"They are aware of Tlnou."

"We know the Mover sent a message. Of course they're aware." His thoughts mill about furiously. "But the test wasn't controllable. It casts doubt on whether the weapon is controllable." But he wonders if they care. Perhaps this whole "deal" is just a ruse to introduce the Mover into the Geodesic.

"They are referring to the results of the original test at Govault, and suggest that geographic isolation is required for control."

Govault!

The blood rushes to his face and he is momentarily dizzy. *These are the murderers of my friends, twice over,* he dares to think. Reed's voice is in his ear. "Don't think about it, Raoul."

"They ask the status of the second test device."

"Tell them I don't know anything new." He snaps.

But Latimer is looking at him and Talbot knows what he is remembering.

"Tell them."

"They say that the weapon is best used in situations where access can be controlled or where the effect is preemptive."

Talbot drags his mind back to questioning. He doesn't dare to go with the flow. "Tell them that there's more. That we want to know their role in an attack on one of our systems. That was not," he hopes, "part of the arrangement."

There is something that may resemble agitation in the group – a massing of risen tendrils that sweep and quickly subside.

Latimer's face mirrors confusion. "They are… saying many things I can't really understand. Perhaps they are talking about…. Autonomic response. Something not planned but ready. A reflex?"

"Get a grip, Latimer. I need you to figure out what they're saying."

Latimer is silent, with just the tips of his star form twitching. Finally… "The additional forces are… distributed and autonomous. This is a state of affairs that has persisted for a long time. More than twenty-five thousand years. They are disclaiming responsibility. The response is normal. When the… Mover… sends the signal that it has… decrystallized? - this is the normal response."

So they really know what happened.

Now things become delicate. Should he threaten them? Break the agreement? Any of those responses might lead to a genocidal impulse.

He settles on a middle course. He has found out enough. It is time to go.

"The automatic response is not acceptable. Our purpose in using the weapon is not to destroy solar systems."

"They claim they can disable the response."

"We require that they do so or the agreement will not be acceptable."

"I sense some kind of desperation they are trying to hide."

And Talbot hears a rising excitement in Latimer's voice. He is suddenly worried that the event is coming apart. "Wanr, stand by." he warns, voice shaking.

340

Reed stares out the window wall watching the group return across the platform. She knows that r*Zaranil is waiting with the antimorphic weapon at the airlock, and she knows that in the next few moments, she will have to decide whether or not to lift ship. Whether or not to leave her friends behind. And Talbot.

Finally, the voice arrives. "Kane."

Reed replies, "Sinclair."

Hallison responds, "Duncan."

Reed continues, "Ixthar."

Wanr replies, "Wells."

Reed smiles suddenly.

341

"Latimer, stay in the lock until r*Zaranil figures out how to check you." Talbot seals the door. Latimer's face is unmoved behind the clear surface, but for a moment Talbot thinks the metal expression is forlorn. r*Zaranil waves the antimorphic weapon across everyone else.

Reed has never seen Hallison so excited. "Jill, you should have seen it. It was... incredible."

"That's fine," Talbot snaps, "but we had better be out of here now."

"Latimer, what kind of desperation?" He senses Hallison at his arm. Hallison asks, "What are you doing?"

Talbot raises his hands. "Wait."

"Hunch?" Hallison suggests.

"Hunch," he replies.

Latimer finally continues. "I sense they do not care for the technology. I can't understand why."

Talbot frowns. "Apparently you didn't either, since you stopped it."

Latimer looks opaque as only a machine can.

Talbot leans forward. "I know you did it. You know how to stop it."

Latimer smiles suddenly. "It has a vulnerability, as you do, as I do. I merely exploited my own organizing transmissions to disrupt it."

Reed cocks her head at a report. "There is a second ship. Approaching."

Latimer sighs and reflows into his usual humanoid shape. "I have been given a complex explanation. I will try..." Talbot does know that if it weren't impossible he could swear that Latimer was about to cry.

"These Companions are the ... descendants of quanta of the Kleztharn, as we thought." He turns to face them, and there is a warm light from somewhere that lines the edge of his jaw. "But some of them are no longer Kleztharn. Oh, Raoul. Some of them gave up the Shape Wars long ago, and retreated here. Everything was dying. They destroyed the Makers, as I suspected. But the Kleztharn technology - the xenophobic technology - was so early released, so long away, that no one knew where it had all gone, or what the missions were.

"Some of them organized and went out on missions of their own... I think to collect what they could, and destroy it, or put it in museums. But when this group met the first negotiators, I think some of them had become more desperate for survival or raw materials, or perhaps were shocked by first contact – and, being less scrupulous, they set up the deal.

"A few of these delegates are afraid. Afraid they are restarting the Shape Wars. They actually remember my information! My person. It is... wonderful. And the other ship - they also remember, and are afraid – they have asked me about the Geodesic and Prometheus."

"And?" Hallison wonders.

"And, well, that is where there is a problem. I have to refuse to tell them. They can use the same ability I used on the Mover. They are about to use it to stop the descendants of the Kleztharn, and they must not follow us or they may do the same to us."

342

The team is irrepressibly talking all at once in the corridor, helmets off, voices perhaps over-cheerful with the release from stress.

But Talbot grabs Reed by the arm. "Time to go," he insists, walking her to the flight deck.

The lights are cool and blue, the spaces dim and quiet. Talbot drops into the left seat and throws windows up on the wall with abandon.

"Left compensators," he intones, excited.

"Check."

"Right compensators."

"Check."

"Power module overloads."

"Check." But her tone is worried. Talbot is obviously looking for a full power takeoff.

"Release the synchronization interlocks, I'll monitor the feed personally."

"Would you like the ritual warning?"

"No time to waste. Auto checklist?"

"Complete."

"Let's light the torch."

"What's going on," she asks.

"They're about to have a civil war. Right now. About us. And the deal. With antimorphic weapons. It's not nice."

He gestures and the thrust reaches through the compensation as they slam upward toward the softly glowing planet.

343

Latimer reads out the story he has experienced and the story he has absorbed as they flee.

Thirty thousand years before, the homeworld of the Manganese-t'la circles its sun, its people enjoying a brisk outdoor existence, a government difficult to understand, and a transport system based on canals. A thousand years later, the Kleztharn have begun to factionalize from the rest of the Companions, and they have responded to the alien influx with a long term plan. Probes are secretly sent out into a vast sphere beyond their territory, with creatures partly morphic, partly biological, programmed with a mission - to keep any species at the destination so primitive it can never be a threat to their stability and shape... and, if that fails, to wage a subversive war. And, if that fails to use their technological power to wage an overt war of holistic destruction.

But the actions of a few cannot be hidden forever, and the plan is discovered. The political turmoil unseats leaders and committees and conclaves until the government disintegrates. Latimer flees into exile, trying to avoid becoming a martyr to the hatred of the Kleztharn. The details are long lost, but it may be that the Kleztharn, in desperation, make an attempt to co-opt the quanta of the others - an act of cannibalism, brainwashing and warfare in equal measure. But it is these actions that unleash the disease. A disease that leads to dissolution. Maybe it is spawned by an accidental or unplanned release of Mover material, as some later contend. Or perhaps it is simply the last defiance. But the disease disintegrates the Companions on the homeworld, and somehow, linked to biology, or close enough to biology, begins to dissolve the Makers as well.

As war and death spread, other hideous weapons are used. A star neighboring the most densely populated Manganese-t'la colony is destroyed by a weapon similar to the fold drive; the resulting supernova remnant expands for the next several thousand years. The colony is depopulated, and its surface, like the homeworld, becomes a sea of incessantly contesting quanta mingling with the scattered remnants of life.

Others, far away, face the shockwave of an antimorphic suicide weapon, and huddle beside the remnants of the star wrecks, merging, gradually losing sentience and becoming the adhele, *living in space alone until discovered by Clu Sherril under the incremental guidance of Latimer who is attempting to relocate his home and who hears the colony of the* adhele *from light years away.*

A few Companions survive in a space station detached from a section of the Web, orbiting a home system Jovian. Their sight of the death is terrifying, and their spirit is crushed. But over the centuries, they begin to regain some will, and start to explore again. They find everything they know has been destroyed, and, staring at the nearby supernova remnant, desperate and anguished, they burn off the contaminated quanta which are all that remain of the colony's Companions, and that world's skin is largely resurfaced with magma.

In remorse, they retreat for a last time to their station, where they live a gradually shrinking life, staring at the tomb that had been their home, endlessly repeating rituals that once had meaning.

But there is a second faction. The factional rifts are reopened, and their emotional instability begins its clandestine work. And then the begins.

Govault is the first test. A new introduction, with a limited life, long enough to generate warfare between an introduced wave of the Companion degenerates and the colony.

Lucax, Talbot thinks sadly.

Then the second test. And a side effect: the testers are able to eliminate one or more of the key survivors of Govault who might learn of the plot.

Atrenn, Talbot thinks grimly. *Or me.*

Finally, Latimer hears a sound he never thought to hear again – the sound of the Vantmar in the Mover broadcast. And so he hurries Clu to a rendezvous with unexpected consequences.

301

344

The engines spin up, and the hammar lifts violently from the pad toward the stars, and then it becomes inertialess and vanishes.

Talbot watches the station receding in the window wall. His hands work the controls like a musician handling a long-loved instrument. For the moment, he is happy to be flying again, but the station behind him is a reminder of a tragedy so large he can barely understand it. In the far distance, a dim mote flashes.

Minutes later, the flashes intensify behind them. Tiny fragments can be seen slowly separating from the station.

Wanr appears at his shoulder with a tray and a bottle of kanar. Talbot watches Wanr with a strange expression. Finally he sighs sadly and takes it. "Thanks."

Wanr fluffs slightly and retreats.

Reed looks up from her work and nods. "I have the course."

Talbot sighs and shakes his head. "Good. I wonder what's waiting for us." He pulls the course over and checks it. "I wish I knew enough to critique this."

"Hey," she laughs and rubs his forearm, "what are you going to do? We either run the course, and get to some waypoint we know, or we stay here with the Kleztharn. Your choice?"

He gestures and the hammar slips into fold.

345

The Tlnou system is swarming with military vehicles, many of them near the wreck of the destroyer, tentatively probing the vast yet scattered remains with active sensors.

But swarming is a relative term, and the space where they unfold is nearly clear for millions of cubic miles.

Nearly clear, because Clu Sherril's morphic vehicle is hanging in space far below them, outlined against a distant nebula.

"Hi, Clu... Hi, Jane," Talbot remarks lightly to no one in particular. His voice is trembling almost unnoticeably. Reed stares. He glances over and smiles a boyish grin, the first she has ever seen. He continues, "You suppose she's going to explain to us why she left?"

"Only if she's planning on doing it after she atomizes us," Reed replies, gesturing up a display that shows the morphic vehicle shifting in space and powering up systems which seem to be weaponry power supplies.

Talbot sighs and glances over his shoulder at Wanr. "Comments?"

"Tactical situation uncertain. Weapons or defenses none we have left. Range of opponent weapons unknown. Recommend presentation of minimal silhouette."

Talbot's hands are already altering the position of the hammer to face the distant vehicle. He uses reverse thrust to start the hammer edging away.

"I can't believe she'd fire on us..." Talbot is muttering. "Why?"

"Good question," Reed replies. "Quarantine?" She begins efforts to establish a communications link, and frowns as the probes go unacknowledged.

346

It has been a long time since the Director has ever felt so powerless. She stalks the brightly lit corridors, dodging the small morphic robotics that clog the halls in waves. Her legs are short, she is tired, and not only is every system of this vehicle denied her, but she is lost.

Until she hears the voices... and, following them, arrives at the opening to the flight deck.

"Lock and prepare to fire," Clu snaps. Her hair is hanging raggedly over her forehead, and clinging in streaked shards across her slightly sweaty cheek.

"Gran, come on, we can't just do that. They're trying to contact us."

"We can't let them," Clu insists. "Check again. Make sure the shell isn't listening to anything except interior messages. Who knows what they may have brought to subvert the ship? And get into your damn suit before something happens. I won't have you sucking vacuum."

Jane walks toward her ancient relative and stops very close, looking carefully at a face that once seemed so familiar and ageless. The faint wrinkles at the corners of Clu's eyes seem to have deepened, her hair has become dryer and more aggressively streaked, and her irises are slightly filmed with a deep tiredness. Jane wonders how long it has been since Clu has slept properly.

"We can't be sure if anything is wrong. What about Latimer? Are you prepared to kill him too?"

Clu blinks hard, twice. "Latimer is dead. I told you, that planet kills. And if they have one single quantum on that ship, and it gets here, this ship is just as dead. And so are we."

The Director steps into the room. "There's more to life than avoiding death. Is this how you will live - cowering in your home?"

Jane watches, eyes flicking between the two. Then she steps to the console, and the words of Gillian Reed echo in the flight deck. "...fire, don't fire, it's us. Please respond. Clu? Jane? Can you hear us? Latimer is with us... we have the story now. We found the xenophobes and we have the weapon we need. Please respond... Latimer?"

"I'm here. Clu, I can guess why you left. But I am still your friend. I was afraid to tell you everything. I was in exile, you know. I didn't know the whole story then. Now I do. The crew here... r*Zaranil and Wanr, at least, found a way to heal me, and to detect any traces of the dissolution virus. Prometheus' morphic technology is in *no* danger. Contact us. Don't destroy us. Talk to us."

Clu's stance is awkwardly bent, as if she has been struck on the hip. She straightens slowly.

"I suppose we'll have to take a chance," she replies, her face expressionless. She turns to Jane. "You and the Director, here, set up a rendezvous. Don't get too close. I'm going to try to get ready with some precautions." A cigar appears between her fingers, lit, smoke faintly coiling in the still air.

347

Curvespace shudders like a reach of ancient earth subsiding. The murmurs echo through realspace in a constant time. r*Zaranil shifts his position, and calls Talbot's attention.

Talbot leans over and watches the mappings twisting slowly. "What could it be..." he whispers, awed and afraid.

Hundreds of light years away, a military action is completed, and the ancient destroyers begin to crack and disintegrate under the pressure of their own unbalanced gravity. Soldiers and police watch carefully from the edges of the system, high above the ecliptic as the last of the overloaded fold drivers whisk instantaneously into their targets and implode. The world sized vessels burn slowly, listing into an uncontrolled rotation amidst the ice.

348

A tall dark human sits at a table looking out over the rim of the station. His coverall is rumpled and his beard is growing in. He broods over the crisp images of stars.

"Drink or inhalant, sir?" the waiter asks, huge golden slit eyes faintly reflecting the galactic spectacle.

Talbot looks up.

"Nothing right now. I'm meeting someone."

"No problem, sir."

Behind the bar, cloaked in the dim haze, a thin man stands, drooping moustaches framing his mouth, straight black hair caught in a gold ring to one side and spilling over his shoulder. He looks up and scans the tables, and then his eyes travel back to where Talbot is sitting. The bartender signals the waiter and they speak in low tones.

Shan wheels over to the table. "Tal, man, I never thought I'd see you again. I hear some strange things have been happening. But here you are. Where you heading, man?"

Talbot's eyes swing up and lock - for a moment, recognition avoids him, and then he remembers from something like three lifetimes ago. And Shan, for his part, sees almost a stranger, only barely similar to the Talbot he had not so long ago seen.

"Hi, Shan. Seems like years."

"Only what, six months, I think?"

"I can't remember, anymore, I'm afraid."

"So, where to, and what can I get you on the house?"

"I'm meeting a friend, and we're catching a flight out to Tlnou. I'm just back from a funeral on Teren."

Shan's face moves to shock and then back to normal. "Sorry. Anyone I know?"

"I don't think so. An old friend of mine, though. Atrenn."

"I knew him. I think. A little. Stopped by when he was transiting. Had some kind of important family in Radelix. Never thought I'd hear you call a Tereniade a friend, though."

"Things have changed."

Jill appears at Talbot's back and rests a hand on his shoulder.

"So I see," Shan replies, leering in a friendly way. "Hi, lady. What would you like? On the house, if you're a friend of Tal."

"Jill Reed," she replies. "Thanks. I'll have a light stimulant. How about coffee?"

"Try some of this new stuff I imported from equatorial Panak on Bosquet," Shan grins, wheeling backward. Talbot smiles. "Shan's got a thing about imports, Jill. But I think you'll like him."

349

"A report was received today that a senior official of the Radelix Geodesic was arrested by the High Constabulary on charges of conspiring to promote an invasion of the Geodesic. Other arrests of senior officials in the Tradeceuz Kin administration have also been announced, including senior legalists. Charges include engineering the Govault massacre and a similar event on a newly opened world named Talith. It is unclear whether or not any other government officials will be implicated.

"In related news, a first contact with a civilization on the outskirts of M4 has been reported. This new civilization appears to be related to the legendary Prometheus space station, and was contacted in the midst of a pursuit led by Raoul Talbot, an exploration lead for Radelix, who was instrumental in uncovering the invasion plot and in establishing the relationship with the Prometheans. Images and interviews are expected within the hour…"

350

The field is warm with slightly golden light of the Tlnou star. Talbot lies in the grass and smiles as swarms of small fuzzy specks buzz slowly amidst the flowers beside his head. He can hear the water rippling, and the sounds of beings wading.

"You seem to be relaxing," a quiet voice remarks in the oddly cadenced inflections of Tlnou. Talbot opens his eyes, and sees Risha's husband. Talbot's smile broadens, and he stretches like a cat unwinding. "You are *so* right," he replies. "Thanks for having us."

He rolls up to sit.

"I'll tell you, this is the place I could sit for a really long time. I don't know about r*Zaranil, he might prefer a cave somewhere, but me? Ahhh…" He sighs, and his eyes narrow, squinting in the sun. He is ragingly happy, watching Jill splash water at Wanr, who recoils with a variety of barking sounds that the translators are unwilling to resolve.

351

Talbot stands in the grass at the lip of the hollow, motionless. Red grass stirs. The old burns are mostly gone, and there is little remnant of the expedition. Talbot looks at his hands, where the sharp edges of the fronds have cut tiny painful slashes over the scars, weeping thin blood onto his palms. His eyes come up to meet the horizon - a line of forest icy red against lime and clouds.

How far I've come, he thinks, *to come back to the center.*

He walks slowly along the rim, thinking sadly of an angry man, who seems, in retrospect, somehow much younger.

He walks slowly out across the plain, and in the distance, as he tops a rise, where he sees a grouping of prey biting and tearing at the tough grasses. He pauses. The wind sweeps a strange fern of cold sensation across his back. He waves to a gaunt white figure near the trees who may not know what that gesture means.

There's plenty of time, he reminds himself. He sends a signal to the shuttle, and notes the location of the response. He heads out across the plain to where the flame settles into the red grass with a burst of white smoke.

Jill is sitting on the ramp as he walks across the ash toward her. He stops below her and smiles. The light shapes her face and her hair is swirling free in the breeze. "Hey, beautiful," he calls. She watches him levelly, but with an amused expression. "Great vacation idea, Raoul," she teases. "Where's the hotel? The pool?" He smiles, walks up the ramp and takes her hand. Together they step inside. The door closes behind them, and then there is the sound of the engines.

In the distance, Deleo stands, watching something end and begin. Then he turns back into the forest, looking for his future.

THE END

Acknowledgements

The Hunt has taken years to develop. It started as a short story, grew to Phase I, and then became the novel you hold. Especially patient was my wife Sue, who provided invaluable support.

In the course of assembling this book I used a variety of tools to help visualize the environments and characters of The Hunt.

Cover and interior illustrations were designed by the author and rendered using the 3D computer graphics programs Cararra and Poser, both currently from DAZ 3D[2], with significant help from the plugins produced by Digital Carver's Guild[3]. Most of the designs and textures are my own, but some clothing was purchased from Renderosity[4] and a variety of public domain astronomical and orbital photos were also used as backgrounds and textures.

The star and planetary orbit maps were designed and rendered (with some postwork) using Astrosynthesis 2.0 from NBOS software[5]. Planetary maps were created using Fractal Terrains[6].

I hope you have enjoyed reading and viewing The Hunt as much as I have enjoyed creating it.

- MARK CASHMAN, 2007

---

[2] http://www.daz3d.com
[3] http://www.digitalcarversguild.com
[4] http://www.renderosity.com
[5] http://www.nbos.com
[6] http://www.profantasy.com

RINGCLIMBER

It is 50,000 miles from the outer edge of the Rings of Saturn to the inner edge. They are a flowing chaos of billions of icy boulders, grit and dust, churning endlessly, rippling with jet streams, channeling electric fields from the magnetosphere into electrostatically active spokes of levitated particles, riddled with flashes of current between charged regions. Moonlets orbit through this destructive environment, carving gaps and braiding flows of boulders and particles into complex sub-rings and ripples...

Imagine climbing through them.

With Saturn a wall beside them, and the Rings a floor beneath, they wait, eyeing the storms on the planet and the jet streams in the Rings; watching the slow procession and mixing of the particles.

Pat is breathing hard with excitement. They are drifting slowly into the shadow of the planet. Erin, beside her, looks over and grins infectiously.

Sharon watches from where she floats high above them, beside the beacon, her outgoing comm down. She doesn't want them to see the tears on her face, or hear the sobs she is unable to control. She can't help but think of Rael's death, now. She looks down at the Rings, wondering what she would do if she saw Rael's suit, drifting there, alone, grinding amidst the particles.

I have this life. Only one, and it's precious. I don't want to waste it. I don't want to die, but someday, I will. In the meantime, I'm really going to live. The best I can.

RINGCLIMBER
mark cashman

PROMETHEUS

"There are a lot of stories. Who knows which is true? The one I like is where five thousand years ago, a hundred men of Earth took the best of their machines and hollowed planets into shells. They linked them into a chain of rock and metal, and hurled themselves and their new home into space."

Clu watches a tear detach and float in the zero-G environment. "I'm going back for Lan," she states over the communication link to Rannart's vehicle.

"Are you out of your mind?" Rannart replies, "I've got pursuit vehicles less than ten minutes behind me. They'll blow you out of space without a thought."

"I can't go without him."

"Let me do my job. I can get him out eventually. Please."

Then it happens in utter silence. The edge of Clu's vehicle is enveloped in a blinding flash that quickly dies away into a vague fog of parts and gas as her vessel tumbles away, shattered. Air roars out of the hull, tearing at her suit. The force of the blast spins the vehicle, and she faints with G-shock as the blaze of the explosion envelops her. The energy vaporizes parts of the seat and the control panel. It washes across her back as she is thrown forward against the restraints. Then… the moon's surface below is disturbed, and something - something huge, massive, and extremely speedy - races upward toward her. Her vehicle is snatched within the maw of the vast object - she is gone and then it is gone.

But even the world that is a myth will not keep them apart.

PROMETHEUS
mark cashman